COME INTO MY PARLOUR

*

Come Into My Parlour is the fifth of seven volumes incorporating all the principal events which occurred between September, 1939, and May 1945, covering the activities of Gregory Sallust, one of the most famous Secret Agents ever created in fiction about the Second World War.

Much of the action of the story takes place inside the Soviet Union, commencing with Russia entering the war against Nazi Germany. There to counter Gregory's plans is his arch-enemy, *Gruppenfuhrer* Grauber, as anxious as ever to settle the long-standing score which has existed between them, and as plot and counter-plot carry the story to a Swiss lakeside villa, the final scenes are played out in a sinister castle situated deep in the heart of a German forest. . . .

BY DENNIS WHEATLEY

NOVELS

The Launching of Roger Brook
The Shadow of Tyburn Tree
The Rising Storm
The Man Who Killed the King
The Dark Secret of Josephine
The Rape of Venice
The Sultan's Daughter
The Wanton Princess
Evil in a Mask

The Scarlet Impostor
Faked Passports
The Black Baroness
V for Vengeance
Come Into My Parlour
Traitors' Gate
They Used Dark Forces

The Prisoner in the Mask
The Second Seal
Vendetta in Spain
Three Inquisitive People
The Forbidden Territory
The Devil Rides Out
The Golden Spaniard
Strange Conflict
Codeword—Golden Fleece
Dangerous Inheritance

The Quest of Julian Day
The Sword of Fate
Bill for the Use of a Body

Black August
Contraband
The Island Where Time Stands Still
The White Witch of the South Seas

To the Devil—A Daughter
The Satanist

The Eunuch of Stamboul
The Secret War
The Fabulous Valley
Sixty Days to Live
Such Power is Dangerous
Uncharted Seas
The Man Who Missed the War
The Haunting of Toby Jugg
Star of Ill Omen
They Found Atlantis
The Ka of Gifford Hillary
Curtain of Fear
Mayhem in Greece
Unholy Crusade

SHORT STORIES
Mediterranean Nights
Gunmen, Gallants and Ghosts

HISTORICAL
'Old Rowley'
(*A Private Life of Charles II*)
Red Eagle
(*The Story of the Russian Revolution*)

AUTOBIOGRAPHICAL
Stranger than Fiction
(*War Papers for the Joint Planning Staff*)
Saturdays with Bricks

Dennis Wheatley

Come Into My Parlour

ARROW BOOKS

ARROW BOOKS LTD

178–202 Great Portland Street London W1

AN IMPRINT OF THE HUTCHINSON GROUP

London Melbourne Sydney
Auckland Bombay Toronto
Johannesburg New York

First published by
Hutchinson & Co (*Publishers*) Ltd 1946
Arrow edition 1960
Second impression 1965
Third impression 1966
Fourth impression 1968
This new edition 1969
Reprinted 1970

*Made and printed in Great Britain
by The Anchor Press Ltd.,
Tiptree, Essex*
ISBN 0 09 002570 9

Contents

1	The Spider's Lair	7
2	The Web is Spun	13
3	The Fly	25
4	The Mission	32
5	The Letter	45
6	The Villa Offenbach	63
7	Midnight Journey	77
8	In the Lion's Den	93
9	The Gestapo Get to Work	114
10	Into Russia	128
11	Perilous Journey	144
12	Strange Interview	159
13	The Truth, and Nothing but the Truth	188
14	Out of the Frying-pan into the Fire	212
15	Floating Coffin	231
16	Warrant for Arrest	254
17	Poison	286
18	Back into Germany	300
19	At the Eleventh Hour	329
20	The Long Night	347

Author's Note

The sequence of the seven books which recount the war adventures of Gregory Sallust is as follows: *The Scarlet Impostor, Faked Passports, The Black Baroness, V for Vengeance, Come Into My Parlour, Traitors' Gate* and *They Used Dark Forces.* Each volume is a complete story in itself, but the series covers Gregory's activities from September, 1939, to May, 1945 against an unbroken background incorporating all the principal events of the Second World War.

Gregory Sallust also appears in three other books: *Black August,* a story set in an undated future; *Contraband,* an international smuggling story of 1937; and *The Island Where Time Stands Still,* an adventure set in the South Seas and Communist China during the year 1954.

1

The Spider's Lair,

At five minutes to ten on the morning of the 23rd of June, 1941, the ugly streets of Berlin were already hot, and a blazing sun in a cloudless sky gave promise of a stifling day. The pavements were far more crowded than in peacetime, owing to the great influx of people brought to the capital of the now swollen Reich by innumerable varieties of war activity; but on this Monday morning the crowds seemed denser than ever and it was clear that they were animated by an unusual excitement.

Its cause was that only the day before the German armies had invaded Russia, and everyone was eager for news of this great new campaign.

Behind closed doors a few old people shook their heads. It was true that for over a year now Britain and her Empire had alone remained in arms to defy the might of Hitler, but those arrogant and accursed islanders still remained unsubdued; holding the oceans with their Fleets, doggedly barring the path through North Africa to the East and, with their ever-growing Air Force, proving a constant menace from the West. Hitler promised that never again should the German people be called upon to wage a war on two fronts simultaneously. Was it really wise, some of the older people asked each other in guarded whispers, to take on the Russian Colossus, however flabby he might appear, before the arch-enemy, Churchill, and all he represented, had been finally overcome?

But such questioning had found no place in the minds of the vast majority. Had not their glorious *Führer* added the Saar, Austria and Czechoslovakia to the Reich without firing a shot; eliminated Poland in one short month of war; forced Denmark and Norway into submission by a single subtle stroke; conquered Holland, Belgium, Luxembourg and France by the most brilliant campaign in history lasting barely six weeks; overrun Yugoslavia and Greece in another blitzkreig of twenty-one days; and in the meantime made Italy, Hungary and Rumania into vassal States? Fourteen nations now acknowledged Germany as their Overlord, and eight of them had been subdued by German arms between two Aprils—since from the invasion of Norway to the surrender of Greece less than thirteen months had elapsed.

Glutted with the loot of Warsaw, Paris, Brussels, Athens and The Hague, the German masses hailed the new campaign against Russia with excited joy and boundless confidence. For them, to expect victory had now become a habit of mind, and defeat unthinkable. In the cafés they were already speculating as to whether Moscow would be captured in one month or two, regretting that they would not get from it the fat dairy produce of Denmark and Holland or the silks and wines of France, but gloating over the thought that the great cornlands of the Ukraine and the oil of the Caucasus could not but still further raise the now high standard of living for themselves—the *Herrenvolk,* and exclaiming joyfully that within another year the German Empire would extend from the North Sea to the Pacific Ocean.

Their confidence was shared by the quiet little middle-aged man who sat at his desk in a spacious second-floor room that looked out on a sunny courtyard at the back of the great S.S. Headquarters on the Alexander Platz.

Both the room and the man were scrupulously tidy. He was a pale nondescript person with fair hair cut short above a sloping forehead. His chin receded sharply and his weak eyes peered through strong-lensed pince-nez at the documents before him. But he worked with sureness and despatch; his delicate hands sorting through the papers with the same swiftness with which they had for years weighed out quarter kilos of currants and sultanas, when he had been a struggling grocer with a poor little shop in a suburb of Munich. In more recent years he had many times, by a single scrawl of his pen, sent to their deaths more people than there are currants in a quarter kilo; and in Germany's new Empire of two hundred and sixty-five million souls there were few who did not regard his name with fear or hatred. It was Heinrich Himmler.

A miniature silver chiming clock on his desk pinged the hour. He signed the paper he had been reading, placed the rest of the pile neatly back in his *in* basket and stood up. Tightening the belt of his black and silver *Obergruppenführer*'s uniform over his plump little paunch, he gave a quick glance in a wall mirror and, apparently satisfied with his appearance, strode with ringing steps across the parquet floor. Throwing open the door of an adjoining room he paused for a moment, dramatically, upon its threshold.

The room was even larger than his office, and was his private conference room. In it nearly a dozen men were always assembled round a gleaming mahogany table. On his appearance they sprang to their feet as though animated by a single lever and, thrusting out their right arms, exclaimed in chorus: 'Heil Hitler!'

Himmler took the salute, advanced to the chair at the head of the table, motioned the others to be seated, and sitting down imself, picked up the agenda that had been ready for him.

He was about to hold the formal monthly meeting, attended y all the German Intelligence Chiefs, at which he made his omments on the separate appreciations that had been sub-itted to him, and issued general instructions about matters n which he required more detailed information.

The three Directors of Intelligence for the Army, Navy and uftwaffe were present, and the civilian Intelligence Chiefs or the Foreign Office and Economic Warfare. At the far end f the table sat Himmler's Principal Assistant, the S.S. eneral Kaltenbrunner; the only man, so it was whispered, of whom Himmler himself was afraid. Behind Kaltenbrunner, t a small separate table against the far wall, two S.S. majors vaited, unobtrusive but observant, to act as secretaries and ake notes of all that passed at the meeting.

On Himmler's right sat a small wizened man in Admiral's uniform. His sparse grey hair only partially covered a fine lomed skull that seemed too big for his body; he had a thin ynical mouth and mild blue eyes. He did not look like a German and his name, Canaris, denoted the foreign extraction of his family; but he had for long been one of the most im-ortant figures in the High Command, and was the Chief of he old, pre-Hitler, German Secret Service. Like the three Directors of Intelligence, his allegiance lay with the *Oberkom-nandantur der Wehrmacht,* and he was responsible only nominally to Himmler.

At Himmler's other side sat another S.S. officer. He was a plumpish man with immensely powerful shoulders, a heavy jowl and hair cut *en brosse*. His thin sharp nose protruded from between what had been a pair of small, light eyes set much too close together; but now the left eye, although an excellent match and detectable as false only through its im-mobility, was made of glass. He was *Gruppenführer* Grauber, the dreaded Chief of Department U.A.-1, and controlled the operations of all Gestapo agents in countries outside the Reich.

Items one to seven on the agenda consisted of the monthly appreciations of 'Future Enemy Intentions', rendered in turn by the three Service Directors of Intelligence; their two civilian colleagues, Canaris and Grauber.

These dealt only with the war against Britain and the salient points that emerged were as follows. It was anticipated that within a matter of weeks both the French quisling, General Dentz, who was endeavouring to hold Syria against the Australians, and the last Italian resistance in Abyssinia, would collapse. Grave concern was expressed by the Airman

over the ever-mounting losses of the Luftwaffe based o
French coastal aerodromes, owing to the R.A.F. dayligh
sweeps, and it was forecast that still further increases i
Britain's air strength would have to be faced in the futur
However, the morale of the British public had fallen sharpl
and Churchill had suffered a considerable loss of prestig
owing to the recent final abandonment of Crete. There wa
good reason to suppose that morale in Britain would fall sti
further during the autumn, owing to the obvious hopelessne;
of ever securing anything but a patched-up peace at best; th
night bombing of industrial centres, a steadily increasin
shortage of consumer goods and what would eventuall
amount to a famine in the luxuries of the masses, such as bee
and cigarettes. Although still shrouded in secrecy, it wa
known that United States 'precautions' were now assuming
warlike status, and that the Americans had landed so-calle
'Security Troops' in both Greenland and Iceland.

Canaris even went so far as to say that, in his view, unles
some special measures could be devised to conciliate publi
opinion in the States, he believed that they would activel
enter the war against Germany before the end of the year. Th
man from the Wilhelmstrasse offset this by forecasting a grea
strengthening of relations between Germany and Japan as ;
result of Vichy giving way to German pressure and agreeing t
accept Japanese garrisons in French Indo-China.

After discussion and a reassessment of certain points these
seven appreciations were taken as the basis of the monthl;
report for submission to Hitler.

It was not until item eight was reached that any reference
was made to Russia. All these key men of the German war
machine had been concerned for many months with th
gigantic preparations for the assault on the Soviet Union
Since early spring they had carried the secret of the D-Da;
fixed for the operation, and they were also fully informed o
the time-table set for the campaign. They all considered it a;
certain that the German armies would be through the Russian-
held half of Poland and in Minsk within a week, and that the
Nazi Swastikas would be flying over Smolensk by the end
of July. Only then did they expect that the main Russian resistance would have to be met, but after a series of big battles
in autumn it was anticipated that Hitler would be able to make
a triumphant personal entry into Moscow by Christmas.

Every scrap of information they could gather regarding
Russian resources had already been passed to the O.K.W.,
and it was now for the Operations Branch of the General Staff
to make the best use they could of it.

Himmler glanced at the one word 'Russia' and prepared to

s the item, remarking casually to Grauber:
I take it you are fully satisfied about your channels?'
Jawohl, Herr – Obergruppenführer,' Grauber replied
ckly, in his high piping voice. 'As you know, the Soviet has
ways been the most difficult of our problems, owing to its
ct control of foreigners, and the fact that it has the best
nter-espionage system of any country outside the Reich.
t I have reliable men in many good places. Owing to dist-
ce and the general poorness of communications, there is
und to be some delay in securing sufficient accurate intelli-
ce to form a true picture of what is going on inside Russia
things develop, but we have many means of sending special
rsonnel in to visit our agents and collect the latest
terial. I shall also go in myself, from time to time, to contact
best men.'

'Any remarks?' asked Himmler, casting a swift, short-sighted
nce round the table.
It was met by a general shaking of heads, so he went on to
other items, despatching each after asking a few questions
d making a brief comment.
At item thirteen, he read out: 'Gregory Sallust'—paused
a moment, frowned, and added: 'What is this? I seem to
ow that name.'
'I had it put on the agenda, *Herr Obergruppenführer,'* said
naris, quietly.
Himmler squinted at him. 'Well, *Herr Admiral*?'
The Admiral looked round, gathering the attention of his
dience. 'As you are all aware,' he began, 'in some respects
e British Intelligence Service has deteriorated since the last
ar. It cannot be denied that they are extremely efficient in
curing certain types of information. For example, captured
cuments prove beyond dispute that their appreciations of
r "Order of Battle" in various theatres of war are uncannily
curate. On the other hand, they seem to have very little idea
to what is going on inside Germany itself. Generally speak-
g, our internal security is highly satisfactory; but the British
possess a limited number of ace operators who, from time
time, have succeeded in penetrating some of our most
osely guarded secrets, and my people tell me that Sallust is
e most dangerous of them all.'
Himmler peered through his pince-nez at Grauber. 'What
you know of this man?'
Grauber's pale fleshy face coloured as he replied: *'Herr
bergruppenführer,* I am surprised that the *Herr Admiral*
ould consider the case of any individual enemy agent of
fficient importance to occupy the time of such a high
owered meeting as this.'

11

'I do so,' countered the Admiral, 'for a perfectly adequa[te] reason. The progress of our "K" series of new secret weapo[n] has now reached a point at which their further developme[nt] necessitates a much greater number of people having kno[w]ledge of them. This will automatically increase the danger [of] the enemy getting wind of these immensely important devic[es] by which we hope to bring the war with Britain to a success[ful] conclusion without undertaking the hazards of an invasio[n]. If a leak does occur, the British will obviously put their be[st] men on to the job of securing for them the secrets of Peer[e]münde. Sallust speaks German as well as if he was born he[re] so all the odds are that he will be allocated to this task. Pr[e]vention being better than cure, I should like to have the He[rr] Gruppenführer's assurance that adequate precautions a[re] being taken against him.'

Himmler looked at Grauber again. 'I asked you what y[ou] knew of this man?'

Grauber shrugged his great shoulders. 'The Herr Admir[al] exaggerates the danger. Sallust is certainly a man to watc[h]. He is resolute and resourceful, and he has pulled off som[e] very clever *coups*. So far he has always managed to elude u[s] but if he puts his nose inside Germany again, I'll get him.'

'Where is he now?'

'He was last reported to me as in Paris, but there is goo[d] reason to suppose that by now he is back in England.'

'He won't stay there long,' the Admiral put in. 'He is far to[o] active, and he is extraordinarily audacious. He even had th[e] effrontery to beard *Reichmarshal* Goering at Karinhall, an[d] got away with it; and I have good reason to believe that h[e] completely fooled von Geisenheim, one of our as[t]ute Generals, less than a month ago in Paris. If the English d[o] learn of our "K" projects I will stake my reputation that the[y] will send Sallust back into Germany.'

'I hope you are right,' Grauber laughed suddenly; it wa[s] a high, unpleasant laugh. 'I have a personal score to settle wi[th] Mr. Sallust, and the one thing I am waiting for is for him t[o] give me another chance to get my hands on him.'

'Why wait?' said Himmler sharply. 'As the Herr Admir[al] says, prevention is better than cure. If this man is so dangero[us] he must be eliminated before he has a chance to do us an[y] further mischief. Lure him here. Set a trap for him and ki[ll] him. See to that, Grauber, or I will make you answer for [it] personally. Within three months, I require a certificate o[f] Sallust's death from you.'

2

The Web is Spun

When, just after midday, the meeting broke up, Grauber went up to Canaris and said:

'Would the *Herr Admiral* be so gracious as to spare me a few moments to discuss the matter in which he has displayed such interest? I refer to the trapping of Gregory Sallust.'

'But certainly, my dear *Herr Gruppenführer*,' the Admiral purred. 'And now, if you like. You Gestapo men are so active that you leave us poor old fogies of the original Service little to do in these days. That, of course, is our excuse for having concerned ourselves in a matter which is really your affair; but to which you have obviously been too busy to attend, owing to the pressure of more important business.'

Grauber showed his uneven teeth in a false smile. 'As things are, a certain amount of overlapping between our Departments is inevitable; but that will be rectified when the two services are brought under one head—as they are bound to be in due course. In the meantime, we always find your co-operation invaluable. May I show you the way to my office?'

'As I was instrumental in having a bomb removed from it last month, I have the good fortune to know it,' replied the Admiral imperturbably, 'but I shall be delighted to accompany you there.'

Having exchanged these honeyed thrusts, the hulking Gestapo Chief and the delicate looking elderly sailor left the room side by side and walked down the long echoing corridor.

They were old enemies, and the rivalry between them was bitter in the extreme. Grauber, with Himmler's backing, had many times endeavoured to bring about the disbandment of the Admiral's department and the absorption of its best men into his own espionage machine, but the O.K.W. had always successfully resisted his attempts, and Canaris was confident that they would continue to do so.

He disliked Grauber personally, regarding him as a gutter-bred thug, typical of the worst elements that had lifted Hitler to power, and despised his brutal heavy-handed methods. He was not the least afraid of the Gestapo Chief, because he knew his own position was secure as long as von Rundstedt, von Räder, von Bock, von Geisenheim, and half a dozen others like them remained at the head of the *Wehrmacht*, and he did not believe that Hitler could wage a successful war without them. In consequence, he took an impish delight in treading on Grauber's corns whenever the opportunity offered; and he had raised the question of Gregory Sallust that morning almost as much for the pleasure of making Grauber appear negligent in front of Himmler as because he honestly considered the matter was important.

Grauber not only hated but also secretly feared the little Admiral. He was shrewd enough to know that most of these top men of the High Command had something that the great majority of the Nazi leaders lacked, and could now never obtain.

Few of the Party chiefs had ever been outside Germany before their rise to power; they knew little of the customs and mentality of other races, and the bulk of their followers, young men, brought up as fanatics in the Nazi tradition and not even allowed to read the true histories of the countries with which Germany had gone to war, were abysmally ignorant of every type of thought that animated human endeavour outside their own political creed.

The Generals and the Admirals, on the other hand, had as young men travelled freely before the First World War and, as they were drawn from Germany's upper classes, had competed at horse shows, sailed their yachts, hunted, gambled and shot on the most friendly terms with their opposite numbers in Britain, France and the United States. They were, moreover, infinitely better educated, as they had been free of all the world's literature in the days before the Nazis had banned a great part of the human race's most important contributions to religion, history, philosophy and ethics.

In consequence, the wizened little Admiral and his middle-aged cronies were far better qualified to understand the enemy's mentality, and invariably made much shrewder appreciations of their future intentions than Grauber's young thugs were able to furnish for him, despite his constant urging to them to apply ice-baths, hot irons and thumbscrews to anyone even remotely suspected of possessing useful information. And Grauber always had an uneasy feeling that one day the Admiral would show up the shortcomings of the Gestapo Foreign Department U.A.-1 so blatantly that in a fit of cold unforgiving rage Himmler would consign its Chief to Dachau.

However, Grauber was far too clever to allow his personal feelings about his rival to prevent his making use of him whenever he felt that he could do so without unfortunate repercussions; and now, having reached his own handsome office, which was only a few doors away from Himmler's, he seated the Admiral in a comfortable armchair, gave him one of his own genuine Havana cigars, lit it, and said:

'It is our mutual misfortune, *Herr Admiral*, that there are times when our interests are not altogether identical, but this is happily not one of them. No one could be more anxious to put Sallust out of the way for good and all than I am myself, but it is you who have taken the initiative in this matter, so I do hope that I may count on your assistance.'

'Assuredly, my dear *Herr Gruppenführer*, assuredly,' agreed the Admiral, puffing contentedly at the long cigar. 'Although, of course, my little organisation has nothing like the ramifications of your own, and I don't suppose for one moment that there is any really worthwhile help that I can give you.'

'You can tell me what you know of Sallust?'

'That would, I am sure, be no more than a repetition of the data that is already in your own files and, unlike yourself, I have never had the questionable advantage of making personal contact with the fellow.' Canaris shifted his glance maliciously to Grauber's pebble-filled left eye-socket, knowing perfectly well that the original eye had been bashed out by Gregory Sallust with the blunt end of an automatic.

Grauber flushed, but went on persistently: 'Nevertheless, you may have picked up something about him, that I have not, so I would like to hear your version of his activities.'

'Very well then. It fills many pages, so I will give only a résumé and you can stop me at any point on which you require further information. Sallust comes of good middle-class stock, but his parents were only moderately well off and both of them died when he was quite young. He was an imaginative and therefore troublesome boy and after only two and a half terms was expelled for innumerable breaches of discipline from his public school, Dulwich College. With the idea of taming him, his uncle sent him as a cadet to H.M.S. *Worcester*. The freer life seems to have suited him, but again, owing to his refractory nature, he was never made a Petty Officer, as they term their Prefects. On leaving he did not go to sea, because he did not consider that such a career offered a sufficiently remunerative future. Instead he used a portion of his patrimony to give himself a year on the Continent. He has a quite exceptional flair for languages so he could soon speak German and French like a native. He was still at an age when he ought to have been at school, but he was already his own master and a handsome, precocious young blackguard. The women adored him and he had an insatiable curiosity about the night life, both high and low, of all the cities he visited, so there wasn't much he hadn't done by the time the war broke out and he returned to England.'

Canaris paused for a moment, then went on: 'He got a commission at once in a Territorial Field Artillery Regiment, and in due course was sent to France. At the age of twenty-one he was serving on the staff of the Third Army. At the battle of Cambrai he was wounded and carries the scar to this day. It lifts the outer corner of his left eyebrow, giving him a slightly satanic appearance. He showed great gallantry at the time he was wounded and was given the M.C.

'After the war he took up journalism; not regular work, but unusual assignments that took him abroad again. As a special correspondent he saw the high spots of the Graeco-Turkish war of nineteen nineteen, and the Russo-Polish war of nineteen twenty. Then he spent a lot of time in Central Europe, studying the development of the new states that emerged from the Versailles and Trianon Treaties—Hungary, Czechoslovakia, and so on. It was through his articles on such subjects, I believe, that he came into touch with that formidable old rascal Sir Pellinore Gwaine-Cust.'

Grauber's solitary eye flickered slightly and he suddenly sat forward. 'So you know about him, do you? My compliments, *Herr Admiral*; he keeps himself so much in the background that I thought hardly anyone here had the least idea of the power he wields behind the scenes on every major problem concerning the British Empire.'

'Oh, yes, I know about him.' The Admiral's thin mouth twisted into a cynical smile. 'He took seven thousand marks off me at baccarat one night at Deauville in nineteen twenty-four, drank me under the table afterwards and sent the money back next morning with a charming little note to the effect that, seeing the poor state of Germany's post-war finances, he did not feel it fair to take such a sum off one of her secret agents at a single sitting. You can repeat that story if you like. I have often related it as a lesson in good manners, to my subordinates.'

'Since there is nothing in it which redounds to the credit of the Service to which we both have the honour to belong, I would not dream of doing so, *Herr Admiral*,' Grauber said pompously. 'But tell me, was that your only meeting with him?'

'By no means; and I am quite certain that he would not have returned the money but for the fact that we were old friends and had had many good times together when we were young. In those days he was a subaltern in a crack cavalry regiment, and he won a particularly well-deserved V.C. in the Boer War. I used to stay with him at his lovely old home, Gwaine Meads, in Shropshire. There have been Gwaine-Custs living there ever since the Romans gave up their attempts to subdue the more savage tribes of Britons on reaching the Welsh Border; and I don't doubt that the place is still maintained in almost feudal state, since he's as rich as Crœsus.'

16

'Yet he had to resign his commission on account of his debts,' put in Grauber. 'It's very remarkable that a hunting and shooting squire, of all people, should have succeeded in amassing such a vast fortune.'

'He is a very remarkable man. But in his young days titles and connections counted. When he left the Army he got himself taken on to the board of a few not-too-sound companies in the City. Before they were much older his co-directors found that they had given a seat to a wolf in guinea-pig's clothing. But they had no cause to regret it. With that hearty innocent laugh of his he did them out of half their profits, but the half he let them keep was ten times as great a sum as they had ever made before. They used to send him to Turkey, Egypt and India. He could twist Orientals round his little finger, enable his companies to pay twenty per cent dividends and keep the rest himself, for "man's time", as he used to call it.'

Grauber shook his head in puzzled wonder. 'These English, they are incredible,' he murmured, as the Admiral went on:

'Yet for over half a century he has managed to maintain his extraordinary fiction that he is just a lucky fool. I've heard him say a score of times in that booming voice of his: "I've an eye for a horse or a pretty woman, but no brains—no brains at all," and he's said it so often that people have really come to believe him.'

'To get back to Sallust, *Herr Admiral,* you were telling me how these two first became associates?'

'So I was. Well, Sir Pellinore must, I think, have read some of Sallust's articles in the more serious weeklies and realised his extraordinary flair for getting to the bottom of complex political situations. In any case, he began to employ him on a series of special missions to assess commercial possibilities in hitherto unexploited markets and in the more dangerous business of finding out the truth about the ramifications of certain cartels. But Gwaine-Cust, as you must be aware, is far from being only a money-spinner. For the past twenty-five years, at least, he has been the friend and confidant of practically every British statesman who has shown any aggressive or Imperialistic spirit. He has got all sorts of queer "off the record" jobs done for them that would have endangered their positions if they had done them themselves. Today his name is still hardly known outside the West End clubs and the city, and he holds no official position of any kind—he is not even chairman of any of his companies—yet I believe him to be the most dangerous enemy we have and the most powerful man in Britain after the Members of the War Cabinet.'

Grauber nodded agreement. 'That is my view, too; and it follows that as soon as war broke out Sir Pellinore naturally

17

switched his ace private investigator on to war problems. I will not bother you for an account of Sallust's war activities as those are well known to me; but I should be interested if you would give me your views on his woman.'

'Which woman?' asked the Admiral blandly. 'He is quite a Don Juan, and has had affairs with many.'

'I know; and that makes the present one all the more interesting to us, as there is some reason to suppose that after the best part of two years he is still in love with her. I only knew her slightly as I—er—never moved very much in *Reichmarshal* Goering's circle, but you must have known her quite well. I refer, of course, to the Countess von Osterberg—or, if you prefer her maiden name by which she was more widely known— Erika von Epp.'

'*Ach die liebe Erika,*' sighed the Admiral. 'Yes, I knew her intimately.'

Grauber bridled: 'The *Herr Admiral* seems to have forgotten that the *Frau Gräfin* betrayed her country to run away with this accursed Englishman and, in her absence, has been condemned to be executed as a traitress immediately she is caught.'

'I forget nothing, my dear *Gruppenführer*; but a beautiful woman remains beautiful whatever she may do, and no laws ever made have been strong enough to control a woman's heart. Your torture chambers must often have revealed to you that a woman's love is stronger than pain, stronger than death, and often stronger than the ties of country too. As we sit here many thousands of girls—French, Dutch, Norwegian, Belgian —have fallen in love with fine young German soldiers, who a few months ago they regarded as the hated conquerors of their race; and many thousands of pretty German girls have fallen in love with the foreign workers we have brought into the Reich, although we regard them as little better than slaves. Even the Gestapo cannot prevent that, and although we may sometimes have to harden our hearts in such cases for the protection of the State, it is absurd to hold the simple fact of anyone falling in love with a foreigner as a crime. Besides, as far as I am aware, Erika did not betray her country, she only gave her lover certain useful information about an organisation which had for its object the overthrow of the Nazi Party.'

'The Nazi Party *is* the country!' bellowed Grauber, striking his desk.

'Of course,' purred the Admiral, 'none of *us* would dream of questioning that. I am only pointing out to you a purely academic difference which may have become overstressed in poor Erilsa's obviously unbalanced mind, Moreover, as I was

18

about to add, she did not run away. She was seriously wounded and evacuated from Dunkirk.'

'You defend this woman?'

'Ethically, yes, but for all practical purposes, no. She has offended against the laws of our country and been condemned; therefore if she is caught she must die, and if I were given the opportunity to catch her it would certainly be my duty to do so. I may add that if your dictaphone is working this morning and you are taking a record of this conversation it will be time enough to hand it over to Herr Himmler when you can prove that I have at any time failed to do my duty.'

With a growl, Grauber sat back. 'I suggest that we are wasting time, *Herr Admiral*. Will you be good enough to tell me what you know of this woman?'

The Admiral drew slowly on his cigar and his mild eyes hardened as he recalled the sufferings that had been endured by his cast after the last war, then he said slowly:

'Like so many of the *Hochwohlgeboren*, Erika's family was completely ruined by the revolution and inflation that followed Germany's collapse in nineteen eighteen. I suppose it was not unnatural that the people should blame the officer class for having led them to defeat instead of victory, but for several years they took it out of us by every means in their power. The financial policy of the Socialist Government reduced our investments to so much worthless paper. Fifty-nine out of every sixty officers who had served in the war were turned off on to the streets and they were the last people to whom anyone would give employment. The Jews are paying today for what they did to us then. We were forced to sell our houses, farms, jewels, furs and cellars to them for a miserable pittance in order to save ourselves from dying of starvation. Thousands of well-bred German women then had to haunt the big hotels and night clubs as prostitutes, as the only possible means of supporting their fathers, husbands and brothers—often gallant officers who were still incapacitated by wounds received in the war. That was the grim background against which Erika was brought up.

'As a child she had known every luxury; by the time she was old enough to go to school she was living with her parents and elder sister in a tiny flat in Munich that was little better than a tenement. I have heard her say that during those winters she used to lie in her little truckle bed so cold that she could not sleep and that by the time she was seventeen she had forgotten what it was like not to be hungry. She got herself a job in a Munich department store and became the mistress of some little floorwalker there in order to get herself a square meal every evening. Who can blame her?'

19

Canaris shrugged, and went on: 'But Erika was made for better things than that, and she knew it. She soon left the shop-walker for a director of the company, and by then the natural ability of the officer class was bringing it back into prominent positions again. By the time she was twenty she had had a dozen lovers, each richer and more powerful than his predecessor. She had an apartment in Berlin, servants, furs, jewels, and it was already recognised that she and Marlene Dietrich were the two most beautiful women in Germany.'

'It would be about then that she tied up with Hugo Falkenstein,' Grauber commented.

'Yes, did you know him?'

Grauber shook his head.

'Hugo was one of the comparatively rare exceptions that justify the existence of the Jewish race. He had the soul of an artist, the brain of a great statesman and the generosity of an emperor. He could be utterly ruthless to his enemies, but I have never known a man who was kinder, more considerate or more gentle, not only to his friends but to all who came to him in trouble. It was not surprising that Erika fell in love with him.'

'Did she? I've always supposed that she was out for his money.'

'No. Before she met him she was already one of the inti-mates of *Reichmarshal* Goering's brilliant circle. She could have her pick of a score of wealthy men, and married them too, had she wished. She would have liked to marry Hugo, and he begged her to, but she wouldn't do it beause she knew that she could be more useful to him as his mistress than his wife. As long as she remained Erika von Epp she was a German aristo-crat; people closed their eyes to her private life, and all doors remained open to her, but if she had become Frau Falkenstein no one who mattered would have received her any more.'

'Nevertheless, she made a great fortune out of her associa-tion with Falkenstein.'

'True, but she earned every *Pfennig* of it by her own fine brain. He soon realised that she was not just a beautiful play-thing, and he employed her in the most secret negotiations of his great armaments concern. She became his principal ambas-sador and he sent her many times to Britain and France, and on several trips to the United States.'

'Yes, I know that. And then Falkenstein was idiotic enough to quarrel with the *Führer* and withdraw the financial support he had been giving to the Government. What insolent folly on the part of a Jew who might have continued to enjoy our protection as long as he was any use to us.'

'He was a fool as far as his own interests were concerned, but one must admire his courage. He simply refused to accept protection for himself if the persecution of the poorer people of his race was to continue. You know the result. He was sent to Dachau, where your people tortured him for six months and drove him insane before they killed him. Can you wonder that Erika swore that she would devote the rest of her life to a vendetta against the Nazi Party?'

Grauber shrugged his great shoulders. 'You say that she would have liked to marry Falkenstein; are you sure of that?'

'Yes. She once told me so herself. That was a year or so after his death. She said that although it would have made her much less useful to him at the time, she regretted having so persistently refused him. She was tired of being a successful adventuress and would have liked to have left the gay whirl of Berlin for a quiet home in the country with children to bring up. I asked her why she didn't marry, and she replied that it was too late now; she would never find another man like Hugo, to give her the sort of children that she wanted born out of real love between two good-looking and gifted people.'

'I wonder if time has changed her views and she now loves Sallust enough to want him to be the father of her children.'

'I should think it highly probable,' the Admiral said meditatively. 'She must be about twenty-nine and the urge to settle down and start a family will almost certainly have increased since she first met Sallust. From what little information I have it appears that they are still devoted to each other, so the odds are that they would get married if they could. But the snag is that she would first have to get a divorce from von Osterberg.'

'Yes. But why, after all you've said, did she marry him? In nineteen thirty-eight she could have married pretty well anybody, so why the devil pick on such a colourless fellow; and there were no children of the marriage?'

'She did it to please her old father, who was practically on his death-bed at the time. His one wish was to see her respectably married into some good old family before he died. I suppose she had given up all hope of really falling in love again, so in order that the old man might die happy she permitted the most easily manageable of all her many suitors to make an honest woman of her. But the marriage was purely one of convenience. Von Osterberg was always hard up for money to carry on his scientific experiments and she could well afford to give him a princely allowance. He is, too, rather weak, a vain type of man, and he admired her beauty so much that he agreed from the beginning that if she would become his Countess he would leave her completely free to amuse herself in any way she liked.'

21

Grauber remained silent for a moment, then he said: 'I could make von Osterberg dance to any tune I like. How would it be if I made him write to her via the Swiss Legation, and dangle before her the prospect of a divorce if she is prepared to come over and meet him somewhere just inside the German border, to discuss the legal aspects of the thing?'

'I agree that if you could once succeed in luring her back into Germany she would make the best possible bait to draw Sallust into the net afterwards. But she would show him the letter, and no man in his senses would allow the woman he loves to risk such a trip simply on the off-chance of getting a divorce.'

'I was counting on her showing the letter to him, and I think you're right that he would not let her come—alone.'

'I see. You think there is a chance of killing these two birds with one stone?'

'Yes. The war may go on for years yet, so if he really wishes to marry her I don't think he will let such an opportunity slip. The odds are that he will accompany her to Switzerland, and with a little luck I shall snare them both in the same noose.'

Canaris shook his dome-like head. 'It's not good enough, my dear *Herr Gruppenführer*. It's much too obvious. I feel sure that two such clever people would realise it was a trap.'

'Not necessarily.' Grauber's solitary eye glinted as the swift thoughts sped through his brain. 'The whole plan would, of course, be worked out very carefully. Von Osterberg could say that he had had to give up his war job on account of some illness and that he was greatly in need of money. He could say that he had heard through some neutral diplomat that she could never come back to Germany as she was now living with an Englishman. He could offer her a divorce in exchange for her making over to him a certain sum, to be agreed, in German securities. He could tell her that he was living very quietly somewhere on our side of the Bodensee, and that he could not make the crossing into Switzerland on account of his illness, but there would be very little risk in her slipping across one night to see him and get the whole thing fixed up.'

'It stinks, my friend, it stinks,' said the Admiral. 'They would never fall for such a story as that. But if you plant von Osterberg on the Swiss side of Lake Constance—that would be very different. It might not even occur to them then that a visit to him would entail any risk at all; but he, or one of your people that you sent with him in the guise of a servant, could give a prearranged signal on the night they came to see him. He would have to arrange to make it a night appointment, of course. Then a squad of your men, that you would have ready for the purpose, could easily carry out a little raid into Switzerland, surround the house, put them both in the bag and bring them back across the lake.'

'*Kolossal, Herr Admiral! Kolossal!* Grauber exclaimed. 'How right I was to ask you for your assistance. But wait a moment. What reason can von Osterberg be told to give for having gone to live in Switzerland? He would not be permitted to do so on grounds of ill-health alone; unless he was a consumptive, and then he would not be renting a house on the lake-side, but in some sanatorium up in the mountains.'

'True. Do you know what sort of war work he is now employed on?'

'Yes, as it happens I do. He was in one of Krupps' laboratories; but I was doing a security check only last week on a list of scientists who have recently been transferred to work on our new "K" weapons—his name was on it, so he must now be up at the experimental station on the Baltic.'

Canaris pulled thoughtfully on his cigar. 'Von Osterberg was always a dreamer and I should think that normally he is a very squeamish kind of man. It would be quite in character for him to have been overcome by horror at the thought of the wholesale and indiscriminate slaughter of men, women and children that these new weapons of ours will cause, once we begin to launch them against England. Instead of illness, could he not give that as his reason for having left Germany? He could say that he felt the *Führer* was going too far in contemplating methods of warfare which ignored all human considerations and, in consequence, had abandoned his post and sought refuge in Switzerland.'

'Good! Excellent! Such a story would greatly strengthen his reason for wanting money, too. If that was his case he would not be able to get any funds from Germany, so he would have a much more plausible reason for offering her a divorce in exchange for a good round sum in cash.'

'There's one serious snag to it, though.' The Admiral paused a moment. 'I don't at all like the idea of giving Sallust even an inkling that von Osterberg has been employed on a new type of weapon. Our gravest concern for the next twelve months, or more, will be to prevent the British from learning that we are preparing to destroy them by the thousand through an entirely new form of warfare; and our present object is to forestall any attempt by this very man to find out about it.'

'True! Yet your idea about Von Osterberg ratting on us for such a reason is so good that it seems a great pity not to use it. After all, we have no firm grounds for our assumption that Sallust and the von Epp woman wish to get married, and would, if she were free to do so. The inference that von Osterberg has been employed on secret scientific work would enor-

23

mously increase the inducement for Sallust to come over. In fact, I am certain that he would not be able to resist such a lure. He is an immensely conceited man and would immediately flatter himself into the belief that he would be able to either bribe or trick von Osterberg into giving him some really valuable information. Besides, our scientists are working on innumerable problems. It would be quite unnecessary to give any indication of our "K" weapons at all. Von Osterberg could hint that he had been asked to work on some new form of gas —something particularly horrifying and against which the British respirator is no protection. It might be gas that sends people mad or causes parts of the body exposed to it to go gangrenous, so that its victims gradually rot to pieces before they finally die.'

'What a horrible mind you have, *Herr Gruppenführer*! However, I think you're right. The double bait of a speedy divorce, if Erika wants it, and providing an apparently easy opportunity for Sallust to pull off another fine feat of espionage, should certainly be sufficient inducement for the two of them to make a trip to neutral Switzerland. I take it, though, that you are quite satisfied about your ability to control von Osterberg?'

Grauber smiled. 'Yes. In the first place I have no reason at all to doubt his patriotism, in the second, by the time I've had a talk with him he will be far too scared to do anything except exactly what he is told; and in the third, I shall send one of my best men with him into Switzerland with orders to watch him at every step.'

The Admiral stood up and made a faintly mocking little bow. 'In that case, my dear *Herr Gruppenführer*, having rendered you such small assistance as lay within my power, like my illustrious predecessor, Pontius Pilate, I wash my hands of this affair. Erika was once a dear friend of mine, and I have never believed that she was a traitor to her country; but expediency demands that I should leave her and her lover to your tender mercies. I pray that God may cheat you in the end and bring them death more swiftly than you would desire.'

3

The Fly

'Vell, glad to see you, my boy. Here's how!' Sir Pellinore
Gwaine-Cust raised his silver tankard to Gregory Sallust and
took a long swig at the champagne that it contained.

'Cheers!' murmured Gregory, taking a somewhat more
modest pull at his tankard of the freshly iced wine.

'Don't sip it as though you were a deb at her first dance,
man,' chided the elderly Baronet disapprovingly. 'Only way to
get the full flavour of this stuff is to take the first half-tankard
non-stop.'

'I agree; but it's too precious to treat like that in these days;
unless, of course'—Gregory's saturnine features lit up with a
sudden grin—'one happens to be a munitions magnate trying
to work off excess profits through the old expense account.'

Sir Pellinore's bright blue eyes opened wide with indigna-
tion. 'Insolent young devil!' he boomed. 'How dare you make
your dirty cracks at me! Admittedly I've a few shares in one
or two companies, but what the Government doesn't take off
as to pay for the war wouldn't keep a baby in napkins. I'm
living on capital. Only thing to do unless I gave up Gwaine
Meads and this place. And at my age I'll be jiggered if I move
into some poky little flat.'

They were sitting out on the terrace behind Sir Pellinore's
London mansion, and Gregory glanced up at the great pillared
façade that rose behind them. Its cream paint looked grimly in
the July sunshine, and here and there it had been scarred by
bomb splinters. The windows of the big library that opened on
to the terrace had been shattered and were now boarded over;
a large chunk of the stone balustrade had fallen on the public
footway below, leaving an ugly gap. But he had known the
house well in peacetime, and recalled its splendid staircase lit
with great crystal chandeliers and thronged with distinguished
people, while a string band played softly in the distance and a
score of liveried footmen served the guests with every delicacy
that money could provide.

Even now, in war-scarred London, he felt that there were
many worse places to live in than Carlton House Terrace, with
its beautiful view over St. James's Park. To the right, at the
extremity of the double avenue of The Mall, the upper storeys
of Buckingham Palace rose white above the fresh green of the
tree-tops. In the left foreground stood the Admiralty, Horse
Guards Parade, the back of No. 10, the Foreign Office, and

the Offices of the War Cabinet. Between them a constant stream of little figures was weaving to and fro, mainly Naval Army and Air Force officers hurrying from conference to conference, at which the next moves in the war would be planned while in the very centre of the scene lay the green sward, made gay with flower-beds and girls' summer dresses; and the lovely tree-fringed lake, upon which swam flotillas of bright-winged ducks, and where the three white pelicans gravely stood knee deep in water for hours on end—so inanimate, but apparently wise, that they had irrelevantly been nicknamed 'The Three Chiefs of Staff'.

Who, Gregory wondered, with a war in progress, would willingly live anywhere but here, right in the vortex of the cyclone, or, in peacetime, not prefer the outlook on this ancient Royal pleasance to view over some dusty London square?

He glanced at his companion. Sir Pellinore stood six-feet four in his socks, and his limbs were big in proportion. He was now over seventy, but he could still have thrown most men of thirty down his staircase. His bright blue eyes were full of animation and his great white cavalry moustache flared up across the rubicund cheeks that it had taken a hundred pipes of port to bring to their present healthy glow.

'We don't breed men like him in these days, more's the pity,' thought Gregory. 'He just wouldn't do in a flat. He'd begin to feel suffocated in no time and he'd be knocking the ornaments down with those great hands of his every time he made one of his sweeping gestures.'

After a moment he said: 'Even in wartime I suppose Gwaine Meads and this little shanty cost you a pretty penny to keep up. Still, you are lucky to have lived in the days when you could salt down a fair part of your ill-gotten millions. No one of my generation will be able to put by anything worth while. In fact, when the State has no more use for us we'll probably spend our declining years in some frightful institution, where the highlight of our existence will be a piece of cake to eat with our tea on Saturdays.'

'Oh, come, that's a gloomy view to take.'

'But not unrealistic. We've had two years of war, and with Hitler in control of a big slice of Europe as Napoleon ever had it may go on for another twenty. Britain has had to sell the shirt off her back to get dollars from America, and to keep our end up against our Totalitarian enemies we're being compelled to Nazify ourselves to a point at which we shall be able to call nothing but our souls our own. Of course, I'm quite prepared to go on fighting in the hills and on the beaches, and all that, until my hand is so shaky that I can no longer hold a gun, but it does seem a bit hard that if I chance to survive to

r age I shall be either in a workhouse or an antiquated
e-slave of the State.'

'Nonsense, my boy! Things won't be as bad as all that. Think
he summer of nineteen sixteen. We were in a pretty pickle
. Yet we got the Jerries down in just over another two
rs; and afterwards there was a mint of money lying about
those who had the initiative to pick it up.'

't won't be like that this time.' Gregory glumly shook his
d. 'Coming events cast their shadows before. The bureau-
ts have at last got us where they've wanted us for years.
s war is being used as an excuse to strangle all free enter-
se, and to prevent any Englishman's home ever being his
tle any more. Last time Lloyd George wanted to give us all
ee acres and a cow. This time we'll have to have a permit
milk the cow, even if we can afford to buy it; another to
ke butter from the milk, and a third to grow the grass that
 cow feeds on. But no, I'm wrong about that. We won't
allowed to have any acres or cows because the Government
 issue us with a ration of powdered milk. We'll all be
ary little people living in dreary little houses and forced
work eight hours a day in some ghastly factory making
ury goods for export to our richer neighbours, and we shall
tain life on a packet of vitamised chemical foods that we'll
ve to queue for once a week at the local Food Office.'

Sir Pellinore took another pull at his tankard, wiped his
gnificent white moustache with the back of his hand and
claimed with a puzzled stare:

'What the devil's got under your skin, Gregory? I've never
own you like this before.'

'Oh, I don't know,' Gregory shrugged. 'For one thing I'd
e to get married and settle down. Of course, I know that's
t of the question until the war is over, and even then Erika
ll have to get her divorce. But these last few weeks, since
got back from France, have pretty naturally increased the
ge in both of us—and it's a bit depressing to think how
mote the chances are of our ever being able to live the sort
 life we'd like.'

'What sort of life had you in mind?'

'Nothing terribly extravagant. Just a comfortable home
mewhere in the country. An old place for preference, with
e sort of rambling outbuildings that children love to play
, and a decent garden. I'd like a south wall to grow peaches,
glasshouse for a vine, and a meadow for a cow. Four or five
res and a house with two spare bedrooms would be quite
g enough. Something large enough to have friends down to
ay in comfort, but that wouldn't need a big staff to keep up.'

'All right, now's the time to buy. The public never can see

further than its nose, otherwise there would never have b
rich men like myself in any generation. Just because thi
aren't too good they think the war is going on for ever. 1
idiots have all got cold feet about house property and the
be fighting each other for it in a few years' time. For five
six thousand today you can take your pick of a score of pla
in any county that would have cost you ten before the v
and will fetch fifteen after it.'

'Yes. You're probably right, and I could just about run
that without making too big a hole in my capital. I must th
it over.'

'Don't think it over. Tell Erika to look round for the s
of place you'd both like, and when she finds it, buy it. Y
can't possibly go wrong; and don't interfere with your inve
ments. I'll give you a cheque before you go.'

'But, hang it all . . .'

'That's all right. Ten thousand ought to do you. Most pla
of any size have been taken over for the duration by the Arr
or the Air Force, and by the time they've kicked hell out o
you'll need a thousand or two extra to make it really hal
able again.'

'It really is terribly good of you.'

'Nonsense, my boy. Consider it as a wedding present in a
vance, if you like. But, anyhow, I was going to give you a go
fat cheque for your last little exploit; and, as I've told y
before, if I hang on to all my money the bulk of it will only
to the Government in death duties when I die. Much bett
give it away to people I like to have a bit of fun with it no\

Actually Gregory had met Sir Pellinore long before he h
started to write articles on international affairs. Twenty-fi
summers ago as a very young subaltern, he had carried S
Pellinore's only son back out of the hell of Thiepval Woo
in the great Somme battle. The young man had died of l
wounds, but the episode had created a strong tie between l
father and his rescuer which had strengthened with the passi
years until Sir Pellinore had come to regard Gregory wi
almost as much affection as he had had for the son that he ha
lost.

As Gregory began to renew his thanks the elderly Baronet c
him short and said:

'That's settled then. Now I'll tell you why I lugged you u
from Shropshire. I want to hear how you think the war
shaping.'

'Oh, come!' Gregory laughed. 'It's you who are talking no
sense now. For the best part of a month I've been buried
the country, whereas you've been right in the middle of thing
Generals, Admirals, Air Marshals, Ambassadors on leave an

Cabinet Ministers are always dropping in to give you the low-down, so you must know how things are going infinitely better than I do.'

'No, no. It's true that a few old cronies of mine look in now and again to talk over the stuff the papers have printed that morning. They never ask my advice, mind you. And they're right. They know that I've got no brains. I've an eye for a horse and a pretty woman, but I never had any brains at all.'

'I know,' said Gregory, his dark eyes twinkling. 'It's just that you're a good listener and they like to pour out their little worries to you, isn't it? I've heard that one before.'

'Drat the boy!' Sir Pellinore grumbled. 'Impudent as ever. Well, perhaps they sometimes do tell me a thing or two, because they know I'm safe. But what I know is no damn business of yours. Trouble is, though, that none of us here can see the wood for the trees. Our minds are so bunged up with detail that we're incapable of making a sound assessment of the big picture. You're outside it all and you're a pretty shrewd young rascal. That's why I want to know how things look to you.'

'Right then,' Gregory sat back and lit a Sullivan. 'Let's take the good side first. The great thing is that we're no longer alone. The Russians are now in this thing with us.'

'Yes, and whether we like the Bolshies or not, Winston was one hundred per cent right to declare that any enemy of Hitler's is a friend of ours. Still, they haven't shown up any too well—so far. Ever since the show started the Nazis have been pushing them back on every front.'

'Nevertheless, they must be killing quite a lot of Germans; and if the main German armies had not gone into Russia this summer they wouldn't be sitting on their bottoms. They'd be on their way through Turkey to the Persian oilfields by now, or perhaps even knocking hell out of Kent and Sussex.

'That's true. We were in pretty low water this spring, after our withdrawal from Greece and Crete. At all events this Russian business has given us a badly needed breather.'

'That's just the point I'm making. If we hadn't gone into Greece Wavell could have used those troops when he had the Italians on the run to go right through to Algeria and join up with the French. They were game to come in with us then and by this time the whole of North Africa would have been in our hands. But in that crazy Greek adventure we threw away the only decent Army that we had, and it's going to take months yet to build it up again. In the meantime, Russia is saving us from the worst results of our folly and enabling us to conserve our forces till we're stong enough to strike again next spring.'

'Yes. If the Russians can stick the pace. Well, what else?'

'The other bull point is the way that the R.A.F. is being built up. It's impossible to say yet if Germany can be knocked out by air power alone, but the pasting that the German cities are getting now must be having a pretty serious effect on their war industries. Anyhow, one thing I do know. The British Army alone will never be able to defeat the main German armies on the continent of Europe. It's not a question of courage or efficiency or even weapons; it's simply that we haven't got the man-power.'

'How about if the United States came in with us?'

'Ah, that would alter the whole picture. Together we might do the trick. But will she? that's the question? This Lease-Lend she is giving us now will be immensely valuable when it gets into full swing, but she may consider that is going far enough. After all, the Prime Minister did say, "Give us the tools and we'll finish the job", didn't he? And even if America came in tomorrow, it would take her at least two years to raise, train, equip and transport to Britain an army big enough to ensure our joint success in invading and conquering Hitler's Empire. On the other hand, the Ruskies are in with us already, and there are best part of two hundred million of them.'

'Yes. They've got the man-power all right, but the problem there is, how much of it can they actually put into the field? Can't fight wars with scythes and pitchforks these days, you know. Still, saying they were equipped with plenty of tanks and all this modern paraphernalia, what were you driving at?'

'Simply that, if I were the War Cabinet, I should use every means in my power to encourage the Russians to keep the German Army busy, while I switched four-fifths of the resources of the Empire over to creating the mightiest Air Armada that has ever been dreamed of. We've already seen what the R.A.F. can do on a wartime increase proportionate to the other two Services. I believe that if its further expansion was given absolute priority over everything else we'd knock such blue hell out of the Fatherland that we'd have the war over in another two years.'

'That's what the airmen say themselves,' nodded Sir Pellinore. 'But there's not a hope of it. The other Services wouldn't stand for that—and they may be right, you know. The Germans are reported to have reached Smolensk already. That's half-way to Moscow. Russia's strategy has always been to give ground but there's a limit to the amount she can afford to sacrifice. Every city that goes into the German bag means fewer munitions for Stalins' armies; every acre lost means less food for the Russian people. If the Nazis push on at this rate the Bolshies may be compelled to pack up by the autumn. Then

e'd have the German Army on our hands again, and with the
resources of all Europe to draw on no amount of bombs on
Germany would put it out of business for good.'

'The Russians have just signed this agreement with us not
to conclude a separate peace,' hazarded Gregory.

'Ah, but will they stick to it if they find they're getting an
onest-to-God licking, eh? That's the rub. I wouldn't trust
most of those fellers with an old top-hat. Talk about a thieves'
kitchen. Why, even the dossiers of the big-shot Nazis are no
worse than the records of most of those Kremlinites. Mind
you. I think Stalin is in a class apart. He is about as unscrupulous as you are, which is saying something; but at least he's a
clean thinker. As a matter of fact, I've always had a sneaking
admiration for old Uncle Joe, and I'm certain he has the sense
to know that it's either Corporal Charlie Chaplin or himself
for the high jump this time.'

'If you're right he'll fight to the last ditch, then?'

'Yes. But where is the last ditch? That's what I'd like to
know. There's another thing. For several years now Stalin's
health has been reported as not too good. Heart trouble, so
they say. Of course that may just be a Kremlin rumour put
out on purpose. Why, God knows, but they're a funny lot,
and always pushing out stuff that doesn't make sense to anyone except themselves. Say it's correct, though, and he konks
out on us. There are still certain pro-German elements in Moscow. They might get control. Then we'd be in a pretty mess.
But I'm butting in on your appreciation. Go ahead?'

'Well, to finish up on the credit side, there's the Italian collapse in Abyssinia and General Dentz's surrender in Syria.
Two more great triumphs for Wavell before his transfer to
India, and two expensive running sores stopped, which enormously consolidates our position in the Middle East.'

'Umph!' grunted Sir Pellinore. 'Only hope the Auk does half
as well there. Winston thinks a lot of him, but time will show.
What next?'

'On the debit side, owing to the wastage of our resources in
Greece and Crete, I shouldn't think we can possibly launch
another offensive against Libya until next spring, and unless
we have a crack at Norway there doesn't seem to be anything
that the Army can do at all.'

'They might; but once bitten, you know.'

'The Navy is stretched to the limit as it is, yet the U-boat
menace is on the increase and conditions in Britain are worse-
ning every month. Things aren't too good in India, and the
Japs are getting more uppish every day. We've lost the Eastern
Balkans, as well as Greece, and Antonescu's *coup d'état* in
Rumania has secured to Hitler his main supplies of oil. Our

going into Syria may have been necessary but it has turned
great part of the French against us so all the prospects that ∿
had earlier in the year of the French Armies in North Afri
declaring for us have now disappeared. By and large, it's not
pretty picture. Our commitments are enormous and our r
sources lamentably few. The Royal Air Force is the on
weapon we've got with which we shall be able really to stri
at Germany for a long time to come; so, as far as I se
it's a pretty hopeless job to attempt to plan our future strateg
until we know the real value of Russia as an ally, and get son
idea as to how long she will be able to keep the main Germa
armies occupied.'

'Excellent, my boy! First-class appreciation.' Sir Pellino∿
swallowed the remainder of his champagne and set the tankaɪ
down with a bang. 'Well. That's why I want you to go ∿
Russia for us and find out.'

4

The Mission

Gregory's face broke into a slightly twisted smile. 'I kneʋ
damn well you hadn't lugged me all the way up from Shrop
shire to ask my opinion of the war.'

'Glad I did though. Couldn't have worked out better.' Si
Pellinore gave a loud guffaw. 'Every point you made brough
us back to the Bolshies and the question of how long they'ɪ
be able to stay the course. Saved me the trouble of having tɪ
convince you how important it is that we should get some
thing straight from the stable about their form.'

'Still working on your old principle of never doing anything
yourself if you can get the other chap to do it for you, eh?'

'That's it. Only exception to the rule is drawing corks ouɪ
of old bottles. Servants don't understand how to handle gooɪ
liquor these days, and if the cork's gone powdery they let it geɪ
into the wine. But how about it? Are you prepared to play?'

The slightly stooping shoulders that were concealed undeɪ
Gregory's well-cut lounge suit lifted in a little shrug. 'As the
only alternative now left to men of my age is a job in a fac
tory, or a seat in an office, with Home Guard in the evenings
and Fire-watching at night, I suppose I'll have to.'

32

'Cynical young devil! You're right, though. It's the middle-aged civilians who're getting the rough deal in this war. The fellers in the Services are better fed, better clothed, get more sleep and have most of the pretty girls with them to tumble around into the bargain. But, joking apart, I felt sure I could count on you, and I'm very grateful. When can you leave?'

'That's for you to say; but I'd like a few more days with Erika, and I imagine it will take you that to make arrangements for my trip?'

'All right. Today's Thursday. Get back in time to dine with me here on Monday night and I'll have everything ready.'

'How do I go? Do I have to risk my neck again by dropping with a parachute, or do you want me to sneak over the frontier disguised as an organ-grinder?'

'Gad, no! You go straight in by the front door under your own name with a perfectly good British passport. No need for any heroics this time. The Russians are now our allies.'

'Yes. That had occurred to me. Also the fact that sending someone to ferret out the military secrets of an Allied Power is, to say the least of it, a bit unorthodox.'

'What's that!' Sir Pellinore drew up his long legs with a jerk. 'When I need any lessons in ethics I'll ask for them, you insolent young cub.'

'I should think the Foreign Office would throw a fit,' smiled Gregory, quite unperturbed.

'Oh, the Foreign Office knows when to mind its own business. Don't you worry about that. But you're right, of course, that they wouldn't dare to monkey with a thing like this. That's why we can't ask you-know-who to handle the job. If one of his people were caught at it there'd be no end of a rumpus.'

'Quite apart from what may happen to me, if I'm pinched by the *Ogpu* there may be quite a spot of bother this end, as I'm to go in on a British passport.'

'I realise that, but the Bolshie counter-espionage system is far too good to chance sending you in any other way. If you are caught, at least they can't check back on you and link you up with our own organisation. I had in mind that you should go as a journalist with a notional job under our Press Attaché. No good journalist can resist poking his nose in where he's not wanted, so if you do get in a mess we ought to be able to laugh you off on that score.'

'That sounds all right. What exactly do you want me to find out?'

'Three things. What proportion of their man-power the Russians can actually put into the field. How much territory they can afford to give away before they would be compelled to throw up the sponge. And the real state of Stalin's health.'

Gregory made a grimace and the scar above his left eyebrow suddenly showed white. 'That's a pretty tall order.'

'I know, but only by having that information can we form a sound assessment of how long they can stick it.'

'What's the matter with our Military Intelligence? They are paid to do this sort of thing in peacetime, and they've had years to collect the data on which to form a proper appreciation. Can't they give you what you want?'

Sir Pellinore's blue eyes were a little blank, and he shook his head. 'I don't think it would be very profitable to go into that. All I can tell you is what some of our senior Generals have told me. Camberley and the War House have always taken a pretty poor view of the Russians. That may be based on sound information or it may be prejudice. Anyhow, when Russia came in most of these wallahs said she'd be finished in a month. Well, the month is up, and the Bolshies seem to have quite a lot of kick left in them yet. Now, when I lunch with the "brutal and licentious" at the Senior or the Rag, the pessimists say the Russian goose will be cooked by the end of August, while the optimists give her three months at the outside.'

'Have you ever read a book called *Red Eagle?*'

'No. What about it?'

'It was a biography of Marshal Voroshilov, published several years before the war, and I remember being particularly interested in what the author had to say about Russia's future strategy, as gleaned from Voroshilov's writings.'

'What line did this scribbler feller suggest that he'd take?'

'He reported Voroshilov as saying that, owing to the tremendous development of air fleets in the Western European countries, frontiers and definitions of front and rear in the countries engaged would no longer have their former significance; and that the Marshal was counting on a great belt of Russian territory, including the cities of Leningrad, Smolensk, Minsk and Kiev, being rendered untenable. In fact, that he was reorganising the whole of Russia's war potential to enable her to give up great areas of territory and yet put up an unbreakable defence. That he was already moving his arsenals and war factories right back behind the Urals where they would be too distant to be bombed; and that this would enable him to fight on in a position from which it would be practically impossible for any European power to dislodge him.'

'Interesting, that.'

'Yes. I thought so, because it was such an entirely different picture to anything that our military pundits ever seem to have visualised; and, after all, if they had only taken the trouble they could easily have checked up those statements by consulting Voroshilov's writings for themselves.'

'Well, I only hope to God my Generals are wrong and your feller's right; but that's what we've got to find out. The hell of a lot hangs on this, Gregory, and I'll tell you why; but you must keep it under your hat.'

Sir Pellinore stood up and thrusting his great hands into the pockets of his penstripe trousers, began to walk up and down. 'We know that the Russian first line units are pretty well equipped, but the show seems to be developing in the way this pen-pusher of yours forecast. Huge battles are raging now at many points between the Baltic and the Black Sea, but there is no longer a continuous line of battle, and half the people fighting know only from day to day which is their front and which is their rear. In that sort of warfare whole formations, even up to divisions and Army corps, are apt to find themselves encircled and cut off. That doesn't matter if you are on the winning side, because a few days later your pals come up and break the ring that the enemy has made round you; but if your High Command is giving ground you find yourself left behind and you're in the bag for good, with everything you've got.'

'You mean that the Russians are not only losing men but a lot of their best equipment too?' Gregory interjected.

'That's it! Remember what we used to hear about the Ruskies in the last war? People who were out there said that they were damn good fighters but so short of weapons that they had only one rifle to every three men; and that when the feller who had it became a casualty the next chap picked it up. Well, if they could do that now with their tanks and guns they might be all right for a long time to come. But owing to this hotch-potch that has resulted from mechanised warfare it can't be done. Stalin says that his war-plant is adequate for normal replacements, but that his losses to date have been abnormal, and that if he's to stick the pace he must have every tank, gun, lorry and radio set that we can send him. See? He's calling on us to do a Lease-Lend to Russia.'

Gregory raised his eyebrow. 'So that's the idea. Well, it seems a very sound proposition.'

'Oh, it fits in with your theory about encouraging the Russians to keep the main German Army occupied on the ground while we hammer hell out of Germany from the air. But if we rob all our new divisions of the weapons they should be receiving to send the stuff to the Bolshies, and they do collapse by the autumn, we'll look a pretty lot of fools, won't we?'

'You certainly would,' Gregory laughed. 'What a problem!

35

I certainly don't envy the people whose responsibility it is to pass judgement on that one.'

'You're right, my boy. To send or not to send this stuff to Russia is probably the most important decision we'll be called on to make during the whole war. No good taking half measures. That's a sure road to ruin, whatever happens. We've got to back the Bolshies for all we're worth and take a chance on being left naked ourselves next spring, or play for safety now with the prospect of having to fight the Germans on our own again in a few months' time. Now you see why the people who have to make that decision are so desperately anxious to know what the real chances are of the Russians being able to fight on through the winter if we hand over our weapons to them.'

'It's taking on the hell of a lot, but I'll do my best for you. There's one serious snag, though, I can only speak about ten words of Russian.'

'I thought of that. I want you to take that tame Bolshevik of yours with you to act as your interpreter, General Kuro-bitch or Kipopoff, or something. Never could get the hang of these foreign names.'

'You mean Stefan Kuporovitch?'

'That's it. How's he hitting it off with that French gel he married? Pretty little baggage. Have they been enjoying themselves at Gwaine Meads?'

'Who could help enjoying themselves at your lovely home? They've been having a marvellous honeymoon, and fortunately Madeleine and Erika like each other, so all four of us have been living on top of the world. Still, I don't think Stefan could go back to Russia.'

'Why? Has that French piece of nonsense tied him to her apron strings?'

'No, it's not that. They've had a longer honeymoon than most people get who marry in the middle of a war, so I don't think she'd stand in his way. And, as a matter of fact, ever since the Germans began to get the best of it he's been itching to get back to fight for his country.'

'Well, here's his opportunity—anyhow, to do some useful work for the cause of the Allies.'

'That's all very well, but if he went back to Russia it's a million to a sack of potatoes that Stalin's boys would shoot him.'

'I thought he was a pal of Voroshilov's?'

'So he was. He started life as a Czarist officer; but like all the more intelligent ones he was a Liberal, and more by force of circumstances than anything else he found himself on the side of the Reds. He served under Voroshilov at Tzaritisn and formed a great attachment to him, so, pretty naturally, from

36

that point he continued his military career. But by the time I met him at Kandalaksha he was fed up to the back teeth with the Union of Soviet Socialist Republics and all its works. That's why he decided to clear out with me. So you see he's really a deserter from the Russian Army.'

Sir Pellinore stroked his fine white moustache thoughtfully for a moment, then he said: 'I've got over worse fences than that in my time. We'll make him a naturalised Englishman and give him a British passport. Thousands of Russians have fled the country in the last twenty years and taken other nationalities. Scores of 'em have gone back too, and been none the worse for it.'

'That certainly is an idea,' Gregory agreed. 'And now that Britain and Russia are allies it's hardly likely that they'd deliberately pick a quarrel with us over an interpreter attached to our Mission.'

'No. At worst they might say that he's *persona ingrata*, and ask our Ambassador to send him home; but if he keeps himself well in the background he may not even be recognised.'

'How is Sir Stafford doing in Moscow?'

'As well as can be expected. Cripps is a clever fellow—very able man. So was Karl Marx, but I can see him as the hit of the season at the court of Queen Victoria.'

'Oh, come,' Gregory smiled. 'That's no fair comparison. Surely it was paying the Russians a pleasant compliment to send them our leading Communist, as they are Communists themselves.'

'Are they?' Sir Pellinore ceased his pacing and fixed Gregory with his bright blue eyes. 'Maybe they were in Trotsky's time, but in all but name they've been National Socialists for years. Anyhow, Cripps may be as patriotic as Winston, but the fact remains that in Russian eyes he does not represent British thought or feeling. The way to have won their confidence would have been to send 'em the Duke of Gloucester. They'd have been so flattered they would have eaten out of our hands, and you wouldn't have been able to see Moscow for Union Jacks. I put that up to one or two people, but they wouldn't listen. And after all, why should they? Everyone knows I've got no brains—no brains at all!'

Gregory's mocking laugh was cut short by the appearance of the elderly butler to announce lunch.

'Well, that's enough of your smoking-room stories, my boy,' Sir Pellinore gave a broad wink. 'Got to get down to business while we eat. This plague rationing is a darn sight more of a nuisance than the bombs, but at least that house-painter feller can't stop us getting lobsters off our shores, and some

37

of those nectarines you brought up won't go down too badly with a bottle of Yquem.'

Having partaken of Sir Pellinore's Lucullan hospitality, Gregory made a few purchases in the West End, spent an hour at his club and caught the six-ten back to Shrewsbury, where a car met him and carried him to Gwaine Meads in time for a late supper.

The major part of Sir Pellinore's stately home was now an R.A.F. hospital. Before the war was twenty-four hours old he had said to one of his friends in the Air Ministry: 'Have the place fitted up for as many convalescents as it will hold and send the bill to me. No commandeering, mind. Everyone who stays, patients, nurses, doctors, gillies, cooks—are all my guests and each one is to be told so individually. It's not that I want any thanks but if they know that they'll have the decency to refrain from burning the Jacobean staircase and making bawdy additions to my Angelica Kaufmann frescoes. Send me a monthly account of what it costs to run and I'll pay the whole shooting match, but the west wing is to remain untouched and at my disposal. I may want to send friends there to recuperate if they've been through a rough time. Understand?'

The Air Marshal, being a man of sense, had 'understood' and, at the price of considerable inroads into even his enormous fortune, the elderly Baronet still enjoyed the amenities of a dozen rooms in his beautiful country home, although he was much too occupied with the war ever to go there himself.

Since Erika had been evacuated from Dunkirk he had insisted on her making her home there, so Gregory also spent nearly all this time at Gwaine Meads whenever he was in England. At the moment, Sir Pellinore's other private guests consisted of Stefan Kuporovitch and Madeleine; an elderly scientist who was recovering from a breakdown due to overwork and a young Guards officers who had recently been cashiered. The others did not know it, but he had acquiesced in fake charges being laid against him for highly secret reasons. None of Sir Pellinore's guests ever enquired into one another's business. It was quite sufficient for them that they had all been sponsored by him, and they got on excellently.

Although Erika lived in the private wing she had long since taken on voluntary duties in the hospital, and Madeleine, being a fully trained nurse had, after a brief holiday, also joined the staff. In consequence, the two girls were busy most of the day, so on the Friday morning Gregory had no difficulty in getting Kuporovitch to himself.

In this second summer of the war the gardens had lost some of their former splendour, but a few old gardeners managed to keep them tidy and a number of the convalescents often amused themselves by running the motor mower over the lawn so the turf on to which Gregory led his friend, in order to be out of earshot of everybody, was still smooth and springy.

'I saw Sir Pellinore yesterday,' Gregory opened up in French, which they still used as a common language. 'And he wants me to do a job for him in Russia.'

'*Mais, mon vieux!*' the Russian's black eyebrows, that contrasted so strangely with his grey hair, lifted, wrinkling his smooth forehead 'You would be crazy to attempt undercover work there, seeing that you can hardly speak a word of Russian.'

'That's exactly what I said, and he suggested that I should take you as my interpreter.'

Kuporovitch's lazy blue eyes remained quite expresssionless for a moment, then he said: 'You know as well as I do that for me to return to Russia is to court death. Yet I am not afraid to die, and would risk my life willingly if by so doing I can serve my country.'

'Sir Pellinore proposes that, if you agree to go, he should take out naturalisation papers on your behalf. You would not only travel on a British passport but enjoy the full protection of our Embassy. He seemed quite confident that then, even if you were recognised, you would remain immune from arrest.'

'That is an idea. I doubt if it would be sufficient protection in ordinary times. The *Ogpu* would arrange that I met with an "accident" and send your ambassador their regrets. But we Russians are realists. We do not cut off our noses to spite our faces. It is unlikely that they would interfere with me if I have taken British nationality and they are also given reasons to believe that I am fulfilling a useful function with their British Allies.'

'Good. I'm sure that could all be fixed up; and I need hardly say how much I'd like to have you with me; but there would still be the risk of their catching us prying into their affairs.'

'*Mon ami,* again I can only say to you that I am willing to risk my life if by so doing I can serve my country. But, on the face of it, to return there as the secret agent of a foreign Power seems a strange way to do so.'

They had reached the long herbaceous border, now a little past its best, but still gay with a multitude of flowers that were just beginning to seed. As they turned back towards the terrace of the house Gregory did not reply and they paced on in silence for a little, two figures apparently much of a height. Actually Gregory was several inches taller than the Russian, but his head was thrust forward as usual in a predatory slouch while Kuporovitch's broad shoulders and bulky torso were largely offset by the fact that a lifetime of military service caused him to carry himself rigidly erect.

Gregory was in a quandary. He wanted to be fair to his friend, yet, at the same time he had the interests of his own country to think of. He knew that it would be impossible to accomplish his mission without a reliable interpreter, and that his chances of finding one who would also prove such a courageous and resourceful companion as Kuporovitch were extremely slender. At length he said:

'What do you think of Russia's chances, Stefan? Do you reckon she will be able to hold this German onslaught and stick it out till next spring?'

'Of course she will,' Kuporovitch replied with quiet confidence. 'We may have to give much more ground, but that has always been Russia's strategy. Her war machine is so vast that it will take months to get it into full operation. I doubt even if her mobilisation will be completed until this time next year. But then you will see. It will indeed be "death to the German invaders"!'

'Yes. I realise the immensity of Russia's resources. But the *Blitzkrieg,* with its armoured spearheads racing ahead at fifty miles a day, is a new form of warfare. Isn't it possible that she might be knocked out by the capture of most of her principal cities before she's had a chance really to get going?'

Kuporovitch shook his round bullet-head. 'No. We have always believed that one day the Germans would attack us, and years ago Voroshilov, as Commissar for Defence, made his plans accordingly. Today our main munition plants are in places like Sverdlovsk, Omsk, Tobolsk, Petropavlovsk and Cheliabinsk, all right back behind the Urals; and a constant stream of reserve formations will be brought forward into the battle. It will be a hard war for many of our poor people, but even the fall of Leningrad, Kiev, Odessa and Moscow could not put us out of the war, and our soldiers will not lay down their arms while there is one Hitlerite bandit left on Russian soil.'

Gregory sighed. 'How I wish our people would accept your word for all that; then it wouldn't be necessary for me to make this trip. Still, if you're convinced of that yourself, Stefan, I can set your conscience at rest. In order to decide on its own future strategy the British Government want me to go out to assess Russia's capacity for remaining in the war. As long as they have any doubt about that they're bound to play for safety, but once satisfied they could take all sorts of risks which should have the effect of bringing about the final defeat of Germany very much sooner. So if you can help me to prove

...at your beliefs are correct you'll be rendering a great service
...o your own country.'

'In that case, *mon vieux*, I am your man. My countrymen
...ave a habit of giving short shrift to people whom they catch
...rying to find out their secrets, so we shall have to be very, very
...areful; but that is all the more reason, knowing something of
...heir methods, that I should go with you.'

'Bless you, Stefan.' Gregory linked his arm affectionately
...hrough that of the Russian. 'I honestly think I'd funk this
...ob on my own, but with you to help me the chances of get-
...ing back to Gwaine Meads again are increased a thousand-
...old.'

'When do we leave?'

'We catch the morning train to London on Monday and
...ine with Sir Pellinore that night. After that it will be up to
...im; but he can get all sorts of things done in a few days that
...ake other people months. So if I telephone to him at lunch
...ime that you've agreed to play he'll probably have your
naturalisation papers pushed through over the weekend. It
...would be as well, I think, to anglicise your name at the same
time. Fewer questions are likely to be asked if the passport is
issued to Mr. Stephen Cooper.'

'Yes, that is sound. I fear though that the little Madeleine
will take my departure badly.'

'So will Erika; but they both know that we're not the sort
of chaps to sit at home indefinitely while there's a war on, and
at rock bottom they wouldn't think much of us if we did.
After all, we're lucky to have had a month here; but I suggest
that we shouldn't say anything about our being off again till
Sunday night.'

'I agree. Then the prospect of parting will not shadow our
last weekend here, and we'll do our damnedest to make it a
super good one.'

'That's it,' Gregory laughed. 'Let's eat, drink and be merry
while we may. What about a visit to the peach houses, to collect some fruit for lunch?'

That night and for the two days that followed they lived
up to their intention and nobody but the two girls who loved
them would have suspected that they had a care in the world,
but perhaps it was their grasping with such fresh zest at every
pleasure that offered which made both Madeleine and Erika
slightly uneasy.

In consequence, when Gregory took Erika out on to the
terrace after dinner on the Sunday night and said: 'I've got
some news for you,' she replied at once:

'I know, darling. You're going abroad again, aren't you?'

'So you guessed,' he smiled, and picking her up sat her on

41

the stone balustrade, so that her golden head came nearly leve
with his own.

'It wasn't very difficult.' She put a soft arm around his neck
'Your going up to London on Thursday and then your love
making having been so hectic ever since.'

His tight-lipped mouth twisted into a grin that brought dee
furrows each side of it to his lean cheeks. 'So I overdid it, eh?'

'No, my sweet. You could never overdo making love to me
but that's how I guessed.'

'Well, there it is. As a matter of fact I had two pieces o
news for you and I've a penny here still clutched in one hand
I was going to ask you to guess which fist it was in, and if you'd
picked the one with the penny you'd have had the good new:
first. Still, you beat me to it and know the worst now. I'm off on
my travels again tomorrow morning.'

'Is it—is it Germany?' she asked, with a little catch in her
voice.

'No. I don't think you need worry overmuch this time. I'm
going to Russia.'

'Russia! But the Russians are fighting Hitler too. You know
I'm not trying to pry but I simply can't imagine why Sir
Pellinore should be sending you there.'

'There's no harm in my telling you, because even if the Nazis
knew they couldn't stop me, or do anything to interfere with
my activities, and there's nothing at all specific about my
mission. I'm simply going to try to find out what everybody
would like to know. How long the Russians can hope to resist
the German armies; how much of their man-power they can
really put into the field; how much territory they can afford to
give away, and that sort of thing; and, incidentally, the state
of Stalin's health.'

'I see. Yes, I suppose it is important that the British should
secure their own really reliable information about that sort
of thing. But everything in Russia is hidden behind a veil of
secrecy, and the Russians are such strange ruthless people that,
even now they are your allies, I shall be frightened for you till
you get back.'

'I'm taking Stefan with me.'

'Oh, I'm so glad. I suppose that's selfish of me, because poor
Madeleine will be heartbroken. She simply adores that dear
old tough. But he's as cunning as a monkey and as courageous
as his national bear; and he knows the ways of those grim
compatriots of his, as well. It'll be a tremendous comfort to me
to know he's with you. But can he go back? I thought . . .'

'We've fixed that. At least Sir Pellinore is pulling the wires
as usual and Stefan is going out on a British passport. Not a

ce, but a real one to be issued as a result of his assuming
British nationality.'

Erika smoothed Gregory's brown hair with her slim fingers.
'You know, sometimes I feel that I ought to accept Sir Pellinore's offer to do the same for me. It's such an anomalous
position, having been evacuated here when I was too ill to
know what was happening, and being under sentence of death
by the Nazis, yet having refused to declare myself a refugee.
Of course if it weren't for the special exemption that dear
old Pellinore obtained for me I'd be behind barbed wire in
the Isle of Man; but I didn't come over to the enemy deliberately, and I won't pretend I did, and it does seem terribly wrong
to rat on one's own country by changing one's nationality in
the middle of a war.'

'Don't fret, my sweet,' Gregory caressed her cheek. 'The
moment we can get married you'll be British anyway.'

'Do you still want to marry me?'

'More than ever. I'd had more than my share of racketing
about before I met you, and so had you. I'm sick to death of
travelling and risking my neck. The minute the war is over I
mean to chuck my pistols in the Thames, get married to you
on a special licence and settle down for good. That reminds
me. You haven't asked me my other piece of news.'

'No, I'd forgotten, but you said it was nice. Do tell me.'

'Old Pellinore has given us a wedding present in advance.
A cheque for ten thousand quid to buy a home to settle down
in.'

'But how marvellous! He is a dear.'

'Yes, every rich man knows that when he dies he can't take
his money with him, but you don't find many of them that
behave with such splendid generosity.'

Erika leant forward and gave him a long, long kiss. As they
drew apart she murmured: 'When you see him tomorrow, give
him that from me.'

'Not all of it,' Gregory laughed. 'But listen, beloved. You
know the sort of place we want, we've talked of it so often.
We ought to be able to pick up something jolly nice now, with
possession three months after the war, for five or six
thousand pounds. While I'm away I want you to write to some
of the best London house agents and find out what they have
to offer. Pellinore's secretary will make arrangements for you
to go to see anything that sounds attractive, and if you find
anything you really like buy it. I'm leaving you a power of
attorney for the cash.'

She nodded and with tears dimming her lovely eyes leaned
her cheek against his. 'Oh, Gregory, darling. What heaven
it would be to really have a home of our own. I'm afraid it's

too like a dream to ever come true. And you seem to ha
forgotten one thing—I'm married already and, as far as '
know, Kurt is still living.'

'That's true,' he murmured, after a moment. 'For mont
at a stretch I almost forget the fellow's existence. But we'll g
rid of him somehow.'

'It may not be so easy, you know. He's just a colourless lit
man and he married me mainly out of vanity I think. His on
real love is his scientific experiments and they positively e
money. As he is a scientist, it's most unlikely that he will
sent into any place of danger where he's liable to be kille
but if I'm able to get anything for my German investmen
after the war we might be able to buy him off. The worst stu
bling block will be his mother. She's rather a fine person; a re
Grande Dame of the old school, and with the exception
Goering she regards all the Nazis as *canaille*. But she is terrib
dictatorial and disapproves most strongly of divorce. Unfo
tunately, Kurt is absolutely under her thumb and it's n
going to be easy to make him stand up to her, even if we ca
get him to agree himself.'

'We'll fix them both one way or another, even if I have
fish my guns out of the Thames and take a last trip to Ge
many.' Gregory smiled, with an attempt at lightness. Then h
lifted Erika off the balustrade and set her on the ground, as h
went on:

'Let's not talk about them any more tonight. Time's to
precious. Look, the moon's just coming up over the yew hedge
of the maze. Let's get ourselves lost in them.' And with the
arms about one another's waists they walked down the ston
steps to cross the moonlit lawn.

When Gregory compared notes with Kuporovitch the fo
lowing morning he learned that Madeleine had taken th
news of Stefan's departure equally bravely. After a year spen
in the French Resistance Movement and as one of the earlies
members of it she was much too courageous to harrow he
man with a scene because he had elected to go back into th
battle.

The two girls stood the test to the end, although their eye
were dimmed with tears as they stood, hand in hand, at th
porch, to watch the car drive off that carried Gregory an
Stefan to unknown perils; but when it had vanished from sigh
round the curve of the long drive they went in and wept to
gether quietly for a little. Then the time came for Madeleine to
go on duty in one of the wards, and Erika went up to her
room.

From the drawer of her dressing-table she took a letter that
had arrived in the post only that morning. It had been re-

addressed to her from London, but it bore the frank of the Swiss Legation and the original superscription was in a thin spidery hand which she had recognised immediately as that of her husband.

5

The Letter

Erika had read the letter immediately on its arrival. She now ran through it again more slowly. It was headed, *Villa Offenbach, Steinach, bei Rorschach, Bodensee, Switzerland;* and said:

My dear Erika,

I expect you will be surprised to hear from me. That is, of course, if this letter ever reaches you; but I hope it may, as I have good reason to believe that you were in England a few months ago. You are much too beautiful to escape remark—wherever you may be—and it is to that I owe receiving news of you.

You will see from the above address that I am now in Switzerland. One of my few friends here is a Red Cross Welfare officer at the camp in which the Swiss intern such Allied airmen as are compelled to make forced landings in their territory. In the course of his work my friend was talking to a young British flying officer who had only recently been put on the active list again, after being wounded and spending some weeks at a convalescent home somewhere on the borders of Wales. They were speaking of the women of various countries and this young man declared that he thought German girls generally plain, but knew of two remarkable exceptions. Then he mentioned Marlene Dietrich and yourself, and it transpired that you had been doing some clerical job at this home to which he had been sent as a convalescent after leaving hospital.

Unfortunately, this conversation took place some time before I left Germany, so my friend could only remember the bare facts, of which he is quite positive; but he has such casual talks with many officers and cannot now recall which of them

45

*it was that mentioned you. So I have no means of ascertaining
the address of this home at which you were, and perhaps still
are, and I am sending this to the Swiss Legation in London, in
the hope that their Red Cross people may be able to trace
you through the British Police Department that deals with
enemy aliens.*

*You will also, no doubt, wonder what I am doing in Switzer-
land. It is a long and sad story. You will remember that when
I last saw you I was working in one of Krupps' laboratories.
That was just before you fled the country. Some weeks later
I saw Goering, and he told me all about that. Apparently you
not only crossed swords with the Nazis, but you got yourself
mixed up with some good-looking Englishman who was spying
for the British, and the Gestapo were out for your blood.
How lucky for you that Hermann is not only such an old
friend of yours, but was in a mood when it amused him to do
down Himmler by getting you out to Finland.*

*Naturally I assumed that you would remain in Finland, or
some other neutral country, for the duration of the war. I
thought you too good a German to go over to the enemy; but
perhaps the good-looking Englishman has something to do
with that?*

*To return to myself. Last spring I was transferred from
Krupps to special, even more secret work, at an experimental
station miles from anywhere. At first I did not fully realise
what the outcome of the work going on there would be; but
as I gradually got to know about the experiments which were
being conducted I was able to form a picture of the final results
at which my colleagues aimed—and I was utterly appalled.*

*No one could be a keener devotee of science than myself,
but science should be for the benefit of humanity, and not
its destruction. I am, I believe, a good German, and would
do anything in reason which might contribute to the victory
of my country; but certain forms of attack are, I consider,
carrying warfare too far; and the use of this new weapon
which I was assisting to bring to perfection would have an
effect so horrifying on an enemy's civil population that no
decent man of any nationality could countenance its use.*

*I thought of asking to be transferred back to my old work,
or even to be allowed to enlist in a fighting unit; but you know
how ruthless the Nazis can be. By the time I had decided that
on no account would I continue to assist in this dreadful task,
I knew too much to be permitted to leave it. Even a request
for a transfer would have been enough to cause them to regard
me as no longer secure, and this secret is of such importance to
them that, rather than jeopardise it even remotely, they would
have shot me out of hand.*

In consequence, I felt that my only course was to fly the country. I made very careful preparations, collected as much ready money as I could and succeeded in getting through to Switzerland. I fear that many of my friends will consider me a traitor, but at least I shall not have the agonised deaths of hundreds of thousands of helpless women and children on my conscience.

I have rented a tiny chalet here on the shores of the Bodensee, under the assumed name of Dr. Gustaf Fallström, and have given it out in the village that I am a Swedish naturalist engaged in making a study of the water life of the lake. The Gestapo has a long arm and even here I am far from safe as, if they could find me, to make certain that I shall not give away Germany's terrible war secret, they would certainly kill me. Needless to say, nothing would induce me to do so, but being completely lacking in integrity themselves they would never believe that.

From fear of being recognised I live very quietly; but, even so, there are so many Germans in Switzerland now, either on war missions or for health reasons, that I am most anxious to get further afield as soon as I possibly can; and if only I can complete the necessary arrangements I shall try to get to South America.

My passport and passage could, I think, be arranged by my friend in the Red Cross, but the main difficulty is money. The small amount that I could bring out in cash is barely enough to support me for a few weeks longer, and all normal sources of obtaining funds are now closed to me. I am wondering therefore, if you could help me?

I do not suggest that we owe each other anything, either on financial or sentimental grounds. I have always loved beautiful things and I derived much pleasure from having the loveliest woman in Germany for my Frau gräfin; moreover you were very generous in enabling me to purchase expensive equipment for my hobby. On the other hand, I gave you the enjoyment of my honourable name and carried out my part of our bargain by refraining from interfering in your affairs. But what of the future?

I think there is a reasonable prospect of my being allowed to return to Germany after the war, but I doubt if you will ever be able to do so. Hermann's love of salacious gossip is sure to have resulted in his having related the story of your affair with the Englishman to a considerable number of people, and the fact of your having taken refuge with our country's enemies is bound to become generally known in due course; and with such matters to your discredit you would be received nowhere.

It seems, then, that you will have to remain abroad for good; and will be faced with the problem as to how you are to live. The Nazis have already confiscated your great private fortune and, in view of our relationship, I do not think you will consider me particularly ungenerous when I tell you that I have no intention of supporting you out of my comparatively slender income. You will still, of course, possess the great asset of your remarkable beauty but, unfortunately, that will decline with the passing of the years. Therefore, the answer to your problem seems to be that, having lost one fortune, you should acquire another for yourself, as soon as it is reasonably possible for you to do so, by marrying again.

The fact that you are at present tied to me should not prove an insurmountable bar to such a prospect if we can come to a satisfactory arrangement. Our both being in exile complicates matters to some extent, but my enquiries through my friend has led me to believe that we could secure a decree through the Swiss courts if we were both resident in this country for three months. The proceedings, would, of course, take much longer, but that period would entitle us to apply for the case to be heard and once it is on the list, if the case were undefended, we could leave the matter in the hands of the lawyers.

If, therefore, you would like to acquire your freedom, I am quite prepared to give it to you; but I make one condition. Somehow or other you must find a sum sufficient to enable me to pay my passage to South America and live there in reasonable comfort until I can find a way to support myself.

At the moment, of course, you may have no desire to marry again, and if you cared to send me this sum of money merely as a gesture of goodwill I should be under eternal obligation to you. But as our ways will be so widely separated in the post-war world there seems little sense in our remaining tied together, and a time may come later when you will wish to re-marry. And by then you might have lost all trace of me, so it would take you years to obtain your freedom legally.

I have no desire to make things difficult for you, so the sum I have in mind is the modest one of £1,000. That you were reported to me, not as in an internment camp, but as a free woman working in a convalescent home for officers, shows that you still have powerful friends in England. With your abilities it should not be difficult for you to raise such a sum and secure a permit to travel to Switzerland.

If you can, it means security for both of us. I should be able to start life again in a country where I could earn a little money without fear of being recognised, while you would have a clear future ahead of you without any entanglement which might, just at the wrong time, spoil your chance of accepting

*an offer of marriage that would guarantee you against a pen-
urious old age.*

*I hope that you are well and will regard my suggestion
favourably, in which case I trust I shall hear from you—or
see you here, fairly soon.*

> *Your affectionate husband,*
> *K.*

Erika laid the letter down with a little sigh. When she had
first read it after breakfast that morning, while Gregory was
finishing his packing, her immediate impulse had been to run
upstairs to him shouting: 'Darling! I'm free! I'm free! I'm
free! Or as good as free. Kurt is willing to give me a divorce';
but after a second she had realised what the results of such an
act would be.

Of course, he, too, would be overjoyed on first hearing this
splendid news, but when it came to the practical necessity of
her going to Switzerland and living there for at least three
months he would begin to worry. Kurt was right about
Switzerland being full of Germans and there was even more
chance that she might be recognised by one of them than him.
If she was, and Grauber got to hear of her presence there, he
would certainly try to get her. She knew of innumerable cases
in which the Gestapo agents had murdered their enemies in
neutral countries or kidnapped them and taken them back to
the torture chambers in Germany.

Gregory was just about to set out on an important mission.
It was absolutely essential that he should leave England with
an unworried mind and all his wits about him. She made up
her mind instantly that she would go to Switzerland. If he
could have gone with her, that would have been a different
matter. But he was no longer free to do so, and it would not
be fair to him to send him away to Russia with the knowledge
that she was risking capture by the Gestapo, however slight
that risk might be.

Personally she did not think the risk a matter for serious
concern. She too would take a little chalet there and live extremely quietly. She would dye her hair, make friends with
nobody and never go further than the village shops. Like Kurt,
she would also take another name and give herself out to be
a neutral, so that neither German nor British agents would be
liable to take an unwelcome interest in her. But all such precautions would mean little to Gregory if he were not on the
spot to take care of her. Out there in Russia he would probably
be thinking of her and worrying himself silly just at the moment he ought to be watching his step, and get caught in consequence.

Her decision once taken she had endeavoured to put the whole business out of her mind during their last hour together; but he had no sooner gone than her thoughts became full of it, even while she and Madeleine were endeavouring to console one another.

Having read the letter again more carefully, she tried to analyse its contents. The long, rather pompous sentences were typical of Kurt, and it was just like him to have thrown his hand in owing to disapproval of inhuman methods of warfare. He had always been a queer mixture of the dreamer with high ethical standards where broad issues were concerned, yet with a canny streak which sometimes led him into, apparently unconscious, immorality in matters that affected him personally.

She felt that when he had been writing this long screed it had not even occurred to him that he was more or less contemplating blackmail; yet, reading between the lines, she felt sure that he really meant 'get me this thousand pounds and you can have your divorce now or later if you want it, but if you fail me now I'm going to refuse to give you your freedom if you ask me for it in a few years' time'.

Yet she also felt that he wanted a divorce too. Obviously he considered that after the war she would be of no further use to him. If she could not return to Germany he would never again get the kick out of strutting after her into receptions and restaurants there, and as she had lost her fortune she could no longer provide him with the expensive scientific instruments he was always hankering after for his private laboratory.

Probably he felt that in the uncertainties of the post-war world it would be a good thing to be free himself. His title was an old one and he still had his castle in Württemberg. With those assets he also might marry again and secure a share of some rich industrialist's daughter's fortune.

But in spite of that he had the instinctive shrewdness to gamble on the fact that a divorce would be as much to her advantage as his own, and demand that she should come to his assistance with a thousand pounds as the price of her freedom.

He was delightfully casual too, in his assumption that, although she was a refugee, she could easily lay her hand on such a sum. He knew, of course, that she had many rich friends in England and no doubt assumed that she had already acquired a wealthy lover. He had always regarded her quite dispassionately and rather as though she were a marvellous *objet d'art* that he was proud to possess but did not mind other connoisseurs handling. When an elderly relative of his had once

50

remarked that it was quite time that he took serious notice of her infidelities, he had shrugged his shoulders and replied: 'My dear Uncle. After all, what is a slice off a cut cake?'

She had been furious at the comparison when the uncle in question, a bibulous old gentleman, had later repeated the story to her one evening when he was slightly tight; but at least she could not complain of her husband's attitude, in view of the life she was leading of her own choice in those days.

Putting the letter in her bag she went over to the hospital wing and endeavoured to settle down to her work, but the thought of it never left her mind all day, and she felt an irresistible urge to talk it over with someone. Madeleine was the only person at Gwaine Meads in whom she could confide, so that evening after dinner she asked the French girl to come up to her room, and translated the letter to her.

Madelaine had changed out of her nurse's uniform for dinner into an afternoon frock which, although it was quite simple, she wore with all the elegance of a born Parisienne. Her eyes were a deeper blue than Erika's, and her dark silky curls above her piquant, tanned little face gave her a warm Mediterranean type of beauty; but her figure, limbs and skin had not the perfection of Erika's, neither did the set of her eyebrows, cheekbones and mouth give her such a striking loveliness.

Having listened to the letter, her first question was typical of her eminently practical French mind. 'Can you get the thousand pounds?'

'Oh, yes,' Erika smiled. 'Gregory left me a power of attorney, and only last night we were saying that we'd give anything to get married, so I'm sure he'd wish me to use some of his money for this. I may have to smuggle it out of England, but I'm not going to let any regulation stand between me and my happiness, and I'm certain that he wouldn't either.'

Madeleine puffed out a cloud of smoke from her cigarette. 'Then it seems fairly plain sailing, *chérie*. If you go to Switzerland and live quietly in some small place under another name it's most unlikely that the Nazi agents there would get to know about it and give you any trouble. I don't believe, though, that he's right about your being able to get a divorce in Switzerland in three months.'

'He doesn't say that. He says that three months' residence there would qualify us to apply for the case to be heard in a Swiss Court. They may have waiting lists there as long as they have in England. Then I suppose there would be another long wait before we get the final decree. I expect the whole thing would take at least a year, or probably eighteen months.'

'Then one of you, anyway, would have to stay there till the

51

case came up. The innocent party, or anyhow the one who brings the suit, always has to appear before the judge. If he wants to get away to South America he'll have to give you evidence and let you divorce him.'

Erika nodded. 'I imagine he is willing to do that. From his letter it looks as if he has been living in Switzerland for some time already, so all he'd have to do would be to go through the usual sordid rigmarole.'

'Yes, he could stay for a few nights with some girl at a small hotel; your lawyers would arrange for the chambermaid to identify him a few days later and you'd have to identify him as your husband too; then he'd be through with his part in the affair and free to clear out, leaving you to do the rest. Do you think he has any idea that you want to marry Gregory?'

'I don't see how he can have. It's twenty months now since Gregory and I were together in Munich and Berlin. He apparently heard of our affair then from Hermann Goering; but until I met Gregory I've never really loved anyone since Hugo Falkenstein died, so none of my affairs in between ever lasted anything like that long, and Kurt can have no reason to suppose my Englishman was anything but a whim of the moment. He is just being practical, I think; and as he no longer has any use for me himself, suggesting that we should both clear the ground so that we're free to make advantageous marriages if we want to later on.'

'I only asked,' said Madeleine thoughtfully, 'because it occurred to me that if he knew you were really keen about it he might try to blackmail you for a much larger sum when you get out there.'

'I don't think he'll try to do that. You see, he has much more to fear from the Gestapo than I have. If they did happen to find out that I was in Switzerland and thought that they could kill or kidnap me without risking serious trouble with the Swiss Government they would do so out of spite, but Kurt's case is very different. He is in possession of very valuable information about this new method of warfare that they are preparing, and they must be terribly worried that he may give away their secret. Nazi agents in a dozen countries are probably hunting for him high and low and if they once find him they'd go to any lengths to ensure his silence. I think his attitude is quite a logical one and that if I say I'm prepared to give him this thousand pounds he won't dream of haggling with me, but do his part as quickly as he can in order to get out.'

Madeleine smothered a little yawn. 'Sorry, *chérie*,' she smiled, 'but last night and saying good-bye to Stefan has taken it out of me rather, and I'm feeling terribly tired. I'm so glad about all this, as I know how happy you must be at the thought of getting your freedom. There certainly doesn't seem to be any really bad snag to it. When will you start?'

'As soon as I can. I don't want Gregory to know anything about it, because I'm sure he'd magnify the very little risk there is and worry about me while he's away. But as soon as he has left England I shall go up to London and ask Sir Pellinore to help me about my journey. I'm sure he will, and I can find out when Gregory is leaving by ringing up Carlton House Terrace tomorrow morning.'

When Erika telephoned to Sir Pellinore on the Tuesday she learned that Wednesday evening was the time fixed for the departure of Gregory and Stefan; so she asked if she might come up on Thursday for the night, and he said he would be delighted to have her.

She arrived at Carlton House Terrace in the afternoon but did not see her host until they met for dinner. Sir Pellinore, as he so frequently declared himself, had an eye for a pretty woman, and while he always treated Erika with an old-world gallantry that she found charming, he expanded under the influence of her smiles and became the most entertaining of companions.

Over an admirable dinner they talked of war-time London, then of the changes in the life of the great metropolis during the past fifty years, after which he amused her with some of the more printable episodes of his own lurid youth in the gay 'nineties. It was not until the butler had withdrawn, leaving a tray of little gilded bottles in silver filigree stands, containing liqueurs, beside her and a full decanter of port in front of him, that he asked the purpose of her visit.

'Well, young woman!' he boomed, picking up the decanter and pouring himself a lavish ration. 'Help yourself to some of that sticky stuff they've put there for you, or there's brandy if you prefer it. No good offering you this, even though it is Cockburn's 'Twelve, I know. And now tell me what's brought you to old London Town. Not to see me, worse luck, although I have got that scallywag Gregory out of the way for a bit.'

'But I have come to see you,' she smiled.

'Ha! Then it's only to get something out of me, I'll be bound. If it's Hitler's head on a charger you want I'm doing my best to get that for you already. If it's money or advice it's yours for the asking.'

'It's advice and help as well,' Erika replied, producing the letter from her bag. 'I had this from my husband on Monday morning.'

Sir Pellinore held his glass to the nearest candle, admired its clear ruby brilliance for a moment, sniffed the wine, took

53

a large gulp of it and, while he was swishing it round his mouth appreciatively, fished out of his pocket a pair of large, horn-rimmed spectacles. Putting them on he gave a swift wipe at his moustache and picked up the letter.

Having read it through, and verified the meaning of some of the German expressions with her, he had another go at his port, then said quietly:

'Erika, you've got something here. This husband of yours is in possession of information which may be of vital importance to us. D'you think you can get it?'

She shook her head. 'I'm afraid there's very little hope of that. You see I know Kurt inside out, and in some ways he's a man with very high principles. As he says himself in his letter, he is a good German, and although he may disapprove of Hitler's methods I feel sure that he would never betray one of Germany's secrets.'

'Principles be damned. I've seen more of the world than you, and one thing I've learned is that every man has his price, or at least ninety-nine per cent of 'em. I'd be selling matches on the corner instead of sitting here if they hadn't.'

'I'm afraid Kurt is one of the odd one per cent, though. Scientists are queer people. They have their own code of honour in addition to the average man's natural patriotism, so they are exceptionally difficult to bribe.'

'I know that. But this feller must want something, and money can buy most things. He's asking for a thousand pounds, but what's the good of that to a German aristocrat who's planning to start life all over again in South America? Offer him any price you like. Twenty thousand wouldn't be too much if he's really got this information. Now, it's up to you.'

Erika drank a little of the Benedictine she had chosen. 'Very well, I'll do my best for you, but I'm not hopeful.'

'Come on now!' Sir Pellinore encouraged her. 'As you say, these alchemist johnnies are queer lot. Stupid as politicians, most of 'em, once they're off their own subject. He's probably too much of a fool to appreciate what money may buy for him and will get on his high horse at the mention of filthy lucre. All right then, offer him an arsenal full of test tubes and stinking chemicals instead. Tell him that if he comes back to Britain with you he'll be really safe from those thugs that are after him, and that we'll let him blow himself up in the finest laboratory money can buy.'

'I am quite certain that Kurt would never take refuge here during the war.'

'Then let him make his stinks in South America, and we'll foot the bill for all the paraphernalia he requires. I tell

54

you, Erika, you've got something here. I can feel it in my bones.'

'All right. Don't look so worried, you poor darling. I really will do my best.'

Sir Pellinore gave her a searching look. 'You've more brains in that little head of yours than most young women, my dear; but I wonder if you really realise how much this may mean. You see, in spite of what people think, just because they can't get enough cigarettes, or soap flakes to wash their undies, the war is not going too badly. The Americans giving us Lease-Lend was the real turning point; Britain can stand up to Hitler indefinitely with that; and now the Russians are in with us the house-painter feller's goose is properly cooked. It may take a bit of time yet, but miracles apart, we've got the Nazis' measure now and their ultimate defeat is inevitable. I said "miracles apart", mind you, and these scientific johnnies are the only gods who are likely to produce one at the present day. It's unlikely, but it's just on the cards that your unwanted spouse may have been working on a war-winner.'

Erika's attention was riveted now, as she murmured: 'D'you really think so?'

'I hope to God he wasn't, but it is a possibility, and it is by ignoring just such possibilities that one loses wars. Say it's a new gas now? All our hocus-pocus men have declared that it is impossible to produce in adequate quantities and manageable form a poison gas that is lighter than air. But say they're wrong? Revolutionary discoveries in science are always being made these days, and the Nazis may have got one ahead of us, eh?'

'Gregory says Hitler will never use gas. He is too frightened of it because we're so much better prepared for gas warfare than he is. Except for the people who can afford to buy them, the German civilian population is still without gas masks and if the R.A.F. put gas down on the big German cities it would bring their war industries to a standstill.'

'That's true enough. But say they had something that could paralyse the R.A.F., eh? Something our masks won't protect us against with which they could drench our airfields. Then they'd be able to put it down on our cities and it would be *our* war industries that would pack up. As long as Britain is a going concern we've got the Nazis set. But if they could knock out our big towns and render them untenable the whole course of the war would be changed. Britain is the only practical base in which a striking force for the eventual invasion and reconquest of the Continent can be built up. Given a new weapon that could paralyse our cities and render our Air Force impotent we will never see the defeat of Hitler in our lifetime. Some such entirely new scientific development is the one and only thing I'm frightened of. Now d'you understand why I want you to get me this information, whatever it may cost?'

'Yes,' said Erika solemnly, 'I do. Is there anything else that strikes you about the letter? Any advice you can give me about the way to deal with him, I mean?'

Sir Pellinore had another go of port and read the letter through again.

'Why has he gone to earth right on the Nazi's doorstep?' he asked, after a moment. 'There's only Lake Constance, or the Bodensee as you Germans call it, between him and the fellers who're out to get him. It's summer, and I should have thought he'd have parked himself somewhere up in the mountains as far from the German frontier as he could get.'

'Perhaps that's on account of the cover he has chosen,' Erika suggested. 'He was always keen on fishing. That goes well with his story about his being a Swedish naturalist, and if he is in hiding with nothing to do all day the fishing would be a godsend as a recreation.'

'Um! Perhaps you're right,' Sir Pellinore grunted. 'Maybe, too, that he is cleverer than we think, and reckons the sleuths are less likely to look for him right under their noses. I thought for a moment that it might be a trap. Don't want you sandbagged and shanghaied back to Germany.'

'That possibility occurred to me, too,' Erika agreed. 'I thought of it only this morning when I was coming up in the train. Do you think it could be a lure to get me there?'

'You know the feller better than I do, so you're the best judge of that,' Sir Pellinore replied non-commitally. He would have been distressed beyond measure if anything happened to Erika, but he honestly thought the chances of that extremely unlikely and, in any case, his every action for the past two years had been governed by the sole consideration of what it would contribute to the defeat of Hitler. In his position he had to steel his heart and follow the dictates of cold logic when dealing with such problems. If it had been one hundred to one that Erika would land herself in Dachau but the one chance offered a possibility of saving a hundred British lives of equal value to her own, he would still have encouraged her to go to Switzerland. As it was, the risk appeared infinitely smaller and the stake immeasurably greater. He had drawn her attention to the only glimmer of a red light that he could see, and felt that was as far as his principles would allow him to go.

'The Gestapo could compel pretty well anyone to write such a letter,' Erika said slowly, 'but I don't think they'd let them out into Switzerland afterwards if they had. What is more, I

on't think they will allow any mention of this new form of
warfare they are contemplating to appear in the letter either.'

'That's true. Still, we can't be too careful. Tell you what.
I'll send that young Guardee out with you. What's his name?
Piers something. Feller who's staying down at Gwaine Meads
now.'

'Piers Gaveston. Oh, I wish you would. He's such a nice boy,
and he seems to have had such terribly bad luck.'

'Yes. Bit impetuous, but he's got his head screwed on all
right. Sound as a bell too. But I can't spare him for long. You
must keep it under your hat, but this bit of a pickle he's been
in was all a put-up job. Very unpleasant, but necessary to
give certain people the impression that he's a bad lot.'

Erika smiled. 'We all felt sure that he must really be innocent
as he was one of your private guests.'

'You did, eh?' Sir Pellinore's bright blue eyes suddenly hardened. 'Never jump to conclusions about a thing like that, I've
got plenty of friends who'd be wearing broad arrows now if
they'd been fools enough to be found out. Anyway, young
what's-his-name is being groomed for a special job and he's
due to start on it at the end of the second week in August.
There should be just time, though, for him to take you out
and have a preliminary snoop round at this chalet place. If
your husband's really there it should be all right for you to go
ahead, but if the place is occupied by anyone else that'll show
there's something phoney about it, and you can return with
Piers to England.'

'Thank you so much. Is there any other point in the letter
that strikes you?'

Sir Pellinore poured himself a second glass of port and
read the letter through to the end.

'I don't think so,' he said, taking off his spectacles and handing it back. 'By and large, the story seems too logical to be
fishy. Reading between the lines, I should say your husband
is just as anxious for a divorce as you are. He obviously thinks
you'll be in no position to support him in the future and would
like to be free to sell his title to some rich man's daughter who
wants to put a coronet on her undies.'

'I imagine it is not easy to get to Switzerland now Hitler
is in control of Northern France and Vichy France is closed
to us, but I take it you will be able to help me about my
journey?'

'Yes. If you wanted to go only on personal grounds, to get
this divorce, it might be very awkward. But in view of this
new type of warfare business I can say with a clear conscience
that you're going out to do a job for me. We send long range
aircraft over now and again with the bags for our Legation,

57

and I can get you a passage in one of them. I'll fix up the mone
side of it for you, too. Get you a credit for twelve hundred at
Swiss bank and have a chit sent to our Minister there that he
to weigh out any bigger sum that you may require if you ca
do a deal over the secret information.'

When Erika had thanked him he finished his port and the
went upstairs, where it was agreed that she should return t
Gwaine Meads the next day and wait there until she hear
from him.

A week elapsed and on the following Thursday morning sh
received a letter in Sir Pellinore's bold, flowing hand. It wa
extremely laconic and simply said:

*A plane will be leaving on Sunday. Suggest you arrive her
early Saturday afternoon. Have written instructing you
escort to place himself at your disposal. You can now te
him whatever it is strictly necessary for him to know. Bles
you.*

P.

Piers Gaveston had also received a brief chit from Si
Pellinore, by the same post; and, glancing up from it, he smiled
at her across the breakfast table. He was a tall fair young mar
with nice brown eyes and a slightly upturned moustache
They made no comment on their letters but as soon as the
meal was over, seeing her go out on to the terrace, he drifted
casually after her.

As soon as they were out of earshot of Madeleine and the
Professor he said with a grin: 'I am instructed to report for
duty, madame! What are your orders for the day?'

'Nothing very onerous,' she smiled. 'Let's walk through
the woods as far as the little Greek temple, and as we go along
I'll tell you why Sir Pellinore has asked you to help me.'

They fell into step, and leaving the gardens, strolled slowly
down the long grassy glade while Erika told him about the
journey they were to make and her husband; but she said
nothing of the secret work upon which Kurt von Osterberg
had been engaged.

'I do hope you manage to fix things up all right,' he said,
when she had finished. 'It must be rotten to be tied up to a
chap that you no longer care about. Anyhow, I'll make darn
certain it's him who is living at this place, and not some of
those Nazi so-and-sos, before you go anywhere near it.'

She told him that Sir Pellinore had let her into the secret
of his cashiering, and that she thought it far braver for a young
man to submit to such an ordeal in the interests of his country
than any heroics would have been that he could perform in

58

ttle; but he replied quite lightly:

'Oh, I wouldn't have missed it for anything. The day after
I had committed myself to Sir Pellinore I would have given
the earth to get out of it. The time while we were setting the
scene for our little act was pretty grim, too; but once the
balloon went up the fun began. People's reactions were so
unexpected and often quite comic. They hurt at times, because
some that I would have put my last quid on as good as
salt in my eye; but others, some of them people I hardly knew,
came forward and practically offered to perjure themselves for
me. There's nothing like a spot of real bother to show you what
your friends are made of.' Then, without disclosing its object,
he gave her an amusing account of the case.

As they were walking back, Erika remarked: 'Gregory
just told me that you have the same name as a famous
character in English history. Are you descended from him?'

'Infamous, you mean,' he laughed. 'Piers, or Pierce, Gaveston was the wicked favourite of Edward the Second. He
used to take the King out to night clubs when he ought to have
been attending to dreary affairs of State. The Barons were a
gloomy lot of killjoys and didn't like poor Piers a bit; they
fought him and did him in, in the end. My family claim to
be descended from this gay young spark and apparently
thought it would be amusing to christen me after him. Fortunately both my parents are dead, so they'll never know how
suitable their choice was, as I, too, shall always be regarded as
a bad hat.'

This confidential chat had the effect of drawing Erika and
Piers closer together than all their casual conversations in the
past weeks had done, and she felt that she was lucky to have
such a likeable companion for her escort.

On the Friday night she told the Matron that she was leaving
to do some secretarial work for Sir Pellinore in London, and
said good-bye to a number of people she had come to know in
the convalescent wing. Afterwards she had a long heart-to-heart chat with Madeleine, and was seen off by her and the
Professor when she left with Piers next morning.

That afternoon she found that Sir Pellinore had made an
appointment for her with the barber who worked for one of
the M.I. Departments. He dyed her hair a deep, rich brown
and took a shade off the corners of her eyebrows. A photograph of her was then taken, and after dinner that night Sir
Pellinore gave her a Swedish passport in the name of Madame
Astrid Largerlöf and all the other papers that she would require. On the morning of Sunday, the tenth of August, he
waved them good-bye from the steps of his house and a taxi

took them to a wartime department of the Air Ministry s
ated in Holborn.

They were there as instructed, at half past nine,
although the journey down to the airfield in Kent, from wh
they were to depart took only a little over an hour, their
craft did not take off till nearly three o'clock in the afterno
The delay seemed interminable, pointless and exasperati
which caused Piers during one dreary wait to remark:

'What extraordinary people airmen are. I've had quite a
to do with them in the past two years and operationally t'
are absolutely wizard. I've seen squadrons go up to fight
the Battle of Britain, and squadrons of bombers leave on l
trips to Germany, and in every case the aircraft took off,
after the other at stated intervals, to the split second; yet
you want them to fly you anywhere, nothing is ever ready. Tl
start to test their engines only when the aircraft is to get
and, like today, often in the end decide to use another, or s'
testing for an hour because it's time for the mechanics to ha
their lunch. In fact, where passenger flying is concerned tl
seem to lose their sense of time altogether.'

'They've inherited that from the Civil Air Lines of pre-w
days, I expect,' Erika replied. 'They had brought time-wasti
to a fine art; but what can the poor passengers do as long
air routes are granted to corporations as a monopoly?'

Piers shrugged. 'Well, let's hope that the British Air Li
run things a bit better after the war.'

By ten to three they were at last emplaned with the o
other passenger who had accompanied them from London.
was a pleasant middle-aged man with spectacles; and althou,
he had said nothing of his business, Piers, having caught sig
of the heading of some documents he had been reading duri
one of their interminable waits, had gathered that he w
something to do with the Ministry of Economic Warfare.

As they were going to a neutral country their pilot was
civilian and the aircraft had civil markings; its windows we
also blacked out in order that the passengers from a belligere
country should not gain knowledge of the Swiss defences.
consequence they could see nothing of the landscape belo
them, but the aircraft climbed and climbed until Erika thoug'
it was never going to stop and the great height made h
acutely uncomfortable, even when she put on her oxyg
mask. But the high altitude at which the aircraft made tl
greater part of its flight was necessary in order to avoid tl
possibility of running into German 'planes while flying ov
France. In due course they dropped and dropped, which gav
her an equally sickly feeling, but the pilot made a good landin
on the Swiss aerodrome, having accomplished the actu;

ourney in considerably less time than his passengers had spent
etween reporting to the office in London and taking their
eats in the 'plane.

After their papers and suit-cases had been examined, Erika
nd Piers said good-bye to their fellow passenger and took a
axi to a small hotel. It proved to be full, so they went on to
he second on a short list that Piers had made before starting,
nd here they secured accommodation. The plain but abund-
nt food, together with unstinted butter and cream, that they
were given for their dinner seemed almost a banquet compared to meals in wartime Britain; and, after it, tired out from
their long day, they went early to bed.

Next morning they drew some Swiss money from the bank
at which credits had been arranged for them, and made a
few purchases. Erika could not help glancing at herself whenever she encountered a mirror in the shops they entered. She
was still very good-looking, but no longer striking, and that
was not due alone to the change from blonde to brunette in
her hair and make-up, or to the fact that the barber had deliberately dressed her hair in a new style less becoming to her.
At length she came to the conclusion that it was mainly the
clever alteration in the shape of her eyebrows; and, although
she felt a natural resentment at no longer looking her best, she
had at least the consolation of being reasonably certain that
only people who had known her well in the past were likely
to recognise her if they now ran into her in the street.

After lunch they caught a train for St. Gall and, during the
afternoon, enjoyed the splendid scenery of the Swiss mountains. On arriving at their destination they went to another
modest hotel—the Pension Julich. Piers also had a forged
Swedish passport and registered there as Olaf Hjelm, their
story being that he was her brother. She found that he could
talk German with considerable fluency, so now that they were
in the Germanic cantons of Switzerland they spoke German
together in order to make themselves less conspicuous.

Having looked at a map before leaving London, they knew
Steinach to be a village towards the east end of Lake Constance, and only about fifteen miles from St. Gall. After breakfast on the Tuesday, therefore, Piers left Erika to sit in a
quiet part of the hotel garden and went off to see what he could
find out.

The previous evening she had given him a very full description of her husband and he had repeated it to himself several
times. 'Forty-four years of age, height about five foot eleven,
medium build with rather narrow shoulders, a thin face, brown
hair greying at the temples, high forehead, brown eyes, straight
nose, thin-lipped mouth, pointed chin, clean shaven, well-

cared-for hands with square fingertips and small feet.'

With such abundant data to go on Piers felt that he cou
not possibly mistake his man, even if the Count had grow
a moustache and beard as a disguise; and when he returne
just after four o'clock, Erika saw from his smiling face befo
he spoke that he had been successful.

'He's there?' she exclaimed, trying to suppress her excit
ment.

Piers nodded. 'The chalet is quite a little place and sever
hundred yards from any other houses. It stand right on th
lakeside and has only a small fringe of garden separating
from the road. As I drifted up they were both geting the
boat out . . .'

'There's someone with him, then?'

'Yes, a tall, thin fellow with blue eyes, who's gone prema
turely bald. I shouldn't think he's much more than thirty, an
he wears what hair he has left smoothed sideways across h
shiny scalp, in the same way as you may have seen some old
fashioned waiters wear theirs. At a guess I should say he's
servant of a rather superior type, but he's definitely not a gen
On the middle finger of his left hand he was wearing a gaud
amethyst ring. I don't know if he's a German or one of th
local German-Swiss. I'm not good enough on accents to hav
been able to tell that. Anyhow, I got a good look at the tw
of them before they noticed me and I'm quite certain that th
shorter one was your husband. Your description fitted hin
exactly, and he hadn't even grown a beard.'

'Did you speak to him?'

'No. After I had been standing at the gate for a minute th
Count looked up and saw me. I leant over it and called out
but he didn't come up to find out what I wanted. He dive
back into the boathouse as though he wasn't at all keen abou
being seen, and it was the other fellow who jumped ashore
and came round to the gate. I said I was an artist looking for a
quiet, inexpensive lodging and asked him if he had a room to
let. He turned me down pretty abruptly; just said the place
was taken for the summer and that they had no rooms to
spare.'

'Thank God,' Erika sighed. 'It seems perfectly all right,
then?'

'Absolutely, as far as I can judge. The Count is there and the
chalet is too small to hold more than the two of them in comfort.'

'Thank you so much, Piers.'

'Not a bit,' he smiled. 'I'm delighted to have been able to
fit this little reconnaissance in for you before starting on my
big job. Will it be all right by you if I leave tomorrow? The

rcraft we came in was returning on Thursday, if you re-
ember, and if I don't catch that, there may not be another
r a week.'

'Yes, of course it will. I can manage quite well on my own
w we've made certain that it's not a trap. I'd better not be
en going there if it can be avoided, though, for Kurt's sake;
I think I'll call on him after dinner tomorrow night.'

6

The Villa Offenbach

ika was sorry to lose Piers. Not only was he an amusing
mpanion who had shown her a nice degree of attention that
kled her vanity without embarrassing her, but his very pre-
nce had saved her from the less welcome attentions that
re the penalty for her good looks whenever she travelled,
stayed in an hotel, alone.

However, he had done the job that he had been sent out
do; it was already the 9th of August, and Sir Pellinore
nted him to start on his own work by the end of the week.
e had no possible reason for keeping him with her and,
en had he been free to remain, she could not have taken him
her visit to Kurt, for her husband's hackles would rise at
ce were he given the least reason to suppose that she had
ne there, not simply to arrange about their divorce, but also
the emissary of Germany's enemies.

Having seen Piers off after breakfast, she ordered a car for
-thirty that evening to take her down to Steinach, then
nt most of the day reading in the garden. For some little
e the night before she had pondered over the best way to
id anyone knowing about her visit. The Gestapo had eyes
d ears in many places and paid all sorts of people to turn
apparently unimportant information. Even with her dyed
r, a description of her might ring a bell in the mind of
ne Gestapo man who knew her, and a report that she had
en to see the recluse at the Villa Offenbach lead them straight
Kurt. Moreover, although she knew nothing about the
iss divorce laws, she thought it possible that if any officious

person gave information that there had been collusion
might quite well prevent the case going through.

Eventually she had decided she would take a car into Ste
bach, tell the chauffeur to put her down at the local hotel
dinner and pick her up again at eleven o'clock. After she h
dined she could then slip out to make her visit, and retu
without him knowing that she had ever left the hotel.

The matter went according to plan. The August night v
clear and warm; the hotel to which her driver took her v
a pleasant little place with a vine-covered terrace, on wh
she dined, overlooking the lake. As she ate the excellent fr
trout which she had chosen from the menu, dusk fell and
stars came out. After dinner she sat for a little while in
covered loggia at the far end of the terrace, but a you
Frenchman's persistent attempts to pick her up gave her
excellent excuse for leaving it, and by nine o'clock she v
making her way along the almost deserted street.

The chalet was about a quarter of a mile outside the to
but, from Piers' description, she had no difficulty in find
it. The blinds were drawn but the music from a radio echo
out over the lapping waters at the far side of the house.
opened the little wicket gate, stepped up to the porch and ra
the bell.

The radio was switched off; there were footsteps in the h
and the door was opened by the tall, prematurely-aged-loo
ing man with whom Piers had spoken.

'I have called to see the gentleman to whom this chale
let,' said Erika cautiously.

'I'm afraid the Professor is working just now,' replied
man politely but firmly. 'But I look after most things for h
so perhaps you could tell me your business?'

'Dr. Fallström is expecting me,' she said. 'In fact, I h
come all the way from England to see him.'

The man took a step backwards so that in the dim light fr
the hall he could see her face better, then he smiled slowly a
stood aside. 'Please to come in. I am sure that the Professor v
be happy to receive you.'

The hall was a small square one with a door on either si
and beyond the staircase, one at its far end. Having closed
front door her guide led her to the one at the end, opened
and followed her inside. The room Erika entered ran
whole width of the back of the house, and it flashed throu
her mind that the smaller ones at the front were probably
dining-room and kitchen. The chalet had only two storeys
there would be three, or at the most four, bedrooms upsta
This was evidently the principal living-room. It was comf
ably though unimaginatively furnished, but its dark bea

64

and wide fireplace gave it a pleasant homely air. Kurt was sitting in an armchair with an open book on his knees.

As she entered the room he started violently, then stood up and came over to kiss her hand. He was greyer than when she had seen him last and his face was more lined. She thought he looked ill and worried, but that was no matter for wonder.

'So you got my letter,' he began, then glanced at her dark hair and smiled. 'For a moment I hardly recognised you.'

'That was just a precaution,' she smiled back. 'I felt that for both our sakes I ought not to risk . . .' Breaking off, she turned her head slightly to indicate the other man, who was still standing impassively behind her.

'Oh, forgive me,' von Osterberg said quickly. 'You don't know each other, do you? Erika, this is Fritz Einholtz, my laboratory assistant. He felt the same way as I did and we escaped from Germany together, so we have no secrets from each other. Fritz, this is my wife, upon whose coming so much of our hopes depend.'

'I am honoured to meet the *Frau Gräfin*.' The tall man drew himself erect, clicked his heels in the approved German fashion and bowed sharply from the waist, as he kissed the hand that Erika extended to him.

'Let me take your fur, and please to sit down,' he went on quickly, and as he did the honours of the house she felt that he had much more life about him than his master. It was clear, however, that he had no intention of being left out of the marital reunion, since as soon as they had seated themselves he placed his hand on the back of another chair and said: 'You permit?'

'This is our only sitting-room,' said von Osterberg hurriedly, 'and Fritz is naturally as anxious as I am to learn if you can help us to get to South America, so you won't mind if he remains with us, will you?'

'Of course not,' she agreed, politely; upon which Einholtz sat down, drew up his long legs so that he could rest his elbows on his knees, and regarded them with speculative interest.

'Did you have a good journey?' enquired the Count.

'Quite good, thanks,' Erika replied.

'I—er—feared that you might find some difficulty in getting here, now Switzerland is more or less cut off from England.'

She shook her head. 'Normally I would have done, but you were right in your assumption that I still have some good friends over there, and they arranged matters for me.'

'You managed to get the money, then?' Fritz Einholtz put in quickly.

Erika gave him a slightly chilly glance. The war often made

friends and bedfellows of masters and men these days, but she felt that was hardly sufficient justification for her husband's laboratory assistant to question her on their private affairs.

Von Osterberg stepped into the breach. 'We thought you might have difficulty about that too—at least, I did; but Fritz bet me twenty marks that you could manage to help us somehow.'

'It is here, in a Swiss bank, and I can draw it at any time,' she admitted.

'Thank you,' said her husband, but did not seem to be particularly pleased or excited, and after a moment she went on:

'Still, willing as I am to help you, Kurt, I think we should regard this as a business deal, and get matters more or less fixed up before I actually pay the money over. I take it that, as you wish to get away from Switzerland as soon as possible, your idea is that I should divorce you, so that you won't have to appear in the Swiss courts later?'

The Count nodded. 'Yes, I think that would be best.'

'Then you'll have to go through the usual unsavoury business with some girl at an hotel.'

'Yes, I suppose so,' he said, slowly.

'Come now, Kurt,' Einholtz cut in again. 'We have talked of this often and agreed that such a step will be necessary, so why show this reluctance to face matters now?'

'Yes, yes, of course!' von Osterberg replied a little testily. 'It was only that such a business is naturally repugnant to me.'

'Well, the sooner you do it, the sooner I'll be able to start proceedings and the sooner you'll be able to get away,' said Erika practically.

'All right. Naturally there was no point in providing evidence until we knew that you were agreeable to do your part; but, now you're here, I'll go into Zurich and try to find an accommodating young woman over the weekend.'

'Have you yet found a solicitor here to act for you, *Frau Gräfin*?' Einholtz enquired.

'I haven't actually seen him yet, but before I left London I obtained the address of one.'

'That is good. The preliminaries are now settled then. All you have to do for the moment is to let your husband have the name of the hotel at which you are staying, and when he returns from Zurich he will let you hear from him.'

'I'm at the Pension Julich, in St. Gall. I thought it better to stay at a small place as there was less likelihood of my running into anyone who might recognise me; and I am passing as a Swede, under the name of Madame Largerlöf.'

As Erika answered, she was wondering how best to prolong the conversation. She did not want to rush her fences in the

66

matter of the secret form of warfare upon which they had been engaged, and any mention of the war might lead to that. On the other hand, there seemed little more to be said about the proposed divorce. Therefore, when her husband suddenly said to her: 'Erika, you must be chilly after your walk, would you like some coffee?' she accepted at once.

Neither of the men made any move to rise and after a moment von Osterberg said: 'Would you mind, Fritz?'

But the lanky Einholtz laughed and shook his head. 'No, Kurt, not tonight. My coffee is not good enough for the *Frau Gräfin*. Yours is always so much better. She will have cause to thank me, I know, if I leave it to you.'

With a shrug of apparent good-nature, the Count got up and left them. For a few seconds they were silent, then Einholtz said:

'Did Kurt say anything in his letter to you of our reason for leaving Germany?'

'He implied that he disliked the work upon which he was engaged,' Erika replied cautiously. She was reluctant to admit what Kurt had said to any other German—even his assistant; and in any case, she did not wish to discuss the matter with Einholtz. She wanted to get Kurt on his own; but her companion was persistent.

'The possibilities of the thing upon which we were working were too horrible to contemplate,' he said. 'I was Kurt's assistant, you know, so I was in it up to my neck, just as much as he was. When we realised where our experiments must finally lead us, it was too much. We talked it over and decided to make a bolt for it together rather than go on.'

'Really!' She raised her eyebrows. 'Kurt didn't say much, but what little he did say, and the fact that he was in Switzerland, on the run from the Gestapo, made me think that it must be something like that. Did you have much trouble in getting away?'

'Not much. We chose our time carefully and two days later arrived at Schloss Niederfels. Kurt felt certain he could trust the servants in his own home, and he was right. We felt, too, that that was the last place where the Nazis would look for us. After a little over a week there, we managed to get in touch with one of Kurt's old friends, *Freiherr* von Lottingen . . .'

'Willi von Lottingen,' murmured Erika. 'Yes, I remember him well.'

Einholtz nodded his nearly bald head. 'That's right. Then you may also remember that the *Freiherr* has property on the German side of the Bodensee, almost opposite us here. He arranged with his old steward to receive us at night and have

67

us smuggled across in one of his boats.'

'I see. Of course, Schloss Niederfels can't be much more than sixty miles from the north side of the lake, so the last stage of your journey was quite a short one.'

He gave her a sharp look. 'Did Kurt mention to you, then the place at which we were working?'

'No. It was what you said just now that gave me the impression that you came from some more distant part of Germany.'

'*Ach so!* Well, yes, we had to come from right up in the north; but it was getting away from the experimental station that was the most risky part of the business.' For a few minutes he described to her the difficulties of evading the check-ups at the camp so as to secure a clear twelve hours' start before their absence would be discovered; then he began to shake his head again over the inhumanity of the method of warfare that the Nazis were preparing to wage.

Seeing that they were now properly launched, Erika asked as casually as she could: 'What was the frightful thing upon which you were working?'

'A new gas,' he replied, without hesitation. 'A poison gas lighter than air. That, perhaps, does not mean much to you *Frau Gräfin*, but it would revolutionise chemical warfare. Of course, we have known how to make such gases for years, but the problems have always been: (*a*) to produce one from a chemical that is easily obtainable, and the use of which in great quantities would not interfere seriously with the manufacture of any other basic war industry; (*b*) to devise a method of making it quickly and cheaply; (*c*) to work out safety measures which would protect our own people from its deadly effects, both during manufacture and when used in battle.'

'But the British have taken tremendous precautions against gas,' she objected. 'Unlike us, everyone there has a gas-mask.'

'Ah!' he sighed. 'But their masks will not protect them against this new gas; and by the time they find an antidote to it, hundreds of thousands of them will have died most horribly. Their great cities will, overnight, become charnel houses The dead will be too many for the survivors in the country districts to come in and bury. In a few months chaos and anarchy will result. Even if they do not sue for peace their powers of resistance will be so weakened that Hitler will be able to launch an invasion that would prove a walkover.'

'There is an antidote, then?' she asked, thinking how right Sir Pellinore had been in his guess as to this new type of warfare upon which Kurt had been working.

'*Jawohl,* counter measures can always be devised against every new weapon; but that takes time. And however quickly

68

the British scientists got to work, new masks, or attachments to the present ones, would have to be manufactured by the million. It would be months before everyone in Britain could be issued with them; and in the meantime, city after city will become a terrible festering sore filled with the dead and untended dying. It was the thought of that which proved too much for Kurt and myself.'

'It's too ghastly to think of,' she agreed. 'But I suppose that if the British had particulars of this new gas they could take precautions beforehand?'

As she was speaking von Osterberg came in, carrying the coffee.

Einholtz's eyes left her face, and he glanced quickly over his shoulder as though he had said too much and the Count would not approve of his talking so freely; but now they were on the subject Erika decided that she would not let it drop.

As her husband set the tray down beside her, she said: 'Herr Einholtz has been telling me about your escape from Germany, Kurt, and the reason why you felt that you could not possibly go on with the terrible work they gave you to do there. I think you're both very brave to have risked your lives rather than go on, but I wonder if that is quite enough?'

'What do you mean by that?' asked von Osterberg.

'I mean that others will be going on where you left off. At least I suppose so?'

'Yes. We were only two in a team of twenty highly qualified scientists and scores of assistants.'

'Then, your having left, won't really make very much difference?'

'No,' he agreed, dully.

'So this ghastly thing will happen in a few months, or next year, anyway?'

'I suppose so.'

'Well, do you two feel quite happy about simply having washed your hands of it? I mean,' she hesitated, 'oughtn't you to do something to try to stop it?'

There was dead silence for a moment, then Einholtz said: 'Are you suggesting that we should give such information as we have to the British?'

'Yes.' Erika leaned forward and began to speak very earnestly. 'Please don't think that because I took refuge from the Nazis there that I want our country to lose the war. Holding nearly all Europe, as she does now, Germany is in a far stronger position than Britain. Surely if she is capable of winning she can do so without resorting to such an incredibly barbarous method of warfare. If we win that way, we Germans will be hated for ever afterwards. Every race in the world will be against us and, sooner or later, they'll all unite to destroy us.'

'I think you're right,' said von Osterberg suddenly. 'Now we can read the neutral papers and listen freely to the radio, it seems to me that things are moving in that direction already.'

'They are,' she agreed quickly. 'And that's entirely due to Hitler and his Nazis. But if he defeats the British with this new gas it will take very much longer to unseat him. The best hope for all decent Germans and the future of our country is that the war should go on until both sides are thoroughly fed up with it. Then there would be some hope of the *Wehrmacht* eventually breaking the Nazi stranglehold and securing a fair and just peace by negotiation.'

Einholtz nodded. 'I believe you're right about that, *Frau Gräfin*. But what would you have us do?'

'I feel sure I could arrange for you to return to England with me.'

Von Osterberg shook his head. 'That I would never do; even if it were possible.'

'What is the alternative?' she asked. 'You propose to go to South America. But how will you get on there? After your voyage is paid for, the remainder of the thousand pounds won't keep you for very long; particularly if you want to buy new scientific equipment to go on with your old work. As a matter of fact I have a far bigger sum. I never told you about it but I had quite large investments in England before the war. That money is frozen at the moment, but this information you possess must be of such value to the British I feel certain that in exchange for it they would unfreeze my capital and allow me to make it over to you.'

'You are suggesting now that I should sell one of Germany's war secrets,' her husband said, coldly, 'and that, I would never do. You came here to arrange with me about a divorce. Let us stick to that and leave this other matter out of it.'

Erika finished her coffee and stood up. 'All right then, Kurt,' she agreed quietly. She had seen a sudden gleam of cupidity in Einholtz's eyes at the mention of her fortune, and thought it better not to pursue the matter further for the moment.

As he held her fur for her, she added: 'I wish you'd both think about it, though; quite apart from any question of the money. It seems so illogical to have sacrificed your careers and jeopardised your lives because you disapprove of this terrible thing, and yet be unwilling to take any steps to prevent it happening.'

'I wish neither to think nor talk of it any more,' von Osterberg replied with a sudden burst of violent feeling. 'And it would be better for you if you didn't either.' Then he formally

issed her hand and Einholtz, maintaining a noncommittal
silence, showed her out into the night.

She got back to the hotel a quarter of an hour before her
car was due to pick her up. The young Frenchman was still
there and made another, rather half-hearted, attempt to get
into conversation with her. She replied to him only in mono-
syllables and a few minutes later, to his considerable disappointment, he saw her drive off.

On thinking matters over she decided that she had not done
so badly. She had always expected that Kurt would, at first,
refuse to even consider the proposal, but he seemed ill, worried
and uncertain of himself; and people in such a condition
are much more easily induced to alter their opinions than the
vigorous and healthy. She had at least sown the idea in both
his mind and in that of Einholtz that the logical outcome
of their refusing to participate further in their hellish work
would be to prevent its ever coming to fruition, and Einholtz
had tacitly agreed with her.

At first, when he had shown no inclination to leave her
alone with Kurt, she had feared that he would prove a serious
stumbling-block; but the contrary had proved the case, and
she felt a strong conviction that he would not need a great
deal of persuading to do a deal on a financial basis. It was
clear, too, that he was much the more virile partner of the
two refugees and had acquired a strong influence over Kurt.
That influence would have rather frightened her in other circumstances, but as things were it looked as if it might prove
greatly to her advantage.

As far as the divorce was concerned, matters could hardly
have gone better. Whatever else happened, Einholtz wanted
to see that thousand pounds every bit as much as did Kurt, and
she felt sure that he would bully his ex-master into going to
Zurich and doing his stuff in the very near future. So it only
remained for her now to wait in patience until events provided
her with another opportunity to go further into the question of
his abominable gas.

The opportunity presented itself much sooner than she expected. On the Saturday afternoon she was sitting in a corner
of the small garden of the Pension, reading a book, and, on
glancing up, saw Einholtz approaching her.

Having secured her address on the Wednesday night he had
got in touch with the secret Gestapo headquarters in Zurich.
They had their means of ascertaining who came and went at
every hotel in Switzerland, and on Thursday evening a report
had reached him. Briefly it stated that a woman answering
Erika's description had arrived at the Pension Julich on the previous Monday, accompanied by a tall, fair, youngish man.

Both of them passed themselves off as Swedes, but they ha
only been heard to speak German together and the man had
slight accent which suggested that he was possibly English. H
had paid his bill and left her, giving no indication that h
meant to return, on the Wednesday morning.

Einholtz had scowled as he read the flimsy. Erika was onl
the lesser fly. It was Gregory Sallust that his chief, *Gruppen
führer* Grauber, was so anxious to catch in his web. Naturally
when Erika had appeared at the Villa Offenbach he had ha
high hopes Gregory was waiting for her in the village, or a
any rate, not far off; and now it seemed that he had simpl
accompanied her to St. Gall, remained there with her for tw
nights and then left her.

But on re-reading the message more carefully he saw tha
the description of Erika's companion did not tally with tha
which had been given to him of Sallust. The big fly they wer
out to catch was not fair-haired, neither was he particularl
young or tall, and it was known that he spoke German lik
a native. However, there was one thing about which Einhol
felt certain. The man had accompanied Erika to act as a
advance guard, to make a reconnaissance of the Villa Offen
bach before she went there, in case it was a trap. He woul
have done that the day after their arrival. That would be Tues
day. Of course, the tall, fair, young man who had said he wa
an artist and asked if there was a room to let in the Villa.

As Einholtz tied that up he smiled with grim satisfactio
Grauber had wanted him to take two or three other men wit
him on this job. His chief had thought that von Osterber
might prove too much for him alone, and that once on neutra
soil without a full-time guard there was too much risk of th
Count escaping. But Einholtz had persuaded him that to hav
a squad of their thugs kicking their heels about the place prob
ably for weeks on end, would be certain to give the sho
away, and had undertaken to be personally responsible fc
their stool pigeon. It was now proved how right he had bee
about that, and von Osterberg had made no attempt at a ge
away. There was very little chance of his doing so, eithe
Einholtz felt, as long as he did not allow him to see anyon
alone and handcuffed him by the ankle to his bed each nigh
and whenever he had to go out himself.

The Count had been pretty difficult at the time of Erika
visit though. Of course, he had been hoping that she wouldn
be able to raise the money, or that if she did, she wouldn
be able to get to Switzerland with it. He had obviously trie
that trick about the coffee in the hope of getting his wife o
his own, so that he could tip her off. Then he had played h
gaoler up badly over the secret weapon, and deliberately trie

72

o head Erika off; instead of acting according to his instructions and, after showing a few scruples for form's sake, agreeing to think it over.

It was on this account that Einholtz had decided to come over and see Erika that afternoon. He feared that she might have taken her husband's blunt refusal to play as final. If that were the case she would probably report to London that there was no hope of getting any information and remain on in Switzerland only to secure her divorce. On no account must that be allowed to happen, as the secret weapon was the special bait designed to draw Gregory into the trap, and he could only be lured to the scene if she reported that together they would have some hope of obtaining it.

As she saw him coming across the small lawn she thought how much younger he looked with a hat on. It was a round, soft felt, with a small feather in the band, and he lifted it to her straight off his head, revealing the thin plastered swathe of hair across his bald scalp, instead of merely tilting it forward in front of his face as an Englishman would have done.

She did not like the look of Fritz Einholtz any better than when she had first seen him. Whatever his real social position might be she had a distinct feeling that he was not a nice person; but she felt sure that he had come to talk to her about the secret gas, so she smiled a greeting and motioned to a chair beside her.

'I hope you don't mind this little social visit,' he began. 'But I know how anxious you must be about your divorce and I thought you would like to know that Kurt has gone into Zurich for the weekend, in the hope of being able to give you the evidence you'll need.'

'It was nice of you to come,' she said. 'I'm so glad Kurt has made up his mind to go through with this absurd formality. He seemed very reluctant to do so the other night.'

Einholtz stretched out his long legs and thrust his thumbs into the armholes of his waistcoat with a self-satisfied air.

'As a matter of fact, he took quite a lot of persuading, but fortunately I have some little influence with him; in the end he usually comes round to my point of view. I'm very happy that in this case I should have been able to help you.'

'I'm terribly grateful,' Erika smiled. 'But I wonder if he's to be relied on now he is on his own. He is not the sort of man who has ever gone in for picking up girls, and he may funk it at the last moment.'

'Yes. I'm a bit afraid of that myself. I did think of going in with him to get him going, but the two of us sitting about in the cafés and dance places of a big city would more than double the risk of some Nazi police spy recognising us from our descriptions. Still, if he doesn't come up to scratch this time, we'll take a chance on that, and I'll go in with him some time next week.'

'I don't want you to run into danger on my account, but if the risk is not a great one I'd be awfully glad if you would.'

'It would be a pleasure to be of service to the *Frau Gräfin*, and after all, the risk of our actually being captured is not very big,' Einholtz replied; and he smiled as he thought of the unfortunate von Osterberg, who instead of making a round of the brighter spots of Zurich that afternoon was, in fact, securely handcuffed to his bed.

There was a short silence, then Erika said: 'I wonder if you have thought over what I was saying the other night?'

'You mean about our work? Yes, I have thought of that a lot, and I am sure there is a great deal to be said for your point of view. The thing that worried me most, though, is the thought that if we turned the information that we have over to the English we should have to give them a full scientific analysis of this gas. Unless we did that they could not take adequate precautions against it. But once they had our secret they might manufacture the gas themselves and use it against our German cities, and that would be even more horrible.'

Erika shook her head. 'I'm certain the British would not do that.'

'Why are you certain? I think they would be very tempted to do so, if they felt that they could bring a victorious end to the war that way.'

'No. I'm certain they wouldn't. The war has been in progress for nearly two years now, and you have only to consider the record of our enemies. We Germans have made a shameless use of the Red Cross to cover military operations; we have sunk both enemy and neutral ships without warning; we have used civilians to screen our troops in battle and we have murdered them by the thousand to create panic and block roads. But the British have done none of these things. After all, we would never do such things either, if it were not for the Nazis. The British know that and they always say on their radio that it is the Nazis and all their beastliness that they are fighting. Anyhow, in spite of all provocation the British have kept their hands clean. Even if some of them would like to take such short cuts to inflicting defeat upon us they never do so, because it is against their policy. Their one hope lies in the sympathy which they have aroused in America for their so-called crusade against brutality and evil. They dare not risk losing that, and the use of any inhuman method of warfare would lose it for them in a week. That is why I am certain that, if they had it, the British would never use your gas.'

'Your argument is a strong one, *Frau Gräfin*,' Einholtz nodded. 'Yes, I think you are right. The British would not use it xcept as a reprisal—if Germany used it first.'

'And perhaps not even then, if they had adequate protec-on from it. The British are often extraordinarily quixotic.'

'That too, is true. If then we can set our minds at rest on at point I feel we should consider the matter further. After ll, what you said the other night about Kurt wishing to go on ith his scientific experiments if we get to South America is so ght. But to do so he would need a pretty big sum of money.'

Erika was quick to see the turn the conversation was king. 'I am so glad you agree with me. Those experiments f his are for the benefit of humanity, not its destruction. In e past I financed him for them pretty lavishly, and I am uite prepared to do so again.'

'That is very gracious, *Frau Gräfin*. I will confess that am very interested in the matter too. You see, I also am a cientist, although I have not the genius or distinction of the ount, your husband. It would mean a great deal to me to be ble to continue to help him with his work.'

As Einholtz made this announcement he feared for a oment that Erika might, from her association with von Oster-erg in the past, know something of the Count's peacetime xperiments, and begin to a talk of scientific matters to him. ince he had never been in a laboratory in his life, this might ave proved extremely tricky ground; so, having made his oint, he hurried on:

'However, to arrange this matter will not be easy.'

'You think my husband will prove obstinate?' Erika asked.

'That, I believe I can overcome. It will take a little time ut I shall reason with him. I had in mind much more serious ifficulties.'

'Such as . . . ?' Erika prompted him.

He stared at his flashy amethyst ring for a moment, and aid slowly: 'As I have told you, the British could not take dequate precautions against this gas unless they had a proper cientific analysis of it. Such things one cannot carry in one's ead, and we have left our notes behind in Germany.'

Her heart sank. 'Then—then if they are essential, that makes impossible for us to pass on this vital information.'

'Not necessarily, *Frau Gräfin*. I do not mean that we left em at the experimental station. On an impulse of the mo-ent we brought them with us as far as Schloss Niederfels; ut it had not even occurred to either of us then that we ight later consider it proper that we should pass them on. n fact, we were so greatly concerned at the thought of the arm which might be done to the German cause should they

75

fall into the hands of the enemy that we decided that in n
circumstances must we expose them to such a risk by takir
them out of Germany. In consequence, before we left, v
locked them up in the safe of Kurt's private laboratory at th
castle.'

'I see,' she said slowly. 'That means, then, that someboc
would have to go back into Germany to get them?'

Einholtz nodded his semi-bald head up and down.

'That is the trouble. Of course it is not far. It could be dor
in a single night's journey, and anyone could easily recross th
lake from the Villa to *Freiherr* von Lottingen's place on th
other side with small risk of detection. But it needs a brav
man to penetrate even so far into Nazi Germany.'

Again there was silence for a moment. Einholtz had no
completed the baiting of the trap. Without appearing to loc
at Erika he watched her from beneath half lowered lids wit
carefully concealed eagerness, as he wondered if she woul
produce Gregory.

Knowing the impossibility of doing that, Erika's though
were running on other lines. At length she said: 'If you coul
induce Kurt to agree to our proposal, do you think we coul
persuade him to go back and collect these notes of his?'

He made a negative gesture with one of his bony hands. '
hate to say so, but Kurt was as nervous as a cat during th
whole of our journey. I am certain that nothing would induc
him to risk returning to Nazi-controlled territory.'

'But you are of a braver spirit,' she said, seizing the chanc
to use a little flattery 'Would you go?'

He appeared to hesitate, then replied: 'No, I don't think so

She caught at the latent possibility suggested by his hesita
tion, and said: 'You are a scientist, *Herr* Einholtz, and n
doubt have your own ambitions. If so they would be easie
of achievement if you were no longer working under someon
else. My money is my own to dispose of as I wish. Kurt wi
get his thousand pounds for the divorce. That is settled. Bu
I want to prevent this terrible thing happening; not only fo
the sake of those wretched women and children in the slum
of the British cities, but also because I am convinced that b
so doing I should have served Germany well in the long run
I will pay to you ten thousand pounds if you will get for m
the full analysis of this new poison gas.'

Again he appeared to hesitate, then he said: 'No. I can'
do it. You see, the people on Kurt's estate are loyal to him
They would not give away a von Osterberg. But I am not a
von Osterberg. I should be alone with no one to depend or
to give me help or shelter if things went temporarily wron
and I found that I couldn't get back the same night after all

76

No, I am sorry, but the thought of Dachau frightens me too much. I will not risk it.'

He was on tenterhooks now. He felt that he had played his hand well and that, having arrived at an apparent impasse, she might at any moment say that she thought she knew a man who, given proper directions, would undertake this dangerous task. But she did not. Instead, she suddenly looked him squarely in the face and said quietly:

'I am a von Osterberg. I know the people at Niederfels; the indoor servants, the outdoor servants, and the tenants who live on the estate. They will be loyal to me. But there must be a lot of scientific papers in that safe, and I don't know sufficient about such matters to be certain of picking out the right ones. If I arrange to give you an order for ten thousand pounds on the Federal Bank of Switzerland, cashable on our return, will you come with me to Schloss Niederfels?'

The thoughts sped like lightning through his brain. For some reason known only to herself she would not make use of Gregory Sallust in this business. But once she was inside Germany, if there was the least hope of getting her out, Sallust would come in to attempt her rescue. It was a cinch; and with careful handling, a fine chance to put ten thousand good British pounds into his pocket into the bargain.

He bowed. '*Frau Gräfin*, I should be ashamed to refuse any proposal made by so courageous a lady. We will go back together into Germany.'

7

Midnight Journey

On his way back to the Villa Offenbach, Fritz Einholtz thought over the result of his visit to Erika with mixed feelings. So far he had failed in the achievement of his object. Not only had Gregory Sallust refrained from accompanying Erika to Switzerland and was, presumably, still ignorant of the situation that was maturing there, but, apparently, she was not even contemplating asking for his help.

It might be, of course, that they had quarrelled and were

no longer in love with each other; or it might be that Sallus had been sent off somewhere on another mission, and so wa not available. If the former were the case, *Gruppenführe* Grauber would have to think up some other way of getting a his enemy; if the latter, then in due course, when Sallust re turned from his mission, no better bait than having his gir friend on a string in Germany could be devised to get him i the trap.

The fact that Erika was clearly anxious to obtain a divorc could not be taken as definite evidence that she wanted t marry Sallust, but in view of their known relationship fo the best part of the last two years it certainly pointed tha way. In any case, she was an enemy of the Reich and a mos dangerous woman, so it would be a good move to put he under lock and key.

Yet, in order to do so, and still leave the trap open for Sallust to follow her inside, Einholtz knew that he had severa knotty problems to solve.

In the first place, he could not leave von Osterberg behind. If he did, the Count would seize the opportunity to rat on them; and, not only disappear, but quite probably go over to the enemy. That would be absolutely disastrous, since, as well as giving away all that had occurred at the Villa Offenbach, and thus preventing Sallust following Erika into Germany by a route upon which he could be seized at any time it suited them, he might also betray the real secret of the 'K' weapons, which was of such vital importance to Germany.

At the thought, Einholtz shuddered slightly, seeing a swift mental picture of himself, weakened from weeks of torture, and bruised and bleeding, as he was finally clubbed to death in the yard of some concentration camp.

Yet, if he took von Osterberg back to Germany with him the sole point of Erika going herself would be washed out; since the apparent function of the one, to assure the loyalty of the people at Niederfels, would cancel that of the other.

Again, the part he had led her to believe that he would play —of securing the right papers—would be redundant if von Osterberg went; and to her it would appear very queer if they both proposed to risk their necks when the job could be done by one of them. For a moment he contemplated sending them in together; von Osterberg ostensibly to get the notes, and Erika, ostensibly, to give him courage. But that would not do either. Within ten minutes of having left the Villa in the launch, von Osterberg would spill the beans and, instead of proceeding to the German shore, they would turn the boat and head for another Swiss village, to land and disappear together.

Einholtz knew that he could easily secure help. It would be easy enough to get someone else to look after von Oster-berg while he accompanied Erika to Schloss Niederfels, but he did not favour that idea. The appearance of a stranger at the Villa would be difficult to explain when they were sup-posed to be living there in such secrecy, and Erika might smell a rat.

The only really satisfactory idea that emerged from his cogi-tations during his short journey was that he had only to pro-duce his rubber truncheon to make von Osterberg agree to say whatever seemed desirable when Erika paid her next visit to the Villa.

On Sunday morning he shackled the Count to his bed again and went into Zurich. There was a small hotel there actually run by the Gestapo, which often proved useful to them for accommodating their agents when they were in difficulties with the Swiss police. In consequence, it was a very simple matter for Einholtz to secure from the Gestapo man who ran it a forged hotel bill, purporting to show that the *Herr Graf* von Osterberg had stayed there with a woman for the weekend, passing her off as his *Gräfin*. If it later proved necessary to produce a suitable girl, that could easily be arranged; but Einholtz did not think it would, as he reckoned that Erika would be in the net long before her solicitors got down to checking up the evidence with which he proposed to provide her. But he took the name and description of the young woman it was proposed to use, if that proved essential, and duly primed von Osterberg with that information that night.

Next morning he made the Count telephone Erika, asking her to pay another visit to the Villa that evening. On the Mon-day night, therefore, she took the same precautions as before, dined at the litle hotel in Steinach, and arrived at the Villa soon after nine o'clock.

She thought her husband looked more ill than when she had seen him the previous week, but as soon as he told her that he had got the evidence she required she put his poor state down to the probability that the whole business had been most repugnant to him and he was now showing the strain he had been under in going through with it.

He produced the hotel bill and also a letter that he had written for her that afternoon. It simply said that since they had not lived together for the past two years he had lost all affection for her and entered into another relationship; that he had now definitely made up his mind that in no circum-stances would he return to her or contribute in any way to her support in the future, and that he enclosed a hotel bill upon which she could act, if she wished.

Having perused the two documents carefully she thanked him and said, 'Can you give me particulars of the girl you stayed with, in case the solicitors say that the court will require her to be identified?'

'She stayed there as my wife,' he replied, 'but her real name is Mitzi Winkelweiss, and she is a German. She was about your height, but dark, and with a small mole on her right cheek. She has a job as a typist in the *Deutscher Reisebüro,* but they don't pay her very much so she makes a bit extra now and again by going to the dance room at the Café Hiller, when she feels like it, and picking up any man who takes her fancy. That is where I found her.'

He reeled it off tonelessly, and Erika felt sorry for Mitzi Winkelwiss, who obviously could not have had a very enjoyable weekend. She hoped that Kurt had at least paid the poor girl well for the uninspiring hours she must have spent with him; but that, after all, was not her business, so she simply said:

'I think you arranged matters very well, as it should be easy enough to find her, if that proves necessary.'

'I don't think it will,' Fritz Einholtz put in. 'As the case will be undefended, it should be quite sufficient if Kurt is identified as the man who stayed at that hotel, with a girl, on the night in question. After that, all your solicitors will have to do is to get you to point Kurt out to them so that they can serve the papers on him.'

'There is still the best part of three months to go before I can start proceedings.'

'That cannot be avoided. But Kurt will not run away.' Einholtz laughed suddenly. 'He cannot, anyhow, until you give him the thousand pounds to do it with. But I think I see at what you were driving. You were about to say that there is not much point in your going to see your solicitors yet; and you are right. Kurt has shown that he means to deal fairly with you by giving you the evidence you will require with a minimum of delay, but no more can be done for the moment.'

'Wasn't it a bit risky to choose a German girl, when you meant to stay with her at an hotel under your own name?' Erika asked, glancing at her husband.

'I was a bit scared about that, too,' Einholtz said, before von Osterberg had a chance to reply, 'but Kurt thought it would seem more natural and look less like collusion. Of course, he didn't learn till later that she was in a German Travel Agency, which increases the risk of her talking to someone who might be interested in us. Still, the odds are that she never mentions her lapses into prostitution to anyone in

80

the office, and, anyway, she has no idea where Kurt lives—so I don't think we need worry overmuch.'

Einholtz was rather proud of this little subtlety and would have been disappointed if Erika had not given him a chance to work it in, because it was just the sort of touch likely to strengthen her belief in their good faith. After a moment, he went on:

'I've been talking to Kurt about that other matter too, and we both feel, now, that there was a great deal in what you said when you were here last.'

'Oh, I'm so glad,' she said, smiling at Kurt, but she left it at that for the moment, as she did not know if he knew of Einholtz's visit to her, so thought it best to say no more until one of them had given her a lead.

Einholtz stood up to get a cigarette and from behind her back made a swift, imperative gesture at the Count, on which he began to speak, although with obvious reluctance.

'It is all very difficult,' he said. 'Fritz and I have agreed that we ought to enable the British to protect their civilian population from this—er—gas, if we can; but I left my notes in the safe a Niederfels. I've been through a lot and my health is not very good, so, to be honest, I'm not really up to undertaking such a dangerous journey—at all events on my own. Fritz is braver than I am, and he is prepared to put his head in the lion's jaws again, but the trouble about that is that I don't like to let him. You see, our people at Niederfels would never give me away, but if he turned up there on his own the risk that one of them might split on him to curry favour with the local Nazis is quite considerable.'

As he paused, Erika felt certain she knew what was coming next, but she was mistaken. He added, rather heavily, 'So it seems, the only thing for us to do is to go together.'

Erika gave an imperceptible sigh of relief. She had been dreading this dangerous venture more than she realised, and now, it seemed, quite unexpectedly, a merciful dispensation of Providence had let her out of it. If Kurt went with Einholtz there was no reason at all for her to leave the comparative safety of Swiss soil. But, once again, she was jumping to conclusions.

Her husband puffed nervously at his cigarette, and resumed: However, this job really needs a third person. I—well—I've got cold feet about entering the Castle alone, in case the Nazis have taken it over in my absence. With someone to stand by me, I'd risk it, but not alone. We should be able to do the whole job in a few hours if things go well. But that depends on our not running into trouble, and being able to make our getaway immediately I've collected my notes. When we get to

81

the other side of the lake we can use one of Willi von Lot-tingen's cars, but we dare not drive up to the Schloss; so before we reach it, we'll have to park the car on the roadside some-where. It's for that we need a third member of our party. If it were found unoccupied by anyone and reported to the police, or stolen, our lifeline would be cut, and we simply daren't risk that. We need someone who will remain with the car while we are away to ensure that it is still there when we get back.'

Erika caught Einholtz's eye, and guessed that he had said nothing to her husband about their meeting, but had mentally designated her for the part which would overcome Kurt's last objection.

'All right,' she said, slowly, 'if that is the way you feel, I will come with you.'

'Erika,' he began, 'I really don't think ...'

But Einholtz had jumped to his feet and, seizing her hand, kissed it, as he cried enthusiastically: 'Then all is well. It is most brave of you, *Frau Gräfin*, to take this risk with us. But to know that the car is there safe and ready for our getaway means so much. Together we will do this thing. Let us put behind us all thought of failure.'

Erika forced a smile. 'Yes, and now we've decided to do it, the sooner we can get it over the better.'

'We can't go while the moon's like this,' von Osterberg said hurriedly. 'There are patrol boats on both sides of the lake They would ...'

Unseen by Erika, Einholtz shot him an angry glance, and he lapsed into unhappy silence. But one look out of the long window which ran half the length of the room on its northern side showed how right he was. Bright moonlight silvered the lake and any boat upon it could have been seen the best part of a mile away.

'That is true,' Einholtz had to admit, 'but the moon is past the full and if we plan the timing of our trip carefully it should not prove a serious disadvantage to us. Say we made an early start in three or four days' time, we could be clear of the coast here before the Swiss boat comes on duty, and sneak in to the German side just as darkness is falling.'

'But we'd have the moonlight coming back, then,' Erika objected.

'Not necessarily. If the Castle has been taken over we shall have had our journey for nothing, anyhow; but if it has not there is no reason why we shouldn't remain there a few hours then start back about half past three when the moon is setting Even if we find the place full of Nazis, we could sit quietly in the woods till the moon is going down, then it would be dark by the time we reached the lake on our return journey.'

'Wouldn't it be better to wait for a fortnight, when there won't be any moon at all?' von Osterberg hazarded.

'If we wait so long, the thought of the risk we are going to run will get on our nerves to such a degree that when the time comes we may funk it altogether,' Einholtz argued. 'Don't you agree, *Frau Gräfin*?'

Erika knew that her husband was right, and that during the dark period of the moon there would be the minimum of risk; but she also knew that the delay of a fortnight might make all the difference between success and failure to the British scientists and manufacturers who would have to design and make the new gas-masks, perhaps at breakneck speed, if they were to be issued in time to be effective. She also felt that there was a lot to be said for Einholtz's view, so she replied, 'Personally, I'm all for doing the job as soon as conditions are reasonably favourable.'

'Right then.' Einholtz consulted a little pocket diary. 'To-day's Monday the 18th, isn't it. Well, on Friday next, the 22nd, the moon sets at four-fifteen. That should still give us ample time to get back across the lake while it is still dark. How about making it Friday night?'

The others agreed and it was arranged that Erika should come to the Villa that evening at six o'clock, so that they could get well out on to the lake by sundown. She then returned to the hotel and drove back up the winding valley to St. Gall.

Next morning she breakfasted early and caught the express via Zurich to Berne. In the Swiss capital she called on the firm of solicitors who acted for the British Legation. Having presented a letter of introduction which Sir Pellinore had obtained for her she had an interview with a pleasant middle-aged Swiss who undertook to handle the proceedings of her divorce. He confirmed the fact that no steps could be taken until November, but filed the hotel bill and the particulars of *Fräulein* Mitzi Winkelweiss that Erika gave him. He did not think there should be any difficulty about the case as husband and wife would both have established residence in Switzerland and the Swiss courts usually granted decrees automatically in undefended cases.

Considerably cheered by this she returned to St. Gall, but the double journey of some hundred and twenty miles each way through tunnels and mountains had made a tiring day and she did not get back until quite late, so on entering the lounge of the Pension Julich she was none too pleased to find Einholtz waiting for her.

He said that he had rung up that morning and learned that she had gone off for the day, but was expected back in the evening, so he had taken the liberty of coming over as there was a certain matter he wished to discuss with her.

While she ate a light supper he sat with her talking trivialities, and when she had finished they went out into the garden As soon as they were seated in two wicker chairs he said:

'You will, of course, have guessed that I have come to talk to you about money.'

'I don't see why I should have,' she replied a little shortly.

'Oh, come, *Frau Gräfin*,' he shrugged. 'You must have realised that had it not been for my persuasive powers your husband would never have agreed to make our contemplated trip By persuading him to come himself, too, I very nearly succeeded in sparing you the danger and anxiety of it. His fear that someone might steal or move the car while we were busy in th Castle was the one thing I could not overcome, but that wa not my fault.'

'Yes, I realise that.'

'Then you appreciate that if we succeed in securing thos notes you will owe that to me?'

'Yes, I see what you mean. You have come to get an under taking from me that if we are successful, in spite of the fac that Kurt is going with us, I still pay the ten thousand pound to you?'

'Exactly!'

'All right.' Erika nodded. 'After all, it is you who have mad the whole thing possible, and will have to lead the expeditior so I think that's fair enough.'

'*Herzlichen Dank Frau Gräfin*. There is, however, one othe point that has occured to me, although I hesitate to mentio it.'

'Well, what is it?' Erika asked a shade wearily. She had neve liked *Herr* Einholtz very much, for all his helpfulness with he difficult husband; and now he was coming out in his tru colours, as a man who was determined to make quite certai that he received a good round sum as the price of preventin an indiscriminate massacre on a giant scale, she liked hir even less; but it was imperative that she kept in with him, s she added with a little laugh, 'I promise not to run away fror you.'

'Please, please!' he protested. 'Such a thought never entere my head. But I'm afraid I had a much more horrible one. I did occur to me, after you had gone last night, that we migh become separated while we are on the other side. On such venture one never knows what may happen. Saying, for e ample, that we were shot up during our return and had scatter.'

'And I were captured or killed,' Erika supplemented.

'Yes, God forbid that such a thing should happen, but

84

it did, and I had the notes on me and succeeded in getting back, what do you wish me to do with them?'

'Take them to the British Legation in Berne. Mention my name and ask for an interview with the Minister. Hand him the notes and give him a week to have them looked at by a competent scientist in London; and, if the reply is satisfactory, he will pay you the ten thousand pounds. I will go into Berne again, myself, before we leave and arrange the matter.'

'Many thanks, *Frau Gräfin*,' Einholtz murmured smoothly. The arrangement did not suit him at all. He had hoped to persuade her to give him a draft cashable on his return, or at least make some arrangement by which the money would be handed over to him in exchange for a packet of papers containing any plausible-looking scientific gibberish; but she had proved much shrewder than he had anticipated. The stipulation that the notes should be examined in London before payment was made completely spiked his guns, and he saw no way round it.

This attempt to get hold of her money was a purely private venture and he was much too scared of *Gruppenführer* Grauber to prejudice the success of his official mission by pursuing it at the risk of arousing her suspicions.

Realising that she was tired, he had the good sense to say, 'That's settled then,' stand up, kiss her hand and wish her good-night.

Next morning Erika wrote a long letter to Sir Pellinore. She told him everything that had taken place and what she hoped to do. He would, she felt sure, be worried about the risk she was running, but at the same time, knowing that no one else was in a position to undertake this vital task, fully approve her decision to accompany her husband and Einholtz to Schloss Niederfels.

On the Thursday she went in to Berne again and called at the Legation. His Majesty's Minister had received a note about her from the Foreign Office and saw her in person. From him she obtained a special label bearing in bold red letters the words 'MOST SECRET' and underneath, in small script, 'To be opened personally by . . .' below which she wrote Sir Pellinore's name. Having put her letter in a larger envelope she sealed the latter with the label and gave it to the Minister for despatch by the next bag. She then wrote out for him full particulars of the procedure to be followed should Einholtz later present himself at the Legation with a packet for the Minister.

Immediately after supper, on her return to St. Gall, she went to bed and took a mild sleeping draught, to ensure herself a good night's rest, against the prospect of being up all the following night; and she stayed in bed till lunchtime next day.

During her lazy morning she thought much of Gregory, wishing almost desperately at times that he were with her, but she was heartily glad that he knew nothing of the dangerous business upon which she was soon to set out. In the afternoon she packed her bag, as a precaution against the grim thought that she might not return, but left it upstairs and told the girl down in the office that she was retaining her room but going off to spend the night with friends.

At five o'clock, clad in her travelling tweeds and with a small automatic in her handbag, she walked down the hill to the station and caught the local train down to Rorschach. The old lakeside town with its red roofs and slated steeples was looking lovely in the early evening light, and she lingered on the quay for a little before she took a bus along the lakeside road the few remaining miles to Steinach.

She found both Kurt and Einholtz ready to set off and all three of them went straight out to the boathouse. *Freiherr* von Lottingen's summer villa lay some four miles south-east of Friedrichshafen, so the crossing was only ten or twelve kilometres and twilight had not yet begun to fall, but Einholtz's plan was that they should appear to be going out simply for an evening's fishing. The rods and any fish that they might catch would also, they hoped, be considered evidence of their innocence if they were halted and questioned on the way to Niederfels. None of them had papers they could show, but Einholtz proposed to say that Erika was staying as their guest in Stuttgart, and they had taken her for a day's excursion on the Bodensee.

The launch was a powerful one and soon took them well out into the lake. Einholtz then shut off the engine and the two men got out their rods, while Erika sat silent in the stern of the gently rocking boat. There was little shipping on the lake and nothing approached them to within hailing distance. Most of the other boats in view were scattered in an arc off Friedrichshafen, which they could now see in the distance as a blur of houses, and tall chimneys belching out smoke in the race to produce German war equipment. In an hour and a half they caught three trout and two bream to go in the creel they were taking with them.

Gradually dusk came down and, switching on the engine to half speed, Einholtz edged the launch a few miles nearer to the German shore. Then he stopped it and they drifted silently again while he produced two thermoses of coffee and some sandwiches, from which they picnicked.

As he put the thermoses back in their basket, Erika said:

That was a good idea. Heaven only knows when we shall get another meal.'

'We'll get one in a few hours' time, I hope,' Einholtz replied lightly. 'If our luck is in we should be able to get a cold supper and a good bottle of wine at Niederfels, while we're waiting for the moon to go down.'

His confidence cheered Erika a little as, one by one, she watched the stars come out and darkness closing down to shut out the splendid panorama of the mighty snow-clad mountains to the south. Friedrichschafen was now hidden, as all its windows were blacked out, but they could still judge its position by the lurid glow that lit the night sky from its blast furnaces.

Einholtz put on the engine at half speed again and ran it for a little, then shut it off for a few minutes while they strained their ears listening for the sound of other boats or any distant challenge. He was almost as anxious as Erika not to run foul of a German patrol boat, as, had they done so, he would have given the game away and resulted in his having to arrest her out of hand. Having got her so far he would have achieved his immediate object by her capture, but he took a pride in his work and wished to complete the job artistically.

By a series of repetitions of this tactic of alternatively nosing the boat in for a few hundred yards and shutting off the engine to listen, they succeeded in getting close to the German shore, then creeping round the big headland that lies to the south-east of Friedrichshafen, without incident. A few minutes later Einholtz turned the bow of the launch towards the land and a dark irregular cluster of buildings loomed up. The launch bumped against a short causeway and they were all thrown sharply forward. Einholtz swore, and a voice from somewhere above them in the blackness cried:

'Wer da?'

Erika strove to hold her breath, and at the same time fumbled in her bag to get out her automatic, in case there was trouble.

'Who is that?' Einholtz asked in a low voice.

'Kestner,' replied the voice.

'Gottseidank,' murmured Einholtz; then he gave his name and added: 'You remember me. I was with the Gräf von Oster-erg when you helped us to get across the lake. The Gräf is with me now, also his Gräfin. We have business that must be attended to. Can you lend us a car, just for the night?'

The man called Kestner came down to the causeway and helped them manœuvre the launch along into a large boathouse, where two other launches were lying. When he had closed the water gate behind them he produced a torch and shone it for a moment on Einholtz's face, then he said:

'Yes, it's you all right. I can manage a car if you wish, but you must be crazy to come back here like this.'

Einholtz gave his colleague a gentle pat of encouragement in the darkness, and muttered something about a job that would take them only a few hours; then they followed Kestner along a garden path and through the double doors of a big garage at the side of the house.

When the doors were shut behind them and the light switched on, Kestner, who proved to be a fat, middle-aged man, was duly presented to Erika as *Freiherr* von Lottingen's steward. She enquired after her old friend and was told that he was now with the army on the Russian front. Von Osterberg merely said good evening to the man, then stood there in moody silence.

There were two cars in the garage, a Mercédès-Benz and a Buick. Einholtz chose the Buick, remarking that it would be less conspicuous. They filled her up with petrol and oil, of which Kestner seemed to have plentiful supplies, and as they were about to get in Einholtz suggested to Erika that she should sit with him, so as to get the hang of the car in case she should have to drive it a short distance after they had left her in it. When they had settled themselves von Osterberg got into the back, Kestner switched out the light in the garage, opened its doors and the gate on to the road. With a wave to him they drove away.

Avoiding Friedrichshafen, they took a by-road inland to Ravensburg then, some miles further on, leaving Wingarten on their right, they passed through the villages of Altshauser, Boms, Saulgau, and Herbetingen to the little Schwabian town of Sigmaringen. On leaving it they followed the north bank of the upper Danube as far as Beuron, then, turning north out of the village, they entered the forest-clad heights of the Heuberg, and by winding side-roads at length approached the straggling single street of Wilflingen above which Schloss Niederfels towered upon its wooded crag.

Their journey from the lake had proved amazingly simple; the night was fine, but on the by-roads they had followed there had been little traffic and not once had they been stopped or challenged.

At the entrance to the village a fork-road rose steeply behind the houses to one side of the street, and this led by a series of corkscrew twists and bends up through the silent forest to the castle. Einholtz drove up it several hundred yards then, on reaching a place where the track flattened and broadened out in a small clearing, he turned the car round, so that it was pointing downhill, and drew up on the wide grass verge beneath the trees.

As they got out he said to Erika: 'It should take us twenty minutes or so to climb the rest of the hill on foot. Soon after that we should know if the place has been taken over or not. If you hear any shooting, start up the engine and get the car back on to the road, so that you'll be able to drive off without a second's delay if we can get back to you. But if it is all clear I'll blow two blasts on my whistle, then you can drive the car up and park it in the courtyard, and we'll have some supper while we are waiting for the moon to go down.'

He slung the creel of fish over his shoulder and, Erika having wished them good luck, the two men set off.

When they had disappeared round the bend she left the car with the door of its driving-seat open, so that she could slip into it at once, and walked to the far side of the clearing. The moon was now well up and from where she stood she could see the great bulk of the castle looming out over the tree-tops far above her.

Standing out against the night sky, with the moonlight glinting on the slates of its tall conical tower, the long roof of the chapel and its many pepper-pot turrets, it looked immense and faintly sinister. It had stood there night after night like that for hundreds of years, since the days when the von Osterbergs, like most of the German nobility, had been robber barons. It had its own grim legends and might well have been the original castle Dracula. Knights in armour had many a time come clanking down the track accompanied by a hundred or more rough retainers on their way to join the Schwabian bands; and through the centuries all the lords and ladies of Württemberg had gathered there in their silks and satins, to celebrate the births, the marriages, and the deaths of the von Osterbergs in the great banqueting hall where, beneath the hanging banners of long-forgotten victories, refectory tables had groaned beneath countless dishes of rich food and big flagons of Rhenish wines.

If Kurt von Osterberg died tonight, she reflected, he would get no stately funeral, and there would be no splendid assembly of his peers to drink a health to the new lord of Niederfels. Some black-uniformed S.S. man would merely stand by smoking a cigarette, while a few of Kurt's old servants were made to throw their master's body, uncoffined, into a hole in the ground.

A slight shudder ran through her. She was sorry for Kurt, he looked so tired and ill. She wondered that he had had the guts to court the vengeance of the Nazis by throwing up his job, and admired him more than she had ever done for doing so. She wondered if his old dragon of a mother was still living in the castle or if out of cruel spite against him some of Himmler's bullies had carried her off to a concentration camp. Knowing how devoted he was to the old lady it crossed her mind that it was strange that he could have brought himself to expose her to such a risk. She was surprised that she had not thought of that before, but she had had so little opportunity to talk to Kurt about himself. At their brief interview Einholtz had always been with them and Kurt's poor state of health had seemed to make him particularly moody and non-communicative.

The time of waiting there seemed interminable. Every now and then Erika glanced at her watch; she could just make out the figures by the moonlight and the hands seemed to crawl. With quick nervous gestures she lit cigarette after cigarette only to throw them away half smoked. At last, after what seemed an age, she heard two faint shrill blasts from a whistle and sighed with relief.

Hurrying to the car, she got it going, turned it round and drove up the steep winding track. At its top the way flattened out a little. The castle was now a huge black mass in front of her but the towers flanking its great gateway stood out in the moonlight, and the big arched nail-studded gates were open.

She drove into the courtyard and turned the car round so that it should be ready for them to leave at once in case of an alarm. Then she got out and, crossing the court, went up the few steps to the central door. It was ajar, and a chink of light came through, so she pushed it open and went in. The light came from along the passage where she knew the great banqueting hall lay. Instinctively she tiptoed towards it.

As she reached the door she saw that the curtains were drawn across the tall windows that, set deep in the thick walls, lined both sides of the big room. At its far end, near the open fireplace, a table was laid and it looked as if one person had dined there. Kurt's mother, the old *Gräfin* was still there then, and how like the old woman, she thought, to continue to dine in solitary state in this great barrack of a place, instead of in one of the smaller rooms. On the table stood two multi-branched silver candlesticks, and it was the soft glow of the candles in them that made an oasis of light in the lofty chamber. The August night was quite warm but a wood fire had been burning on the hearth and Kurt was putting more twigs and logs on to its smouldering embers to get it going again. Einholtz was nowhere to be seen.

At the sound of Erika's footsteps von Osterberg looked up, and said, 'You've been very quick.'

'The second I heard the whistle I drove straight up the hill,' she replied. 'Where has Einholtz got to?'

90

The Count glanced nervously over his shoulder at a curtained door that led to his own sitting-room. 'He—he's telephoning.'

Erika's eyes widened with surprise. 'Telephoning!' she echoed. 'But why? Who to?'

Von Osterberg held out his hands in a little helpless gesture, then let them fall limply to his sides. For a moment he seemed to struggle for words. Suddenly they came with a rush: 'Erika, I couldn't help it! I swear I couldn't! I tried to warn you! I begged you not to concern yourself with this secret weapon. I flatly refused your offer of money for it. I even tried to persuade you to put off coming here, hoping that if I had a fortnight I might be able to find some way to let you know the truth. But that devil headed me off every time. He never allowed me to get a moment with you alone, or to leave the Villa. I've spent whole days handcuffed to my bed.'

During his outburst every muscle in her body seemed to stiffen with apprehension. As he paused for breath, she gasped: 'You—you mean that they used you to lure me into a trap? That Einholtz is a Gestapo man?'

He nodded dumbly, then burst out again. 'I wish I'd killed myself, but I hadn't the courage. I think I would have if it hadn't been for my Lady Mother. That's how they got me down. They threatened to send her to a concentration camp. You know what that would have meant? I couldn't bear it. I gave in.'

Erika was no longer listening to him, but thinking desperately: 'I'm trapped! I'm trapped! Any second he'll have finished telephoning and be back here. What shall I do? Oh, God, what shall I do?'

She suddenly felt very cold and small and helpless, and, as the horror of the things that the Gestapo did to their prisoners flooded back into her mind, fear gripped her heart so fiercely that she felt as though she was paralysed and incapable of moving from the rug on which she stood. The blood had drained from her face leaving it chalk-white, except under her high cheekbones where the slight dusting of powdered rouge now stood out unnaturally. Her hands had gone faintly clammy, and as she stared unseeing at her husband her eyes were distended by terror.

The hanging of the door behind which Einholtz had been telephoning swayed and the brass curtain rings from which it hung rattled.

As though galvanised by an electric shock Erika let out a piercing scream, stepped back, then darted forward to run past it.

Even as she moved, she knew that she was too late. The

door swung open and Einholtz stood there, tall and grim, wi
a sardonic smile playing about his thin mouth.

At a glance, he had taken in the situation. He had unde
estimated the time it would take her to get up the hill by
trifle, and in those few minutes von Osterberg had given hi
away. That was rather a pity, as he had quite a lot of fu
acting his part that evening and he had wanted to play h
little comedy out to the end. He had planned for them to su
together of the fresh trout they had caught and a few bottl
of the best wine from the cellar of his unwilling host. Durin
their drive he, had been conjuring up an amusing picture
that supper in the great hall, with Erika, beautiful in the candl
light and her miserable husband wriggling like a fish on
hook as he wondered when the blow of her arrest woul
come, yet knew himself incapable of doing anything to sto
it. Still, that he had been deprived of that culminating scen
was of no great moment, and it was Erika who would suff
most, since he would now send her supperless to bed in th
chilly dungeon that he had already earmarked as her priso
while she remained in the castle.

As the door swung open Erika pulled up with a jerk. Sh
was cursing herself frantically now for having stood starin
at Kurt like a gaping fool when she should have taken advan
age of those few precious moments. If she had fled at onc
she could have got past the door where Einholtz now stoo
and down the passage, perhaps even half-way across the cour
yard, before she appeared. The engine of the car was still warn
those few seconds' lead would have given her time to jum
in and start it up. By now she might be half-way down to th
village, and at least still at liberty with a chance to make a bi
for her freedom.

But now it was too late. If she attempted to reach the pass
age Einholtz had only to step out and grab her as she passed

In jerking herself back one of her high heels twisted unde
her and she toppled sideways against the table. Swinging roun
she grasped its edge to keep herself from falling. As she hung
balanced there for a second she found herself staring into the
flames of the candles. Recovering her balance, she stretched
out her hand and grabbed one of the silver candelabra. Heav-
ing it up above her shoulder she flung it with all her force at
Einholtz.

He threw up his arm to cover his face but the heavy missile
hit him on the chest. As he recoiled the candelabra crashed to
the floor, its lighted candles scattering in all directions. Most of
them went out, but one rolled across the polished parquet and
came to rest against the fringe of the heavy damask door curtain. It was dry as tinder and Erika had scarcely turned again

fore it suddenly flared into a great sheet of flame.

Slipping round the tables she darted towards the row of windows at the other side of the room.

'Stop her!' Einholtz shouted to von Osterberg. 'Stop her, or I flay the hide off you.'

The Count made a half-hearted move to bar her path, but she struck him violently in the face with her clenched fist.

As he reeled away from her she saw that one of the window-curtains was billowing slightly from a gentle breeze. Confident that the window behind it must be open she ran towards it, wrenched the curtains aside and sprang on to the alcove seat, which brought her to within two feet of the broad sill.

Einholtz had pulled a gun from his pocket. Ignoring the flames that now lit the lofty chamber and the smoke that eddied about him, he levelled it at her back and bellowed:

'Halt, damn you! Halt, or I fire!'

It was at that instant, staring out through the open, lower half of the tall window, Erika realised that her unpreparedness and fear had once again betrayed her. In her desperate panic she had momentarily lost her sense of direction. Instead the window facing on the courtyard, as she had thought, it was one of those on the opposite side of the room. It looked out above the tree-tops of the forest-clad gorge.

8

In the Lion's Den

Einholtz's shout to halt was still echoing among the rafters as Erika, carried forward by the impetus of her own movement, pitched from the window-seat on to the broad stone sill.

Appalled at the outlook which had so suddenly loomed up before her, she stood there swaying for a moment.

The window was tall and narrow, twelve feet in height and worked on pulleys, so she was able to stand upright in the opening below its two now overlapping halves. Straight ahead of her there was nothing for a mile or more, until the starlit sky was broken by the wooded crests of a line of hills, on the side of the valley. Below her lay a seemingly unbroken sea of tree-tops shelving steeply to the valley bottom, then rising again in the distance. The upper branches of the nearest tre were not far below her but about twelve feet away. Betwe them and the wall of the castle there yawned a dark fifty-fo gulf, at the bottom of which the great stones with which t wall was built merged into the rock of the mountain to Moonlight silvered the whole scene, making it a vista of st unearthly grandeur that a landscape painter would have tr velled many miles to see; but for Erika it now held no beaut only stark menace and the terror of a leap to death.

'Come down from there!' Einholtz shouted. 'If you jun you'll break your neck.'

His voice recalled her instantly to the peril that lay in h rear. She knew too much of the Gestapo's dreadful work have any illusions that they might treat her well. If she st rendered it meant a concentration camp, starvation or fended off by scouring the dustbins for potato peelings a scraps of offal; lice, dirt and disease, beatings and unbeara humiliations; being thrown naked into an ice cold bath th having paraffin rubbed into the tenderest parts of one's bod Such things were not propaganda stories invented by Go many's enemies. She had lived for six years in Germany und Hitler and she knew the vile unvarnished truth.

Yet, she still hesitated. The tree-tops seemed so far awa Their upper branches were too slender for there to be a hope that if the leapt and caught at one of them it would be her weight.

Suddenly she caught the sound of heavy footsteps behi her. Einholtz was running across the room to grab at h skirt and pull her down. She swayed again with terrible certainty, trying to nerve herself for the jump, but funking at the last moment.

'Come down!' he bellowed as he ran. 'Come down, or shoot you as you jump.'

She swayed once more. Her knees seemed to be giving und her. She let them go, slipping down to a crouch instinctively avoid his threatened shot. Then, thrusting herself forward w every ounce of her strength, she launched herself out of window.

As she hurtled through space she heard a sharp report a the tinkle of glass behind her. Einholtz had fired too late a too high; his bullet had shattered two of the overlapping pa that a moment before had been just above her head.

Next second the nearest tree-top brushed her arm; anoth instant and pine-needles pricked and stung her face. Then s was falling . . . falling . . . falling. On every side of her branch rustled, bent and snapped, as she plunged downwards amo them. Frantically she tried to grab at them as they flew pa t only succeeded in tearing away a few handfuls of foliage. bigger branch hit her behind the neck, jerking her upright, other caught her under the legs, and for a moment she hung ere suspended from it, upside down. Then her feet flew up d she slipped from it to continue her terrifying descent head wn. A moment later a blow on the shoulder knocked her f unconscious, her body was twisted as it fell and a fright- l jolt in the ribs drove the breath out of it. For a count of enty she gasped agonizingly as she strove to get her breath ck, no longer realising where she was or what had happened; en her mind cleared and she found that she was doubled up th her head and arms dangling over one side of a big branch d her feet and legs on the other.

In the stillness of the night she could clearly hear Einholtz rsing somewhere high above her. Furious at having been ulked, he suddenly let fly a spate of bullets from his auto- tic, firing downwards through the lower branches of the es. One of his bullets struck a chip out of the bough upon ich she was hanging, then whined shrilly as it ricocheted ay into the darkness.

Still struggling to get her breath, Erika wriggled into a ghtly more comfortable position and peered downwards. e branch on which she hung was only about ten feet from · ground. Adjusting her grip, she lowered herself cautiously swing and then drop from it. As she took her whole weight her hands a stab of pain went through her right shoulder, d she realised that she must have wrenched it in her fall. The n made her let go sooner than she had intended and she pped sideways to land with a thud on the ground.

Hitting the thick carpet of pine-needles gave her another nising twinge. For a moment she lay there, bruised, sore d still breathless, her heart pounding heavily and her dyed r hanging in a tangled mass over her badly scratched face; n she started to pick herself up.

Only then did she realize that luck had been with her. Not y had she escaped serious injury but her bag which held money and a little pistol was still dangling by its straps m the crook of her arm. In order to conceal the gun she l specially chosen a good stout leather one which had a ety device to prevent it from flying open inadvertently. She s thankful now that she had forgotten all about the gun, l not attempted to get it out, as, had she done so, Einholtz uld as like as not have shot her before she could have shot n. As it was, she had simply thrust her arm through the ps of the bag while running to the window and, by the rcy of God, the clasp had held.

On getting to her feet she found it difficult to stand upright

owing to the slope of the ground; and her instinct urging h
to put as great a distance as possible between herself and t
castle she at once began to stumble downhill towards t
valley.

The moon gave little light under the thick branches, t
carpet of pine-needles was soft but treacherous, being und
mined here and there by rabbit holes and concealing partia
decayed logs beneath its undulating surface. Slipping a
slithering, she made her way downwards, often having to gr
at a low bough or tree-trunk to stop herself from falling. Af
about ten minutes she paused, and feeling that she was n
safe for the moment, sat down to rest. It was the first chan
she had had to wonder what her chances were of retaining h
hard-won freedom and to endeavour to formulate some de
nite plan of action.

About her chances of ultimate escape she was far from sa
guine. Einholtz was probably already busy on the telephor
arranging for a special announcement to be made which, wi
in a few hours, would result in every policeman in Württe
berg being on the look-out for her. The pains at which she h
been to have her hair dyed and her eyebrows altered wo
now go for nothing, since her description, as given by h
would be an up-to-date one. Her quickest way out of G
many lay in a return across Lake Constance, but even th
was sixy miles distant and she had no means of transport.

It occurred to her that she might work her way round to t
village, break into some garage and steal a car, but she aba
doned the thought almost as soon as it came to her. The villa
was on the other side of the castle and at least three mi
away. Long before she could reach it people there wo
have been warned to keep watch for her, and for the n
twenty-four hours every vehicle on the roads for miles arou
would be pulled up and searched whenever it passed a po
post.

If she stuck to the forest it might take them days to find h
but the Gestapo were tenacious people and they would
troops or the local peasantry to beat the woods acre by a
until they ran her to earth in some ditch or tangle of brambl
or, more probably, the fact that she had no means of proc
ing food would starve her into raiding isolated farmsteads u
she was caught and given up.

Yet she was certain that any attempt to reach the front
while the hue-and-cry was at its height was foredoomed
failure. In a few days the excitement would die down, a
as other matters arose to occupy the police, their net wo
slacken. If only she could find a secure hiding-place and eno
food to sustain her strength for a week, as a German in G

96

many with ample money, she should stand a fair chance of reaching the frontier and slipping across it undetected.

She searched her mind for anyone in the neighbourhood who might give her shelter, but, apart from the village people, she knew no one who lived within the radius of a night's tramp through the woods and along by-lanes. She had never lived for any great length of time at the castle, either, so the village folk were more acquaintances than friends. There were several couples who she felt sure would give her a bed for the night, but the trouble was that they all either had children or were old people. And it was perhaps the most terrible of all the evils Hitler had brought upon the German race that the minds of its children had been deliberately perverted to such an extent that they formed a vast legion of spies for the Nazis and were ready to betray even their own parents. The presence of a visitor in the house would undoubtedly be reported to the Nazi schoolteacher or youth leader first thing in the morning. As for the old people who lived alone, Erika could not bring herself to take advantage of any of them. She knew too well the terrible price they would have to pay if the Nazis learnt later that they had harboured a fugitive.

The trees were slightly less dense at the spot where she had stumbled to a halt and, on glancing over her shoulder at the sound of some small animal scurrying through the undergrowth, she caught a glimpse of the moonlit tower of the castle piercing the sky between two tree-tops. If only she were inside it she knew a score of good places in which she could have hidden for a month without being discovered. The huge, rambling pile was full of disused rooms, lofts, garrets and secret stairways; and now that the war was within a few days of two years old the staff must be so reduced it was doubtful if the curtains were pulled back each morning to let the sunlight into even a tenth of its many chambers.

The idea of hiding there gave her mind a sudden access of new energy. There was something both bold and shrewd about seeking refuge from the lion in the lion's den which she knew would have appealed to Gregory. But, even as she made up her mind to attempt it, two knotty problems still faced her. First, she had to find a way in unobserved and, secondly, when she had selected her hiding-place how was she going to get on for food?

She thought that she would manage to get in all right. She was now to the west of the castle and for the whole of its length on that side it rose in a sheer wall of stone; but to its south, in the early eighteenth century, by which time castles had outworn their usefulness as strongholds, a von Osterberg had broken down part of the great rampart and made a garden on a succession of terraces that ran down to meet the woods. Above them lay most of the rooms that had been modernised and Erika felt fairly confident that she would find a way in through one of them.

But the question of securing enough food to feed herself for a week was a much more difficult one. If she sneaked down to the larder each night and raided it for supplies, now that the household was so greatly reduced it was certain that her theft would soon be discovered, and if Einholtz used the place as his headquarters while the search was being conducted for her, he would soon tumble to it that she must be the thief. Even if he left the castle the servants would miss the food and one night lay in wait for her. She would be caught in the act and her fate would then lay in their hands. It was one thing to rely on their loyalty when descending on them out of the blue for a visit of a few hours, but quite another to rely on their protection when they knew that the Nazis were scouring the whole countryside for her.

She wondered then if there was one among them that she could really trust; someone to whom she could tell the truth; who would bring her food each night in secret. But her marriage to von Osterberg had been one of convenience and they must be aware of that. She had always preferred her own lovely house outside Munich and her apartment overlooking the Tiergarten in Berlin, so, on her brief summer visits to the castle, although they had accepted her as its mistress they had always really remained Kurt's servants.

Her pity for Kurt was mingled with contempt and anger. Even if he did not love her she had always been a good and generous friend to him. His weak and futile attempts to warn her counted for nothing since he had actually let her walk into the trap. Surely, by the use of a little imagination he could have found a way to open her eyes before allowing her to set foot on German soil, or at least found some remnant of manly chivalry to help her in her bid to escape, instead of obeying Einholtz's orders and attempting to stop her.

She was glad that she had struck him. He had deserved it. A German nobleman who deliberately betrayed his wife to a bestial gang of torturers was less worthy of respect than his meanest churl. She wondered, almost, that the ghosts of the past von Osterbergs had not materialised in that old hall and risen up to slay him where he stood. If dead men's bones could move, theirs, at this moment, must still be rattling with fury and disgust under the great stone slabs in the castle vault. What, she wondered, would his old mother say to him, if she ever learned of the depths of palsied cowardice to which her son had sank?

At that thought Erika stood up. A new idea had suddenly occurred to her. The von Osterbergs had got her into this frightful situation and, if it were humanly possible, they should get her out of it.

It took her twenty minutes of hard going to climb the uneven slope that she had plunged down in ten. On reaching the edge of the trees below the window from which she had jumped she craned her neck back to see if she could discern any signs of life in the banqueting hall. Evidently the fire had been got under control soon after it had started, but it had perhaps delayed them from coming out to search for her for a few moments. They would certainly have done that, believing her to be either dead or injured, but the fire had probably given her enough time to get out of earshot before they arrived on the scene; so they probably believed that she was either lying there with a broken neck and they had failed to find her in the darkness, or that she had been stunned by a bough and was still caught up in one of the trees. If so, that was all to the good.

The curtain had been redrawn and the window was still open, but no sound came from it; only the little noises of the forest disturbed the stillness. Turning right, Erika made her way along the fringe of trees parallel to the wall until she reached a great square bastion which jutted out from the main block. Its base was gripped by arm-thick trunks of ivy and smothered in dense clusters of brambles, so she had to make a considerable detour, but ten minutes later she had made a half circle round the bastion and came out on its other side where the terrace garden began.

The lowest terrace was formed by a stone balustrade set on a four-foot wall. Some distance away Erika could see the break in the middle of it where a flight of steps led down into the woods; but that was still in moonlight and she meant to keep in the shadows. She was already so dirty and bedraggled that her appearance could hardly be worsened so, heedless of her clothes, she forced the toe of her shoe into a cranny of the wall and, gripping one of the balusters, round its middle, heaved herself up. Her right shoulder gave her another angry twinge, but biting her lip, she suppressed a cry of pain, threw a sadly laddered silk-stockinged leg over the coping and scrambled down the other side.

For a moment she paused there to regain her breath, thinking as she did so of the gay parties she had known that in times past had lazed about this lower terrace on summer afternoons drinking Peach Bola and iced Hock. Little had she thought then that would ever be called upon to scale it like a thief in the night, with her hair dyed, in clothes torn to ribbons and with the fear of death in her heart.

This terrace garden consisted only of three shallow stages that did little more than replace the great rampart which had once stood there. Had it been made by a British nobleman of the eighteenth century the terraces would have been extended deep into the woods, so that fine lawns with herbaceous borders and ornamental trees might be planted upon them; but the German mind has always lacked both the craving to create beauty from a wilderness and sufficient appreciation of flowers to cultivate them in any but the crudest manner. The von Osterberg who had made the terraces had done so on returning from a campaign in Italy and, following the Italian fashion, had contented himself with laying out a few small formal beds on each with two fountains on the middle stage.

Keeping well in the shadow, Erika went up a flight of side steps to the second terrace, passed one of the now silent fountains, and climbed over the balustrade to the third, which was merely a broad stone-flagged walk with neglected standard rose trees set in it at intervals.

It was on to this that most of the modern living-rooms of the castle opened, and she crept cautiously along, examining every window as she went for any chinks of light which might show through the blackout curtains; but, as far as she could ascertain, every room was in darkness. On reaching the far end of the façade she tiptoed up a narrow stone stairway let into the great wall. It brought her out on to another smaller terrace, formed by the battlemented top of the south-eastern bastion which lay at the opposite end of the garden to the one she had circumvented. At the inner side of the bastion the central block of the castle rose again and the storey she was now facing had five modern windows and a glass door looking out on to the leads. This, Erika knew, had always been the *Gräfin* Bertha's suite, and there was small reason to suppose that in the past two years the old lady had changed it.

The moon was now sinking towards the distant tree-tops, and Erika reckoned that about two hours must have elapsed since she had made her escape. As she had seen no lights she thought it a fair assumption that, after a quarter of an hour's search for her and notifying the police of what had happened, Einholtz and Kurt had had their supper and gone to bed, so the odds were that they were asleep by now. All the same, if her mother-in-law was suddenly startled into wakefulness, by hearing someone enter her room, her cries for help might quite well arouse them; so Erika decided to get in unheard if she could and wake the Countess very gently.

Removing her high-heeled shoes, she stuffed them toes down into the pockets of her tweed jacket. The solid leads gave out

100

not the faintest sound as she crossed them. Reaching the door, she grasped its handle and tried it very gingerly. Under the pressure it turned and with only the faintest creak the door opened outwards. Stepping inside, she found herself faced by a heavy curtain. Having paused there a moment to still her breathing she edged gently sideways to get out from behind the hangings but, as she did so, the brass curtain rings jingled a little.

Instantly a light flicked on and a deep voice said angrily: 'Come out from behind there, whoever you are.'

Pulling a curtain back, Erika stepped into the room. For a moment she was dazzled by the light, then she saw the old lady sitting up in bed, staring at her. The *Gräfin* Bertha was a small, stout woman of over seventy, but still hale and hearty. Her grey hair had never gone white but always retained the black threads in it that it had had when Erika had first known her. She wore it in the severe German fashion, parted in the centre and plastered down each side with its ends twisted into a bun at the back. She had never used make-up in her life and her face was dry as parchment, having the slightly raddled appearance which often affects old ladies. Her sharp black eyes stared at the world aggressively from beneath heavy, arched unplucked brows, and her fleshy nose overhung a full, determined mouth.

'So you're a woman, eh?' she said sharply. 'What do you mean by entering my room like this?'

In view of her dyed hair and bedraggled state Erika could hardly wonder that her mother-in-law had failed to recognise her, but the fact at least showed that she knew nothing of what had taken place in the castle earlier that night.

At the sight of this formidable old woman Erika instinctively slipped back into the habit of the past and made a formal little curtsey as she replied: 'I am sorry to disturb you, my lady mother, but I am in great trouble and I come to ask your help.'

'*Teufel nochmal!*' exclaimed the Countess. '*Es ist die kleine Erika.*'

Erika shook her hair back from her face and advanced into the room. After her ordeal, the fall through the trees and her long tramp, she was now feeling desperately tired, but it would never have occurred to her to sit down without her mother-in-law first having asked her to do so. She stood there as the deep old voice went on:

'This is extraordinary! What sort of trouble have you got yourself into now? Have you seen Kurt? He got back tonight and is in the castle somewhere. I suppose you know that the

101

Nazis want to kill you? I thought you were safely abroad. Where have you come from?'

Without waiting for answers to any of her questions the old woman pointed to a thick woollen garment that lay near her feet, and added, 'Give me my bed-jacket, child.'

As Erika draped it round her mother-in-law's shoulders, she said, 'Yes, I was abroad, but I came back because I understood that Kurt wanted me to do so.'

The black eyes gave her a sharp look. 'You must have changed a lot then, to pay any attention to the wishes of my son. And what a sight you look, girl. How did you get yourself into that state?'

'I jumped out of one of the windows of the banqueting hall, into the trees below, and for the past two hours I've been tripping over roots and rabbit-holes as I made my way round here through the forest.'

'Hum!' the old Countess gave a grunt of grudging admiration. 'It must have taken some pluck to jump into those trees from that height, but you always had plenty of that. Still, you're looking very shaken, but I don't wonder. In my bedside cupboard, there, you'll find a small flagon of *Branntwein*. Give yourself some; then sit down and tell me what you have been up to.

Erika found the little wicker-covered bottle of brandy, poured a good tot into a medicine glass, drank it, gave a quick shudder and then, as the warm spirit coursed through her veins, felt better. While trudging through the forest she had worked out the story she meant to tell if, as she supposed, the *Gräfin* Bertha was ignorant of the trap which had been sprung that night. Knowing her mother-in-law's aversion to divorce she meant to say nothing about that, and she also wished to spare her, if possible, full knowledge of the cowardly way in which her son had acted. Sitting down she began her explanation:

'I've been in England. I didn't go there from my own choice but I was seriously wounded just before Dunkirk, and they evacuated me while I was still unconscious. About a month ago I received a letter from an old friend through the Swiss Legation in London. It said that Kurt was living here, that he was very ill and desperately wanted to see me. It's getting on for two years now since the Nazis were hunting for me in Germany and they must know that I've been living abroad. I thought that if I dyed my hair and changed my appearance a bit there would be comparatively little risk of my being recognised if I just slipped across the Bodensee and came by byroads as far as Niederfels and back. There's no point in going into my relationship with Kurt, but I felt that I ought to come f it could be managed, and I arrived here just before midnight onight.'

'So the loving wife returned,' said the Countess sarcastically. It is true that Kurt has been ill. I have been worried about him for some time, but, thank God, he has not been ill enough to wish for a death-bed reconciliation. There was nothing to be reconciled about for that matter. You always were a fly-by-night and I only let him marry you because I had a great respect for your father. I knew well enough that you'd continue your old tricks of slipping out of one man's bed into another's, but as you come of a good family I thought you'd have the good taste to conceal your amours after you were married, and I proved right about that. Still you and Kurt married one another only because it suited you both to do so, and I don't believe a word of this story about the fond wife risking prison or worse to smooth her husband's pillows. You had some much more pressing reason for putting that pretty neck of yours under the executioner's axe.'

'You may believe it or not, as you wish, lady Mother,' Erika replied quietly, 'but the fact remains that I left England because I was given good reason to believe that Kurt wanted to see me.'

'You have seen him, then?'

'Yes; but I found that he is no longer his own master. He is virtually a prisoner of the Nazis in his own house. Naturally I had no idea of that, and I don't suppose you knew it either?'

'No.' admitted the old lady with considerable asperity, 'I certainly did not. He seems to have got himself mixed up with these undesirable people recently. Towards the middle of last month he brought one of them here to stay for a few days; a man named Einholtz; and, I must say, he had better manners than most of Hitler's scum, although, of course, he was not the sort of person that I should ever have been willing to receive in the old days. Afterwards, they went off together on some mission to do with the war. Kurt returned only tonight and came up to see me about an hour before you came in from the roof. He seemed more ill than ever, and he stayed with me only a few minutes, but he told me he had accidentally set fire to some curtains in the hall, and also that he had brought *Herr* Einholtz back with him. But I had no idea that he was this man's prisoner.'

'I'm afraid he must be, as he was obviously in no position to prevent Einholtz trying to arrest me, when I appeared. The fire was my fault. I threw one of the candelabra at him before I jumped out of the window.'

'You suggest then that the Nazis made use of my son's name to lure you back here?'

Erika nodded silently.

'Of course, he could not have been aware of what they were up to,' the old lady supplemented.

'I can hardly think so,' Erika lied, 'although he must have realised the situation tonight. If he did have some idea of what was going on he probably felt that he was powerless to prevent it, or it may be that they threatened him with sending you to concentration camp if he made any attempt to interfere. They are capable of any beastliness when they mean to get their own way, you know.'

'Yes, I realise that. How our sensible German people can have allowed themselves to be led away by such a set of scoundrels is still a mystery to me. But what are you going to do, child? I suppose you want help to get back over the frontier.'

'Please. I'd rather kill myself than let them catch me.'

'How did you come here?'

'In a car. I left it in the courtyard, but I dared not go back to it. I felt that Einholtz would expect me to try that and be certain to set another trap for me with it.'

'Have you any plan in your mind?'

'Yes. Hours ago Einholtz will have telephoned the Gestapo headquarters in Stuttgart, and every road in Württemberg will be patrolled by police cars on the hunt for me by now. For the next few days the whole countryside, right down to the Boden see, will be much too hot for me to stand any chance of getting through it uncaught. But, after a bit, the excitement will die down. They'll think I've managed to get away on a train to some distant part of Germany. It's a lot to ask, but if you would let me hide in one of the disused rooms of the castle for a week, and could bring me a little food every night, I'd stand a much better chance of getting away safely in a week's time.'

'It is very little to ask,' retorted the old lady with rough kindness. 'If Kurt's name was used to get you here, and for some reason he is unable to protect you, the least we can do is to shelter you here for as long as you wish.'

Erika sighed with relief as the *Gräfin* Bertha went on: 'You have been through a bad time tonight, child. You had better clean yourself up in my bathroom, then you must get some sleep. I will make you up a bed next door where my old fool of a husband used to sleep whenever one or the other of us was ill. You will be quite safe there, as no one ever comes to this part of the house except my maid Helga, and she can bring you your meals.'

'Thank you—thank you so much, but—' Erika hesitated. 'One never knows whom one can trust in these days. Wouldn't

104

it be safer if you could manage to smuggle me up something to eat at night? I could make do on very little.'

'Don't be a fool girl,' was the prompt reply. 'A pretty picture it would make if I were seen carrying a leg of goose out of my larder. Helga is a lazy little good-for-nothing, but she won't give you away.'

'All right then,' Erika stood up. 'You won't mention my being here to Kurt, will you.'

'Why not?' The old woman's eyes sparkled with a gleam of amused malice. 'Are you afraid that he'll tell me the real reason you came back to Niederfels? It was on account of some young man that you're in love with, I'll be bound.'

'No, it wasn't that. But to tell Kurt I'm still here, after what happened tonight, would embarrass him terribly, I'm certain that the Nazis have got some hold over him and I'm sure he would hate having to admit that to you.'

'Very well. What you have been up to is no concern of mine. It is enough for me that the Nazis are after you. I'll not allow one of my own kind to fall into the hands of those guttersnipes, if I can possibly prevent it. Off you go, now, and get those twigs out of your hair before you lay your head on one of my good linen pillowslips.'

Gladly enough Erika retired to the bathroom. Like its owner, it was a relic of the past, having a mahogany framed marble bath the size of an Egyptian sarcophagus in one corner and an ugly cylindrical wood-burning stove in another. The fire under the stove was out but the water in the cylinder was still warm, so Erika was able to have a good wash and bathe her sore feet. As she was completing her ablutions the *Gräfin* Bertha opened the door a few inches to thrust in a pink flannel nightdress and a brown woollen dressing-gown that had seen better days. With her lovely limbs encased in these strange garments and carrying her own clothes in a bundle under her arm Erika emerged to meet her hostess again.

The old woman led her through to her late husband's dressingroom, where she had made up a bed that in most British homes would have long since gone to a junk shop. Like her own, it was of black painted iron, garnished with a soul-shattering variety of brass knobs and trimmings, and had upon it as its upper layer one of those mountain-like oblong bags of feathers under which all nineteenth-century Germans kept themselves warm at night. Nevertheless, Erika sank very gratefully into the soft depths of this monstrosity, although she gave a little moan of pain as part of her weight was taken by her wrenched shoulder.

On the Countess learning the cause of this, she hurried off to get some embrocation, and the unwilling Erika had to submit to some ten minutes' drastic treatment before she was finally allowed to sink back on the huge square pillow. With a 'Schlaf gut, Erika,' her mother-in-law put out the light and left her. Two minutes later she was sound asleep.

When she awoke it was broad daylight and she lay for a little while grimly thinking over the events of the previous night. The trap had been so cunningly devised, with its double lure of a divorce for her and the information of vital importance to Hitler's enemies, that she did not see how anyone in her own situation could have avoided falling into it. That she had temporarily escaped was due as much to luck, in having been left alone with Kurt for a couple of minutes, than to her own blundering effort to get away at the last moment, but she could at least congratulate herself on having appealed to the *Gräfin* Bertha for shelter as that had been her own idea and had proved one hundred per cent successful. She felt that her chances of getting back across Lake Constance were not too bad, but the thing that maddened her was the thought that any prospect of securing the information she had come into Germany to get, or her divorce, was now extremely remote.

It seemed certain that all this talk about a new gas had simply been part of the set-up, and that it existed only in Einholtz's imagination. As for her freedom she doubted if Kurt had ever had any intention of giving it to her and, in any case, even if she could get back to Switzerland the evidence she had been given would now prove valueless. From what the *Gräfin* Bertha had said it was clear that Kurt had not gone with Einholtz to Switzerland until the middle of July, and August yet had over a week to run. That meant that he could not have been living there for much more than five weeks, and a minimum of three months' residence by both parties was an essential requirement before application could be made for the case to be heard in the Swiss courts.

Erika was aroused from her gloomy thoughts by a dark-haired maid in a brown uniform entering the room with a tray. This was evidently the old Countess's personal maid, Helga, and knowing that her life would now lie in this woman's hands, Erika gave her both a friendly smile and a look of the keenest interest.

She was about twenty-five, tall, well made and, despite her rather heavy jowl and full, sensual mouth, by no means unattractive. After murmuring a formal greeting she set the tray down on the bedside table and, without looking at Erika again, began to tidy up the room.

As Erika did not recall having ever seen her among the castle staff in pre-war days, she asked:

'Have you been with the *Gräfin* Bertha long?'

'I have been here just over a year, *gnadige Frau*,' the girl plied. 'The former maid of the *Frau Gräfin, Fräulein* Patz, as knocked down in the village by a car and died. I had en just left a situation in Berlin and my godfather, Herr chnaffer, who is head keeper here, recommended me for this ost.'

Erika was just about to say: 'I remember old Patzie—how ragic for her to have been killed like that,' but she checked erself in time. The fact that the maid had addressed her imply as 'Lady' instead of 'Lady Countess' showed that she vas not yet aware of her identity, so the less she said about erself the better; and with no further remark she began the neal on her tray.

Half an hour after Helga had left her the *Gräfin* Bertha came in. Having enquired after Erika and learned that, apart rom the ache in her shoulder, she felt none the worse for her nidnight adventure, she said:

'I've told that girl of mine that you're my niece and that ou arrived here late last night in a shocking state, having just un away from your husband; and that it would teach him a esson if for a week or two he didn't know where you had got o; so I intended to keep you here very quietly, and on no account was she to mention your presence to anyone. I have always most strongly disapproved of discussing such matters with servants, or giving reasons for anything I do, but as she will have to bring your meals up to you it was necessary to tell her something to stop her tongue wagging.'

'I think that was very clever of you,' Erika smiled. 'Perhaps it is just as well that she hasn't been here very long, and so didn't know me.'

'Umph!' grunted the old woman dubiously. 'We would have been better off with Patz. She had been with me ever since my marriage and knew how to mind her own business without any telling. This girl is good with her needle and has learnt now not to speak until she is spoken to, but she's too fond of the men. I don't miss much and I've caught her more than once making sheep's eyes at my chauffeur when her mind should be on her work.'

Erika felt sorry for Helga. She could imagine few mistresses more exacting and tyrannical than her mother-in-law, and would not have applied for the post of personal maid to her had it been the last job on earth. Having no suitable comment to make, she said:

'I suppose most of the men have gone to the war by now?'

'All the young ones left on mobilisation, and a number of the others have been taken since. But Hans, he is the fellow that Helga has her eye on, is getting on for forty, and he was

returned to us on account of some internal trouble. They ha
him and all the older men out to help search the woods for yo
this morning.'

'Then they told you about last night. Have you seen Kurt

The old lady nodded. 'It was he who told me; but he sa
nothing about you. He simply said that they had brought
woman back with them to the castle because Einholtz wishe
to question her on a matter connected with their secret mi
sion, and that she caused the fire by throwing a candelabra
him, and had then thrown herself out of the window. His su
pressing the fact that you were the woman gave it away th
he wasn't telling me the whole story, so I think you were rig
now in saying that he is not to be trusted.'

'If the Nazis *are* exercising some form of pressure on him
Erika said slowly, 'it is much better for his own sake that
should not know about my still being here. And, in any cas
he would naturally shrink from telling you that they had use
him as a stalking-horse to try to catch me. The description the
will issue of me, with my hair its present colour, wouldn't co
vey to you that I'm the woman they are after, and I expe
Kurt felt least said soonest mended.'

'It worries me, though,' the *Gräfin* Bertha confessed. 'Ku
has always been a good son to me, and it is not like him
conceal his troubles from his mother. God will scourge tho
Nazis one day for the way they have broken sacred family ti
and sown distrust between those who love one another. Th
morning Kurt said that he and this man Einholtz would pro
ably be staying here for a few days now; but I shall speak
him and give him a stern warning that if he continues to m
himself up with such people trouble is bound to come of
That may have the effect of stiffening his back sufficiently
determine him to break off this most undesirable association

Erika shook her head. 'If you would permit me to advis
lady mother, I would not do that, I feel sure that the Naz
have only made use of Kurt for the attempt to catch me. On
they are convinced that I have escaped Einholtz will leave t
castle, Kurt will go back to his scientific work, and you w
have no further cause to worry about him.'

'Perhaps you are right, child. But I have never tolerate
deceit of any kind and I am loth to do so now. Still, I will wa
a little and see if it turns out as you say. You had better ha
a bath now, and attend to those scratches on your face.'

When Erika stood naked in the bathroom she found th
her body was mottled, as though she had some terrible diseas
with a score or more of multi-coloured bruises; but apart fro
their tenderness when she touched any of them, and the ach
in her shoulder, she felt remarkably well, and realised that s

had got off extremely lightly. On returning to her room she saw that Helga had cleaned, ironed and mended her clothes, so she dressed and sat down to read some of the magazines and books that her mother-in-law had put there for her.

This continued to be her principal occupation during the week that followed, as, to avoid suspicion, the *Gräfin* Bertha kept to her normal routine, and rarely came in to talk to her for long, except for an hour or so in the evenings before going to bed.

She thought the old woman had mellowed and softened a little with age, but she was still dogmatic and assertive, *Kirche, Kinder und Küche* were her Germanic gods, and while she was worldly enough to accept the fact that many married women of her generation had had lovers and proved none the worse for it, she was wholeheartedly with the Church in condemning divorce because it broke up the home. Until his death only ten weeks earlier, she had still regarded Kaiser Wilhelm II as her legal sovereign, and attributed all ills to the Hohenzollerns having gone into exile. The present war was, for her, merely the logical continuation of a struggle that had been forced on Germany in 1914, as the only possible alternative to eventual annihilation by a diabolical combination of the treacherous French, the greedy British and the barbarous Russians. She hated all three nations with equal intensity and, while she deplored Hitler's methods in his own country, every time she saw in the paper that a U-boat had sunk another British merchant ship or that an English city had been bombed, she exclaimed with fervour: *'Das ist gut! Gott strafe England!'*

In consequence, she and Erika had few subjects in common, except their detestation of the Nazis, and it took all Erika's tact and forbearance during her week in hiding to prevent herself entering on an open dispute with her mother-in-law on a score of matters concerning religion, international relations and the war.

They had both hoped that Einholtz would depart in the course of a few days but he still showed no signs of doing so; and on the eighth day after her arrival at the castle Erika was so weary of these pointless discussions, which called upon her for endless white lies and evasions, that she was quite relieved when it was decided that she should make her bid to recross the frontier that night.

Her shoulder no longer pained her, the scratches on her face were healed and only the worst of her bruises still showed as brownish discolorations. The order of her going had been discussed and settled some days before, and her courageous old hostess, despite the danger to herself, had proved unshakable in her determination to take the fugitive back to the

Bodensee in her own car. She had also dug out some clothes which had once belonged to her long since married younger daughter, so that no keen-eyed young policeman might recognise Erika from her Harris tweeds.

The question of her getting to the lake having been settled for her, Erika had thought a lot about how best to attempt to cross it. As there had been two launches in *Freiherr* von Lottingen's boathouse, in addition to that in which she had arrived it seemed reasonably certain that at least one of them would still be there. She knew how to start and steer a motorboat, so she did not see any reason why she should not cross the lake in one. There was the danger that the *Freiheer's* villa might have been taken over by the Nazis; on the other hand, it might be occupied only by his servants, who had been made use of by them. In either case they would probably have put a guard on the boathouse for the first two or three nights after her escape but it was unlikely that they would keep one there indefinitely.

The only alternative was to lie low in Friedrichshafen, or one of the lakeside villages, until she could find a boatman willing to smuggle her across for a considerable payment; but any such delay would confront her with innumerable dangers as she had no papers that she dared show if questioned, no food cards, and there was the ever present risk that someone might recognise her from her recently circulated description. An attempt to get away in one of the *Freiherr's* boats, therefore, seemed a far better bet.

Having set her hand to the task the *Gräfin* Bertha entered into the plan with all her accustomed vigour. In the afternoon she told her chauffeur she wished that night to make a visit without the court's guest, *Herr* Einholtz knowing that she had left the castle, and that he was to take her car down to the local mechanic in the village to have some minor repairs done then collect it again in the evening and wait for her with it at the entrance to the forest road. She also instructed Helga to prepare a large packet of *Brötchen* for Erika to take with her on a journey, and to bring her up a really substantial meal at eight o'clock.

In due course she went down to dinner herself, as usual, while Erika ate hers upstairs, and afterwards discarded her own darned but still elegant attire for the heavy brogues, thick woollen stockings and ugly cloth costume that had once hidden from view the ungainly figure of her sister-in-law.

At half past nine the *Gräfin* Bertha joined her, and made her own preparations for the journey, which consisted of putting on a strong pair of lace-up boots and enough woollens, topped by a fur coat, for a trip to the North Pole, although it was only the end of August and the night was fairly warm.

110

At about a quarter past ten they set off, the idea being to reach the north side of Lake Constance a little after midnight. The old lady took Erika down a back staircase and along several gloomy, echoing corridors which eventually led to a heavy oak postern gate that opened on to the courtyard.

There was now no moon and a slight wind rustling the trees fortunately drowned the sound of their footsteps, as the old Countess plodded heavily along, apparently having temporarily forgotten the necessity for caution. They crossed the court without mishap and after a quarter of an hour's trudge down the steep, winding forest road found the car at its appointed station.

'You remember *Freiherr* von Lottingen's place on the Bodensee, Hans?' said the *Gräfin* Bertha, as she climbed in. 'It is there I wish you to take me.'

The man silently tucked a rug round them, bowed to his mistress, and got into the driver's seat. The car was an incredibly old Rolls of a pre-1914 vintage, and it had the usual glass screen between the chauffeur and its occupants, so that the man could not overhear the conversation of his passengers.

As soon as it was under way the old lady said: 'Now remember, child, if we are pulled up and questioned, it is I who will do all the talking. No one in Württemberg will dare to detain me for long, once they know who I am; you may be certain of that.'

Knowing that her mother-in-law still lived mentally in another age and that the new regime was no respecter of persons, Erika did not altogether share this admirable optimism, but she felt that by sheer arrogance and personality the *Gräfin* Bertha might easily bluff her way past anyone less than a fairly senior S.S. officer, and that was no small comfort.

As the shortest route between Schloss Niederfels and *Freiherr* von Lottingen's summer villa lay mainly through by-roads, they met little traffic until they reached Friedrichshafen and, passing safely through it, they arrived without accident within rifle-shot of their destination.

A few hundred yards before they reached the villa Erika tapped on the glass screen, and Hans drew the car up at the side of the road. As he was doing so she squeezed the old woman's hand and leaning over kissed her withered cheek; then she said:

'It is hopeless for me to attempt to thank you, lady Mother. You have been an angel to me, and I shall never forget your kindness.'

'Think no more of it, child,' replied the *Gräfin* Bertha brusquely. 'But don't get yourself carted off to England again. It is not fitting that a von Osterberg should accept the hospitality

111

of our enemies while we are at war. Now get along. God be with you.'

Erika got out, spoke a word of thanks to Hans and, leaving the car, was soon swallowed up by the darkness. Her mother-in-law had suggested waiting for a while, until it could be assumed that she had got safely off, but Erika knew that if she was spotted at all she would have to run for it, and that any attempt to regain the car would have involved the old lady. This being the last thing she wished to do, she had dissuaded her from waiting on the excuse that even if she found the boat-house guarded she would no longer need the car, as she meant to try to find a night's lodging in the nearest village and could quite well walk there.

As she walked down the road she heard the car turn, reverse and drive off, and somehow the sound gave her an extraordinary lonely feeling. But within another two minutes she was opposite *Freiherr* von Lottingen's villa trying to still her mounting heartbeats as she nerved herself for the most dangerous part of her undertaking.

The garden gate stood slightly open. No one was about, so she slipped through it. In the faint starlight she saw that the paths were weedy and the flower-beds overgrown from two summers of neglect. There was just enough light for her to see the black silhouette of the villa against the night sky and make out the roof of the boathouse to its left and a little way below it. Pausing for a moment, she listened intently. No crack of light showed at the side of any window in the villa, and it was so silent that she could hear her own breathing. A gentle rain had begun to fall, and she tried to think that this was a sign the gods were with her, as it would decrease visibility on the lake and make the launch she hoped to get out less likely to be seen from one of the patrol boats. Getting her torch and her little automatic out of her handbag, she put the torch in the left and the other in the right hand pockets of her coat, then slung the bag over her left arm, and stuffing her hands in both pockets, went cautiously down a side path that led to the boathouse.

It took her five minutes, treading very gently, to reach the back of the broad, squat building. She could now hear the water lapping against its far end and the faint hissing of the rain as it spattered softly on the roof. It suddenly occurred to her that she ought to have brought some kind of jemmy in case the place was locked, and she cursed herself for this stupid omission which might prove the ruin of her plan. But next moment she found the door, and it gave noiselessly at a touch from the toe of her shoe.

Slipping inside, she closed it carefully behind her and, with

112

her left hand, brought out her torch. As she snapped it on she saw the three launches were lying there motionless in the water.

Next second her heart missed a beat. Beyond the low cabin roof of the nearest boat a man was standing. Instinctively she raised the torch a little, but even before the beam lit his features she knew that it was Einholtz.

He was standing there quite still, grinning at her, and it flashed through her mind that, somehow, he must have known that she had gone to earth in the castle all the time, found out about her plan and, with deliberate malice, let her carry it out until freedom was almost within her grasp, simply for the fun of coming ahead to wait for her there, with the certainty of catching her as she took the last fence.

Her right hand was still in the pocket of her coat. He lifted his right hand to raise his soft hat in mocking salutation. It never touched the felt, but the hat lifted all the same. As he raised his hand she fired twice, through the pocket of her coat.

The two sharp reports were still echoing round the boathouse as one of her bullets whisked his hat from his head. She heard him cry out, then saw him spin round and fall with a crash on to the floor boards. A whiff of the burnt cloth of her pocket came strongly to her nostrils.

Her mind was quite clear and now working like a dynamo. If there were other Nazis in the villa her shots would have roused them and they would be down there within a few moments. In any case the steward must be somewhere about and he might be armed. There was still a chance that she might get out on to the lake and yet elude pursuit, but that or all the horrors of a degrading death in a Nazi concentration camp hung on the swiftness of her actions in the next sixty seconds.

Jamming the torch back into her pocket, she ran to the loop of rope that secured the stern of the nearest launch round a low bollard. Breaking her nails on the coarse fibre of the rope she tore at it until she had wrenched it back and thrown it clear. As it splashed into the water she sprang forward to unloose the bow painter.

She had just grasped it when a quiet voice behind her said:

'*Guten Abend, Frau Gräfin*. How fortunate that I allowed that dolt Einholtz to go ahead, or it might have been me lying there now.'

At the first sound of the voice, Erika swivelled round as though she had received a lash from a whip. Outlined in the faint light of the doorway loomed the heavy figure of a very broad-shouldered man. In his right hand she glimpsed a big pistol which was pointing straight between her eyes, and above

113

the pale blob of his face she could see the high crown of an S.S. cap.

As her hand went towards her pocket again, he snarled: 'No you don't. And you needn't bother about undoing that rope We shall not need the launch tonight. You remember me, don't you? *Gruppenführer Grauber.*'

9

The Gestapo Get to Work

Erika would have known that high-pitched lisp anywhere. It was for ever coupled in her mind with the big pasty face and cruel solitary eye that had mocked her, day after day, as she had squirmed on the floor of a squalid hutment while its owner spent an hour by the clock every afternoon gently flicking the muscles of her arms, legs, thighs and buttocks with a little whip, until he had half flayed her.

She was still crouching beside the bollard, her hand hovering within a few inches of her pocket, but she was staring straight into the muzzle of his heavy gun. He had the drop on her just as she had only a few moments ago, had the drop on Einholtz. Had she had her pistol in her hand she would have squeezed the trigger, taking a chance that her shot would get in first and deflect his aim, and accepting the possibility that they might kill one another, as then, at least, if she had to die she would have had the satisfaction of dragging this fiend down to death with her. But she knew that before she could even get her hand on the butt of her pistol his gun would flash, and its leaden slug smash through the bone of her skull.

She did not want to die. Her whole soul cried out in revolt against it. She *must* feel Gregory's strong arms about her again before her body went to moulder in the grave, and only by continuing to face whatever terrors life had in store for her could there be any hope of that. Yet Gregory was in Russia, thousands of miles away, and close at hand there were underground chambers where the Gestapo's victims moaned for the devil to take their souls if only he would release them from their pain. She had sworn to herself never again to fall alive into their hands. Perhaps time really did not exist, and if she

114

net death bravely now, in what would seem to her no more than a few moments, Gregory would be with her in some other world lovelier than this by far. Her hand twitched once and dived into her pocket.

Grauber did not fire. In two strides he was upon her. His heavy boot lifted and caught her, still crouching, under the chin. As she spread-eagled backwards, she thought for a moment that he had kicked her head right off her body. The darkness became intenser; red stars and circles flashed before her eyes; there was a frightful pain where her spine met the base of her neck. She was only semi-conscious when she felt him grip her wrist and give it a frightful wrench that made another pain shoot through it like a knife, as she released her hold on her pistol.

As though from a great distance she heard his voice. 'You little fool! Surely you didn't think I'd shoot you? After all the trouble you've given us that would be much too easy a way to let you out. We are going to have lots of pretty little games together before they shove what's left of you into a furnace. Do you remember the little games we used to play in Finland? That is quite a long time ago and I have invented a lot of others since, which I must show you. Get up!'

Her mind still swimming and only partly there, Erika made no move.

'Get up!' he repeated, and kicked her savagely on the shin.

The fresh pain brought her round completely, and knowing that other kicks would follow if she did not obey, she made a great effort which brought her lurching to her feet.

As she stood there swaying weakly, she heard a loud groan. Grauber heard it too. He looked towards the place where Einholtz had fallen and snapped at her:

'Stay where you are. One move from you and I'll smother every hair on your body in mutton fat, then light them up as candle wicks.'

Leaving her leaning for support against the side of the boathouse, he strode over to his subordinate. When he had kicked her under the jaw she had bitten the side of her tongue, it was rapidly swelling and hurt her terribly. The blood from it tasted salt in her mouth and the back of her neck ached atrociously.

Time had ceased to exist for her. How long she stood there she did not know, but Grauber's voice, and after a time that of Einholtz's answering him, vaguely penetrated to her dulled senses. She gathered that one of her bullets had seared Einholtz's scalp, temporarily knocking him out, but that he was now rapidly recovering and intensely angry.

After a while Grauber came back to her, and Einholtz was beside him. Erika's eyes had now become accustomed to the

115

dim light, so she could see that the latter's face was very pa'
and that a trickle of blood from his wound was running dow'
it.

When he was within a yard of her he suddenly raised h'
fist and struck her in the face. With a little whimper she wer
over backwards; he then began to kick her.

'Stop that!' grunted Grauber. 'I mean to make her talk, an
if you give her too much she won't be able to.'

Erika lay there, moaning, where she had fallen. Already sh
was wishing that she were dead, yet knew that she had not ye
gone through one hundredth part of what they meant to d
to her. When Grauber again ordered her to get up she mad
no attempt to do so, hoping now that if he kicked her enough
it might result in some internal injury that would carry her of
quickly.

Instead of kicking her again he stooped, thrust his grea
hand into her mop of tumbled hair, clutched a big handful o
it and began to drag her bodily towards the door.

She screamed, but he paid no attention to her yells. Lever
ing herself up with one foot, she swung her head round and
bit him savagely in the hand.

He let go her hair with a curse, sucked at his hand for a
minute, then, stooping again, grabbed one of her ankles. A:
he pulled her after him once more her head and shoulders
bumped along the boards, then out on to the gravel path.

'Let me go!' she panted. 'Let me go and I'll walk! I'll walk
I promise you!'

'Let me go!' she panted. 'Let me go and I'll walk! I'll walk,
ing to her feet, Erika lurched up the path between them.

At the gate a Mercédès-Benz, with a uniformed chauffeur
at its wheel, was waiting. Grauber said to Einholtz:

'We had better go into Friedrichshafen and have that wound
of yours attended to at the local headquarters.'

'*Jawohl, Herr Gruppenführer,*' muttered Einholtz, sullenly

With a word to the driver Grauber pushed Erika into the
car and climbed in after her. It was a big car but he was such
a bulky man that there was not room for more than the two
of them on the back seat, so Einholtz let down one of the
small seats opposite. The two men pulled down the blinds of
the car, Grauber switched on a little blue light in its roof, and
the driver let in the clutch.

Einholtz wiped some of the blood that was still trickling
down his face away from the corner of his mouth, glared at
Erika, and suddenly jabbed his heel down hard on her instep.

'You little bitch!' he snarled, as she jerked away her foot.
'You thought you'd been so damned clever, didn't you, getting that old woman to hide you? But I had the tapes on you

116

from the very first morning. If you'd had any sense you might have guessed that any maid who had to serve that old cow would hate her guts, and that Helga would prove no exception.'

He chuckled suddenly, and went on. 'Anyhow, that girl would give away her own mother for a good healthy man like me. How we laughed up in her room every night, to think of you down there so smugly thinking you'd put a fast one over the Gestapo. I could have pulled you in any time, but there was no hurry about that, and as I was having my fun I thought I'd wait till you made your breakaway. There's no sport like catching the bird just as it thinks it's out of the cage.'

'If you're not careful you'll try that once too often,' lisped Grauber.

'I knew you were behind her, *Herr Gruppenführer*,' grunted Einholtz sourly.

'Perhaps. But that wouldn't have stopped you getting a bullet through your brain instead of through your hat. You wouldn't have had a headache now if you had been willing to stop their car at the crossroads where I picked you up. I let you have your way because I know this little spitfire better than you do, and I had an idea that she might teach you a lesson.'

Einholtz relapsed into sullen silence and neither of them spoke again until in a back street of Friedrichshafen, the car sounded its klaxon twice, upon which a pair of high gates were opened for it and, driving through it, pulled up in a courtyard.

'Out you get,' said Grauber, as the driver threw open the door nearest Erika, so she followed Einholtz from the car and up a few steps into a hall where several smart S.S. men were lounging. The moment they saw Grauber they sprang to rigid attention, but he was in a good humour, and piping: *'Guten Abend, meine Herren,'* motioned them to relax

With a muttered word about seeing the doctor, Einholtz went up a stone staircase, while Grauber laid a hand on Erika's shoulder and gave her a push towards the open door of one of the ground floor rooms. As she entered it she saw that it was just a bleak sparsely furnished apartment which might have been the interviewing room in any police-station. Closing the door behind him, he waved her to one of the wooden chairs, then took out a cigar, lit it and sat down himself.

Leaning his elbows on the bare table he stared fixedly at her for a full minute, then, at last, when her eyes dropped before his gaze, he said:

'I want some information from you, and you know enough about the sort of thing that goes on in such places as this to imagine what will happen to you if I don't get it. So you'd better talk, and tell the truth, bearing in mind that I have

117

enough facts already to check your story. Now! Where's your boy friend—that snake Sallust?'

'I don't know,' replied Erika.

'Oh yes you do. Why didn't he come with you to Switzerland?'

'Because I couldn't get in touch with him. I don't know where he is.'

'When did you see him last?'

'A little over a month ago.'

'Where were you then?'

'In a hospital, at which I was working in England.'

'Did he tell you that he was going away again?'

'Yes.'

'Did he say where to?'

'No.'

'You're lying!'

'I'm not.'

'Yes, you are. Let me refresh your memory. He told you that he was going to Russia. You see, I know where he's gone. Do you remember Karl Zensdorff who was with me in London? But no, that was before you met Sallust. Anyhow, Karl was one of my men and a very fine professional knife-thrower. He and Sallust ran across one another at the house of a little Jew called Rosenbaum up in Hampstead. Karl crucified the Jew and practised his knife-throwing on him afterwards, very prettily, I remember. Well, Karl is now in Damascus. He reported to me only two days ago that Sallust had just passed through and, according to our French friends in the passport control, is on his way to Russia. You see how small the world is and how we get to hear of these little things. Naturally, my agents in Russia have been duly instructed to keep an eye on Mr Sallust, so I shall be able to verify a great part of the statement you are about to make to me. Now—you'd better not try to lead me up the garden path.'

He paused, obviously, expecting Erika to reply to him, so, after a moment she said, dully: 'I can't make any statement about that. How can I, when he didn't even tell me where he was going?'

Grauber stood up. 'Now listen to me, Sallust is in love with you, and you've been in the game with him, so he tells you most things—everything, in fact, that he does not consider to be a vital secret. He wouldn't be human if he didn't; and I am confident that he would not regard this mission to a country allied to Britain as of particular secrecy. I am now going to leave you for ten minutes, while I have a drink in the officers' club upstairs, I give you this last chance to think matters over.

118

When I return, unless you are an imbecile, you will tell me what I wish to know.'

His jack-boots rang heavily on the boards as he strode to the door. As it slammed behind him Erika let her head fall forward on the table. Her jaw ached, the back of her neck ached, her shin ached, her instep ached, and her left eye was rapidly losing up from the blow that Einholtz had given her. She tried to collect her thoughts, but she felt absolutely ghastly, and her mind remained blank to everything except the pains shooting through her body. It seemed to her only a moment before she once more heard Grauber's heavy footfalls as he came in again.

A carafe of drinking-water and a glass stood on the table. Filling the glass, he flung its contents over her bowed head. As the cold water splashed on to the back of her neck and ran down her spine she shuddered and straightened up.

'Well,' he said, 'are you going to talk?'

She knew that she would have to sooner or later. They would do things to her that no human will could resist; but she felt that she owed it to her own integrity to refuse as long as she had the power to do so. She mutely shook her head.

At that moment the door opened and Einholtz came in, his face now clean and the top of his head swathed in a turban of white bandages.

'There's a show on downstairs,' he said to Grauber. 'If she's proving stubborn it might soften her up if we took her down to see it.'

Grauber considered for a moment, then he nodded. 'Yes, that's a good idea,' and taking Erika's arm he jerked her to her feet.

Between them they hustled her out into the hall and down a flight of stone steps into the basement. The corridor was lit only by small red electric bulbs at intervals along its ceiling. Einholtz pushed open a door flush with the wall and they entered a large, low-ceilinged room. It was furnished only with a table, upon which stood some electrical apparatus, a kind of wooden throne that stood in the middle of the floor, and a few hard-seated chairs. In one corner there was an iron stove, roaring away, which made the place stiflingly hot and on the far wall there was a rack upon which hung a score or more curious-looking iron implements.

A man in a white surgeon's smock, with heavy lensed spectacles, sat at one end of the table and at the other sat an S.S officer with a writing-pad in front of him. Two S.S troopers were standing near the throne, and between them stood a woman of about thirty, stark naked.

The officer stood up as Grauber came in but the *Gruppen-*

führer signed to him to get on with his business. He then pushed
Erika into a chair, took another himself, and the show began

The woman was a German and a coarse-looking creature
but she had a decent, honest face, and as the interrogatio
proceeded Erika learnt the cause of her being there. She was a
local prostitute and she had sheltered a British airman wh
had made a forced landing after his aircraft had been hi
during a raid on Friedrichshafen. She had not known tha
when he picked her up, as he had already secured workmen'
clothes by breaking into a farmhouse, near which he had lan
ded. He also spoke fairly good German and had represente
himself as a Belgian who had been brought into Germany fo
forced labour. He had quite a bit of money and had treate
her much better than most of her casual customers. Later
when he had been trying to get a boat to smuggle him acros
Lake Constance, the truth had come out, but by that time h
had been living with her for a week and she had grown to
fond of him to betray him to the authorities. With her help h
had arranged about a boat, but they had both been caugh
just as he was leaving.

The Gestapo thought it possible, though improbable, tha
the man had talked to her about his job as an R.A.F. pilot, so
she might be able to give information about the technique of
the British air raids and the station upon which his squadron
was based. Although the woman protested again and again
that he had said nothing at all about such matters, they thought
it worth while to go right through with a routine grilling on the
offchance that her ravings might disclose something of interest.

The oral examination having produced nothing, at an order
from the officer the two troopers seized the woman and thrust
her on to the throne. While they were strapping her wrists and
ankles to its arms and legs, the man in white left the table and,
uncoiling two rolls of electric flex as he went, walked over to
the woman carrying their large specially fashioned terminals.

Erika saw with horror that the throne was a form of electric
chair but that instead of the shock being administered as usual
by knee bands and a headband the terminals were designed for
the impalement of the wretched woman. The two troopers
stood by making lewd jokes while the other man thrust them
into her writhing body.

Having adjusted them so that she could not force them out,
he went back to the table and flicked over a switch. Instantly
the woman was galvanised.* Her mouth opened and let out a
piercing scream. Her eyes started from her head.

* This ingenious German toy was used at Gestapo headquarters
in Paris, and one such instrument is now in possession of the
Sûreté.

120

The operator switched off the current and the investigating officer said: 'Well, what have you got to tell us?'

The woman was tough, and instead of inventing any story that might have postponed further torment, let fly a spate of obscene curses at him.

They were abruptly cut short by the current being turned on again. As the woman's limbs went rigid, Erika closed her eyes to shut out the awful sight and put her hands over her ears, but she could not shut out the screams that echoed round the sombre chamber. The current was kept on for longer this time, and when they turned it off the woman hung limp for a moment, only held in place by her hands. Her body was glistening all over, and the sweat was streaming down it. Suddenly she vomited.

'Now!' came the staccato voice of the officer. 'Another two goes of the heat and you'll never again be any good for your old job. Out with it.'

'He was an Australian,' she moaned. 'I told you that—and it's all I know.'

'Think again!' The officer leant over and this time turned on the current himself; but he kept his finger on the switch and for a full three minutes alternately flicking it up and down. During the whole ghastly proceeding the victim never ceased to jerk convulsively and emit heartrending screams except when the current was cut off, and then she gibbered and moaned with her head rolling piteously from side to side.

In the brief intervals of applying the current the officer had continued to hurl questions at her, without result, and apparently coming to the conclusion that he was flogging a dead horse, he suddenly sat back; barking out an order to the guards to release her.

As they undid the straps she fell forward, a flabby mass of writhing pink flesh, on to the floor. Unceremoniously they picked her up, flung her on to a stretcher, and carted her away.

At the slam of the door Erika took her fingers from her ears and opened her eyes. She found Grauber looking at her.

'Well,' he said, 'how would you like to try a taste of our new toy?'

She shuddered, lowered her eyes and made no reply. The room was appallingly hot and now stank foully from a mixture of sick, sweat and excrement and iodoform. There were beads of perspiration standing out on Erika's forehead and her chemise was sticking to her back.

Grauber's voice came again. 'If you're not prepared to talk now, in ten minutes' time you'll be carried out of here in the same state as that woman.'

Erika felt that she was going to faint, but she still sat silent

121

with her head hanging down on her chest.

'What you've seen isn't one tenth of it,' Grauber's voice went on. 'Those toys inflict internal burns, you know. For months afterwards you'd wish you'd never been born, and you'd never be fit for much again.'

She closed her eyes, swayed slightly, and slid sideways to the floor.

'*Donnerwetter!* She's fainted,' growled Grauber.

But Erika was not quite out. As she lay there, sweating and terrified, she could still hear the voices above her.

'Bring your things here, *Herr Doktor*,' Einholtz called. 'We'll pull her clothes out of the way and give her a shot where she lies. That will soon bring her round.'

As Einholtz stepped forward to grasp the edge of her skirt Grauber said sharply: 'Stay where you are, both of you.'

There was a pause, during which Grauber seemed to be considering, and Erika could feel her heart pounding in her chest. Then he spoke again in a lower tone, evidently to Einholtz.

'I know this woman. I've had her through my hands before. She's the highly strung type and needs special treatment. We'll do better with her in a more artistic setting.' He raised his voice: '*Herr Doktor*, I wish you to come with us, and bring your instrument.'

As he finished speaking, he stooped, seized Erika in his strong arms and lifting her, flung her over his shoulders like a sack of potatoes.

Directly the fresh air from the ground floor reached Erika's nostrils she began to feel slightly better, but she gave no sign of returning consciousness, as her apparent faint seemed to be a temporary protection.

In the hall Grauber lowered her to a bench. There was a short wait while he left her to give some orders about his car, then, on his return, as she still showed no sign of coming round, he shook her.

She opened her good eye—the other was now almost entirely closed. 'Come on,' he said, 'we're going to take you for a little midnight excursion.'

With an effort she got to her feet and stumbled before him down the steps out to the now waiting car. They sat side by side in the back, as before. Einholtz and the doctor took the smaller seats. The high gates were opened, the blinds of the car were pulled down, and it drove off.

Her pains had now merged into one dull ache that gripped her whole body, with occasional stabs from the specially tender places whenever the car swayed or jolted. Her mind was still half bemused by terror and physical exhaustion, but the fresh night air gradually cleared it a little. She could neither

122

nor guess where they were going but knew that wherever
might be their journey boded no good to herself. Any
empt to escape would have been so utterly hopeless that it
not even occur to her. She lay limp in her corner with the
d perspiration drying on her body. The car droned on and
until it seemed that she had been sitting there for hours,
t she had lost all sense of time, and to her the journey was
e some never-ending nightmare.

She was roused from her semi-stupor by a more violent
ies of twists and jerks than usual, and it came to her vaguely
it the car must be winding its way up a steep hill. Two
nutes later it pulled up. Einholtz and the doctor got out and
auber pushed her after them. She saw then that she was
nding in the courtyard of Schloss Niederfels.

The shock of the unexpected stimulated her brain a little.
e had thought they were taking her to some concentration
np. Why, she wondered, should they bring her here? Then,
t of the corner of her eye, she caught sight of the sinister
ctor, standing only a few feet away from her with the big
ther case that contained the fiendish instrument. Of course,
y could use it at Niederfels as well as anywhere else, and
auber's remark about a 'more artistic setting' came back to
·. Yet why should he have the idea that she would yield up
ore readily any secrets she possessed in the banqueting hall
r well-furnished bedroom of the castle than in a reeking
ncrete cellar?

She was given no chance to speculate further at the moment
Grauber's hand closed on her arm again and they all moved
wards the main door. Perhaps Einholtz had left it unlatched;
any case it opened at his touch and, switching on the lights
he went, he led them down the short passage to the ban-
eting hall.

'I think we might start by having some supper,' Grauber
nounced in his high voice. 'I'm quite hungry after our drive.'
'Jawohl, Herr Gruppenführer,' Einholtz replied quickly
you will keep an eye on the woman, I will arrange it. We
n't want her jumping out of the window again.'

Grauber glanced at the doctor. 'He will see to that. I'd like
word with you before you go.'

They had automatically gone forward to the big open
arth. While the doctor remained near Erika the other two
lked back towards the passage and stood for a few moments
nversing in the doorway to it.

As Erika sat down in one of the high-backed armchairs her
nce fell upon the big, brass-faced clock that was ticking
ay above the carved wood mantel. The hands stood at a
arter past three. It seemed inconceivable to her that barely

five hours had elapsed since she had left the castle; since nea[r]
four of those must have been occupied by her journeys to a[nd]
from the shores of the Bodensee. Yet, actually, her attempt [to]
get the launch, her arrest, the short run into Friedrichshaf[en]
and her soul-shattering experiences at the Gestapo office h[ad]
all been encompassed in little more than an hour.

She wondered vaguely what had happened to Kurt. Perha[ps]
having no more use for him, Einholtz had shot him before lea[v]-
ing the castle; or possibly he had been handcuffed to his o[wn]
bed and locked in his room. Then, for the first time, the que[s]-
tion entered her mind as to what had happened to the *Grä[fin]*
Bertha. Somehow she had taken it for granted that the ga[llant]
old woman had got safely back. But had she? On the way [to]
Friedrichshafen Einholtz had disclosed that he had known t[he]
part she was playing all the time. The terror Erika had felt [in]
the Gestapo office had put that out of her mind, but now s[he]
suddenly became anxious for her mother-in-law. Grauber a[nd]
Einholtz were not the sort of men to neglect their habit [of]
exacting a bitter payment from anyone who sheltered a[nd]
aided any fugitive from the mockery of Nazi justice.

The clock had ticked through ten minutes when Erika hea[rd]
footsteps in the passage, and with a fresh surge of apprehe[n]-
sion saw the old Countess come in.

She had a heavy dressing-gown over her nightdress and s[he]
was followed by Helga, who was similarly, if more attra[c]-
tively, clad. Einholtz brought up the rear.

Grauber, who had sat down near the entrance to the ha[ll]
came to his feet, clicked his heels and bowed from the wa[ist]
with ironical politeness as he presented himself:

'*Gruppenführer* Grauber, I have heard quite a lot about y[ou]
tonight, *Frau Gräfin,* and I am most interested to make yo[ur]
acquaintance.'

The old lady had her chin in the air, and her dark eyes su[r]-
veyed him as though he was something that the cat had broug[ht]
in.

'What do you want with me,' she snapped. 'How dare y[ou]
get me out of bed at this time of the night.'

'I want some supper,' he purred. 'And you, *Frau Grä[fin]*
are going to get it for me. As you cannot have been in bed f[or]
much more than an hour, it is quite fitting that you should g[et]
up again; so that, unexpected by you as the sequel to yo[ur]
recent adventure may be, you should not be deprived of w[it]-
nessing its results.'

As she made no reply he brought down the short whip th[at]
he was carrying with a smart bark on the leather of the cha[ir]
behind him, and barked, 'Supper, you old cow, or the ne[xt]
time this whip falls it will be your hide that it will lash!'

For probably the first time in her life the *Gräfin* Bertha showed fear. She had seen Erika, dishevelled, battered, and with one eye banged up from a great purple bruise, slumped in a chair at the far end of the room, so she needed no telling what had happened. The blood drained from her face and without a word, she silently turned about.

Einholtz grinned at Helga, and gave the lush-looking maid a friendly slap on the bottom. 'Go and keep an eye on the old witch,' he laughed, 'and make her put her back into it. You've got nothing to worry about. You'll be leaving here tomorrow. We can use a girl like you.'

With an answering laugh Helga followed her ex-mistress out of the room.

The clock ticked metallically on for another quarter of an hour. Erika was wishing that instead of shooting Einholtz ineffectively in the boathouse she had turned her pistol on herself. She did not know what was going to happen, but the atmosphere of the place was now heavy with the foreboding of some unbelievably ghastly scene that was soon to be enacted there.

Then there were footsteps again and her mother-in-law came back, carrying a tray so heavily laden that her aged arms could scarcely bear its weight. Helga walked jauntily behind her carrying three bottles of Hock.

Suppressing a sob, the *Gräfin* Bertha set the heavy tray down on the table. With palsied hands she set out the plates, cutlery and three dishes containing the best cold food the larder had to offer. When she had done, Helga snapped at her:

'Get the glasses, quick now!'

'Go with her, Helga,' said Grauber, quietly. 'I don't want our charming hostess to rat on her own party.'

While the two women were away the men drew chairs up to the table. Grauber set one for Erika and bowed to her. 'The *Gräfin* von Osterberg will not refuse to join us in her own home I'm sure.'

During the past half hour Erika's limbs had stiffened as she sat. When she stood up a score of pains seared through her and she gave a little moan, but she tottered to the table and sank down in the high-backed Jacobean elbow chair that Grauber was holding for her.

The *Gräfin* Bertha returned with another tray. While she set the glasses on the table Helga uncorked the wine. The three men helped themselves to the food and all of them offered the dishes to Erika, but she shook her head. Her swollen tongue was now dry in her mouth and a morsel of food would have choked her, even had she been willing to eat with them.

Helga took a chair next to Einholtz and began to help her-

125

self lavishly to the cold meats. As she was munching her fir
mouthful she grinned maliciously up at the *Gräfin* Bertha a
said:

'You stay where you are and wait on us. Come on, give
some wine.'

The old lady picked up one of the bottles of Hock, walk
round to behind Erika's chair and poured her a full gla
'Drink that, child,' she said gruffly, 'you need it.'

It was the only time she had spoken since her first appea
ance and the sound of her voice did Erika good. She felt c
tain that the old woman understood it was through no fault
hers that the Gestapo men had come to the castle and we
inflicting these indignities upon its aged chatelaine. She gra
fully drank the golden wine. It stung her sore tongue a lit
but eased the dryness of her mouth and its warmth made h
feel slightly better. Having poured out for the others, t
Gräfin Bertha walked quietly to an armchair by the de
embers of the fire and, picking up her workbag, began to kn

The nightmare meal seemed to drag on interminably, y
barely twenty minutes had passed when Grauber pushed aw
his plate. The others followed suit, lit cigarettes, and pass
round the third bottle of Hock.

In the ensuing silence Erika became a prey to the mo
frightful fears again. What were they going to do now? He
would this night of horrors end?

Gauber tipped back his chair, looked across at her and sai

'After the feast, the entertainment. That is the proper ord
of things, isn't it, *Frau Gräfin*? Tonight, in this marvello
old hall, which makes so perfect a setting for such a scene, v
shall be privileged to witness a somewhat unusual spectac
Herr Doktor, oblige me by getting out your apparatus.'

The soulless eyes behind the heavy lensed spectacles show
no trace of emotion. Like an automaton the Gestapo-train
operator, who had not uttered a single word since Erika h
first set eyes on him, stood up. Walking over to the big leath
case that he had brought with him, he produced a set of b
teries, the coils of flex and the two poker-like terminals. E
holtz pushed aside some plates for him and he set them on
table. After making a quick test he spoke at last:

'All is ready, *Herr Gruppenführer.*'

The blood had drained from Erika's face as Grauber look
at her again, and said:

'As I was remarking to *Herr Oberstleutnant* Einholtz earli
tonight, you do not stand up well to physical torture. You a
one of those highly strung women who are damnably obstina
yet faint as soon as some trifling persuasion is offered to the
No information can be extracted from an unconscious bo

126

as far as the *Herr Doktor*'s apparatus is concerned, and her similar treatments, you are a very poor subject.'

Erika felt certain that he was playing a cat-and-mouse game with her. He was deliberately encouraging her to hope for mercy in order that she might be plunged into greater depths of despair when, as she knew already, it emerged that not a trace of mercy existed in his perverted and evil heart. But he went smoothly on:

'I have seen many women under examination with various scientific aids, and the sight of your paroxysms would hold nothing new for me. But I promised our friends an unusual spectacle, and I will give it to them. It would interest me to see how a really aged woman reacts.'

Turning away, he added suddenly to Helga: 'You are the *Gräfin* Bertha's personal maid. Strip her of her clothes.'

'Stop! Erika's cry rung round the hall as she sprang to her feet. 'I will not have it!'

Grauber looked up at her, his single eye lit by a self-con-gratulatory smile. 'I had an idea that might bring you to heel,' he purred. 'It never fails to intrigue me that people who are prepared to die rather than talk themselves will often cave in rather than see others touched; although I confess that I don't pretend to understand it myself.'

'You wouldn't, you swine,' she flared at him.

He shrugged. 'Now you feel differently you may as well get it over. Tell me what Gregory Sallust is up to in Russia and I will send the *Gräfin* Bertha back to bed.'

Erika slumped down in her chair again and buried her face in her hands. She knew that she could not possibly sit there and let them strip that hidebound, dogmatic, but courageous old woman naked, far less allow them to practise upon her the vile indignity that had turned the Friedrichshafen prosti-tute from a stalwart woman into a quivering, slobbering jelly. It was unthinkable, and Gregory himself would be the first to agree to that.

Frantically she wondered what the effects of giving away the reason for his journey into Russia would be to him. But she could not see that it would in any way jeopardise his safety. His mission was so wide and general in its scope that to dis-close its object would reveal no vital secret.

Suddenly Grauber brought his great fist crashing down on the table. The plates were still rattling as he shouted: 'I've wasted enough time on you. Are you going to talk, or am I to make that old bitch jump around as she hasn't done since she went on her honeymoon?'

Erika started upright. 'Yes! I'll tell you!' she gasped. 'Greg-ory has gone to Russia to find out three things. How much of

their man-power the Russians can arm and put in the fie
How much territory they can afford to give away before th
are forced to either make a stand or surrender; and the state
Stalin's health.'

Grauber's solitary eye opened wide, then an amazed sm
spread over his heavy features.

'But this is marvellous!' he cried. 'Sallust is the best age
that the British have got. If I can capture him now he w
have that information. And those are the three things that
would give half my private fortune to know.'

10

Into Russia

In the summer of 1939 a specially chartered aircraft cou
easily have carried a passenger from London to Moscow in
single day, but in the summer of 1941 such a journey was on
of the most difficult, hazardous and wasteful of time that any
one could undertake. It would have been easier, safer and fa
quicker to travel to Honolulu or Mandalay, since direct strat
sphere flight had not yet been established between Britai
and Russia, and the great swathe of Nazi-held Europe cut th
two Allies off from all normal means of communication.

As it was, Gregory and Stefan Kuporovitch had to wait fo
a suitable day when an aircraft could fly them from Souther
England far out into the Atlantic, to avoid the unwelcom
attentions of enemy aircraft based on the French Biscay coast
and so to Gibraltar. From Gibraltar they had to run the gaunt
let of the Western Mediterranean to besieged Malta, th
single foothold still retained by the Allies in the centre of th
inland sea. Thence, in constant danger from German an
Italian war 'planes, they had to make another thousand-mil
flight to Cairo. Having safely accomplished these three lon
hops they could congratulate themselves on having got through
the most risky part of their journey, but the worst of its delays
discomforts and uncertainties still lay ahead.

Anxious as Sir Pellinore had been that they should reach
Russia as soon as possible, he had not dared to make a request
for any special priority to be accorded to their travel permits

fter Cairo. The Russians having been virtually barred out of
:urope for so long and then having of their own choice, for
nany years restricted all but official contact with the outside
vorld, were extremely suspicious of their new Allies. Even
nembers of the Military Mission, sent to help them, found
nemselves subject to the most infuriating delays and scru-
nies, and if the least indication had been given that Messrs.
allust and 'Cooper' were *en route* for the Soviet Union on
natters other and more urgent than routine work under the
3ritish Press Attaché, a score of excuses would have been
roduced to prevent them entering Russia at all.

In consequence, from Cairo onwards, the two travellers had
o make the best arrangements they could for themselves and,
s civilians of no apparent importance in a military zone, their
ath was far from being strewn with roses. Their cover, as
ournalists, which they had perforce to disclose wherever they
vent, proved, in most cases, a hindrance rather than a help, for
he majority of responsible officers live in perpetual, and not
ltogether unfounded, dread that any visiting pressman might
ater write up some 'human interest' story which, while inno-
ent enough in itself, would give away to the enemy informa-
ion prejudicial to forthcoming operations. But the worst of
heir troubles arose from the fact that German agents, French
uislings, and anti-British schemers of the Arabic world had
etween them, succeeded in making the Near East a seething
auldron of unrest throughout the whole of the summer.

In May, the pro-Nazi Premier of Iraq, Raschid Ali, had
taged a *coup d'état,* kidnapped his boy king and declared
gainst the British; necessitating offensive operations which had
eft a certain bitterness in their wake. In June, the Vichy
rench in Syria had given the Germans facilities to establish
ir bases there, and although the bitter resistance of the Petain-
sts had been overcome by the 12th of July, they were still
loing all they could to sabotage British interests. The situation
here was now further complicated by the high-handed actions
f the Free French and the hatred of the Syrian Nationalists
or all Frenchman irrespective of their politics, which led to
iots, shootings and every sort of trouble for the unfortunate
3ritish, who, on the one hand, did not wish to antagonise
heir Free French allies, and, on the other, were appallingly
mbarrassed by the recently published 'Atlantic Charter', un-
ler which the Syrians claimed their right to independence.
)n top of this the violent, avaricious and despotic Shah of
ersia had sold himself to the Nazis, refused to expel the
undreds of agents they had established in his country and had
leclared his intention of resisting by force of arms any at-
empt by the British and Russians to use his territory as a

military supply route in their common struggle against Germany.

During the middle and latter part of August, Gregory and Kuporovitch were tempted a score of times quietly to fade out and, ignoring the British military controls, make their own way to the Russian frontier. They would certainly have reached it more quickly, but the trouble was that they would then not have the requisite number of rubber stamps on their passports to show that they had arrived there by orthodox means, and it was absolutely essential that they should enter Russia without the least suspicion attaching to them. In consequence, they had to kick their heels in transit camps and small hotels for days on end in Cairo, Haifa, Damascus and Baghdad while awaiting the okays of security officers.

On 25th of August, British and Russian forces entered Iran and on the 28th, the Persian Army, having offered only a token resistance, was ordered by the new Premier, Ali Faranghi, to cease fire. By pulling a fast one, that their status as pressmen entitled them to go to the front as much in Persia as it did in Russia, the two travellers succeeded in entering Iran with the British forces operating from Khaniquin; but when they linked up with the Russians advancing south from the Caspian they were not allowed to proceed further. Luckily, however, a genuine war correspondent decided to make for Teheran and gave them a lift in his car to the Persian capital.

Here they were able to make direct contact with the Russian authorities in the Soviet Legation. Their passports and visas were all in order but they met with a sponge-like combination of politeness and procrastination which resisted all their effort to get any satisfaction for ten days. Gregory had little doubt that, in the meantime, their suspicious allies were making enquiries about them in Moscow, but he knew that it would be futile to leave Teheran for the frontier until they had secured the special permits without which, visa or no visa, no one was now allowed to cross it.

At last permission to proceed was granted; a Russian courier was attached to them and having accompanied them to the border, saw them safely into an old-fashioned but comfortable broad-gauge train on the Soviet side, with strict injunctions that in no circumstances were they to leave it until they reached the capital. On Friday the 12th of September, six weeks after leaving London, they arrived in Moscow.

On presenting their papers at the British Embassy, a junior secretary took them to an annexe, that had recently been acquired to house the additional staff necessitated by the new alliance. Here they were introduced to a number of people given a bedroom between them and made members of the Press Section Mess.

During their journey they had held many discussions as to how they should set about their mission once they arrived in Russia. Kuporovitch had been pessimistic from the beginning, and had declared on half a dozen occasions that, while it was just possible that they might find means of getting reliable information as to Stalin's health, any attempt to assess Russia's resources would prove far beyond their scope, and that the chances of their finding out the final line upon which the Soviet armies must stand or surrender were positively nil.

The fact that Gregory had never lived in Russia, and knew nothing of the special difficulties which would confront them there, made him much more optimistic. He reasoned that as two unusually shrewd observers, both having considerable military knowledge, they ought, provided they were allowed reasonable freedom of movement, to be able to see enough and talk with enough people to form a pretty sound appreciation of the proportion of soldiers to men of military age who were still civilians, of the rapidity with which new classes were being called up, and of the length of time it took to convert the intakes into battle-worthy troops. To find out about Russia's future strategy would obviously be a much more difficult matter. But here, he felt, that if only he could meet enough people, particularly Soviet officers, and discuss prospects with them, in time the pieces of the jigsaw would fall into place. Then, if he could get the impression he had formed himself tacitly confirmed in casual conversation by one or two talkative senior officers, he would at least have something well worth reporting to Sir Pellinore.

In pursuance of this policy of securing a sort of 'Gallop Poll' by talking to anybody and everybody whose views might be worth hearing, at dinner that night they entered into conversation with every member of the Press Section Mess, and obtained quite a useful collection of miscellaneous information as a background for their further specific investigations.

The official rate of exchange made the *rouble* incredibly expensive to foreigners. It was easy to get a far higher rate 'round the corner', but even then there was little that one could purchase with one's *roubles* when one got them. Such things as could be bought, including the personal services of the Muscovites, male and female, could however, be had for a song if the purchaser was in a position to pay for them with cigarettes, soap, perfume or lipstick.

At this point, Gregory and Stefan found it difficult not to smile, since the latter, knowing perfectly well what sort of conditions he was likely to find in his own country, had taken appropriate measures, and from Cairo onwards each of them had been lugging an additional suit-case crammed with just such priceless commodities.

Their new acquaintances went on to inform them that the Ballet was as superb as ever, the Opera excellent and the cinema shows, apart from the high quality of the technique, lousy, as they had practically no humour or story value and were, one and all, simply vehicles for Government propaganda. The public went regularly and made no complaints, because they were conditioned to this, and not one in ten thousand of them had ever seen anything different; but these endless documentaries and films with a moral were a poor form of entertainment.

Nevertheless, the Bolsheviks' long experience in the art of propaganda was now proving of enormous value, both in keying their own people up to make the maximum possible efforts for the war and as an insidious weapon against the enemy. They were absolute realists and, knowing that they were fighting a completely unscrupulous enemy, they arranged their broadcasts with no regard at all to the truth, but solely on their calculated effectiveness—a game at which they were daily making rings round Dr. Goebbels. Yet, wherever possible they made the truth serve them too, and every programme included accounts of the spectacular heroism or high production feats of individual soldiers or war workers as well as of units, divisions and factories; a policy that filled the British pressmen, who, after two years of war, were still muzzled on such matters, with envy, and an added contempt for their own amateurishly-run Ministry of Information.

They all agreed that Russian morale was excellent and did not believe that this was due only to the skilful internal propaganda. Various factors were advanced to account for this. In the first place the Russians had certain qualities in common with the British. The two countries alone, of all those in Europe, had never been entirely overrun and subdued by an enemy in the whole of their history; therefore it was impossible for either people to envisage defeat. Both peoples were also essentially home-dwellers, as opposed to the café-frequenting nations of the Continent; both were intensive cultivators of their own soil, the British in their millions of small gardens and the Russians on their farms; and this attachment to home and land gave them an additional incentive to fight desperately in their defence. Added to this it was clear that, whatever the shortcomings of the Soviet régime might be, it had at least caused the Russian masses to feel that they now were the real owners of their country, and that not only the land and the cities

132

but also the parks, palaces, theatres, stadiums, museums, and even the works of their artists, scientists and writers, were in fact the personal property of each and every one of them.

This high morale was, moreover, by no means attributable to the type of blind patriotic neurosis which had gripped and given a spurious self-confidence to many nations during the first stages of the 1914–18 war. The Russians had now been waging a gigantic conflict on a thousand mile front for nearly three months, and if enemy claims were to be believed, their losses in dead and prisoners already ran into millions. Even on the most conservative estimate they had taken appalling punishment and, so far, with only brief local successes here and there, been thrown back in every sector.

When Gregory left London, at the end of July, they had already been driven out of the greater part of the protective belt of foreign territory that they had secured as a screen for their own frontiers during their Machiavellian alliance with Hitler. Russian Poland, Lithuania and Bessarabia had been overrun. The Germans were pouring north into Latvia and west into the Ukraine, and were only being held with difficulty at Smolensk.

Their initial defeats had compelled them to divide their long front into three commands, under Voroshilov in the north, Timoshenko in the centre and Budenny in the south; but this had not saved them from further disaster. During August, von Leeb had driven through from Latvia to Esthonia, taken Novgorod, reached Lake Ilmen and forced Voroshilov back against the Valdi hills; while von Rundstedt had proved more than a match for Budenny, hurling him back through the southern Ukraine, encircling Odessa, capturing Nikolaieff and thrusting towards the Crimea; Timoshenko alone had managed temporarily to stem the German torrent in the centre, but von Bock had smashed his southern flank, taken Gomel and almost cut him off from Budenny.

Since leaving Baghdad, Gregory and Stefan had been able to follow the news only with difficulty, but now their new friends brought them up to date as far as they could do so as, apart from the fact that the Soviet communiqués were often intentionally misleading, it was doubtful if even the Kremlin had more than a rough idea of the general situation throughout the whole length of their vast front.

In the north von Leeb had driven a wedge between Voroshilov and Timoshenko, cut the Moscow-Leningrad railway and now claimed to have reached the shores of Lake Ladoga, to the north-east of the latter city, while the Finns, supported by several German divisions, had resumed their war against the Russians, forcing them to withdraw from the thinly-held

Karelian isthmus to the north-west, gained from the Finns by the armistice of March 1940; so the Russian Marshal and his northern army were now surrounded and beseiged in Leningrad.

In the south Odessa was still holding out, but von Rundstedt had inflicted further defeats on Budenny, the most serious of which had been the spectacular break-through of von Kleist's armoured columns to the Dnieper. By it the Russians had been deprived of the huge hydro-electric plant, powered by the giant dam at Dnepropetrovsk, that supplied one of their greatest manufacturing areas, and the blow was a heavy one. The penetration towards the Crimea had deepened and Kiev, the capital of the Ukraine was now semi-circled.

In the hope of relieving the pressure on his two colleagues, Timoshenko had launched a desperate counter-offensive in the centre. Under him General Koniev had defeated the German Panzer expert Guderian, and the whole of von Bock's Army Group had been badly mauled in the neighbourhoods of Smolensk and Gomel; but with both his flanks now in the air, it was doubtful if Timoshenko would be able to hold the ground he had recaptured for long.

The only hopeful feature of the campaign appeared to be the Russians' determination to stick at nothing that might eventually help to defeat their enemy. In all the previous German *Blitzkriegs* it had proved sufficient for them to send their armoured columns forging ahead to the limit of their endurance for all resistance to collapse behind them. But the Russians were made of sterner stuff than the other people that the Panzer armies had overrun. Army corps, divisions and even companies that found themselves cut off had no thought of surrender, but fought on to the last, knowing that by so doing they were giving invaluable help to their comrades further east, who were still opposing the enemy spearheads. Their stubbornness resulted in thousands of German troops designated for the front line having to be held back to deal with them; but even when their formations were cut up and they ran out of ammunition the survivors took to the woods, from which they issued as small, desperate bands at night to sabotage the enemy lines of communication.

Many thousands of women had joined those bands in the enemy rear and were fighting shoulder to shoulder with the men; and wherever the Germans appeared other women were deliberately setting fire to their own homes and crops in pursuance of Stalin's 'scorched earth' policy. It was this nation-wide determination not only to die if need be, but to beggar oneself and even see one's children starve, rather than allow food or shelter to fall into the enemy's hands, which provided an offset of incalculable value against the actual territorial gains of the German armies.

In their room that night, Gregory and Kuporovitch talked the situation over. The Russian was as confident as ever that his country would emerge from the struggle victorious, but Gregory was not so sanguine. It was obvious that these 'Maquis' operations, which were being carried out behind the German lines on a scale never before envisaged, must be creating a heavy drain on the enemy's resources, but with so many Russian cities either captured or cut off the reduction of Russian resources must be even greater. If the Germans could maintain the momentum of their advance for another three months the whole of European Russia would be in their hands, and Gregory did not see how the Russians could possibly continue to keep their armies in the field if they had to rely entirely on their Asiatic territories for munitions and supplies.

Against this Kuporovitch argued that, even if it were early summer, no army could keep up the pace the Germans had set themselves for a further three months, and that now that winter was fast approaching offensive operations would be rendered doubly difficult. He forecast that the Germans would continue to have gradually lessening local successes for another month, that the heavy snows would then bring about conditions much more favourable to the Russians, and that during the long winter new armies would be built up which would roll the Germans back after the ground had dried in the late spring.

However, they at length agreed that they were both only theorising, and went to bed.

The following morning they went over to the Embassy and the Press Attaché presented them to the Ambassador, Sir Stafford Cripps had already been informed by a 'Most Secret' cypher telegram from London that they were being sent to Russia for special duty. However, in accordance with the Protocol, no Ambassador is ever embarrassed by being made aware of activities which might mitigate against his own standing with the foreign Power to which he is accredited, so Sir Stafford neither knew nor enquired the real reason why they had been sent out to him. His instructions were simply that they should be given some employment in his Press Section which would leave them such freedom as they might desire yet at the same time qualify them to seek interviews and be granted travel facilities as members of the Embassy staff.

The Ambassador gave his Press Attaché suitable instructions and enjoined secrecy upon him regarding the dummy posts that were to be created for the two new arrivals, then he formally wished them luck in their undertakings, and they left him to his papers.

The Press Attaché proved both amiable and helpful. He was clearly intrigued by these two 'cloak and dagger merchants' for whose arrangements he had been made responsible and, taking them to his own room, he enquired if they had any suggestions as to suitable cover for themselves. Gregory replied that their work could best be accomplished under some apparent activity which would necessitate their visiting a number of Russia's principal cities and, if possible, making a few trips to various parts of the front as well.

'I'm afraid that is asking for the moon,' the Attaché smiled. 'You can move about in Moscow quite freely and I can probably get you permits to visit some of the larger cities that are still a long way behind the battle zone, but visits to the front are absolutely out of the question. Our Allies are almost unbelievably cagey about everything to do with their military operations and even General Mason MacFarlane, the head of our Military Mission has not been allowed to see anything of the fighting yet.'

'Visits to some of the big reinforcement depots, where the new intakes of recruits are being mustered and trained, would probably serve just as well,' Kuporovitch remarked.

'That could possibly be arranged, but what excuse could we put forward as your reason for wishing to visit such places?'

'Statistics,' said Gregory thoughtfully. 'An enquiry into statistics would cover an interest in a multitude of subjects. We'd have to keep off figures which might be liable to reveal important military secrets, of course; but we could say that we represented certain important British scientific journals and were gathering data to write articles for them on the war potential of the Russians as a people. A lot of it would be semi-medical stuff. Average height, weight, age and general state of fitness of the recruits; prevalence of various hereditary diseases among them; their powers of resistance to cold and heat; typical diet upon which they have been brought up; percentages of pre-war types of employment; ratio of single against married men; average number of children; numbers in family, and so on. By and large, the Russians are an extraordinarily healthy looking lot, so their authorities should not object to that.'

The Attaché nodded. 'No, that sounds a good idea. But of course, they'll lie to you like blazes, and let you see only the crack troops that have been specially hand-picked to reinforce their Guard Divisions. It's always like that here. They keep special hospitals, crêches, factories, in apple-pie order solely to impress visiting foreigners, and over what happens else-

...ere an impenetrable veil is drawn. It's not done with any
...liberate intention of misleading one, but just because they
...nt everybody to think well of them, and they honestly be-
...ve that in showing the sample they are only anticipating a
...le the high standard they will have throughout the whole
...untry one fine day.'

'I don't mind how many lies they tell us,' Gregory grinned,
only they'll let us get a round a bit under our own steam.'

So the matter was arranged, and Gregory and Kuporovitch
...re given a small office at the top of the building, with two
...les, four chairs, pens, inks, pencils, stationery and a card
...the door bearing their names, underneath which was writ-
...'Statistical Department (Press Section)'.

They had arrived in Moscow on a Friday and, having made
...ir arrangements on Saturday morning, they spent the rest
...the weekend wandering about the capital. Gregory found
...t having Kuporovitch with him now proved an enormous
...vantage, as the Russian could drop into casual conversa-
...n with all sorts of people who, regarding him as one of
...mselves, talked perfectly freely, and were not put off by
...own presence, since he had adopted the expedient of wear-
...a bandage, as though he had been wounded, over his
...uth.

The Russians are a talkative lot and will argue with anyone
...out anything, until any hour in the morning, but despite the
...neral garrulousness of the people with whom Kuporovitch
...aped acquaintance they learned nothing that was of any
...lue to them in connection with their mission. These personal
...ntacts only confirmed what their Press colleagues had told
...m; the people were as uncompromisingly anti-Nazi as the
...tish and just as confident in final victory. Uncle Joe Stalin,
...th his battle cry of 'Death to the German Invaders', was as
...pular as Winston Churchill was in Britain, and the masses
...re more solidly behind him than they had ever been before;
...t they knew nothing about his health and they had no idea
...the size of their Army.

As Kuporovitch pointed out rather glumly, this was not
...lly surprising, as the Soviet Government issues no Army
...st and no details of the expenditure on the Fighting Services
...e ever published; but Gregory was not unduly disappointed,
...ce he was more or less killing time until he could contact
...re promising sources, and mooching around like this helped
...fill in his background and gave him a good idea of the lay-
...t of the city.

The weather was becoming distinctly chilly and, it was re-
...rted, the first snow had fallen in Leningrad on the Friday;
...on Monday morning they took some of their store of soap

and went in search of furs, and the goloshes without whi[ch]
the Russians never move abroad in the winter. On their
turn with their purchases they found a message from th[e]
nominal master saying that he would like to see them, so th[ey]
went along to his office.

'You are in luck,' the Press Attaché told them immediat[ely]
they presented themselves. 'It might have taken two or th[ree]
weeks to get permission for you to visit the sort of places y[ou]
want to see; but I ran into General Alyabaiev this morni[ng]
He used to be on the staff of the Russian Embassy in Lond[on,]
so he speaks English, and he is now one of the big shots in t[he]
Moscow garrison. I told him about you and he has offered [to]
show you round some of the reinforcement depots pers[on]
ally.'

'Splendid!' smiled Gregory. 'Thank you so much. When [is]
this likely to happen?'

'He is completing a round of inspections tomorrow and w[ill]
pick you up here in his car at eight o'clock. You will find h[im]
very easy to get on with. All the soldiers are. I don't kn[ow]
why it is, but they are always far more cooperative than t[he]
Russian Civil Servants.'

'Perhaps that is because the civilians come under the s[ur]
veillance of the secret police,' Gregory hazarded, 'Wher[e]
the service people don't—at least not to the same degree—
they can afford to be more matey without drawing suspici[on]
upon themselves. Anyhow, that suits me, as most of my busin[ess]
will be with the soldiers.'

When they had left the room Kuporovitch said: 'Si[nce]
this General speaks English it will be unnecessary for me [to]
accompany you tomorrow. Although I know him only [by]
name it is just possible that he might remember me. Some[one]
is bound to do so sooner or later, but the longer we can av[oid]
anyone raking up my past the better.'

In consequence it was decided that Stefan should develo[p a]
chill on the liver, and the following morning Gregory wai[ted]
alone to meet General Alyabaiev, who was well over an h[our]
late.

The Russian proved to be a short, thick-set, dark man, w[ith]
merry black eyes and a ready laugh. He had spent eight[een]
months in London during the early days of the Soviet E[m]
bassy, when it was housed in Grosvenor Square, and had [en]
joyed himself immensely; as the amenities of Moscow bef[ore]
the era of the Five-Year plans had been few indeed, and L[on]
don, by comparison, an absolute Paradise. His sense of [hu]
mour had prevented him from feeling resentment at some [of]
the more stuffy English, who, he said, had clearly regard[ed]
him as a professional assassin, and he had met enough of t[he]

138

ore broad-minded kind to secure for himself a thoroughly
ood time; and the memory of it had made him one hundred
er cent pro-British.

Gregory was soon on excellent terms with him, and they
ent the morning inspecting a number of depôts, at which the
isitor could not help but be impressed with the fine physique
d high morale of the new intakes. He asked a great many
uestions, all of which were answered promptly and with ap-
rent frankness, but he noted down the statistics he was given
ly because it was necessary to the rôle he was playing, since
ey had little bearing on the broad strategic picture that it
as his object to obtain.

As they were driving back he remarked on the excellent
scipline of the men he had seen training and their obvious
spect for their officers.

'Ah, it took a war to do that,' laughed the little General. 'In
e old days of peace we 'ave the Political Commissar to every
giment, an' 'e push the nose in everywhere, so that 'alf the
ficers are frightened to 'ave firmness with the men. But we
ght the Finns an' these little people give great big Russia a
ack eye. The Marshals say to Stalin, 'Without discipline wars
nnot be won. You take away the Political Commissars an'
e will soon have the war finished,' so the Commissars were
ook, a new spirit was quickly there, and the war was won.
Now, ef a sub-lieutenant gets in a tramcar every soldier jumps
p to offer seat. That ees good, an' right, because the officer
s passed 'igher tests than the man an' more is expected of him,
o it ees proper that they should pay 'im respect.'

Just as the General was about to set Gregory down in front
f the Embassy he said: 'I can arrange for you to visit some of
ur intake centres further east, ef you are wanting that. But I
hink you waste your time, now I have shown you our routine.
t ees much similar in all other places.'

'I suppose so,' Gregory agreed. 'Still, my articles would carry
ore weight if I could write on data that I've acquired in other
laces as well as Moscow.'

'Perhaps,' the General shrugged, not very enthusiastically.
All right then; let me 'ave an outline of such programme as
ou propose yourself, at the reception tomorrow night, an'
will tell you then what ees is possible.'

'Thanks very much, but I'm afraid I haven't been asked to
ny reception.'

'It ees given at the 'otel Metropole to receive the Polish
Generals in exile. Many were our prisoners from the Polish
campaign of nineteen-thirty-nine, but now they become Allies
an' they will form a Polish Legion to fight the Germans with
us. The Corps Diplomatic ees invited to send its representa-

tives, but ef you are not of those selected I will 'ave sent you special card.'

Having thanked him for his kindness on parting, Grego lunched in the Press Section Mess and afterwards retired w Kuporovitch to their office.

'You know, Stefan,' he said, tilting back his chair and p ting his feet up on his desk, 'we're not getting anywhere.'

The Russian raised his black eyebrows. 'Did you expect my friend, so quickly? These matters take time.'

'Of course,' Gregory shrugged impatiently. 'It's not that. T trouble is that we're not going to work the right way. Th little general was nice as pie this morning, and he gave a all the information I could decently ask for about seve bunches of stalwart hayseeds who were going off quite che fully to give their lives for old Mother Russia; but what hav got out of it? Damn all. What is more, just before I left h he said a mouthful. He told me that if he fixed up for me visit similar depots in other cities I'd see exactly the sa sort of thing, so I'd simply be wasting my time. If they let go I wouldn't see the same sort of thing, of course. At lea not quite. The chaps I was shown were trained reservists called to the colours. One could see that with half an e Whereas out in the Provinces the intakes would be mainly r material. But that's neither here nor there. I want to know h many of these birds can be trained *and* equipped in the wh of Russia during the next six months, and no amount of snoo ing round regimental depots is going to give me that.'

'*Mon Vieux,*' Kuporovitch protested, 'if you visited the He quarters of the Sussex Fusiliers in England, would you exp to find your Adjutant-General there to give you the figures the British Army's potential for nineteen forty-two?'

'Damn it, Stefan, no. But Alyabaiev is one of the Russ A. G.'s people, and quite a high-up. I thought it an incredi lucky break to have got on to a man like that so quickly. H ing tried him out with chicken-feed questions I went on qu smoothly to the wider problems of mobilising, training, a equipping huge numbers of men, but he didn't seem to kn anything about that at all. Of course, he may have been cov ing up. Security is pretty good in Britain, these days, and probably even better here in Russia, where people who w their tongues too much are liable to get a bullet in the mou But I definitely formed the impression that he had no idea all what was going on outside Moscow. He just shrugged shoulders and said: 'Every man in Russia will fight and ev woman too. We shall draw on them as we need them as lo as there is one living enemy on Russian soil." Well, that's f but it doesn't give an inkling of how many Divisions they ho

140

o have under arms by Christmas, and if a General of Alyabaiev's standing doesn't know that how the hell are we going
to find anyone who does?'

Kuporovitch smiled. 'It is, as I have often told you before,
that Russia is different from other countries. In Britain, France,
and the United States, thousands of people have a say in the
running of affairs. Every new policy is explained to the public
and argued out in the Chambers of Representatives and in the
Press. In peacetime everyone who desires it has ready access
to a mass of information about their fighting services, and
even in wartime all officers of fair seniority can form a reasonably good appreciation of the extent to which their services
are being expanded. But it is not like that here.'

He lit a cigarette and went on: 'The Russian people are
told nothing, except what their rulers require them to do. The
Supreme Council, which is elected from all the other so-called
Councils of People's Commissars, does not mean a thing. It
is simply a megaphone to announce the decisions of the little
Camorilla that really runs the country. This is composed of
three small Committees—the Secretariat, the Polit-Bureau and
the Organisational Bureau, Stalin and a few others have seats
on all three of them, but the total membership numbers only
sixteen. The real truth about what goes on in Russia, the actual
progress of the Five-Year Plans, her relations with foreign
States, the strength and condition of her fighting services, her
secret aspirations and future intentions, have, for years past,
been known only to this small handful of men; so, although it
may seem strange to you, it is really quite natural that a man
like Alyabaiev should have very little idea of his country's
military resources.'

'But surely the General Staff must know about such things,'
Gregory argued. 'How, if they don't, can they possibly hope to
run a war successfully?'

'The Marshals would know,' Kuporovitch conceded, 'and
a few of their personal staff officers would get a glimpse of the
big picture but no more. You see, Russia is ninety times the size
of England, Scotland and Wales together, so it is possible, and
from the dictatorship point of view desirable, to run it in
watertight compartments. A dozen different Generals are, no
doubt, now raising and training armies each bigger than those
of say, Holland or Sweden, in various parts of the Soviet Union,
but this little group in the Kremlin alone knows what their
efforts will all add up to. Believe me, Gregory, that is so. As a
General myself I have held many commands, but never was I
allowed to know a single thing about policy, plans or resources
that did not concern me personally.'

Gregory grinned. 'I must confess that I thought you were

just being pessimistic when you've said this sort of thing before. It seems, though, that I owe you an apology.'

'Forget it, *mon ami*. I am only distressed that here is so little help that I can give you; but I have always felt that this task is one which should have been given to the head of your Military Mission, and not to a private individual.'

'That would not have filled Sir Pellinore's bill, because he wanted an entirely independent report. Still, say General Mason Mac had been charged with the job, what could he have done that he won't certainly have done already—namely ask in the most diplomatic language for any information that his opposite numbers care to give him as to what future defence lines are now being prepared and what resources are likely to be available to man them. You know, as well as I do, that they won't tell him anything, or, if they do, it will have no relation to the truth.'

Kuporovitch's lazy blue eyes showed a slight animation as he leaned forward and tapped the table. 'That may well be but your General will at least have the chance of meeting some of the Marshals; then, just between good friends when a bottle or two of vodka has been drunk, he might get something off the record.'

'Then it all boils down to getting hold of one of these twenty-odd top boys. You're convinced that is the only way in which we can get the information we require?'

'Absolutely.'

'Do you know any of these big shots personally?'

'I have never met any of the political leaders, but I have served under most of the Marshals—Budenny, Yegerov, Blücher and, as you know, Voroshilov was my friend and protector for many years.'

'Budenny is in the field commanding the Southern group of armies. Blücher is watching the Japs in the Far East and Voroshilov is boxed up in Leningrad; so they are all ungetatable. How about Yegerov?'

'I haven't the faintest idea where he is. He may be dead now for all I know. Hundreds of high officers were executed for complicity in the Tukachevsky conspiracy years after it happened, and I had heard nothing of Yegerov for a long time before I left Russia, so he may quite well have been implicated by some belated confession, and duly eliminated.'

'Then, by hook or by crook, we must get to the headquarters of one of the others. As Voroshilov was a personal friend of yours, he is obviously far and away the best bet.'

Kuporovitch grunted. 'He *was* my friend, but Clim is not the sort of man to look kindly on a deserter. If I walked into his ffice tomorrow the odds are that he'd shout for a firing squad o have me shot.'

'If you could stay his hand for the first five minutes you'd be all right,' Gregory replied. 'He may be impetuous by nature, but he is quick to grasp a situation and very reasonable to talk to. At least, that's how he struck me when I met him in Finland.'

'You were then passing as a German, under the name of Colonel Baron von Lutz,' Kuporovitch remarked.

'That's true; so his first instinct would be to have me shot too, if I suddenly bob up again flourishing a British passport.'

For a moment they sat silent, then Kuporovitch stubbed out his cigarette and said: 'You are right about Voroshilov being the best bet; not because he was once my friend, but because, Stalin apart, he could give you more accurate information than any other man in Russia. As Commissar for Defence and Supreme Commander of all the Soviet fighting forces it was he who laid down Russia's programme of re-armament and finally settled our strategy in the event of a war with Germany. Moreover, he is the only Marshal who has a seat on any of the three key Committees that control the destinies of the U.S.S.R. However, to see him we shall have to get to Leningrad, and since it is now besieged that will not be easy. If we succeed in that, the chances are that, in a besieged city, our British passports will not be the slightest protection and he will have us both shot. Even if he does not, the odds against his talking freely to either of us about Russia's resources and strategy are simply fantastic. On the other hand, if you kick your heels here till doomsday I am convinced that your will learn nothing of the least value, so if you really feel that you should take on this outrageous gamble, I'll go to Leningrad with you.'

Gregory took his feet off the desk and leaning forward, laid a hand on the Russian's shoulder.

'You marvellous old devil,' he smiled, giving his friend an affectionate little shake. 'All right. We'll both gamble our necks against British arms for Russia. Let's go to Leningrad.'

Perilous Journey

'I wonder if we shall have great difficulty in getting through to Leningrad now?' said Gregory after a moment.

Kuporovitch shrugged. 'The German wedge that has curved round the city is, I should think, already too deep for parties still to be attempting to slip through it, except as an emergency measure, but Russia is holding her own in the air. Of course the risk of running into German fighters and being shot down must be much greater than we found it when flying through the Med, because it is certain that the Nazis will have strong concentrations of the Luftwaffe in the neighbourhood of the city for their siege operations; still, that's a risk which must be accepted. The real trouble will be to persuade the authorities to give us permits for our journey and seats in an aircraft.'

'I've no doubt Alyabaiev could fix it for us, if only we could think of a sufficiently cogent reason for wanting to go there. It is a pity we are not posing as military correspondents, as then we'd be able to plead a desire to report the siege.'

'I don't agree. I think our best hope of getting there is the very fact that we are not supposed to be concerned with military affairs, except in so far as the impinge on the health and general well-being of the people. The authorities have not yet allowed your war correspondents to go anywhere near the front, so it is most unlikely that they would let them go to besieged Leningrad.'

'That's true, but I wonder why? Perhaps they think some of their Generals are mucking things up, and they don't want any foreigners to see their blunders—let alone report them. Von Rundstedt is certainly making rings round old Budenny in the South and I suppose it is only a matter of weeks before Voroshilov will be compelled to surrender.'

Kuporovitch shook his bullet head. 'You are wrong there. At least, as far as Clim is concerned. Semyon Budenny, as I've told you before was one of my sergeants in the days before the Revolution. When the trouble came he saved me from being murdered by hotheads in the regiment, and it was owing to that I willy-nilly lined up with the Bolsheviks. Naturally I've a great personal regard for him, but I know his limitations. He is a fine cavalry leader, popular with the men, pig-headed and courageous, but mentally he is still a Sergeant of Dragoons, and he has not the brains to conduct the operations of a great modern army. But Clim Voroshilov—*sapristi!*—Clim is very different.'

'Why? He was only a mechanic. As a young man he even evaded his military service. He became a General only because he had the gift of the gab, and at a time of crises one of the Soldiers and Workmen's Councils elected him to be their leader overnight.'

'True, true, but what a leader he became! That was in the spring of nineteen-eighteen, when the Germans held much more of the Ukraine than they do now. The Red Army had fallen to pieces. There was no command, no plan. He insisted that they must elect one man to be their General and give him implicit obedience. He was utterly amazed when they elected him. The Germans were pressing on from the north and west; to the south and east the country was held by General Krasnov's White Cossacks. The position seemed utterly hopeless, but he took the job on.

'He ordered all the scattered bands of Bolsheviks to concentrate on the great railway centre of Lugansk. There, he collected scores of trains, loaded them with munitions and the civilian population, which he refused to leave behind; and, Heaven alone knows how, managed to fight off the enemy all the time he was organising the huge convoy. Then he began to move east in an attempt to cut through the White Army to Stalingrad, or Tzaritsyn as they called it them, which was still in the hands of the Reds. After ninety days and nights of unceasing battle he reached his goal. By sheer will-power, organising ability, and indomitable courage, he succeeded in conveying thirty-five thousand non-combatant refugees across seven hundred miles of enemy territory and bringing five hundred trains, with a great store of munitions, and fifteen thousand fighting men to the relief of Stalingrad.'

Gregory nodded. 'Yes, I seem to remember you telling me about that once, and even comparing it with Marshal Ney's retreat from Moscow as one of the greatest fighting retreats in history. But after all, the Germans were pretty well spent by then, and it was only guerilla warfare. To hold a great city is a very different matter.'

'*Sacré nom*! And did he not hold Stalingrad? That summer it was still touch and go for the Bolsheviks. They controlled only Moscow, Leningrad and a triangle extending about two hundred miles south of the capital. Stalingrad was at its southernmost tip and surrounded on three sides. That's why it was known as the Salient of Death. But it held all the grain of the Ukraine, and Moscow was starving; so its retention was absolutely vital. The place was in a state of anarchy and near surrender when Voroshilov arrived there; but they saw at once that he had a head on his shoulders and made him Commander-in-Chief of the whole area. His spirit infused new energy into everyone and he brought order out of chaos. From July to December he held the "Red Verdun", kept the Volga open, fed starving Moscow and saved the Revolution.'

'I know, Stefan, I know.' Gregory sought to check his friend's enthusiasm. 'I'm not trying to belittle these splendid feats but they're ancient history now and warfare was a very different business in those days. Voroshilov was holding Stalingrad against a few thousand disgruntled, ill-equipped Czarist officers and a horde of Cossack cavalry; whereas today he is up against a magnificently trained and disciplined German Army plentifully equipped with aircraft, tanks, and every other device of modern war.'

Kuporovitch brought his clenched fist down on the desk with a bang. 'You do *not* know,' he exclaimed angrily. 'You have not the faintest idea of Clim's capabilities. He is not only a great leader of men and a born commander, he has a brain that seethes with original ideas. It is that which earned him his proudest title—"Organiser of Victories". Look what he did in nineteen-nineteen when the Whites were at the very gates of Moscow. He realised that their successes were due to the fact that they still had organised cavalry which could get round our flanks, whereas we had none—only little bands of a score or so of horsemen with every company or battalion of foot. He went to Lenin and demanded permission to form a Cavalry Army, by collecting these little bands together. Lenin was at his wits' end and he agreed. That October Clin formed a Cavalry Corps while the battle was at its height. By November, fighting all the time, he had formed the First Cavalry Army of the Republic. In sixty days we rode six hundred miles, from Tula to the sea. On January eighth, nineteen-twenty, with the hooves of seventeen thousand horses ringing in our ears, we charged into Rostov, having split the White armies completely in half, and having put an end to the last hope of a Czarist restoration.'

Gregory held up his hand, but in spite of that the Russian went on.

'You will no doubt say, "But that was only another old-fashioned campaign." All right; perhaps it was. But remember that this First Cavalry Army was formed not by a horseman of the Steppes but by a mechanic, and that he forged his weapons because it was the one must suited to our dire need at that moment. And now listen to what he did in his own element. At Stalingrad we had not half enough troops to man our perimeter properly. As attack succeeded attack the men became almost too tired to fight after marching ten, twenty, and often

146

forty miles from one threatened point to another. At that time no one had ever heard of mechanisation, but Voroshilov commandeered every lorry, truck and car in the whole area and mechanised his army, so that it might ride from battle to battle. Not content with that, he laid down railways to all the most vulnerable sectors, then mounted all his artillery on sixty trains that were armoured by the Stalingrad factories while under shell-fire. So, owing to his originality and dynamic energy, our defence became flexible, and with a few hours two-thirds of our fire-power could be brought up to smash an assault on any sector.

'He has not been asleep since then, either; but for the past twenty years has been the first to examine and try out every new device for the strengthening of our army. That is why I tell you that whatever may happen elsewhere, Voroshilov will prove a match for the Germans; and that, as long as he is in command, Leningrad will never surrender.'

'You win,' smiled Gregory, 'and anyhow, I pray to heaven that you're right. If Voroshilov can keep a big German army tied up there in the north all through the winter he'll have done the whale of a fine job. But let's get back to our own pigeon. You think we stand a better chance of getting a permit to visit Leningrad because we're not supposed to be interested in the military side of the war, eh?'

'Yes, I am convinced of that.'

'How about our going to collect starvation statistics, then? Since you are so certain that Leningrad will hold out no doubt General Alyabaiev believes that too. But the amount of food there must be limited and, as the siege progresses, rations will have to be further and further reduced. Britain is up against the U-boat blockade, and if the battle of the Atlantic goes badly for us the same sort of thing might happen there. Statistics concerning the gradual decline of fighting and working ability caused by the lowering of various essentials in a diet might prove very valuable data.'

'That sounds pretty good,' agreed Kuporovitch. 'In fact, I doubt if we could think of any more plausible and harmless idea on which to hang your request.'

That evening they went to the Ballet, and while watching the superb technique of Russian artists experienced their first air raid in Moscow. For the past eight weeks the Luftwaffe had launched a raid against Moscow every few nights, but Gregory had noticed very little damage in the centre of the city, and now he learned the reason.

When the air-raid warning sounded no special measures were taken; the show continued and no one left their seats. Soon afterwards there came the familiar drone of approaching enemy bombers. Suddenly there was a roar as though a dozen volcanoes had erupted. It went on for about three minutes, blanketing every other sound and making the whole building vibrate continuously.

This thunder ceased as suddenly as it had began and, in the ensuing silence, the rattle and clack of innumerable Ack-Ack splinters could be heard like the patter of heavy hail upon the roof. A few bomb explosions sounded in the distance, then the guns opened again with a second synchronated burst. Again there came the clattering of the splinters, a longer silence, then the 'All Clear'.

To Gregory the episode was a terrific eye-opener. As an old artillery officer he had always thought that it was absurd to dignify the sporadic gunfire heard during London's first year of raids as a barrage. But this had been a barrage in the real meaning of the word—a fire so devastating that nothing could live in it—and to create that unbroken pulverising roar he estimated that anything from one to two thousand heavy anti-aircraft guns must ring the city. It was no wonder that only an occasional German aircraft managed to slip through and that the rest were either destroyed or compelled to drop their bombs on the outskirts. On the face of it, such a terrific concentration of cannon solely in defence of the capital argued well for Russia's armament production.

His card for the reception duly arrived the following morning and he noted that he was bidden for nine o'clock, but several members of the Embassy Press Section, who had also been invited, told him that it was quite useless to put in an appearance until ten, at the earliest, as his hosts would not have arrived themselves. The Russians, it seemed, were always an hour or two late for their appointments and kept the most extraordinary hours, often summoning people to important conferences at three or four o'clock in the morning.

The reception proved another eye-opener. Russia was already said to be faced with the certainty of a food crisis in the coming winter, and the whole population had been graded for rationing. The allowances for services personnel and essential workers were quite liberal, for children and adolescents sufficient, for office workers on the near side, for all other civilians of any war value at all meagre, and for the elderly or useless near the starvation line. Yet here the long tables groaned under a vast and varied cold collation, including practically every fish, meat and bird one could think of, jellied in aspic or garnished with appetising delicacies. Caviare in huge silver ice-surrounded buckets was being ladled out on to plates in quarter-pound dollops, and men-servants in a smart livery were handing round silver salvers on which there were little glasses of vodka of a dozen different flavours.

The gathering was mainly military with a sprinkling of naval officers and civilians, but no hint of war pervaded the assembly. None of the officers wore anything resembling war kit, and their uniforms were as spotless and well-pressed as if their wearers had been about to attend a peacetime ceremonial parade.

Gregory could not help smiling as he thought of the truly democratic manner in which a similar affair would have been conducted in London. The menu would have been 'Strictly in conformity with the regulations of the Ministry of Food' and the representatives of the mighty British Empire would mostly have appeared in well-worn office clothes or battledress. Nothing that could possibly impress the visitors to honour whom the feast was given would be allowed, and it would be considered preferable that they should go away hungry, sober and depressed, rather than any opportunity should be given for some Socialist demagogue to accuse the Government in the House of squandering the nation's resources.

Like the Russians, Gregory was sufficient of a realist to appreciate that everything there not eaten by guests and hosts would certainly be finished up by the servants, and that for a few score people to occasionally eat and drink of the best while improving the foreign relations of their country could not make one iota of difference to the general scale of rations. It seemed to him, too, far better for morale that the people should see their Generals dressed as Generals and not slinking about the capital disguised as nearly as possible to look like privates.

Gregory was introduced by his companions from the Embassy to a number of Russian officers. Few of them spoke English but he was able to converse with quite a number of them in French or German. Their comments on the war situation were invariably optimistic but most of them soon switched the conversation to England, a subject in which they were all now keenly interested and about which they could not hear enough. Without exception they asked him when Britain would invade the Continent, and aid Russia for forming a Second Front, and it was clear that none of them had the faintest conception of the colossal strain under which Britain had laboured during the war in which she had stood alone against Hitler, or the immense difficulties to be overcome before a cross-channel operation could be launched with any hope of success. However, they accepted with the best of goodwill his assurance that, even if they had to wait a bit, the day would certainly come when the forces of the Empire and the Soviet would meet in Berlin; and to that day, he had to knock back with them innumerable small glasses of vodka.

While he was searching for General Alyabaiev he went out into the hall, where he noticed the armed sentries were posted, not only at the main doors to the street, but also on the stairs leading to the floors above and down to the basement. On his enquiring the reason for this he was told that the whole ground floor of the hotel had been taken over for the evening, and his informant did not appear to think it at all strange that the people living there should have been confined to their rooms for the night. The Soviet General Staff, who were giving the party, had adopted this measure as the simplest means of ensuring against gate-crashers.

It was half past eleven before Alyabaiev turned up and after a couple of drinks with him Gregory tackled the General about the possibilities of getting to Leningrad. He listened patiently to the reasons on which the request was based, then said:

'Such information as you 'ave a wish to collect would certainly be of big value to your country, an' for us I see no 'arm in your going. But Leningrad ees now forbidden to all foreign correspondents, so our Press Bureau would, I tink, refuse permission. You see, to make exceptions of yourself an' your friend ees to ask for jealousies with the others.'

Gregory grinned at him. 'Leningrad is now in a state of seige, so, surely, what goes on there is solely the concern of the military authorities. I'm much too keen about this thing to tell the other correspondents anything about it; so wouldn't it be possible to side-step the Press Bureau for once and let me go in with my interpreter on a military pass?'

Alyabaiev grinned back. 'That would be possible, yes.'

'Well, I can easily tell my people at the Embassy that a trip has been arranged for me to some of your bases on the far side of the Urals. If I disappear for a few weeks they'll simply assume that I'm getting on with my job and won't worry in the least about where I've got to.'

'A few weeks you say? But eef you go to Leningrad you may be very much stuck there, for months, or all winter perhaps. In no case could I make any promises to get you out.'

'That is a risk I'm quite willing to take, and the longer I am there the more informative will be the figures that I shall obtain.'

'There will be much shelling an' air-raiding of the city. You an' your interpreter will sign a paper that you go there at your own wish, so that eef either of you are killed we can eventually present to your Embassy when they make enquiry about your disappearing.'

'Certainly.'

'Good then, I will consult with a friend who ees of the Operations Staff. Eef 'e make no objection it will be all right with the Security Office. Later tonight I will let you know eef this can be done.'

When the General had left him Gregory mingled with the crowd again. At midnight a pair of double doors at the end of the room were thrown open and a fine selection of hot dishes was wheeled in on trolleys. Gregory had already done ample justice to the cold spread and could not have eaten another sausage, but the Russians crowded round, helping themselves to great plates of bortch, poliviack and chicken fried in butter. Sweet Caucasian champagne had now replaced the vodka on the silver salvers that were being handed round. No one was the worse for liquor but everyone was laughing and talking at the top of their voices, and the Polish officers, who had been very stiff and correct when they first arrived, were now as merry and apparently carefree as their hosts.

About one o'clock in the morning Molotov came in, and stayed for about three-quarters of an hour. He shook hands with all the Poles, made a short speech which was translated into Polish, and then drank a toast with their senior General. Gregory would have given a lot to be able to wave a magic wand and change the sleek, black-haired, pale-faced Commissar for Foreign Affairs into little bright-eyed Uncle Joe, so that from a distance of only a few feet he could have made his own assessment of the great man's health; but in other ways, before the night was out he had no reason to complain of his luck.

Soon after Molotov had gone Alyabaiev led a young Brigadier up to him and reopened the matter of his going to Leningrad. As he had supposed the Russians were much more elastic in their dealings with such situations than the British would have been, and his suggestion of ignoring the Press Bureau was accepted as a short cut to getting the job done instead of a matter for head-shakings and fears of possible inter-Ministerial repercussions. The Brigadier proved to be in charge of communications with Leningrad and told Gregory that if he and his friend would hold themselves in readiness to leave their Embassy at short notice he would have them flown into the beseiged city during the course of the next three days.

Several other officers joined them and were told about the project. All of them were anxious to get to one of the fronts, so none of them thought it strange that Gregory should be prepared to risk his life by making a long stay in a city under bombardment. On the contrary, they congratulated him on his luck and another half-dozen rounds of drinks were tossed off to the success of his venture. It was nearly five in the morning before he got home, but he went to bed well satisfied.

Next morning he told Kuporovitch how things had gone

and they set about their preparations for departure. These were simple, as they had only to repack two of their suit-cases and place the other two, containing the bulk of their wealth in soap and cosmetics, in the care of the Press Attaché. But they were now also faced with the far more difficult task of deciding what their policy was to be when they reached Leningrad; and they spent the whole of the forenoon discussing it.

The salient difficulties were that Voroshilov must know that his old companion-in-arms, Stefan Kuporovitch, had disappeared from the Castle of Kandalaksha in March 1940, and presumably abandoned his command to become a deserter; and that, on the previous occasion when the Marshal had met Gregory, that worthy had been posing as the German Colonel Baron von Lutz. Somehow these matters had to be accounted for and a plausible explanation offered as to why they both now reappeared carrying British passports.

This was the barest necessity which would enable them to escape being handed over to a firing-squad, but, if they were to succeed in their mission, they had to do far more. It would not be enough merely to convince the Marshal that the one was not a traitor or the other an enemy; in addition they must provide some subtle inducement for him to place his complete trust in them, and, still further, impel him to take the quite extraordinary step of confiding to them the full truth about Russia's resources and future strategy.

At first the problem seemed so hopelessly insoluble that they were inclined to regret the rashness of their decision to voluntarily push their heads into the lion's mouth; but they both felt that Gregory's activities the previous night had practically burnt their boats and, although it might have been possible to wriggle out of the trip at the last moment, they were impelled to go through with it on account of their earlier decision— that it offered the only slender hope that they could see of succeeding in their mission.

Having argued round the matter for an hour, Gregory suggested that they should put the cart before the horse, and, instead if trying to think up ways of explaining away the past and their new roles to the Marshal, they should endeavour to assess to whom he would be likely to divulge the information they were seeking.

'He would certainly not tell you anything at all if you appeared before him in your old role as a German,' remarked Kuporovitch.

'No, and I think it most unlikely that he would tell me the truth if I approached him as an Englishman,' Gregory replied. 'He must know that Russia is asking Britain for armaments, so naturally he would make Russia's case out to be better

…an it is, and say that time is on her side and that she has …ractically unlimited numbers of trained men to use them. …e'd be a fool if he didn't.'

Kuporovich leant forward and his lazy blue eyes narrowed … little. 'Listen,' he said. 'We have to think of the *circum-…ances* in which he would speak freely, more than the sort of …en to whom he would do so.'

'That's true,' agreed Gregory, thoughtfully, and after a mo-…ent, he added: 'It might have something to do with the time-…ctor. He knows how far the Soviet armies can afford to re-…eat and must have a pretty shrewd idea how long it is likely … be before they are forced back to their final line. If someone …as able to offer him really important assistance—some blow … the Germans which might shake them badly and throw them …f their balance—'

'Yes, yes. I get your idea. He would then have to show his …wn hand in order that the blow might be delivered at the …ost critical point in the campaign.'

'It would have to be something that could be used only once.'

'For instance, a British landing on the Continent.'

'That's the sort of thing.'

'If it were put to him that the opening of a Second Front …as in active preparation, but that the longer the British could … given the more powerful their blow would be, it would then … in Russia's own best interests for him to disclose the abso-…te maximum for which he considered she could hold on un-…ded.'

Gregory nodded. 'Those are the sort of circumstances in …hich he would tell the real truth all right. I think we're get-…g somewhere now. But I'm not certain that a Second Front … the right bait for our line.'

'Perhaps not. You mean it would need a great deal of ex-…aining as to how we had been sent as emissaries on such a …atter, instead of its being handled through the Embassy and …e British Military Mission? Then too, why should Clim, who … beseiged in Leningrad, be consulted, instead of the question …ing referred direct to Stalin in Moscow. Those points would …rtainly be very difficult to get over.'

'They would; and there's another thing. Most of the officers …at I met last night seem to have very little idea of the dam-…e the collapse of France and the equipment we lost at Dun-…rk did to Britain. They obviously believe that we could launch … Second Front at any time we chose. They don't realise that …'re still only half armed and half trained, and that even …en the job is completed Britain's man-power is so compara-…vely limited, that with her huge commitments in the Mediter-…nean and the East she could never find an army large enough to tackle the Germans on the Continent. But Voroshilov is in different category.'

'You mean that as he is a member of the Camorilla th[...] runs Russia he has access to much secret information that th[...] Generals would not see? In fact, that he probably has a pret[...] good idea of the true state of things in England and knows, th[...] any prospect of a Second Front is right out of the question— at least, for some years to come.'

'Exactly! So however plausible our story might be in oth[...] respects he'd smell a rat, and hand us over to his gunmen.'

'We must rule that out then,' Kuporovitch sighed. 'But wh[...] other outside blow against the Germans could occur that wou[...] need careful timing?'

For a little they sat in silence, drawing heavily on the[...] cigarettes. At length Gregory looked up and said:

'I believe I've got it it, Stefan. What do you think of this?'

For another half an hour they talked, first one, then t[...] other, adding a detail or rounding off a thought, to clothe t[...] bare bones of the idea that Gregory had produced. By lun[...] time they felt that they really had the groundwork of reasonably plausible story, but they worked on it again [...] through the afternoon, until, when they went to the Mess f[...] the single before-dinner whisky and soda that was all ea[...] member was allowed, they were satisfied that, although th[...] would be taking their lives in their hands, they would at lea[...] be doing so on a brilliantly audacious and very careful[...] worked-out plan.

Now that they had settled matters, for better or for wor[...] they were anxious to be off; and when no message came [...] them during the second day after the reception Gregory beg[...] to fear that the Brigadier had forgotten his promise; but th[...] night, Friday, 19th of September, just as they were thinki[...] of going to bed, a box van called for them. In anticipation possibly having to leave in a hurry, they had already said go[...] bye to their nominal master, the Press Attaché, and the oth[...] friends that they had made in the Embassy annexe duri[...] their eight-day stay in Moscow, so they had only to put their furs and carry their bags out to the waiting car.

It bore them through the dark, deserted streets to a big off[...] block. The driver, beckoning them to follow him, took the[...] up in the lift to a waiting-room on the third floor, where a g[...] messenger motioned them to sit down. During the twen[...] minutes that they waited there, three officers and a civili[...] with the black eyes and high cheekbones of a Tartar, join[...] them, each giving his name to the girl on his arrival. Th[...] Gregory's friend, the young Brigadier, came hurrying in, a[...] the three officers immediately sprang to attention.

It was a critical moment, as although the great size of the [So]viet Army made it unlikely, there was always the possibility [th]at he might at one time have served under Kuporovitch. If [so], recognition would be certain to result in a postponement of [th]eir departure until the Soviet authorities had made full en-[qu]iries as to how their ex-General came to be on the staff of [th]e British Embassy. But the Brigadier gave Gregory a quick [sm]ile, nodded amiably to Kuporovitch when he was intro-[du]ced as Mr. Cooper and handed each of them an envelope [co]ntaining the necessary papers for their journey.

He then called one of the officers over, and introducing him [as] Major Makhno, said that he would look after them on their [tri]p and secure accommodation for them in Leningrad. Cut-[tin]g Gregory's thanks short he gave them a quick handshake, [w]ished them a safe passage over the enemy lines, and hurried [ba]ck to his own work. The Major said something to the others [in] Russian and the little party all went downstairs.

In the street the box van was waiting for them. They [cl]imbed into it and an hour later it set them down in front of [so]me hutments on one of the military airfields some way out-[si]de Moscow.

In one of the huts an officer examined the papers of the [p]arty, then they were shepherded into another and left to [w]ait there three quarters of an hour. At length, a little after [o]ne o'clock in the morning they were led out onto the airfield [a]nd across to a big bomber. Having climbed in the passengers [w]ere directed down into the bomb bay. There was no room to [s]tand upright there and no seats, only a double tier of tem-[p]orary racks, across which wire netting had been nailed, on [w]hich they could lie down.

It was both cold and stuffy down there, and extremely un-[c]omfortable, as each individual had only just enough space [t]o turn round, and could not even raise his head more than a [f]ew inches. They were told that smoking was forbidden and [w]hen the doors were closed the bay was lit only by one dim [li]ght.

Gregory was far from happy, as, at times, he suffered from [m]ild claustrophobia, and few things could have been better [c]alculated to bring it on than being packed like a human sar-[di]ne in a tin. Moreover, he knew that if the aircraft ran into [tr]ouble its passengers stood little chance of surviving. Down [t]here in the belly of the 'plane they would be more exposed to [a]nti-aircraft fire than in any other part of it, and if the machine [c]aught fire the crew might bale out but there would be small [h]ope of anyone in the bomb bay being able to extricate them-[s]elves from their narrow quarters in time to do so; in addition, [i]f the aircraft had to make a forced landing there was more

155

than an even chance that its passengers would be crush
trapped and, if they survived the crash, burnt to death.

The fact that the great majority of staff officers of all natio
who made night journeys by air in wartime had to travel t
way, and that most of them reached their destinations in safe
was small consolation. The ensuing hours were the most mise
able that Gregory had spent for a long time, as he could neith
divert his mind by watching the night landscape over which th
were flying nor, owing to the roar of the engines, even hear t
sound of the guns when they entered the war zone, so he cou
only lie there in a cold sweat visualising all the horrible thin
that might happen to him at any moment.

After what seemed a dozen hours at least, the aircraft beg
to drop sharply and for a few moments Gregory wonder
wildly if they were being forced down; then it banked and t
engine stopped. He clenched his teeth and waited for the cras
Then there was a sharp jolt that threw him half out of h
makeshift bunk, a lesser bump, another and another, the
with a sigh of relief, he realised that the machine was runnir
smoothly along the ground.

When they had climbed out of their grim prison Maj
Makhno led them across the airfield on which they had lande
to the reception office. While their papers were being examine
again Gregory saw that it was a quarter past four, so th
had done their four-hundred-mile trip in just over three hour
He was now conscious, too, of the sounds of distant gunfir
and as the little party were taken out to a waiting charabar
he could see the flashes of sporadic bombardment lighting u
the night sky. A heavy shell trundled overhead with a roar lik
the passing of a train, to burst some miles away in the centr
of the city. Suddenly a Russian battery quite near by opene
up with a series of staccato cracks, and it was still firing whe
the charabanc drove off.

Twenty minutes later they were set down outside a larg
building which the Major told them had been the old Hot
Astoria, but was now an officers' club. In spite of the latenes
of the hour a number of people were still sitting about the bi
lounge, and, having arranged about accommodation, the
guide procured some very welcome sandwiches and vodka fo
them.

Fuel was now being husbanded for the worst months of th
winter, so the hotel was unheated, but the vodka warmed ther
up a little and half an hour after their arrival they went up t
bed. The place was very crowded so they had to share a roor
on the fourth floor with Major Makhno and two other officers
who were already installed and sleeping there. Undressing a
quietly as they could, they lay down on the truckle beds unde

156

me blankets and piled their furs on top of them. Occasionally a shell whined over to explode with a loud bang, which as followed by the rumble of falling debris, but they were too red to take much notice and soon dropped off to sleep.

In the morning they went downstairs with the Major and artook of the meagre breakfast which was all that was now llowed, and, after it, he told them that they must come with m to report to the office of the garrison commander; upon hich Gregory said that they first wished to write a letter for elivery to the Commander-in-Chief.

He had already discussed with Kuporovitch the exact form aat the letter was to take, but they had felt it best not to write in Moscow in case, through some accident, it fell into wrong ands. Paper and pens were available in the lounge, so Kuprovitch sat down by a desk and wrote the letter, while Gregory mained near by talking to the Major.

The letter to Voroshilov ran as follows:

y dear Marshal,

No doubt you will be surprised to hear from your old omrade after this long time, but from the letter I left behind r you when I departed so hurriedly from Kandalaksha in [arch 1940, you will have understood the reason for my ence.

However, I am now happy to report that my self-imposed ission has been crowned with success and will, I trust, enable e to make a contribution of real value to the defeat of the itlerite bandits.

After escaping many dangers, and a most hazardous journey, have succeeded in bringing back with me to the Soviet Union a officer to whom you rendered a considerable service when ou were commanding our army in Finland. He represents rtain people who can be of incalculable help to us, and, upon ceiving your instructions as to the most suitable time to rike, he will return to convey them to those who sent him.

For reasons which I will explain when I have the honour to port to you in person, this officer and myself are at present lleted at the Astoria under the names of Mr. Sallust and [r. Cooper respectively, and are carrying British passports.

May I solicit the honour of an interview for my friend and yself at your very earliest convenience?

Your old comrade and brother-in-arms of the Revolution,
                                        Stefan Kuporovitch.

Having finished his letter, unobserved by the others, Kuprovitch swallowed hard, raised his eyes to heaven and crossed mself. He knew that this was but the beginning of the series

157

of lies he would have to tell with absolute assurance and con viction if he and Gregory were to live out the week; but h also knew that only by practising the most shameful dece tion on his old friend Clim would Gregory get the informatio he wanted, and that unless that information was forthcomin there was little chance of Britain supplying the weapons whic might prove the salvation of his beloved country.

After addressing an envelope he added, 'Most Secret an Personal' across its flap, then put it in another marked 'Mo Immediate, for the Marshal Personally'. Seeing that he ha finished, the other two stood up and they left the hotel to gether.

The light snow of early autumn had already made Lenir grad's streets slushy, but a bright sun was shining, and, as th siege was still in an early stage the people in the streets looke well fed and cheerful.

The Germans were being held at some distance from th eastern side of the city and to the north it was largely pro tected by the great inland sea of Ladoga, while to the west th naval base of Kronstadt and the upper bays of the Gulf o Finland were still in Russian hands, so the only perceptibl signs of the fighting came from the south. Field-Marshal Ritte von Leeb was now making a great effort to penetrate th southern suburbs and force a surrender before winter close in, so the dull rumble of his artillery was almost continuous but the Germans were concentrating mainly on the Russia defence lines and only an occasional heavy burst with a resoun ding crump in the city's built-up area.

While they waited for a tram on the broad Nevski Prospek they watched the white vapour trails of a dog-fight up in th sky almost directly above them. One of the aircraft suddenly flared like a struck match, hovered for a second, then came spiralling to earth with a great plume of black, oily smok gushing from its tail. Confident that it must be a Nazi the people in the street cheered lustily, but just as the flaming machine disappeared behind a tall building a shell came hurt ling over, causing them to break off and run for the neares cover.

Without further incident they reached the Garrison Com mander's office. The officer who examined their papers pro mised to have the letter to Marshal Voroshilov delivered without delay. He then told Gregory and Stefan that they were to return to the Astoria and were not to leave the hotel until the Chief Intelligence Officer sent someone to collect them even if that meant their remaining indoors for two or three days, as it was not considered desirable for foreigners to go about the city unescorted.

Major Makhno volunteered to see them safely back to the
Astoria, and when he had done so left them to go about his
own business; but as they thought it quite possible that instructions had been telephoned to the military staff of the club to
keep an eye on them, they made no attempt to evade the order
confining them to it.

As they had nothing with which to occupy themselves they
sat for some time staring out of a window at the passers-by,
and the aircraft from which the sky was rarely free for long,
but both of them were anxiously wondering what the results
of the letter to Voroshilov would be. After a thin lunch in the
canteen, having had very little sleep the night before they went
upstairs and spent the afternoon dozing on their beds. In the
evening they endeavoured to keep their minds off the letter by
playing six-pack bezique, both before and after a far from
satisfactory dinner, but the lack of heating in the club rendered
it cheerless and the cold increased as the night drew on, so at
ten o'clock they decided to go to bed.

They were both still sound asleep at half past two in the
morning when they were suddenly aroused by a rough voice
calling out their names. The other occupants of the room also
woke, and as the light was switched on everyone sat up to
stare at an officer who stood in the doorway. Behind him were
two armed soldiers.

The officer advanced into the room, his hand resting casually on the automatic in his belt, and, having identified Gregory
and Kuporovitch, he stood there while his two men searched
their clothes for weapons. They were then told to dress. This,
they knew was the answer to their letter. It had come, not in
the form of a friendly summons, as they had hoped, but with
all the harsh abruptness of undisguised arrest. Their hands were
steady, but their nerves were stretched as taut as piano-wire,
as they accompanied their guards downstairs and out to a
waiting car.

12

Strange Interview

The car took them only a short distance and pulled up before
a large block of flats. Outside the entrance a fur-clad soldier
was standing in a sentry-box, and on going inside it was clear

that the whole building had been taken over by the military.

Since leaving the Astoria, the officer by whom they had virtually been arrested had not spoken a word, but on entering the hall he dismissed the two soldiers and said to Kuporovitch in Russian:

'I am Colonel Gudarniev, and a member of Marshal Voroshilov's personal staff. The Marshal ordered me to bring you to him: he lives on the top floor of this building. Please to get in the lift.'

'On the top floor!' echoed Kuporovitch, as he obeyed. 'Surely that is a bad place for anyone to be whose life is so precious, now that the city is under bombardment?'

Gudarniev shrugged. 'The Marshal occupied the apartment in the old days, when he was Governor of Leningrad, and it has a magnificent view over the Neva. Naturally we all wished him to live in the rooms prepared for him at his battle headquarters, far underground, but, despite our protests, he elected to reoccupy his old flat, because up there he can see quite a lot of the fighting through a powerful telescope mounted on the roof.'

'How like him,' sighed Kuporovitch. 'I have served under him myself and he was always the same. Reports were never good enough and he must see things for himself. Nearly every day he would visit some part of the front, and he often declared that any General who devoted more than a few hours at night to meetings and paper work was in danger of losing both touch with reality and the personal direction of his men.'

Their escort brushed up his dark moustache and gave them a more kindly look, but the lift stopped, so no more was said and they got out. On the top landing another sentry was stationed outside a plain oak door. He came to attention, then pressed the doorbell. After a moment it was opened by an orderly who, instead of a uniform tunic, wore a white, high-necked blouse belted at the waist. Evidently he was expecting them, as he stood aside, closed the door, took their furs, led them down a passage, knocked twice on another door and without waiting for an answer, threw it open.

As they followed Colonel Gudarniev into the room they saw that it was in semi-darkness. A moment later they realised the reason. Along the greater part of its southern side ran a long low window; from this the blackout curtains had been pulled back; the room was lighted only by the reflection of the snow on the adjacent roofs and the intermittent flicker of artillery fire. Silhouetted in the centre of the gap between the curtains stood out the short, thick-set figure of the Marshal as he gazed over the uneasily sleeping city towards the unceasing battle.

On hearing them enter behind him he pulled the curtains to, then Gudarniev switched on the light. As he did so the Marshal spoke. 'I wish to talk to these men alone, Ivan. You had better go and get something to eat now, then come back to collect them in an hour or so.'

In a single glance Gregory had taken in the room. It was low-ceilinged, of medium size and furnished in a comfortable modern style without any trace of ostentation. In its centre was a large table, at one end of which was a tray bearing the remains of the Marshal's supper; the rest of the table was strewn with maps. Near the window there was a large radiogram and, at the far end of the room, a bureau-bookcase, on the top of which were photographs of Stalin, the beautiful ex-ballet dancer Caterina Davydovna, whom Voroshilov had married, and several children. Grouped round the stove were a rather worn leather settee and two armchairs.

Gregory's eyes switched almost instantly towards the Marshal. Voroshilov was just sixty years of age, but he still appeared to be in the prime of life. His dark wavy hair was grey only above the ears, his eyes were bright and his square-jawed forceful face still had all the characteristics which had caused him, when a younger man, to be regarded as such a handsome fellow. His military tunic, with its big Marshal stars on the high collar, was undone and hung open, showing his white shirt. While Gudarniev left the room he stood with his hands clasped loosely behind his back regarding Kuporovitch with an intent, searching look, and even after the door had closed he continued his silent scrutiny for a full half minute.

'Well,' he said at last, in a sharp tone that boded no good to his visitors. 'What have you to say to me?'

'First, Marshal, permit me to recall to you my companion.' Kuporovitch waved a hand towards Gregory. '*Herr Oberst Baron* von Lutz.'

Voroshilov favoured Gregory only with a swift scowl, then turned back to his compatriot. 'Yes, I remember him now. He was one of the German Military Mission attached to my headquarters just before the Finnish surrender. There was some business about saving a woman from extradition by the Gestapo, and I ordered sledges to be provided for him so that he could cross the ice of Lake Ladoga by night. But, of course! It was to Kandalaksha that he was going and you were then Governor there. That was just before you disappeared from your post, and we all thought that you must have been murdered.

'But, Marshal!' Kuporovitch's dark eyebrows shot up in feigned surprise. 'Did you not get the letter that I left behind for you?'

'I got no letter. And, let me tell you, since you are alive you have no small amount of explaining to do. It is clear now that while commander of a fortress you deserted your post in the face of the enemy, and—'

'Not in the face of the enemy,' interrupted Kuporovitch stoutly. 'There was not a Finn within five hundred miles of me, and of all the dead-alive holes Kandalaksha—'

'Silence!' snapped the Marshal. 'Do you think that we send our Generals to garrison places for their own amusement? Wherever a soldier of the Republic is sent he should be proud and honoured to serve his country.'

'Yes, Marshal, yes. No one would dream of disputing that. It is only that I was hurt by your suggestion that I could ever be capable of deserting in the face of the enemy. After all, you should know me better than even to consider such a thing possible.'

'In any case, you admit that you deserted,' Voroshilov said, now slightly on the defensive. 'And you know the penalty for that.'

'On the contrary,' lied Kuporovitch boldly, 'I did not desert as you would know if only you had received the letter that I left for you.'

'Well, I did not!'

Never having written such a letter, Kuporovitch knew perfectly well that the Marshal could not possibly have received it, but he went on brazenly: 'That is most unfortunate, but it is not my fault. Had you done so you would be aware that I simply left one employment where, whatever I did was of little moment, for another, in which my work could be of the utmost value.'

'And who gave you permission to change your employment?'

'No one. The matter arose very suddenly. There was no time to consult my immediate superior. I had to take the responsibility for the decision myself. It was not easy, but I said to myself:

"Stefan Kuporovitch your country's interests come before everything else. This is a chance in a million to be of real service to the Soviets. This castle in the backwoods is well garrisoned, well provisioned and in no way threatened. Your real duty lies elsewhere. There you will meet sterner trials and carry your life in your hand; but what matter when true patriotism demands that you should seize this opportunity so amazingly thrust in your way? Never mind if you die unhonoured in a foreign land. Your old comrade of the Revolution, Clim Voroshilov, at least, will continue to have faith in you and if you are fated never to return, he will guess the grea thing that you died in attempting to do, and shed a silent tear for you." '

Gregory could not understand a single word they were saying to each other, but he felt from Kuporovitch's tone that his friend was putting up a remarkably good show, and he saw that the Marshal was visibly weakening as he muttered a trifle testily:

'How the hell could I guess what you were attempting, since I had never had this letter of which you speak?'

'Ah, tragedy, tragedy!' muttered Kuporovitch. 'But as you thought me dead, you wept for me all the same, no doubt? Anyway as there was no time to consult anyone, I simply gave myself leave of absence and—'

'What? For eighteen months!'

Kuporovitch spread out his hands and opened wide his blue eyes with an innocent expression. 'How was I to know how long my self-imposed mission would take? I wrote telling you of my decision and hinting at what I hoped to achieve. I naturally supposed that having known me all these years you would be only to pleased to regularise the position for me. It needed only one stroke of your pen to appoint a successor to my command at Kandalaksha, and another to place my name on the special employment list.'

'All right, all right. For the moment let us forget this precious letter of yours. Your having written makes no difference to the fact that leaving your post without permission to do so renders you liable to court-martial and a traitor's death.'

'But, my dear Marshal, if I were a traitor, is it likely that, of my own free will, I should have returned here to be shot?'

This argument seemed unanswerable, so Voroshilov murmured : 'Well, where have you been all this time?'

'Why, in Germany, of course!'

'The devil you have!' The ill-humour vanished from the Marshal's face and it suddenly lit up with intense interest.

'At least,' Kuporovitch amended, 'I was in Germany for most of the time, but I have spent the last few months in England, and have only just managed to get back from there.'

'And what were you doing in Germany?'

'Intelligence work on the highest level.'

'Explain yourself.'

'It was this way. Kandalaksha is a lonely place. No one worth talking to arrives there from year's end to year's end. Naturally, therefore, when Colonel Baron von Lutz returned from your headquarters in Finland I had him to dine with me. At that time, you will remember, the Germans were not "Hitlerite bandits". We had done a deal with them over Poland, and to all intents and purposes they were our "Gallant

163

Allies". But old hands like you and I knew that was only window-dressing and that the Germans and ourselves were only waiting for the word to cut one another's livers out.

'Well, it seemed to me too good an opportunity of pumping a high German staff officer to miss, so I filled the Baron full of vodka and got him talking. Far from being a Nazi, as I had supposed, it transpired that he hated Hitler and all his works. He even went so far as to say that he was one of a group of highly placed officers who considered Hitler had become a menace to Germany's best interests. They felt that his lust for power had unbalanced his mind, and that unless he were stopped in time he might saddle the German people with a greater weight of armed opposition than even they could stand up to and so, finally, bring them down to irredeemable defeat and ruin. In consequence, when the time was ripe, this group was determined either to remove or kill him.

'Naturally I was intensely interested in all this. I became even more so when the Baron said he was convinced that Hitler would break his promise to the German people about not waging a war on two fronts simultaneously, and meant to attack the Soviets. The Baron went on to say that then would be the time to strike at Hitler. As long as he was victorious he would have the support of the great mass of the German people and, even if he were eliminated, one of his colleagues with similar ideas would take his place. But once the Germans were given cause to doubt the final outcome and their casualties became really heavy, then a reaction would set in, and a *coup d'état* to restore peace before Germany had crippled herself seriously would become a practical possibility.'

The Marshal gave a quick nod. 'Such reasoning was sound enough. Well, what then?'

'It seemed to me that if Hitler was planning to attack the Soviet Union it was my duty to find out as much about his intentions as I possibly could.'

'So you went to Germany.'

'Yes. At first, I pretended not to believe the Baron, but he said to me:

' "All right then; come back to Germany with me and I will prove to you that I speak the truth. I can introduce you to a dozen high officers who are already working on the plans for the invasion of Russia. They are one and all opposed to the mad idea of launching a war in the east before the war in the west has been brought to a successful conclusion, because they are convinced that it must lead to Germany's ultimate defeat. But for the time being they must either continue to do as they are told or be disgraced and be removed from the positions of

164

authority in which, later, they can be of great service to their country." '

'That I understand. But surely it was not seriously suggested that these German staff officers would be prepared to disclose to you, a Soviet General, their plans for the invasion of the Soviet Union?'

'Indeed it was, Marshal. It was, and still is, the Baron's view that the Nazi régime could not be overthrown until the German people had lost their faith in it through the German Army suffering a series of reverses. He and his friends were prepared to accept such reverses as the price that Germany must pay if she was to escape far greater disasters later on. They were convinced that these reverses would not only provide them with the popular backing to overthrow the Nazi régime, but also furnish a new German Government with a suitable excuse to call off the war while Germany was still so formidable a power that she could insist on a peace which would leave her as strong, if not stronger, than she was before the war started. It follows that the sooner this series of reverses could be stage-managed the sooner the *coup d'état* could be brought off and the greater the strength Germany would still have left in reserve with which to bargain. Therefore it was the Baron's idea that I should return with him to Germany, and there be given the plans for the Nazi invasion of the Soviet Union, in order to ensure this series of defeats being inflicted on the German armies as soon as the invasion was launched.'

'You amaze me!'

Kuporovitch spread out his hands. 'I was amazed myself, but the whole conception was so logical that it seemed to me criminal not to accept such an offer.'

'But why should the Baron have made this suggestion to you, an isolated Fortress Commander, instead of getting into touch with our Intelligence people in Moscow?'

'The suggestion was quite unpremeditated. It arose spontaneously from this long talk that we had while drinking glass after glass together, far into the night. It was only through unforeseen circumstances that he arrived at Kandalaksha, and his plans were so immature at that time that he had not even considered approaching anyone in Russia about them. But we took an immediate liking to one another, and he insisted that I was the very man to undertake this great task.'

'Why you, rather than another?'

'For one reason, Marshal, because, as you will recall, I started life as a Czarist officer, and in my youth I travelled fairly widely. He felt that I talked the same language as these friends of his to whom he intended to introduce me, and that I should prove more acceptable to them than an officer of solely Bolshevik antecedents. But there was more to it than that. Had this mission been entrusted to an ordinary agent he might not have grasped the full significance of the German plans and failed to absorb certain important technical details, whereas that risk could be eliminated by confiding them to a Soviet General of many years' standing like myself.'

'But, surely, for a matter of such great importance, you could have found some way of delaying the Baron's departure until you had time to communicate his proposals to Moscow and ask official permission to undertake this mission?'

'Short of arresting him, which would immediately have destroyed his confidence in me and sabotaged any prospect of my securing this vital information, there was no way to do so. The ice was just breaking up in the Gulf of Finland. He had made arrangements to sail from Leningrad on a Norwegian tramp that was leaving immediately the channels were reported free of ice. He offered to take me with him to Oslo, and said that from there he would have no difficulty in making arrangements for me to enter Germany with him; but he was absolutely adamant in his refusal to delay his departure for even a few hours, as, had he done so, he might have missed his ship. I had to go with him or lose the magnificent chance to render my country a signal service. Having made up my mind to go. I realised that if I waited till morning the Political Commissar who was attached to my command might prevent my leaving, so we got him out of bed and locked him in the grain store—'

Voroshilov's eyes twinkled, and suddenly he laughed. 'Stefan you old devil! Surely you realise that many a Soviet General has been shot for less.'

'Kuporovitch smothered a sigh of relief by a loud guffaw. After this incredible tissue of lies that he had been compelled to tell he had at last got the Marshal laughing, so it looked as if they were almost out of the wood. With a happy, expansive grin, he replied:

'Hang it all, Clim! Who but yourself taught me the way to treat these snivelling spies that the *Ogpu* put upon us soldiers? Shall I ever forget how you chased War Lord Trotsky out of your headquarters at Tzaritsyn when he tried to interfere with you, and told him that he was no true Russian man, but only a dirty Jew scribbler! And later, in this very flat, when you were Military Governor of Leningrad—you can't have forgotten that pretty little girl you used to keep here—and how, when you found out that she had been set to spy on you by the Chief of the Leningrad *Ogpu*, you marched round to his office, blacked both his eyes and threw him down his own stairs.'

'Enough, enough!' The Marshal brushed these memories

166

aside with a wave of his hand and tried, not very successfully, to regain his dignity. 'We were young in those days. Things are different now. The Politicals have a difficult task and most of them do it well. Their work is a necessary part of the organisation of the State, and they are entitled to our cooperation and respect.'

'Yes, Marshal, yes,' Kuporovitch agreed smoothly. 'But this fellow was one of the stupid, officious kind, and not the sort of man I could possibly take into my confidence. It must have been he who suppressed the letter I left behind on my desk to be forwarded to you; no doubt to revenge himself on me for having locked him up. I suppose he simply put in a report that I had absconded during the night?'

Voroshilov nodded. 'As far as I remember, that was what happened. At all events, all I heard was that you had just disappeared, without leaving any indication as to whether you had met with an accident while out hunting early in the morning, been murdered, or gone off of your own free will. The Commissar probably thought he would look a fool if he admitted that you had locked him up in the grain store, so he burnt your letter and omitted the locking up from his report.'

'Exactly!' exclaimed Kuporovitch, with inward delight that this most satisfactory explanation should have been volunteered. 'And you will appreciate now why it was that I left Kandalaksha in the way I did.'

'You have at least made clear your object,' the Marshal agreed. He had relaxed his stern, judicial air and was now obviously intrigued. Turning to a side table on which were some bottles and glasses he added: 'Perhaps you and your friend would like a drink, while you tell me how it came about that you failed to achieve it.'

Murmuring their thanks, they joined him at the table while he mixed three brandies and sodas, then he motioned them towards the armchairs, and as they sat down, Kuporovitch replied:

'Ah, Marshal, my failure to get back before the invasion started was sad indeed; but it was through no fault of mine. I had the bad luck to be arrested by the Gestapo.'

'You're lucky to have got back at all then,' commented Voroshilov.

'I certainly am, and I owe my escape to the Baron here. But for nearly thirteen months I was in a Nazi concentration camp.'

'Could he do nothing to help you during all that time?'

'Very little, unfortunately. We got back to Germany early in April, nineteen-forty. I had been there about six weeks and had managed to assimilate most of the information regarding

German plans then available, when, by an unlucky fluke, a Gestapo man came to live in the same house as myself. His suspicions were aroused owing to my indifferent command of the German language. One night towards the end of May I was arrested without warning. They could find no fault in my cover story but apparently they were still unsatisfied; as, instead of letting me go, they sent me to Dachau.'

Kuporovitch took a long drink and went on: 'After a few weeks the Baron succeeding in finding out where I was and secretly got in touch with me. On three occasions my escape was planned but each time it was frustrated. The Commandant there was a fanatical supporter of Hitler, so nothing could be done through him, and after my unsuccessful attempts to get away he tumbled to it that people outside were trying to assist me. In consequence, my detention was made more rigorous and nothing could be done for me until the Commandant was changed. That did not occur until early June, but fortunately the new man could be bought, and he connived in my escape the week before Hitler launched his attack on the Soviet Union.'

'And then?'

'After my escape my description was, of course, circulated to all Gestapo and S.S. units, so the Baron and his friends would not accept the risk of allowing me to attempt getting back through Poland, and, in any case, it was then too late for them to pursue their original idea of my returning with plans to counter the invasion. They kept me in close hiding for a bit, then it was decided that the Baron should accompany me to Norway, and so round by the northern route to Russia. You see, it was felt that after my long absence I might no longer be believed when I got back, so he agreed to come with me in order to substantiate all that I am telling you.'

'But if you reached Norway early in July you should have been back here weeks ago!'

'Yes, yes. We should have been, had we not had the misfortune to be captured by the English!'

'Captured by the English!'

'Yes, Marshal,' Kuporovitch nodded solemnly. 'The Baron smuggled me out of Germany in a small tramp steamer that was scheduled to ply up the coast of Tromsö. It should have proved a convenient method of accomplishing the most dangerous part of our journey, but at dusk one evening, off Stavanger, we fell in with a British destroyer that was carrying out a reconnaissance of the Norwegian coast, and we were both taken prisoners.'

'And they took you back to England?'

'To Scotland first, and then to London. Fortunately, the

aron and myself were not separated, so we had a chance to
nsult as to what we should say. By that time Britain and
e Soviet Union had become Allies, so we decided to tell the
uth to the extent that I was a Soviet General and the Baron
a anti-Nazi, and add that we had a plan for sabotaging the
erman war effort which we would disclose only to one of the
niefs of the British Intelligence Service. This secured us
a interview with a Brigadier, to whom we felt we could talk
eely, and we told him about having been on our way to
ussia, and why. At first he obviously did not believe us, but
e was no fool; and at the end of our third meeting he agreed
at, while we might conceivably be of considerable value to
e Allied cause if he arranged for us to be sent to Moscow,
e certainly could be of no use to anyone as long as we re-
ained in a British prison.'

'How did you come?'

'Via Gibrlatar, the Middle East and Persia.'

'I find it surprising that the British should have allowed a
erman officer to travel freely through their war zones, what-
er he might have said about being an anti-Nazi.'

'They did not. During the six week's trip from London to
eheran we were under escort the whole time. What was sur-
ising is that they furnished us with English names and British
.ssports for our journey from Teheran to Moscow. But the
itish are a very peculiar people. It is intensely difficult to
nvince them of anything, except their own superiority. Yet,
ice you have got them to see your point of view they adopt
 as their own, and they will stick at nothing to carry it
rough. Our Brigadier was like that. Once he had made up
s mind that if we could reach you we might prove of real
lue, he made no difficulty about acceding to my request
at our real identities should not be disclosed to the Soviet
mbassy in London, and providing us with the means to
.vel incognito.'

'But why,' Voroshilov enquired with a puzzled frown, 'did
u wish to do that?'

Kuporovitch's dark eyebrows shot up. 'But, my dear Mar-
al, we could never have got here in any other way, or at
.st only after a further delay of perhaps months, while all
rts of enquiries were being made about us. Just imagine
at would have happened if we had presented ourselves at
e Soviet frontier in our true colours—a German staff officer
d a Soviet General who mysteriously disappeared from his
st eighteen months ago. They would never have allowed
 to proceed to Moscow. We should have been held up for
dless interrogations by the *Ogpu* and perhaps even shot as
ies. It was, of course, to prevent our mission being jeopar-

dised in such a way that the Brigadier gave us our Briti
passports and arranged for us to be attached to the Press se
tion of the British Embassy in Moscow until we could get
touch with you.'

Having at last completed this account of his long absenc
Kuporovitch finished his brandy-and-soda and sat ba
Every phase of the story had been worked out and dove-tail
by him and Gregory beforehand, with the cunning of tv
Machiavellis, so he had not had to think up any of his answe
to the Marshal's questions on the spur of the moment or mal
rash statements which might later cause him to contradict hir
self. All he had been called on to do was to say his piece wit
out hesitation and with complete assurance, and this, he fe
he had done.

At first sight such a series of unforeseen happenings, dela
arrests and expedients might seem extraordinary, but, spre
over eighteen months, they were no more extraordinary th
the hazards which were now befalling scores of people of
nations who were attempting to carry out secret missions co
nected with the war. Every point concerning his disappearan
from Kandalaksha with Gregory and their reappearance
Russia as British citizens had been fully explained, and the
was no incident upon which the Marshal could bowl them o
should he decided to institute a check-up.

The one and only weakness in the fabrication was the fa
that, had the story been true, Kuporovitch would certain
never have left Kandalaksha without leaving behind a lett
to one of his superiors to explain his disappearance, and th
of course, he had not done; yet, even if by some most unluc
chance his old Political Commissar happened, of all places
Russia, now to be in Leningrad, and the Marshal produc
him, it would still be only his word against that of his ex-Fc
tress Commander. But the odds against having to brazen o
this point were at easily a thousand to one.

However, the Marshal now appeared perfectly satisfied an
giving his old friend a pat on the shoulders, said with a smil
'Well, Stefan, you certainly seem to have had an excitir
time. It was hard luck being caught like that by the Naz
and if only you could have got back to us with all the infc
mation you had, before Hitler launched his armies, it wou
have been invaluable. Still, no doubt the information you ca
give us now will also be of great value.'

'Alas, Clim,' Kuporovitch sighed, 'events robbed me of t
rôle I had hoped to play. It is now over three months since
left Germany, and the strategic picture has changed out of
recognition since then; so there is little I can tell you of Ge
man intentions which would now be of any use. But at leas

ve brought the Baron back with me. Hitler is still victorious.

o series of reverses has yet occurred to shake the faith of the

erman masses in the wisdom of their *Führer,* but the Baron

d his friends remain unshaken in their view that only his

moval can save Germany from disaster in the end. I am con-

nced that if you can come to an understanding with the

aron the war could be immensely shortened and hundreds of

ousands of Russian lives would be saved. But it is better that

should put his ideas before you himself. Unfortunately he

eaks no Russian, but you speak a little German, do you

t?'

'*Nur ein kleines bisschen,*' replied the Marshal, with a self-
precatory shrug.

At this, the first words that Gregory had so far understood

the whole half-hour's conversation, he smiled at the Mar-

al and, raising his glass said, '*Prosit, Eure Exzellenz,*' before

allowing the remains of his drink.

Voroshilov courteously acknowledged the toast, then turned

ck to Kuporovitch. 'Please tell the Baron to speak slowly,

d to make his expressions as simple as possible. Such re-

arks as I do not understand I will ask you to interpret.' He

used for a moment, then added, 'But wait, before we start

me get you both another drink.'

Standing up, he went over to a little table by the window,

cked up a nearly emptied bottle, set it down and, muttering

mething to himself, left the room.

He was away for only a minute, and on his return hunted

rough the drawers in his desk until he found a fresh box

cigarettes from which to refill his case. He had hardly fin-

ed when his servant came in carrying three drinks, already

ured out, on a tray. The man offered them first to Kuporo-

ch, who took one, then to Gregory, who quite thoughtlessly

etched out his hand for the glass to his left, whereas he

ght normally have been expected to take that to his right.

noring the direction his hand was taking, the man turned the

y a little, so that, except by making a fresh movement, he

uld not avoid picking up the right-hand glass after all.

He took it and, instead of drinking from it at once, set it

wn beside him. The servant's movement of the tray had

en so slight that it might quite well have been accidental,

t, nevertheless, Gregory was vaguely perturbed. That sixth

nse which had so often before warned him of impending

nger now conveyed to him an insistent impression that the

ght-hand glass had been deliberately forced upon him.

On the face of it the idea seemed absurd. All three drinks

oked exactly the same and appeared to be a second round

the brandy-and-soda that they had had before. It then came

back to him that the almost empty bottle the Marshal h
held up just before leaving the room had not looked like
brandy bottle.

Voroshilov and Kuporovitch were now talking togeth
again in Russian. Unnoticed by either of them, Gregory stu
bed out his half-smoked cigarette and thrust his hand do
his hip pocket for his case, to get out another. The moveme
enabled him to turn quite naturally, so that he could get
swift glance at the little group of bottles which were alm
behind him. He had not been mistaken; the almost emp
bottle looked as though it had held some kind of red wine a
the brandy bottle was still half full. Why, then, should
Marshal have gone out to tell his servant to open a fresh o
and bring in this second round of drinks instead of maki
them up himself at the table?

The more Gregory thought about the matter the m
puzzled he became. The idea that the Marshal intended
poison or drug them was simply fantastic. If through some f
tor outside their knowledge he was aware that Kuporovi
had been grossly deceiving him, he had only to press a bell
order to have his visitors thrown into prison or, if his rese
ment went that far, shot out of hand. With such resources
his immediate disposal no sane man would dream of litteri
up his flat with corpses or unconscious bodies and there co
be no doubt about the Marshal's sanity. Yet Gregory wo
have wagered a fortune now that Voroshilov had gone outsi
to give some special instructions to his servant and that
the drink he had been given had been tampered with.

Gregory's two companions were now laughing heartily
gether over some good joke, and Kuporovitch had obviou
completely won his way back into the good graces of his
Chief; which seemed to make the matter even more unacco
table. As they stopped laughing Kuporovitch turned to G
gory and, explaining their hosts' limited knowledge of G
man, asked him to go ahead.

Smiling encouragement, Voroshilov raised his glass and sa
'Prosit, Herr Baron.'

Compelled to follow suit, Gregory raised his, but he to
only a small mouthful, suddenly pretended to choke, a
whipping out his handkerchief, coughed the liquor into it, th
avoiding having to swallow any.

It was brandy-and-soda all right, although much stron
than the first one he had had. As the stuff had been in
mouth for only a moment it was difficult to judge if anyth
else had been mixed with it. He thought he detected a swee
flavour than had been noticeable in his first drink, but t
might easily have been accounted for by the fact that it v

172

sweet Caucasian brandy and he had been given a much stronger proportion of it than he had had before.

With a smile of apology he set down his glass, and, speaking very slowly and clearly, began:

'My friend will have told you, Marshal, of our adventures and how we came to set out upon them. In Germany the situation has altered little from what it was eighteen months ago. Hitler gained great additional prestige through his victorious campaigns in Norway, Belgium, Holland and France last summer. This spring, too, he added further to his laurels by his conquest of Yugoslavia, Greece and Crete. But these victories have now to some extent been offset by his campaign against Russia and the considerable increase in the British air raids against German cities. It is true that the German armies have overrun great areas of Russian territory, but, for the first time, they are meeting with casualties in sufficient numbers to cause considerable concern to the German people. Again, the war has now been actually brought into the German homeland by R.A.F. raids of really serious proportions. These factors—'

Gregory was suddenly interrupted by the shrilling of the telephone. With a murmured apology Voroshilov got up and walked over to his bureau to answer it. As he did so his back was turned towards them, and remained so for a few minutes while he carried on a low-voiced conversation. Gregory's suspicions had been lulled but not entirely satisfied by the one sip of his drink. Instinctively, on the principle that it was better safe than sorry, the moment he saw that the Marshal's attention was fully engaged he leaned forward and swiftly exchanged their drinks.

Kuporovitch stared at him in amazement, but he quickly motioned him to remain silent. The Russian took a sip of his own drink, tasted it with his tongue, then, evidently finding nothing wrong with it, shook his head and shrugged his shoulders, as though to say that his friend must be crazy.

Having finished his conversation Voroshilov rejoined them. As he sat down he picked up the glass that Gregory had just placed beside his chair and took a long drink from it. Gregory followed suit. He felt sure now that the liquor he had first been given was slightly sweeter. A sudden awful thought came to him. Suppose by exchanging their drinks he had poisoned the Marshal? If he had they would soon find themselves in a most ghastly mess. Still, even that was better than being poisoned himself. In any case the next ten minutes now looked like being as acutely anxious as any that he had ever experienced. He could only pray to all his gods that he had been imagining things.

173

'You were saying ...' prompted Voroshilov, as he set down his glass.

'Oh, yes,' Gregory recalled himself with a start to the business in hand. 'I was saying that the result of the heavy casualties this summer and the increased bombing of German towns has largely nullified the effect of Hitler's more recent victories, so that the German people are neither more nor less conditioned to accept an anti-Nazi *Putsch* than they were when Stefan and I left Kandalaksha. In short, that a considerable amount of working up is still required before they can be brought to a state of mind satisfactory to our purpose.'

'You still have, though, a reliable nucleus that would be prepared to act when the time is ripe?' enquired the Marshal.

'Certainly,' Gregory nodded. 'Most of the key personalities of the Great General Staff and about half the garrison commanders in Germany itself are definitely committed to give us their support; and the inner ring, which will be responsible for the actual *coup*, is so dispersed that no betrayal could affect more than a small number of its members.'

'All you need then is a period of adversity which will bring discredit on the Nazi régime and dispose the people to accept its replacement by another?'

'Yes. Or, if that is not forthcoming, some critical phase of the war which could be turned to our advantage.'

The Marshal took another drink, but to Gregory's anxious gaze he showed no indication whatever of being adversely affected; in fact, he seemed, if anything, more alert and more lively than before, as he said:

'Explain that please, I do not quite understand you.'

Kuporovitch repeated what had been said in Russian, and Gregory added: 'For example, if the Soviet armies suddenly stood firm, that would produce the state of tension and uncertainty I have in mind. The German nation has become so accustomed to victory that any serious check would come as a great shock to the people. If your armies dug their toes in and every attempt at a break-through was frustrated it would argue an enormous hidden reserve of power in the Soviets upon which the Nazis had not reckoned. Once there emerges any real doubt about Germany's ability to win hands down it would spread with great rapidity and its results might be catastrophic. The shock of the very idea that the war might finally end in Germany's defeat would be swiftly followed by a period of acute anxiety. If the Nazis were then replaced by a Government favouring an immediate peace by arbitration a feeling of heartfelt relief would be certain to sweep the country.'

'The entry of the United States into the war on our side might also have that effect?'

174

'It might, Marshal, and it certainly looks now as if the Americans mean to come in before the year is out; but I doubt if that would have any immediate influence on the situation. It would take two years at least for them to train and equip an army of sufficient size to make a successful landing on the continent.'

'You mean that only a major check or defeat of the German Army would bring about the loss of confidence in the Nazi Government that you require?'

'Yes, and it seems to me that for a long time to come Russia is the only country capable of inflicting such a check.'

For some minutes they talked on quietly reviewing the world situation. Here and there Kuporovitch put in a sentence in Russian, making clear to the Marshal something that Gregory had said, and all the time Gregory, concealing his uneasiness, watched him like a lynx, not knowing exactly what to expect, but fearing some change of expression or manner which might indicate that he was right in his belief that something had been put into the drink.

After a little he became aware that there was a change, but it was not of the kind that he had vaguely feared. When they had arrived the Marshal, although evidently in excellent health had appeared a little tired from the strain of command and the long hours he worked, but now he had become much more animated. He was talking more freely, laughing at frequent intervals and evidently giving his views with complete candour on every subject that arose.

Having reviewed the war fronts right round from Norway, through the Mediterranean to Persia, they came back to Russia and, feeling that the time had come to take the plunge, Gregory said:

'My purpose in making this long journey and seeking this interview with you, Marshal is to see if we cannot agree on an appropriate date for my friends inside Germany to strike. Naturally, the *coup* itself will need very careful preparation and that will take a little time. On the other hand, it would be highly dangerous to set the wheels in motion too early. Do you feel that, without disclosing more of Russia's strategy than you would wish to do, you can give me some idea of her prospects?'

'At present we are faced with many difficulties,' the Marshal admitted frankly. 'But these will be overcome. It would be of great assistance to us if the Second Front could be opened sooner than you consider possible, but even if it is never opened at all the Soviets will defeat Germany. About that I have not one shadow of doubt.'

'May I ask upon what you base this complete confidence?'

'For one thing, on our man-power. Germany is a nation of eighty million people; even with her satellites Finland, Hungary and Rumania the total is only one hundred and thirty million, whereas our population is over two hundred million.'

'You will forgive me remarking that numbers alone count for little in modern war. Russia's great reserves of manpower will be of no appreciable value to her unless she can train them and put them in the field with the most up-to-date weapons.'

'The Soviet arms factories have already surpassed their planned production.'

'But is that enough. Can they produce nearly double the output of the German factories; as that is what they will need to do if your preponderance of man-power is to be made fully effective?'

Again the Marshal answered with complete frankness. 'No, they cannot. But America will help us under a Lease-Lend arrangement similiar to that which she has with Britain, and we also have hopes that the British themselves will send us large quantitites of tanks, lorries and aircraft.'

'Even so, there is one thing you seem to have left out of your calculations. In addition to her satellites Germany also now controls Czechoslovakia, Norway, Holland, Belgium, Yugoslavia, Greece, Poland, and more than half of France. In consequence she now has at her disposal a huge reservoir of slave labour. This can be used not only in war factories but in mines, agriculture, transport and innumerable other employments on the Home Front which would otherwise have to be filled by Germans. In Russia, on the other hand, every single thing, not only for the war effort but also to keep the country going, must be done by your own people. The inevitable result is that Germany can afford to draft a far higher percentage of her man-power into her armed forces than you can.'

Voroshilov laughed. 'But my dear *Herr Baron*, your statement shows how little you Germans really know about the Soviet Army. It is organised on lines completely different from that of any other state. Listen, and I will tell you about it.'

Gregory needed no enjoinder to do so. He could hardly believe it himself, but the vital information which he had always thought would be so difficult to obtain was now being handed to him on a plate. With vivid, enthusiastic gestures Voroshilov began to describe the general layout of the great force in the creating of which he had played such a decisive part.

'Our Army,' he said, 'is composed of three stratas. First, there are the Shock Troops. These form an army in themselves

176

—an army far larger than those maintained in peacetime by Britain and the United States put together. Every man in it is a regular who has done at least four years' service. They are highly paid, extremely well disciplined, trained to perfection and armed with every weapon that science has so far devised. Even Germany cannot put better troops in the field, and their artillery is unquestionably the finest in the world.

'The second strata consists of Holding Troops. These form the great bulk of our Army. They are regulars with some training, or reservists. Their equipment is of a good modern standard and they are capable of giving battle to the average troops of any European power. In many instances they have already proved their ability to launch successful local attacks and, generally speaking, they put up a good tough resistance when they are on the defensive, which is their main rôle at the present time.

'The third strata consists of our new intakes—the huge volume of raw material that in most cases has had no military training: but I will speak of these in a moment.'

Voroshilov finished the rest of his drink and, his face now flushed a little, went on: 'All other armies integrate their forces. A few crack divisions are pushed in cheek by jowl with less reliable ones for the launching of each new offensive, or if a break-through is threatened, they are brought up to stiffen resistance. But we have evolved an entirely different principle of warfare. Our second strata alone is responsible for manning the entire front, whether we are advancing or falling back. The first strata is used entirely as an army of manœuvre and is always kept at the Commander-in-Chief's disposal. It is never split up, and bits of it used to stop gaps or to form a spearhead for a local offensive. It works intact as an Army Group itself and must be used only for the launching of a major strategic offensive or for the defence of some vital point which it would be disastrous to sacrifice.'

'Has it been used yet?' Gregory asked boldly.

'Only once. At the beginning of this month it was considered necessary to delay the German advance on our central front, so it was placed under Timoshenko. In the fighting round Smolensk and Gomel it fully justified the confidence we had placed in it. Not only did it carry out its mission, but it smashed General Guderian's Panzer Army—the finest troops that the Germans could send against it—and recaptured a great area of territory. It tore a great gap in the German line and could have gone clean through, but its flanks would have been exposed them; so, having done what was required, it was recalled and placed in reserve again. But you see the immense advantage of this new system. While other armies fritter away their best troops by using them all the time, just because they are the best, we use ours only for some special effort which is of real importance to us.'

'Indeed I do,' Gregory agreed, as he thought to himself that this alone was proof enough that Russia, far from being on the verge of defeat, as was generally believed in London, still had many months, if not years, of fight left in her.

'You were going to tell me,' he prompted, 'about your intakes.'

'Oh, yes. We are speaking just now of the man-power question. Here, again, the Soviet principle differs from that of all other modern armies. I came to the conclusion a long time ago that other nations had lost all sense of proportion in the numbers of troops they were allocating to non-combatant duties. In the wars of the Revolution every man was as good as a bayonet or a sabre, but the organisation of the armies of the western Powers has now become so complicated that it takes twenty men to keep one soldier in the field. The Red Army was also developing along those lines, so I eliminated practically the whole of the administrative and supply services.'

'But Marshal!' Gregory almost gasped. 'How could you possibly run a modern war machine without them?'

For some little time Voroshilov had been speaking so fast that he had difficulty in finding German words to express himself, and occasionally he broke into Russian, but Kuporovitch understood all he said and frequently put in a quick word so that Gregory could follow his meaning.

'It is quite simple,' the Marshal smiled. 'The life of every man in Russia belongs to the Soviets. When a man is called up he says good-bye to his family and, although they may hope to see him again one day, they do not expect to do so. It is better both for them and for him as a soldier that all such ties should be forgotten. Therefore, no parcels are sent and no letters are exchanged. We have no army postal service in the Soviet Union.

'Again, pay is redundant—at least in the accepted sense of a regular remuneration. Soldiers do not need money while they are fighting. All commanders are simply issued from time to time with funds in bulk, and when a formation is resting, or in some area where money can buy recreation, they are responsible for distributing lump sums to their various units. But no books are kept, so we are not burdened with a Pay Department.

'Records, too, have been practically eliminated. How long an officer or man has been in the Army is not of the slightest interest to us. It is what he does during his service that matters. Stalin himself, in consultation with the Marshals, nominates the senior commanders, but from the Army Groups downwards it is left to the man on the spot. I pick my own subordinates down to Divisional Commanders. They pick their Colonels, and Colonels have authority to make officers, as required, from the most promising men in their units. In this way the promotion of the best men is never blocked for long, and a really intelligent fellow can reach quite a high rank in a very short time. In addition this is achieved without waste of time, personnel or a single scrap of paper.'

'It is amazing,' Gregory murmured. 'And, of course, there is no reason why it should not work. Still, I don't see how you manage to get on without supply services.'

'We have them, but in an immensely simplified form. As with pay, so with munitions. All types of arms and equipment are sent to senior commanders in bulk. They divide them up, and lower formations receive them as required. But no records are kept and no forms are used. There is a certain wastage, but that is more than counter-balanced by the swiftness with which the fighting units receive their urgent requirements.'

'How about rations?'

'There again everything is simplified. Nine-tenths of our men were born on the land, so they know how to live on it. Bread is, therefore, the only ration issued to the Soviet troops, apart from exceptional cases in which formations are fighting in areas which cannot possibly support them. As they retreat, meat, corn, oil, wine, root crops are all consumed so that none shall be left for the enemy. The supplies of bread are also issued in bulk and no record is kept of its disposal.'

'Such a method may serve while your army is retreating, but it could hardly be so if you launch a counter-offensive and it is successful.'

The Marshal nodded. 'We may then have to send bulk supplies of meat with the bread trains, but, generally speaking, the principle will be adhered to. If a break-through occurs the Germans will not have time to destroy all their food dumps, and in any case our armoured formations are specially organised for just such a penetration. They will work in groups of five tanks, each group being independent and with orders to race ahead, entirely irrespective of what may be happening on its flanks, to the limit of its endurance. Every five fighting tanks will have a supply tank attached to them. This will be loaded to capacity with bread and petrol, and a girl—'

'A girl!' exclaimed Gregory.

'Why yes, a girl to cook whatever food the twenty-five men in the group may capture, and render them other services.'

Voroshilov's eyes were shining with excitement. He picked up his glass and, seeing that it was empty, got up and mixed

179

himself another drink. It seemed to Gregory that his movements were a little unco-ordinated, as though he were slightly drunk, but he was in tremendous spirits and his mind seemed perfectly clear as he came back, and went on:

'You see everything—every conceivable thing—has been thought out to save time and paper work, and prevent useful officers and men being wasted sitting about behind the lines in offices, or being employed in a non-fighting capacity. That even applies to training. The Germans, the British, the French, treat their new intakes as though they meant to make regular soldiers of them. They are given courses in this and lectures on that and months of rigorous drill on their barrack squares. Then they are made to participate in endless exercises, just as though they were a peacetime army. But in a war like this all that nonsense is entirely unnecessary. Now that is what happens to our new intakes.

The Marshal sat forward eagerly and Gregory strove as he had never striven before to get the gist of his mongrel German interspersed with snatches of Russian, and Kuporovitch did all he could to interpret the sense of his old friend's rapid monologue.

'Our call-ups are entirely arbitrary. We don't bother about age groups and all that sort of thing, except locally. Every district commander behind the lines draws on the local population as required each week. Our only concern is that every one of them should keep his depot filled to capacity. The raw material is bathed, shaved, clothed and paraded. They are not taught to form fours or any such useless idiocy, but on their second day they are given a sub-machine gun apiece and taught how to clean, oil and use it. Their only training is in how best to take cover and what to do with a hand grenade. On average they get about three weeks of that; after which they are considered fit to fight in defence of their country.'

'Do you mean to say that you take men off the land and in less than a month send them into battle against the Germans?'

'Why not? A small percentage, who show more than average intelligence, are selected for the signal schools or sent for additional training in other specialised capacities, but for the great majority further training would be sheer waste of time. From their depots they are despatched direct to Army Group Pools, and from there they are issued in the same way as munitions and equipment—to any formation commander who is in need of replacements.'

'But when they reach the front they can hardly be more than a rabble, and they cannot have absorbed even the rudiments of discipline.'

Voroshilov laughed. 'A rabble perhaps, but an armed rabble

180

As for discipline, they know that either disobedience or cowardice is punishable by death. But we very rarely have to resort to such measures. Perhaps you have not realised, *Herr Baron,* that the one desire of nine hundred and ninety-nine of every thousand of these men is to get at and kill some of your country men.'

'All the same. I should have thought that it would have proved terribly difficult for the officers to handle such material effectively.'

'Not at all. If an advance is in progress all they are required to do is to go forward as far as their legs and such food as they can collect will carry them, shooting at any German they may see. If they are sent to a sector where a retreat is in progress they are told to find the best cover they can and that they are not to fall back until they have accounted for at least one of the enemy. Those who survive for a few weeks become better soldiers through their actual experience in battle than any we could make by keeping them for a year in schools and training camps.'

'Your casualties among these learners must be pretty heavy, though?'

'They are, but not exceptionally so; and the flow of replacements is unceasing. At the present rate of wastage we could go on filling the gaps for years without being seriously affected and think of the enormous advantage we gain by this system. Instead of slaughtering fifty per cent of our best troops in the first few months of battle we have been able to conserve them for employment at a time of our own choosing; while we make the Germans pay for every yard of territory they gain by using our second strata troops reinforced by almost untrained man-power.'

Gregory was thinking that already, and he had been quick to realise that he now had a most definite answer to one part of the riddle he had set out to solve. This entirely new conception of using raw material to waste away the best forces of the enemy while keeping your own crack troops up your sleeve was positively staggering. He did not think it could possibly have worked anywhere except in a vast land like Russia, and with the special circumstances in which the Russian people had been nurtured for the past twenty years. But if they found it practical to put farm hands into the front line after only a month's training there could obviously be no question at all of the flow of replacements for the fighting units drying up.

In the meantime the Marshal was going on again. 'You will appreciate too, the enormous advantage that our simplification of the supply system and virtual abolition of administra-

181

tive departments gives us. You were contending just now that owing to the employment of great numbers of slave workers the Germans could put a higher proportion of their manpower into the field than we could, but our elimination of noncombatant establishments more than cancels that out, so, in actual fact, the boot is on the other foot.'

'I certainly begin to understand now your unbounded confidence in ultimately defeating my country,' Gregory admitted. 'But the question remains as to how long it will take you to do it. And, of course, a change of Government here might undermine the will to fight in your people, just as much as one in Germany would adversely affect the morale of our armies.'

'A change of Government!' exclaimed Voroshilov. 'But such a thing is impossible here. The situations in Germany and in the Soviet Union are not comparable. The bulk of your General Staff apparently regard Hitler as a dangerous maniac, whereas the whole of ours looks up to Stalin as a wise and brilliant leader. If you are thinking of the Trotskyites, or the pro-Germans who conspired together under the leadership of Marshal Tukachevsky, forget them. All such traitors were liquidated by us years ago.'

'All the same, Marshal, a change might be forced upon you. I understand that for some years past Premier Stalin has been suffering from trouble with his heart. The very fact that from the highest to the lowest you have such faith in his leadership would make his loss all the more serious.'

Voroshilov put his hands to his sides, sat back in his chair and roared with laughter. When he had recovered a little, he gasped: 'Forgive me, *Herr Baron*, but the joke was too much for me. Just to think that you highly-placed Germans should still believe that old story. It was nothing but a rumour deliberately put out by us during the months that the Tukachevsky conspiracy was being cleared up. We decided in the Polit-Bureau that until all who had been involved had been traced and liquidated we could not allow our beloved Comrade to make any public appearance, and so expose himself to possible assassination. The story that he was suffering from an affection of the heart was simply an excuse for his absence for a time from all important functions. No, you may rest easy on that score. Stalin is only two years older than myself, and as fit a man as I am.'

The second part of Gregory's secret questionnaire had now been answered in the same unequivocal manner as the first. He could only pray now that he would meet with equal good fortune regarding the third; yet he approached it with considerable trepidation, since, staggeringly frank as the Marshal had been on other matters, it still seemed almost unbelievable

182

that he would be prepared to disclose Russia's future strategy to a man whom he believed to be a German officer shortly about to return to Germany, and for whose integrity he had only the word of his old friend Stefan Kuporovitch.

It was, however, now or never, so Gregory took the plunge and make a skilful lead in.

'All that concerns me, Marshal, is that we should work together to bring this war, which is wasting both our countries, to an end as speedily as possible. That can best be achieved by co-ordinating the time when I and my friends should strike at Hitler, with a major Russian victory, or at least a definite check to the advance of the German armies. Can you give me any indication when such an event is likely to occur?'

Voroshilov shook his head, then wiped his forehead with a handkerchief, as he was now perspiring slightly, before he replied. 'No, it is almost impossible to forecast at the present time. While the Germans continue to hold the initiative and we rely on a high percentage of practically untrained troops to maintain some sort of line, we are in no position to plan counter-offensives in advance.'

'But you have this magnificent reserve Army Group of first strata troops, which you can use at any time.'

'True, and we have used them to slow down the rate of the German advance in our centre, but we dare not gamble them in a full scale counter-offensive on any one sector while the rest of our front remains unstable. However, time will adjust that, in two ways. Firstly, every day that passes a few thousand of Germany's first line troops become casualties, and, secondly, ever greater numbers of our new levies are rapidly becoming old soldiers from their battle experience and qualifying themselves for transfer to artillery, engineer and tank units. The time must come, therefore, when the German advance will be held, and we can use our crack troops in a counter-offensive of real strategic importance.'

'You may have to use them before that,' Gregory hazarded. 'Germany's campaigns in Poland, Norway, the Low Countries and the Balkans were so short and swift that her losses were almost negligible, and she has now had two years of war to train her reserves, so when the German Army marched into Russia it was more powerful than ever before. I am convinced that it will be able to campaign for many months yet without showing any perceptible loss of vigour.'

'I think you are probably right about that.'

'Well then, how much more territory can you afford to lose? You have already been deprived of Minsk, Smolensk, Novgorod, Pskov, Bryansk, Gomel, Zhitomir, Roslavel Dnepropetrovsk, Cherkasy, Nikolaiev and Kherson, all valuable manufacturing towns, while Leningrad, Odessa and Kiev—three of your seven biggest cities—are now surrounded and can no longer assist your war effort, except by holding out. I know that in recent years you have created great armament plants behind the Urals, but a war cannot be fought on men and armament plants only. An innumerable variety of products are required to keep a great army in the field, your plants supplied and your munitions workers fed, housed and clothed. With every town you lose, your command of certain war essentials lessens and, if the Germans continue to force you back, a time must come when you can no longer carry on the war from lack of vital necessities.'

'You are right again. Look! I will show you!' Voroshilov jumped up, lurched slightly, and fumbled among the maps on his table. Finding one that showed the whole of European Russia, with the approximate front marked on it, he spread it out while his visitors stood up and looked over his shoulder. Then, stubbing down the square tip of his forefinger on Baku, he went on, still speaking fast but a little thickly:

'Oil is the most important of those war essentials of which you speak. But the Germans still have eight hundred miles to go before they reach the shores of the Caspian, and personally I believe that their effort will be spent long before they can menace our principal oilfields. Yet, if our armies were cut off from the main producing centres that would be almost disastrous. Look now how the oil comes to us.'

His thick finger traced the line of the Volga from its mouth on the Caspian at Astrakhan in a great sweep northwestward to Stalingrad, then north and slightly east to Saratov; after which the great river turned north-eastwards to Kubishev but further up curved back again in a huge arc to the north of Moscow.

'You see! In peace the Volga is the greatest commercial highway in European Russia, and in war it forms the backbone for our lateral communications. All the oil comes up it in barges, and from it there radiate canals and railways to all parts of the front, by means of which the armies are supplied. Therefore the retention of the line of the Volga is vital to us. Now, observe the great bend that it makes westwards towards the Ukraine. The arc of that brings the river much nearer to the Germans than it is at any other point, so, if they still have strength enough left when they get there, that is obviously where they will attempt to cut it. On the apex of the bend stands Stalingrad. Twenty-three years ago this autumn, the defeat or victory of the Russian working-man in his war against tyranny depended on the retention of this city. It was

en called Tzaritsyn. Well, we held it, and the Revolution
iumphed over the forces of reaction.

'We now fight a still greater war against a new tyranny. It
ay be that once again victory or defeat will hang upon the
tention of Stalingrad. The loss of Moscow would be a great
ow to us. Naturally we shall hold it if we can, but even the
ss of the capital would not prejudice the final outcome of the
ar. The loss of Stalingrad and all that it implies would de-
itely do so. Therefore, of one thing you may be certain. If
e Germans get near enough to menace the city the flower of
e Soviet Army will be thrown in without reserve. Even if
lf a million of our finest troops have to lay down their lives
ere, the German armies will break themselves upon that
ck, the Volga will be kept open and the People's Republic
ll emerge victorious.'

As he finished speaking there was a brief silence, then
regory said: 'Thank you, Marshal. You have given me all
at I require. If the German armies reach the approaches of
alingrad that will be my cue. During the month or six weeks
at it will take to make the final preparations for our *Putsch*
ey will be held there and, for the first time, the German
:ople will begin to lose their faith in Nazi leadership. That
ll be the psychological moment for us to strike, and as soon
my friends are in power we shall propose a general armis-
:e. We shall have saved Germany from the fate to which
itler's crazy ambition is leading her, and you, I hope, will
:ver be called upon to sacrifice the finest of your Russian
uth.'

Voroshilov passed his hand over his eyes and swayed
ghtly. For some time Kuporovitch had been regarding him
ith puzzled anxiety. Now he said: 'You're tired, Clim. You've
en taking too much out of yourself.'

'No,' replied the Marshal, with a quick shake of his head.
m all right.' And he turned back to Gregory.

'You realise, *Herr Baron*, that your troops may never get
thin a hundred miles of Stalingrad. What happens then?'

'Once it becomes obvious—making the allowances for winter
that the general advance has begun to lose its momentum,
e shall start our preparations, then a fortnight or so after the
st major German defeat we shall act.'

'Good, I am glad of that, as you Germans are tenacious
hters and otherwise it might mean another year of war be-
re we could drive your troops right out of Russia. You know
am only a soldier by accident. I am really a man of peace. I
e to make things, not break them; and I want to see the
ung people of our new Russia happy and prosperous, not
ring by the thousand, years before their time.'

185

There was a sharp knock on the door and Colonel Guada niev came in.

'Hello, Ivan!' the Marshal greeted him with a vague smil 'Have you come to collect our friends? Well, I think we' settled everything. I've told them all that they want to know

A look of surprise came into the Colonel's dark eyes as th took in his Chief's perspiring face and the marked maps sprea out on the table and he asked: 'What is it that you've bee telling them, Clim?'

The question was put with the easy familiarity of a person staff officer, and the Marshal answered at once:

'Oh, all sorts of things about the build-up of our force and how we mean to beat these Hitlerite bandits. It has bee a very valuable talk and I hope great things will come of it.'

The Colonel's face showed some concern as he said quickl 'Are you feeling quite all right? You don't look too good. anything the matter with you?'

'No,' Voroshilov stagged back to his chair and flopped dow into it. 'I'm a bit tired now, that's all. I'll get to bed as soon you've all gone.'

Gregory had known for the past half hour that somethi was radically wrong with the Marshal, and he could see th Gudarniev sensed it, but there was nothing he could do or sa as they were talking in Russian again, so he could not unde stand what was being said.

In an attempt to set the Colonel's mind at rest Kuporovit laughed and remarked: 'We've all had quite a drop to drin and after such a long day a last brandy often makes one a t unsteady on the legs.'

'That's it,' agreed Voroshilov with tired cheerfulness, th he turned to Gudarniev. 'Take our friends back to the clu Ivan, and give orders that they are to have everything th want. Tomorrow we will make arrangements to get the He Baron out of the city, but we must discuss first what route he take. It would be best if we dropped him from an aircra somewhere in Esthonia, I think. He should be able to make l way back to Germany quite easily from there.'

'Back to Germany!' repeated Gudarniev, with a puzzl glance at Gregory. 'The Herr Baron?'

'That's right. That's where he wants to go. Well, I must g to bed.'

They said good night to him, then Gudarniev politely show them out to the lift and down to the main hall of the buildin

As they accompanied the Colonel their feelings were extr ordinarily mixed. Both of them were filled with elation at t thought that they had got the information they had come Russia to get. Every ounce of it and more. But they were co

ous that some quite abnormal agency had helped them to
tain it. No words of theirs could normally ever have caused
e Marshal to speak to two people, whom he had only an
ur or so before regarded as most dubious characters, with
ch complete disregard for the dictates of security. They
d hoped to pick up just a hint or two out of which they
ght afterwards make something tangible; but to be given
 whole picture had been beyond their wildest dreams. It
d almost seemed as if Voroshilov had been temporarily out
his mind, or under the influence of a spell. But their feeling
triumph was undermined by a most disconcerting uneasi-
s, since they felt certain that Colonel Gudarniev was also
are that the Marshal had not been himself.

Their perturbation grew when, down in the hall, the Colonel
mmoned two soldiers to accompany them out to a waiting
. It might be a regulation always to escort visitors to the
ieged city in this way, but armed guards seemed redundant
en the visitors had been referred to by the Marshal as his
ends.

In the semi-darkness outside it was difficult to make out the
ite that the car was taking, but after a little it seemed to
em that the journey had already lasted longer than it had
 their coming from the Astoria. A few minutes later the
 pulled up, but the block before which it had halted was
t the Officer's Club.

As he stepped from the car Gregory had half a mind to bolt
 it. He was now in the possession of secrets of inestimable
lue to his country. It had already occurred to him that Gud-
iev might have decided to disobey the Marshal's order.
at seemed unlikely, yet why had he brought them to the tall
oomy building that now loomed up across the pavement,
tead of taking them back to the Astoria? If it was some
m of trap and he once allowed himself to be caught in it,
 might never get back to London with the invaluable in-
mation that he had obtained. On the other hand, if he took
 his heels one of the armed guards might shoot him in the
ck. Then he would never get back to London anyway.

He was still hesitating when Gudarniev said to Kuporovitch:
have brought you here because I felt that I could provide
ich more suitable quarters for you than you had at the
toria.'

Kuporovitch, who had also been acutely apprehensive of
at the next few moments might bring, translated to Gregory,
d, with a sudden easing of the tension that both had been
ling, they turned and followed Gudarniev, while the two
ldiers brought up the rear.

As they passed through the heavy doors of the building they

187

saw that the hall had a bleak, official look. A man in the u
form of the *Ogpu* sat at a desk at its far end and two m
stood near the doorway, the second Kuporovitch caught si,
of the uniforms he took a quick step back, turned, and wit
shout to Gregory, attempted to regain the street.

But the two guards barred the path. As Gregory swu
round, they found themselves looking down the muzzles
sub-machine guns.

Gudarniev had turned too. While Gregory was aware o
of the sudden hostility in his voice, his low fierce whis
hissed into Kuporovitch's ears with the venom of a rat
snake.

'You filthy Nazi spies! How you did it, I don't know. I
somehow, tonight, you managed to administer to our Marsh
the Truth drug.'

13

The Truth, and Nothing but the Truth

The street, freedom, and all that freedom meant were st
only a couple of yards away, yet a barrier as impassable as
steel wall now shut Gregory and Stefan off from it. Even
they had instantly flung themselves upon the two fur-cla
troopers and borne them down, before they could have g
the heavy doors open again Gudarniev and the armed me
inside the hall would have shot them from behind. As it wa
the two soldiers already had their fingers on the triggers (
their weapons. At one word from Gudarniev they could hav
filled the prisoners full of lead. There was nothing they coul
do but obey their captor, as he snapped at them:

'Come along. I promised you more suitable accommoda
tion, and, by heavens, you shall have it! Two cells in the base
ment are the place for you, for the rest of the night; tomorro
we'll find you two yards of earth and a bucket of quicklim
apiece.'

'I protest!' declared Kuporovitch, turning swiftly back t
him. 'You heard the Marshal's orders. How dare you disobe
them!'

The Colonel's dark eyes had gone black with anger. 'That is my responsibility,' he flared.

'Damn you!' roared Kuporovitch. 'You seem to forget that I am your superior officer. I demand to be released and taken back to the Astoria.'

But his bluff was useless. Gudarniev's only answer was to draw his pistol and jab it in the ex-General's ribs, as he yelled: 'You're a lousy traitor. Get over to that desk now, or I'll shoot you where you stand.'

As they walked the length of the stone-floored hall, Kuporovitch muttered to Gregory in German. 'Because the Marshal looked ill when we left him, and had apparently been telling us so much, we are suspected of having given him the Truth Drug. It has sometimes been used at trials to make witnesses talk freely. Anyhow, that's what Gudarniev thinks.'

At this announcement a great light dawned in Gregory's mind. Like most people, he had heard that the Russians possessed such a drug, but he had always supposed that it was administered by means of a hypodermic. Evidently they had now found a way of giving it to people in liquid form. Voroshilov must have decided to give him a dose of the drug in his drink; and, by changing the glasses, he had caused the Marshal to take it himself.

Gregory did not blame his recent host in the least for his attempted breach of hospitality. After all, he had sought out the Marshal with the view of attempting to trick him into giving some indication of Russia's future plans, so he had no right to complain if the Marshal had tried to trick him, or at least to make quite certain that he was telling the truth. He had, too, presented himself as a German, and his own first principle was that 'All is fair in love and war.' Since he had come ostensibly to disclose a project for the overthrow of Hitler, and had sought Voroshilov's co-operation in the timing of his plan, he felt that the Marshal had the right to investigate his visitor's integrity by every possible means at his disposal before he talked to him at all.

One thing was now clear beyond all doubt. If anything could have set the seal of unqualified success upon his mission, this was it. The Marshal's extraordinary talkativeness was not only fully explained but there was now the best possible reason to believe that all he had said was the truth, the complete truth, and nothing but the truth.

Yet, by the most damnable piece of misfortune, at the very moment of achieving this staggering success Colonel Gudarniev had tumbled to what had happened; and now it looked as if Gregory's exchanging those two glasses was about to cost him and his friend their lives.

When they reached the desk Gudarniev asked for the night duty officer to be summoned. The man behind it rang throug on a telephone. They waited for a few minutes in tense silence A fat man with eyes in slits that seemed to turn up at th corners and the high cheekbones of a Mongolian appeared Gudarniev gave his name, showed a headquarters pass, an then said to him:

'I am one of Marshal Voroshilov's staff officers. These tw men are under suspicion of being spies and saboteurs. The have gained possession of important military secrets. The are to be confined in such a way that they can neither tal together nor to anyone else. By that I mean that they are no even to be allowed to exchange remarks with any member o the staff here. You will have triple guards placed on their cel to watch one another and see that this order is obeyed. The are carrying British passports in the names of Stephen Coope and Gregory Sallust. You will enter them in your register un der those names and give me a receipt for them, but they ar not to be searched. In no circumstances are these men to b released, except on an order signed by the Marshal in person

Kuporovitch again began a vigorous protest but the fa Mongolian took not the slightest notice. He pressed a butto on the desk, a bell shrilled, and some more armed guards cam hurrying out of a room at the side of the hall. In a guttura voice he gave instructions to an N.C.O., then sat down to writ out a receipt. He was still writing it, with Gudarniev besid him, when two of the guards placed themselves on either sid of the prisoners, and at an order from the N.C.O. marche them away.

They were taken down a passage, through another heav door beside which a sentry was lounging, and out into a bi high-walled courtyard.

'Ah, now I know where we are,' Kuporovitch murmured t Gregory. This is the old Lubianka prison, but they must hav built a new office to it and that infernal Colonel brought us i that way.'

'Silence!' barked the N.C.O. 'My orders are that you ar not to talk,' and he prodded Kuporovitch with the barrel o his pistol.

As they proceeded, Gregory thought grimly that this mu be the courtyard in which the Bolsheviks had massacre thousands of innocent men, women and children during th Revolution, for the sole crime of belonging to the educate classes.

They entered a door on the far side of the courtyard, passe another sentry and were led down a flight of iron stairs to th basement. There, the N.C.O. passed on his instructions to

ead warder and saw the prisoners locked into cells some dis-
ance from one another.

Both of them had hoped that they might be able to communicate with each other on the alarming turn that events
had taken, if only by tapping out messages in morse on the
partition of two cells; but since even this hope had been frustrated, after sitting gloomily on the edges of their beds for a
time, they lay down and went to sleep.

Their sleep was fitful, not alone owing to the desperate
plight in which they knew themselves to be; but also on
account of the intense cold in the underground cells. Fortu-
ately they had their furs, but even so, after a few hours rest-
less dozing the cold was such that they found it unendurable
to lie still any longer, and, getting up, began to stamp up and
down the narrow confines of their prisons.

In due course a hunk of bread and a mug of something that
passed for coffee was brought to each of them. The brown
liquid was an unappetising brew, but, in spite of that, they
were grateful for its warmth. A few hours later they were
given a bowl of greasy stew apiece, and, still later, another
mug of the coffee substitute. They then tried to get some
sleep again, and were semi-comatose when they were roughly
roused and called outside by a little group of warders.

Glancing at his watch Gregory saw that they had been incarcerated for the best part of twenty-two hours, so it was
now the middle of the night again. He wondered miserably if
an order had just arrived for them to be shot.

To his immense relief they were not halted in the sinister
courtyard but taken across it, and through to the main hall
in which they had been received. They were then taken up in
a lift to the second floor and marched into a large, comfortably
furnished office. In it were four men.

One of them, a grey-haired fellow in a smart uniform with
silver rank badges, who appeared to be the prison commandant, was seated behind a heavy desk. Marshal Voroshilov
occupied an armchair to one side of him, while Colonel Gud-
niev and another officer, who it transpired was an interpreter, were standing side by side behind the Marshal.

The guards were ordered out of the room. Voroshilov lit a
cigarette and began to address Kuporovitch. Evidently he had
given instructions to the interpreter beforehand, as, after each
sentence he paused, and the officer translated it into German
for Gregory's benefit. The Marshal said:

'You two beauties have landed yourselves in a fine mess.
One of you, I don't know which, had the bright idea of changing a drink that my servant handed to the *Herr Baron* last
night for mine, so that I drank it instead. I don't see how you

191

could possibly have known at the time what was in it, bu
later it must have been clear to you that the drink had bee
doctored with our Truth drug.'

'I can only offer my profound apologies, sir,' Gregory sai
quickly. 'I changed the drinks, and I did so only because I fe
certain that your servant had forced that particular drink o
me.'

'Did you think I meant to poison you?'

'No. Even the idea of your drugging me didn't seem to mak
sense. I could see no earthly reason why you should wish t
either poison or dope me. If I had known then what the dru
was I should naturally have seen the reason for your wantin
me to drink it. But as I didn't know, the whole thing seeme
quite pointless. My impulse was rather like ducking when on
thinks one is being shot at; I simply changed the drinks over o
the spur of the moment.'

'Well, in this case you ducked too successfully, *Herr Baron*
If you had left well alone, and it was the truth that you wer
telling me last night, your story would have been exactly th
same, drug or no drug, and no harm would have come to you
But as it is, your act has placed you in possession of informa
tion which, whether you are an honest man or not, is mor
dangerous than poison.'

'You must admit that it's not altogether my fault,' Gregor
argued, risking a mild grin.

'No,' the Marshal admitted, 'and I can see the funny sid
of it. As a matter of fact, that liquid preparation of the dru
is quite a new thing. One of our scientists gave me a little as
present with the idea that it might be amusing to give it t
somebody at a party. But I hardly cared to play that sort o
joke on one of my friends, and I had forgotten all about th
stuff until you turned up last night. Then it occured to tha
it would be interesting to try it out on you, and learn just how
much of this conspiracy to liquidate Hitler is the truth. The
joke, of course, turned out to be on me, but there is a sayin
that "he who laughs last, laughs best." '

'I certainly don't regard it as a laughing matter,' Gregor
assured him hastily.

'No,' said the Marshal drily, 'you have no cause to—now.

'But, Marshal, has any real harm been done?' reasone
Gregory. 'After all, the information you gave me was essen
tial to the successful carrying out of the plan I put before you
The fact that you gave it to me unwittingly is surely of no
serious account. If you had not done so, one way or the other
the whole point of my coming to Russia would have been lost.
I am no more a danger to you now, if you allow me to go

192

back to Germany, than if you had told me all you did of your own free will.'

'That remains to be seen. In any case I should not have talked to you as freely as I did, and certainly not before having found out much more about you. However, that oversight can fortunately be remedied. It will be doubly interesting to ascertain just how much of your story really is true.'

As he finished speaking Voroshilov took a small phial from his pocket. Two glasses and a carafe of water had been placed ready on the desk. He poured a little of the brownish fluid from the phial into each of the glasses, added some water and said:

'Come along, both of you. Drink up.'

Gregory was still cold from the long hours spent in the chilly cell, but he felt the perspiration break out in little beads on his forehead. He had no doubt at all what was in the phial. It was the remainder of the drug, and the Marshal meant to play it for tat.

He wondered wildly what he would say under the influence of the drug. Then, if he ought to refuse to drink it, and accept the obvious, although unannounced, alternative, of being led down to the courtyard and shot. If he did drink it and the stuff made him answer all questions without the least reserve he could hardly expect much mercy. But one swift consoling thought came to him. It bashed into his mind how wise Sir Pellinore had been always to insist that he should work on his own. He had never been a member of the official British Secret Service. He knew no one in it and nothing whatever of the methods used. At least, even if they poured the drug into him by force, they would never get any information about that.

Kuporovitch had already stepped forward. With a faint grin he shrugged his broad shoulders and picked up one of the glasses. He knew perfectly well that by drinking it he would give away the tissue of lies he had told, but he was convinced that it was now only a matter of hours, or perhaps only moments, before he would be shot in any case. With Russian fatalism he was quite prepared to die, and it appealed to his sense of humour that he should provide his old friend Clim with half an hour's fun before doing so.

Gregory was still frantically trying to think what he would give away that might compromise British interests with the U.S.S.R. The reason for his mission must come out, of course, but that was entirely unofficial, since Sir Pellinore, who had sent him, was a private individual. Moreover, he would not involve the British Minister in Moscow as Sir Stafford Cripps knew nothing about it. Yet he was still terrified lest something that should remain a secret would come out. He had so little time to think and, with that awful thought agitating his mind, he took a step forward to grab his friend's arm.

But Kuporovitch was, after all, a Russian, and it had not even occurred to him that he might damage British interests. He felt certain, too, that if they refused to drink the potion would be forced upon them both; and although he would never have willingly let Gregory down he saw no reason to suppose that he would compromise him any more than his friend would compromise himself.

His arm jerked up; Gregory's outstreched hand missed it by an inch, and in another second Kuporovitch had swallowed the draught. Gregory saw that his own scruples were now quite pointless. The two of them had been together ever since they had left Kandalaksha eighteen months before, so there was no point in one making a fighting attempt to preserve secrets which the other would now, inevitably, give away. Picking up the other glass, he drank the sweetish brown liquid.

'Good,' said Voroshilov, pointing to two chairs near a big porcelain stove in a corner of the room. 'Now you can go and sit over there and smoke a cigarette, while we give the drug a little time to work.'

'I'm afraid I smoked the last one I had on me hours ago,' said Gregory.

As the interpreter translated, the grey-haired Commandant pushed forward a box that was on his desk and motioned them to help themselves.

Having thanked him and lit up they went over to the stove and, grateful for its warmth, settled themselves as near it as they could. Voroshilov, meanwhile, had turned to Gudarniev and said: 'Let me have that analysis of the shell position, Ivan, I'll run through it while we are waiting.'

The Colonel produced some papers from a brief-case he was carrying and the Marshal set to work upon them, making pencil notes here and there in the margins.

Gregory and Stefan were now entirely concerned with trying to analyse their own feelings. For some moments neither of them were aware of any difference in their mental or physical reactions, but they waited with a mixture of anxiety and interest to see what would happen.

Gradually the anxiety faded from their minds. The warmth from the stove was very pleasant. It seemed to them both that their pulses were beating faster, but in spite of that they felt comfortably relaxed and filled with a strange sense of well-being. For the best-part of the past twenty-four hours they had been acutely conscious that the next hour might prove their last, but now they were no longer worried about that. After a time they forgot all about it; then, when Gregory made

194

fresh effort to think of things that he ought to try to prevent himself from talking about, he found that he could not do so. With a sudden sense of panic he realised that his mind was becoming hazy, and that he could no longer remember events clearly, even in the immediate past. Then the sense of panic left him and he became possessed with a strange, happy exhilaration. He knew vaguely that his conscious mind was lapping and that the subconscious was taking charge. But that did not seem to matter. All idea of resistance left him, and was replaced by a happy docility which made him as incapable of co-ordinating his thoughts as though he were in an opium dream.

The Marshal finished with his papers and said: 'Now let us talk again. Bring your chairs over here.'

His voice and that of the interpreter came to them quite clearly. They stood up at once and obeyed. As they sat down again in front of the desk both smiled amicably, thinking what a fine fellow he was and how much they wanted him and everyone else, to think well of them.

He looked first at Kuporovitch and enquired: 'What was your reason for leaving the Soviet Union? I would like you to tell me about it again.'

'Well, Clim, it was this way.' Kuporovitch answered with easy familiarity. 'You know my history. You know that as a young man I was a Czarist officer and that I only became a Bolshevik through force of circumstances. Before the war and the revolution came, life was good for young fellows like myself. We used to stay at the big houses where there were plenty of good horses and pretty girls to flirt with; good food, good wine, shooting in the autumn, bear hunts in the winter, and all that sort of thing. We were free men and we could even say that the Little Father and his Ministers were fools, if we thought it. But best of all, on our long leaves we were free to travel. I used to go to Paris and Monte Carlo every year, and what a time we had! You'd have loved Paris, Clim. You were always one for a gay life when you could get it, and I bet you would never have come back until your money ran out. The lights of the cafés in the Rue Pigale made the place like a fairyland. You'd have loved the Moulin Rouge, the Rat Mort and all those places. At the Abbaye Thélême, we used to get the girls dancing on the tables without any drawers on, while we drank wine out of their slippers. Champagne was only a few roubles a bottle in those days, and at Voisin's or Larue's, for a golden louis d'or, you could get the sort of dinner you'd never had the chance of eating in your life. Then in the daytime there were the races at Auteuil and Longchamp, and drives in the Bois, and boating parties at St. Cloud.

195

And always there were girls—scores of them—beautif[
women exquisitely gowned and perfumed; lovely as sprin
itself in their silks and laces and jewels; real girls whose who[
life was love and laughter—the sort that we have not seen i
Russia for nearly three generations.'

He paused for a moment to wonder what he was talkin
about. His own voice rang in his ears, gay and enthusiasti[
yet he had no idea of the sense of what he had been saying.

'Go on,' prompted Voroshilov. 'You were telling us abou[
Paris.'

'Yes, of course. Well, I wanted to see it all again before
died. You know how it is here in the Soviet Union. Everyon
works all the time and is terribly earnest about some drear[
subject or other. Everything is shoddy and second-rate, an[
nobody ever has any fun. That's what you and your friend[
have made of our wonderful Russia. I daresay things will b
all right in another twenty years or so and that the childre[
who are growing up now may live to see good times again[
but I was getting on in life and I couldn't afford to wait unti[
all your dreams of the future came true.

'Then, after the Tukachevsky *Putsch*, God knows how
many officers you shot. It must have run into thousands and
the purge went on for months. Everybody who was even re[
motely suspected of being a reactionary came under suspicion[
My hands were clean enough, because he had been your life-
long enemy, and nothing would ever have induced me to be
disloyal to you. But, even so, somebody remembered that I
was an ex-Czarist and they packed me off to a fifth-rate command in a fortress right up on the White Sea. Even there, I
never knew from one day to the next if someone in the Kremlin wouldn't put me on a list to be liquidated, without your
knowing anything about it. So I decided to collect foreign exchange and, when I'd got a useful sum together, to get out. I
was nearly ready to quit when my friend here was brought to
the fortress as a prisoner, but he had a big sum in *valuta* on
him and a plan for getting safely out of the country; so we did
a deal and got out together.'

'You went back to Germany with him?' Voroshilov hazarded.

'*Sacré Tonerre,* no!' Kuporovitch exclaimed with a laugh.
'Why should you think that? We had a girl with us, and a
lovely one. A lady called the Countess von Osterberg. We went
first to Norway, and, while my friend stayed there a time, I
took her to Holland, then to Brussels. We met there again,
and soon afterwards Hitler's *Blitzkrieg* on the Low Countries
broke. I took her to England while he remained behind but I
joined him once more in Paris the day before the city fell to

the Nazis. By a stroke of great ill luck I was knocked down by a car and nearly killed, so he left me for dead and made his way home, via Bordeaux, to England, while—'

'To England!' the Marshal interrupted with a puzzled frown.

'Yes, of course. For the time being, after the collapse there was nothing more that he could do in France. I recovered and stayed on in Paris. Some months later he came over and we joined forces again. We did not leave until early June this year—a week or two before Hitler invaded Russia.'

'And what were you doing in Paris all that time?'

'We were plotting against the Germans. I was one of the earliest members of the French Resistance Movement.'

'And then?'

'We managed to get safely back to England, and I got married. You should see my little Madeleine, Clim. She is as sweet as a peach, and as plump as a partridge. Ah, *Sacré nom,* it makes my old heart beat quickly even to think of her. She is a little Parisian and it was she who nursed me back to health and strength after my accident.'

'Where did your travels lead you after you got to England?'

'To Russia, of course. When I heard that Hitler had attacked us I naturally wanted to get back and fight. It is one thing to leave one's country because a lot of politicals have turned it into a lousy hole, and quite another to stay away from it when foreign soldiers are polluting its soil. My friend here offered me an opportunity to get back, and although I knew that there was a good chance of my being shot for my long absence, I felt that I must chance it, if there was some hope of helping my country at the same time as I helped him with his mission.'

Voroshilov's glance shifted to Gregory. 'I should like to hear about this mission. From what has been said, it seems that you live in England. Is Colonel Baron von Lutz your real name?'

'Oh, no,' Gregory smiled. 'The real Baron died a long time ago. I simply assumed his identity for the purposes of my work.'

'You are, then, an anti-Nazi agent? What is your Nationality?'

'British.'

'I see. What is your object in coming to Russia?'

In the twenty minutes that followed the whole story came out. By a series of shrewd, quietly asked questions, the Marshal extracted all the information of any value that Gregory was capable of giving. For a little he kept on insisting that his prisoner must, in some way, be connected with the British Secret Service, but Gregory's denials were so positive and his account of himself so circumstantial that, bearing in mind he was under the drug, Voroshilov could not possibly disbelieve him.

When the examination was concluded the prison commandant pressed a bell, the guards came in and the prisoners were taken back to their cells. They were both sweating freely and were so hot that they did not even notice the cold. They would have certainly have caught pneumonia and, quite probably, died of it, had not a doctor visited them shortly afterwards. He made each of them swallow a draught and get into their beds, then he piled extra blankets as well as their furs on top of them, and left them.

By that time they were both feeling extremely sleepy, so they soon dropped off, and did not wake again until the doctor came to visit them, round about midday, next day.

When they awoke they remembered their interview with Marshal Voroshilov perfectly up to the point where they had taken the drug and gone to sit by the stove; after that their impressions were blurred and uncertain. They knew that they had talked a lot about themselves and their mission, but actual particulars as to what they had said escaped them. It was exactly as though they had dreamed the latter part of the scene. Their memories of most of it were vague, but isolated episodes stood out with the clarity of a flashlight photograph and these with little to connect them, were all telescoped together in an almost senseless sequence.

Their apprehension of the peril in which they stood had been neither lessened nor increased by their interrogation. Before it they had known that all thought of escape from the Lubianka was quite hopeless and that an order for them to be shot might arrive at any time. Now, it seemed, if anything, more certain that the next time they were led out of their cells, it would be to die.

After the doctor's visit they got up to eat their midday soup, but as time went on the chill of these cells began to worry them again; so, as soon as their evening coffee had been handed in, they repiled the furs and blankets on to their beds and got back into them. Once more they were aroused in the middle of the night, and this time neither of them doubted that they were about to be taken for their last walk.

It was almost with a sense of surprise that they found themselves on the far side of the dread courtyard, and realised they were being taken up through the modern block to the room in which they had been examined the night before. The same four officers were present and Marshal Voroshilov opened the proceedings without any waste of time.

'I have been thinking a lot about you two in the past twenty-four hours,' he announced. 'I find the cases of both of you quite exceptional and intensely interesting. First, Stefan Kuporovitch, I will deal with you.'

Kuporovitch was already standing to attention. He now drew himself rigidly erect and with soldierly impassivity waited for sentence to passed upon him.

'You must be aware,' the Marshal went on, 'that you have merited death on half a dozen different counts. You abandoned your command, which technically, at least, was within the war zone. You deserted from the army. You betrayed the trust of your superiors and have clearly shown that you despise the régime that placed that trust in you. Your return to the Soviet Union was made under a false identity. You have screened yourself under the diplomatic privileges of a foreign power in order to undertake your subversive activities. You have aided and abetted the agent of a foreign power to obtain the military secrets of the Soviet Union. You connived in that foreign agent administering a drug to myself, a high officer of the Republic. Have you anything to say in your own defence?'

'Nothing, Marshal,' croaked Kuporovitch hoarsely.

'And you,' Voroshilov looked at Gregory. 'You, too, have laid yourself open to the death penalty on more than one count. By assuming a false identity, as a German officer for the purpose of obtaining access to me, you have forfeited any protection that you might normally claim as a member of the British Embassy staff in Moscow. By an amazing fabrication of lies and false pretences you obtained from me Soviet military secrets of the first importance. Moreover, although you may think that you had certain justification for doing so the fact remains that, on my having granted you an interview, you took advantage of an occasion that arose to give me what you had reason to believe to be a drink containing either poison or a drug; so, technically you are guilty of an assault on the Garrison Commander of a beleagured city, upon the holding of which much may depend. Have you anything to say in your own defence?'

'Yes, Marshal,' Gregory replied boldly. He had nothing to lose and everything to gain by talking, and was still amazed that any opportunity had been given him to do so; but, since it had, he meant to make a fight for it, however slender his chances of influencing the Marshal's apparently already made decision might appear.

'In the first place,' he began. 'Whatever the technical aspect of this business of my swopping drinks with you may be, I think any impartial judge would agree that you were to blame every bit as much as I was. It just could not have happened if you had not first attempted to drug me. As for the rest. I submit that everything both Stefan Kuporovitch and I have done has been in the interests of the Soviet Union, and with the object of more rapidly defeating our common enemy. That is my defence; and if you will be kind enough to allow me, I am prepared to prove my case point by point from beginning to end.'

'You have no need to do so,' the Marshal replied quietly.

For a moment Gregory felt deflated. All the wind had been taken out of his sails by this calm admission, which seemed to render any defence he might put up not only pointless, but farcical. Yet a second later his alertness was rekindled as Voroshilov went on:

'That has been my trouble each time I have tried to snatch a few moments during the day to consider your case. By all the laws of the Medes and Persians you should both be shot. I have no doubt at all that you would be if we were all in Moscow—where it would be my duty to hand you over to the *Ogpu*. But here, as Garrison Commander, I am the supreme authority in such matters; and I find it difficult to strike a balance between the illegal acts of which you have been guilty and the fact that they were committed for the purpose of securing proof that Britain would be well advised to supply arms and munitions to the Soviet Union.

'You, Stefan Kuporovitch,' the Marshal's voice suddenly became scathing, 'have shown yourself to be unworthy of the high rank conferred upon you. It is expected, and rightly expected, that all persons in the Soviet State who are elevated to positions of authority, whether in or outside the armed forces, should devote their whole energy and every inspiration to the well-being of the State. You know the desperate plight in which our country was left after the Civil Wars. Every city and town in Russia either lay in ruins or had fallen into decay. From end to end the country was devastated; the railways almost ceased to run, the canals were blocked, and ninety per cent of our bridges were down. Out of that chaos we brought order; and you have only to look around you at the fine new cities with their universities, hospitals, factories, theatres, airports, hydro-electric plants and canal systems, to realise the immense amount that has been done. Yet you complain that you are no longer able to live here the easy, slothful, wasteful life of a petty noble, who spends most of his money abroad instead of in his own country. Instead of putting your shoulder to the wheel in order that a time may more quickly arrive when all of us can enjoy some of those relaxations and luxuries you hanker after, you behave like a spoilt, irresponsible child and bandon an honourable position because you wish to go whoring in Paris.'

Kuporovitch hung his head. 'You are right, Marshal. I had
t looked at it in that way. It is, perhaps, because I was born
a generation which knew a happier, freer life than can be
d in the Soviet Union today. No one who has ever had the
ance to be an individualist can take easily to the idea of
coming one of a colourless multitude, and denying himself
y fullness of life in the vague hopes of improving the lot of
 majority.'

'I understand that,' replied the Marshal more kindly. 'I also
preciate that, although you have remained an individualist,
u have not lost your love for your country. It is clear that
u could have remained abroad with your English friends
d your young French wife in ease and comfort for the rest
your days, had you chosen to do so. Yet you deliberately
ve up all that and returned to Russia, knowing quite well
at all the chances were you would be recognised and shot as
deserter; because you believed that in doing so you could
lp bring immensely important aid to the Soviet Union.'

'I take no credit for that,' said Kuporovitch simply. 'How
uld I do otherwise? Any decent man would have done as
ich, given the same opportunity.'

Voroshilov looked at Gregory. 'And you, Mr Sallust. From
ur involuntary disclosures last night it emerged that you
ve rendered great services to your country. You are a very
ever, unscrupulous and dangerous man. None of us here
uld take exception to that, as long as you continued to em-
oy your talents against our common enemy—the Germans.
it you elected to ignore the conventional trust which exists
tween Allies and came to Russia in the capacity of a spy.
though you are not officially connected with the British
cret Service, your activities are calculated to have a gravely
verse effect on the relations of our two countries—and that
a very serious matter.'

'There, I'm afraid I can't agree,' Gregory protested mildly.
was sent here simply as an independent observer. Had I got
vay with the material I managed to collect the relations of
itain and Russia would be greatly strengthened. The British
uld have far greater confidence that, whatever reverses
issia might suffer, she was determined to fight on with them
til the Nazis were finally destroyed, and the Russians would
el a far stronger bond with Britain when they saw great con-
inments of British tanks and aircraft reaching them. And
at most satisfactory situation can still be brought about if
u are prepared to release me and help me to get back to
gland.'

'What! Release you, now that you are in full possession of
l the important secrets of Russia's future strategy.' The

201

Marshal shook his head. 'There is a limit to the trust whi
even the best of allies can afford to place in one anoth
Your government does not trust us with information as
when and where they propose eventually to open a Seco
Front. Why should we trust them with our plans for ensuri
the final defeat of the Germans? No. You and Kuporovit
now know far too much for it to be possible for me even
consider releasing you. I can see no alternative but to pass t
death sentence on you both.'

As the Marshal paused, the hearts of the two prisoners sar
During the past few moments it had seemed that he accept
their plea of a pro-Russian motive as a justification for wh
they had done. But apparently their urging of extenuating c
cumstances, and all the weighing of pros and cons in whi
they had indulged, counted for nothing; as the central fact
their case had been known to him from the beginning, and
had evidently made up his mind to condemn them in advanc

Then he went on: 'But you are a brave man, and you plac
your life in jeopardy only through a desire to serve yo
country. Therefore, if you are prepared to accept my cond
tions, I will suspend the sentence.'

Gregory's eyes quickened with a new light. 'That's ve
generous of you, Marshal. For my part, I will agree to ar
conditions short of giving you an undertaking to work agair
my own country.'

'You should know that I would not ask it of you,' repli
Voroshilov coldly. 'On the other hand, you will have to for,
any prospect of serving your country further in the prese
war. This is the situation. The information you have acquir
must at all costs be kept secret. The easiest way to ensure th
would be to have you liquidated. The only possible alternati
is to hold you prisoner until the war is over. I could keep yo
confined in a cell here, but that would entail certain risks.
shell or a bomb might destroy a part of the prison, thus e
abling you to escape in the resulting confusion. If that happe
ed you would almost certainly attempt to get away through tl
German lines and might be captured there. Again, one mu
envisage the possibility that the Germans may take Leningra
As long as I live I shall never surrender. But I might be kill
and, even if I am not, such immensely superior forces mig
be brought against me that our defences would be overwhelm
and what was left of the city occupied. Once more in the e
suing confusion you might fall into the hands of the enemy.'

He lit a cigarette and continued: 'Therefore, I must g
you out of the city, to some part of the Soviet Union where
is impossible for you to be captured by the Germans. I ca
have you flown to a remote prison in Siberia. The death ser

ice is only suspended, you will remember, and any attempt
escape would result in its immediate execution. It is ex-
mely difficult, but not absolutely impossible, to escape from
ch places. In consequence, my conditions are that, if I sus-
nd your sentence, you will give me an additional guarantee
r your security of your word of honour that in no circum-
ances will you attempt to escape; and you will also give me
ur word that while you are in prison you will not communi-
te anything that you have learned from me to any living
rson. Do you agree?'

Gregory barely hesitated. If he gave his word he felt that he
ould have to keep it. That would mean not only that his
ission would remain uncompleted, but also that he would be
at of the war for good. Yet the alternative was a bullet, and
at just the possibility of a bullet a month hence, or in a few
ays' time, but the definite certainty of a bullet in the next
alf-hour. Not an hour would be given him to try to think out
way of escape, no second chance to alter his mind. He must
ve his parole now, at once, or die.

'Yes,' he said, 'I accept your conditions and give you my
ord of honour to stick to them.'

All this time Voroshilov had been addressing Gregory, who
ad formed the impression that his case was being dealt with
eparately, and that the conditions applied only to him. The
Marshal's look now shifted to Kuporovitch, and Gregory gave
quick glance sideways at him too. He knew that the Russian's
ase must be far worse than his own, in the Marshal's eyes,
nd felt that he must make every effort to save his friend.

Before Voroshilov could speak again he said: 'I am in no
osition to make conditions on my side, sir. But I do want you
o know that Kuporovitch was led into this thing entirely by
he. That is true from the very beginning, when we first met at
Kandalaksha. It is true that he was already toying with the
dea of leaving Soviet Russia—but only toying with it; and I
doubt very much if he would ever actually have done so if I
ad not come on the scene. It was I who persuaded him to
eave and I did so because I felt that he would be of great help
o me in my own work against the Germans. That had definitely proved the case, and I—well—I don't think I want to
accept my life if you will not also give him his.'

From having remained silent for a long time, Kuporovich
suddenly burst into a spate of words:

'*Sacré nom*, but this is absurd! Do not believe him, Marshal!
He does not know what he is talking about! I may not be an
intellectual, but I am no child to be led. What I did, I did of
my own free will. He is lying now, out of friendship; but I
will not have it. I deserve to die, and I am not afraid of death.

203

I insist that you ignore—'

'Silence!' barked the Marshal, cutting him short. 'I ⟨ dealing with this matter, not either of you!'

He lit another cigarette and went on more quietly: 'It i fine thing to see the loyalty of good comrades. There is no ing finer in this world. But in this case the efforts of you b to protect one another were unnecessary. I had already ma up my mind about Stefan Kuporovitch.' His glance shifted Gregory.

'He may, perhaps, never have told you of it, and it is prai worthy in him that he should not have recalled the affair an attempt to influence my judgment now; but many ye ago, in the old war when we were fighting the white reacti aries together, he once saved me from being cut down by Cossack. It is to his strong right arm that I owe the fact tha lived to become a Marshal of the Republic.'

Kuporovitch shrugged and smiled awkwardly. 'Oh, it v nothing, Clim. You mean when we broke Deniken's army Novocherkassk, don't you? But it all occurred in a mêlée, a it was the sort of thing that might have happened to anyc in any battle.'

'Nevertheless, one does not forget such things.' Voroshil replied. 'And in return, I am prepared to give you your l on the same conditions as I have just given Mr. Sallust his.'

'Why, that's mighty generous of you!' Kuporovitch laugh suddenly. 'I must confess that I never expected to get out this place alive. Of course I'll promise not to try to esca and I won't breathe a word to anyone.'

'You will not write it either, or seek in any way to co municate any message, however seemingly harmless, to a one at all,' added the Marshal with a sudden access of cauti

'I promise,' nodded Kuporovitch cheerfully.

'That applies to you, too,' Voroshilov looked at Grego 'It is implied in the undertaking you have already given r Is that understood?'

'Yes, I agree,' Gregory said, concealing his reluctance concede this last promise. His agile brain had already been work while the Marshal was talking to Kuporovitch, and it h occurred to him that somehow, some way, he might j possibly be able to get a message through to Sir Pellinc simply saying: 'Am a prisoner in Siberia, but mission success go ahead.' It would not have carried one hundredth part the weight of the personal report that had he been free to turn he could now have made, but it would have been bett than nothing, and would not have contravened the prom he had made not to disclose Russia's future strategy. No the last hope was gone. His life was safe, but he was comm ted to remain as silent as the grave—in fact to pass into oblivion—until the end of the war.

Voroshilov looked from one to the other of them and said: 'I would add only one thing. Since you have faced peril together and have this strong bond of friendship, whatever your political ideologies may be, I hope that when the war is over you will use your appreciation of one another as individuals to bring your two countries closer together, in order that the fruits of victory may not be lost.'

He signed to the prison commandant, who pressed his bell, and the guards came in. The two prisoners thanked the Marshal again for giving them their lives, and were marched back to their cells.

Kuporovitch lay down on his bed and gazed at the ceiling. He could still hardly realise that not only would he be alive tomorrow and the day after, but probably, all being well, for years to come. The idea of being sent to Siberia had no terrors for him. It was no colder there than it had been at Kandalaksha; and although it did not sound so good to be a prisoner as the governor of a fortress, the former rôle had certain compensations. In a political prison there would be no hard labour, but indefinite leisure to think and plan for the future, and probably quite a passable library of books to read. In any case, unless a prisoner was fool enough to assault a warder he was in no danger of losing his life. Whereas a Soviet Fortress Commander was never certain, from one day to the next, that a political commission might not arrive with the object of holding a court-martial on him, owing to some rumour that the Kremlin had got hold of, and having him shot.

He accepted the fact that they were debarred from completing their mission philosophically; feeling much more sorry about that on Gregory's account than on his own. From what he had seen in Britain and now knew of his own country's resources he had no doubt at all which side would win the war. The Germans would be licked to a frazzle in a year or two, then he would be able to get back to his little Madeleine.

Gregory was far from being so resigned to the fate that had befallen him. He still felt a rather breathless sensation from having so narrowly escaped paying the final penalty, but to him the idea of being incarcerated for an indefinite period seemed grim in the extreme. He knew far more about the strength of Germany and the relative weakness of Britain than Kuporovitch, and was by no means so optimistic about a comparatively early Allied victory. He saw himself, day after day, for weeks, months, years, performing some sort of forced labour in the most miserable conditions. He would be cold, ill-clothed, ill-fed and almost certainly subject to a harsh discipline. It was a nightmare picture of a soul-destroying existence that he conjured up; yet to save his life he had readily accepted it, and, by his promise, he had definitely burned his boats as far as any attempt to escape was concerned.

The fact that he had been so astonishingly successful in his mission, yet was now unable to get away from Russia, or even to pass on to Sir Pellinore some inkling of the facts he had gathered, made him livid with rage, but he knew that there was no way out. He tried to console himself with the thought that during the past two years he had been able to do far more to damage the Nazis than most of his countrymen would have the opportunity to do, even if the war went on for another three or four years. He knew, too, that he had been fantastically lucky not to have been caught and shot long before this. Even in his last venture his luck had not entirely run out, as a prison in Siberia would be incomparably better than a Nazi concentration camp. He had been lucky, too, in having to deal with a man like Voroshilov, instead of some official of the *Ogpu*, who would most certainly have had him shot out of hand.

His recent contacts with Voroshilov had engendered in him a great admiration for the Soviet Marshal, although he felt that he had been a bit harsh in his condemnation of poor old Stefan's wish to spend his declining years in the ease and comfort still offered by the bourgeois cities of the West. After all, Stefan's talk of nights on the spree in Montmartre was mostly froth, arising from memories of a hectic youth. He was very happily married now and, given a chance to settle down, would make a respectable and useful citizen in any country of the Old World.

As an intensely strong individualist himself Gregory did not agree with much that the Marshal had inferred. The doctrine of ensuring every child a good start in life and equal opportunities was fair and right, but the intelligent and hard-working would always rise above the rest, and it did not seem to him a practical proposition that the few should be expected to devote their lives exclusively to making things easy for the majority. In time, such a system was bound to undermine the vigour of the race. If the rewards of ability and industry were to be taken from those who rose to the top they would cease to strive, and if the masses were pampered too much, they would regard protection from all the hazards of life as their right and become lazy. There was only a limited amount of wealth in every national kitty. If it was not added to year by year by vigorous enterprise, made possible through the majority of the people doing an honest day's work, but instead, gradually drained away in bettering the condition of the masses without their making an adequate return, the nation that followed such a policy was bound to go into a decline; then, the general standard of living would fall, instead of the country becoming a Utopia, as the theorists fondly imagined.

The Marshal was, Gregory knew, an idealist, and no doubt he still believed in the principles for which he had fought so desperately when he was young; but even in Russia the theories were not working out. The Communist leaders had achieved great things, but to do so they had been forced to enslave the people. In theory they were cared for from the cradle to the grave, but free education, medical services and coffins were small compensation for the fact that they lived in conditions, and were made to work hours, that would have appalled the working classes of any other country. And now that they were at war they were being herded like cattle to the slaughter, without those they loved even being given the opportunity to learn if they were still alive, wounded or dead.

Gregory thought it curious that Voroshilov should know that, yet persist in his belief that all must come right in the end, and condemn Stefan for his lack of desire to remain in the service of such a State, However, his political convictions apart, he had treated them with a justice and humanity that commanded the greatest respect. And it was that respect which made Gregory feel that, having freely given his word to such a man he could not possibly break it.

The cold of his cell was now worrying him again, and made him more gloomy as he thought of the still greater cold he would inevitably be called upon to endure in distant Siberia. He realised too with almost physical pain that it would be a long time—a very long time—before he would again see Erika. That she would wait for him he did not doubt at all, but it was desperately hard on them both that they should be condemned to a separation which could hardly last less than several years. She would, he knew, worry about him terribly, once his disappearance had been reported to London by the British Embassy in Moscow and his return became seriously overdue. A merciful providence spared him the knowledge that for nearly a month she had been a prisoner of the Gestapo, as, had he known, the thought would have driven him crazy.

In his cell, further down the line, Kuporovitch was still thinking about Madeleine. He wondered if, after the war, she would want to go back to Paris to live. He was not altogether certain that he wanted to himself, now. When he had been brought before Voroshilov he had very sensibly refrained from producing his British passport and endeavouring to screen himself behind it, knowing that to do so would have been quite futile and might only have made matters worse; but that did not affect the fact that he was now a British citizen. True he had accepted British nationality only for the purpose of this mission; but now he had it he did not think that they would take it away from him, except at his own request.

He still thought it a tragedy that there had been a revolution in Russia. There had been abuses of power before it, of course, but nothing like the abuses of power there had been since. The 1914–1916 war had already brought about a great change in the attitude of the Government and many reforms; practically the whole of the middle and upper classes had become convinced liberals and even the Grand Dukes had been for forcing a constitutional monarchy on the Czar. Had it not been that the weak-willed Czar was under the thumb of his German wife, and she, in turn, under the influence of the evil Monk Rasputin, Russia might have been spared those five years of bloodshed and anarchy; and by this time her liberal intellectuals would most probably have led her into a new era of individual liberty and prosperity.

He felt that Clim had behaved darned decently but, at the same time, had his limitations. The Marshal did not know everything, and one thing that was a closed book to him was the pre-war way of life in the great democracies of the West; since he had never even visited them. Kuporovitch had taken his dressing-down in good part, but he reserved his right to his own opinion. One thing, however, was now quite clear. He had returned to Russia only in an endeavour to serve her when she appeared to be in peril, but from now on she had no use for him. Therefore he would stick to his new nationality. After all, if one could not be a Russian the next best thing was to be a Britisher. Perhaps Madeleine would want to live for part of each year in France. Well, that would be all right with him; but he would make his home in England, and settle down somewhere near Gregory and Erika. After all, things had not panned out so badly. The year or so in Siberia would soon pass. The simple but adequate food, the regular hours of prison routine and the enforced abstinence from drink would make him marvellously fit by the time he got out, and probably add ten years to his life. On this comforting thought he went to sleep.

But not so Gregory. He was pacing his cell like a lion in a cage and brooding miserably upon the incredibly depressing prospect that loomed ahead of him. Yet, whichever way he looked at it, there was no escape. He had been caught before and thrown into prison, but, then, he had always been able to occupy his active wits in seeking a way out. There was no prison in existence from which escapes had not been made by men possessing courage, resource, patience and determination. Tunnels could be bored under floors, the iron bars of windows gradually sawn through, and guards coerced or bribed. But now, all such thoughts were futile. It was no consolation to think of the thousands of soldiers, sailors and airmen who had become prisoners of war for the duration. They, at least, could still make plans and attempt a getaway; he was out of the game for good.

Eventually the hunk of bread and mug of brownish liquid that constituted his breakfast were brought to him. He ate the bread and swallowed the muck with the appallingly grim thought that his food for years to come would consist only of such miserable fare. He would not have minded that so much if only there had been one ray of hope that he could devise a way of bringing about his release within a not unreasonable time. But there was no way. He had got himself into a trap and in it he must remain, like a live man in a grave, until, years hence, the ending of the war brought about his resurrection. At last, more depressed than he had ever been in his life before, he flung himself down on his bed and sank into a heavy sleep from sheer mental exhaustion.

The guards who brought his midday and evening meals set them down inside his cell, but did not disturb him. He was still sleeping when they came again, roused him, and roughly ordered him out. Gazing at his watch he saw that it was close on ten o'clock, and realised that he had slept all day. Grimly he thought that, where he was going, he would at least have plenty of time to sleep in, and that he must try to learn to sleep as long as he could, because sleep brought forgetfulness.

He greeted Stefan as cheerfully as he could in the corridor, and they were both taken upstairs and out into the courtyard. They no longer had the fear of it that they had had the night before, and obediently got into a Black Maria which was waiting there for them. The van had a row of six cells on each side and they were locked into two of these. the other cells appeared to be empty, but there was a tip-up seat for a guard at the rear end of the narrow passage that separated the two rows of cells, and when a soldier with a machine pistol had taken it he was locked in with them. With a jolt the van started off and drove out of the courtyard.

The prisoners assumed that they were being driven to an airfield somewhere outside Leningrad, from which they were to be flown to Siberia. It seemed that the Marshal had lost no time in arranging for their departure; but that was hardly surprising seeing how anxious he had been that no mischance should occur which might possibly result in their capture by the Germans. Remote as such a possibility might be, he had ample justification for taking immediate steps to guard against it, as the capture of an Englishman in a Russian theatre of war would have been certain to lead to a particularly rigorous examination of the prisoner and, under torture, even Gregory himself could give no absolute assurance that he would not give away the vital secrets he had learnt about Russia's future strategy.

During their three days in the basement cells of the Lubianka they had hardly been conscious of the unceasing battle that raged in a great arc round the city. On a few occasions they had heard a dull crump as a bomb or heavy shell had landed in the vicinity of the prison, and twice the floors of the cells had seemed to rock slightly from a nearby concussion. But now, as the van drove smoothly through the almost deserted streets they could again hear the distant rumble of the bombardment, punctuated here and there by a louder explosion.

After about a quarter of an hour the Black Maria came jerkily to a halt. There came the sound of muffled voices. A moment or two passed, then the guard in the back of the van shouted a question. A shell burst in the near distance with a reverberating roar. Another shout came in reply and they started to move again.

As the van ran on Gregory thought of the many types of blitz which he had heard during the past two years of war; the sporadic shelling across the Maginot Lines, the devastating bombardment by the Russians of Vipuri in the Finnish war, the spectacular but comparatively harmless demonstration by the Luftwaffe against Oslo on the first night the Germans had gone into Norway, the concentrated fury that had devastated Rotterdam; the tragically light fire of the British artillery as they retreated on Dunkirk; the roar of the first month's blitz on London and the thunder of the terrific anti-aircraft barrage that he had recently heard in Moscow.

And now he was leaving it all. Once the muffled booming was drowned by the drone of the engines in the aircraft which was to take him to Siberia, the odds were he would never hear another bomb or shell explosion in his life. He disliked physical danger as much as any sane man, but his escape from it now was no consolation. He could not reconcile himself to the thought that he had been compelled to throw in his hand while the war was still unwon; but it was no good crying over spilt milk now, and he supposed that he would get used to a safe but monotonous existence in time.

The van seemed to be taking them further out of the city than the airfield lay at which they had arrived, but Voroshilov

210

still held a dozen or more airfields within the wide perimeter of his defences, and there was no particular reason to suppose that they would be taken to the one which was used by aircraft going to and from Moscow.

They had been on their way over three-quarters of an hour and must have covered, Gregory thought, well over twenty miles, when the van slowed down and pulled up.

Both he and Kuporovitch heard the rear door unlocked, then a sharp plop, as though a cork had been drawn from a bottle of champagne. There followed a curse, the sound of stumbling, a fall and more hearty cursing. Evidently the guard must have missed his footing in the darkness as he opened the door, and taken a tumble. He, or someone else, scrambled in, there was a jangling of keys and the two cells were unlocked. The man with the keys snapped a handcuff on Gregory's right wrist and linked him to Kuporovitch by snapping the other bracelet on the left wrist of the Russian. Then he gave them a push towards the open doors of the van.

A little awkwardly they scrambled out of the back of the Black Maria. There was no moon but snow was falling gently, and by its faint light they realised at once that they had not been taken to an airfield. The van had pulled up at the far end of a mean back street, or rather, a *cul-de-sac*, since it terminated abruptly in a tumbledown wharf, beyond which could be seen the glimmer of lapping water.

Facing them, as they jumped down, was a burly, fur-clad figure, with a big automatic clutched in one hand and a lightless torch in the other.

It was not until their feet were on the ground that either of them noticed another fur-clad figure, but this one lay face downwards in the snow, quite still, a few feet away where it had rolled into the gutter.

The man with the torch suddenly flicked it on and shone it in their faces.

'It's them all right!' he said. 'Quick now, and we'll get them down to the boat!'

Every muscle in Gregory's body stiffened. The light was too dim for him to make out the big man's features, half-hidden as they were by the fur hood he wore, but he had spoken in German.

Gregory would have known that voice anywhere in the world. They had been rescued, if one could call it that, but only to fall, manacled, into the hands of his bitterest enemy— *Herr Gruppenführer* Grauber.

14

Out of the Frying-pan into the Fire

For a moment it seemed to Gregory that he must be dreaming—or the victim of some nightmare aftermath from the strange drug he had recently taken. Yet the height and the great hulking shoulders of the figure that faced him tallied exactly with his vivid memories of the Chief of Gestapo Department, U.A.—1.

Next moment the voice came again: 'Schuster; *Kommen Sie her! Schnell!*'

That high-pitched voice was Grauber's without a doubt; and now Gregory's eyes were more accustomed to the half-light he could just make out the heavy jowl, cruel mouth, and sharp nose of his old antagonist.

The impulse to make a dash for it had seized him at the first sound of Grauber's voice, but the second he moved he felt the pull of the handcuff that attached him to Kuporovitch, and realised the futility of such an attempt. Shackled together as they were they could neither fight nor run with any hope of succeeding in either. Grauber loomed in front of them with his big automatic at the ready, the man who had released them from the cells had just jumped down behind them from the van, and a third man, Schuster, no doubt, came hurrying round from its front.

Gregory's eyes fell on the cylindrical attachment that stuck out from the muzzle of Grauber's pistol. It was a silencer, and it explained the noise as though a bottle of champagne had been opened, that they had heard just after the van door had been unlocked. He now recollected hearing a short succession of similar sounds just after the Black Maria had halted some half-hour before. They must then have been somewhere on the edge of the city. Evidently at some lonely spot Grauber's two men had held up the van, shot the driver and the N.C.O. carrying its keys, taken their places, and brought the van to this waterside slum, Grauber must have been waiting there and, immediately his man now impersonating the N.C.O. had unlocked the door at the back of the van, shot the remaining guard as he was about to get out.

Somehow the Gestapo chief had found out that they were prisoners and were being taken to a certain airfield that night. He had laid his plans accordingly, and with his usual efficiency. In consequence, Voroshilov's plans had suffered a most appalling miscarriage. Gregory knew that, rather than this should have happened, the Marshal would have shot every prisoner in the Lubianka. His worst fears had been realised; two men who knew all the secrets of Soviet strategy had fallen into the hands of the enemy.

As the driver joined them, Grauber addressed his two men; 'Fels! Schuster! You have done well. I am pleased with you. Before we leave we should hide the van—also the body of this brute I shot just now. I do not want the *Ogpu* nosing about this wharf. Pick him up and throw him in the van. You Schuster, will drive it to the end of the street. On the left is a warehouse that we have rented. It has nothing in it except a few cases of explosives. There is plenty of room for the van, and we will leave it in there. Fels, you will come with me.' After a second he went on, speaking for the first time to his prisoners.

'Mr. Sallust, we meet again. Your companion is, I believe General Kuporovitch. You will both walk down the street in front of me. Any monkey tricks and you know what will happen.'

Apart from Grauber's party, the *cul-de-sac* was entirely deserted. A wood yard occupied one side of it and some lightless buildings the other. The Russian lying in the gutter was quite dead. Schuster took his feet and Fels his shoulders. They heaved the body into the Black Maria and slammed-to the door. As Gregory watched them he was praying that a patrol of Soviet police or troops might come on the scene. Some unforeseen interruption resulting in a mix-up might still provide a chance for him and Stefan to get away; but it was now nearly eleven o'clock and all the inhabitants of this grim district seemed to have gone home for the night.

Schuster ran round to the front of the van and Fels, drawing an automatic, turned to help Grauber guard the prisoners.

'Quick march!' snapped the *Gruppenführer*, and they set off down the street.

At an opening through a tumbledown paling he gave the order to halt, and kept them covered with his pistol while Fels left them for a few moments to unlock and drag open the doors of the wharfside warehouse. The Black Maria was driven in, Fels and Schuster closed the doors and rejoined their Chief. The temperature was well below freezing and a crisp carpet of snow covered the ground. Their footfalls made no sound, apart from a faint crunching. A lorry rumbled past the far end of the street, then there was silence again.

'This way,' Grauber muttered, and led them diagonally across the wharf to a place where a flight of wooden stairs led down to the water. Tied up at their bottom a small launch was gently rocking.

'Take care, the steps are slippery,' Grauber warned them. 'I don't want my men to be put to the trouble of fishing you out of this ice-cold water.'

At the sound of his voice two figures emerged from the cabin of the launch; one held it in to the steps with a boat-hook while the other began to untie the painter.

'Ready?' murmured Gregory to Stefan as they reached the bottom of the stairs—since the handcuffs now linked them like Siamese twins—and together they stepped on to the narrow deck of the boat.

'Get in the cabin,' ordered Grauber, following them on board. Then he turned and looked back to the top of the stairs where Fels and Schuster were still standing. 'Gute Arbeit Jungens! Auf Wiedesehen.'

'Danke, Herr Gruppenführer,' the men's voices came back. 'Heil Hitler!'

'Heil Hitler!' repeated Grauber, and the boat pushed off. He settled himself on the after edge of the cabin well, where he could both keep a watch on his prisoners and a look-out over its low roof. The man in the stern started a motor and the launch nosed her way out to sea. She was showing no lights, the exhaust had been muffled and the falling snow limited visibility, so there seemed little prospect of her being spotted and challenged by a harbour patrol.

After they had been going for a few moments, Gregory said: 'I congratulate you, Herr Gruppenführer, on this very remarkable coup.'

'Silence!' piped Grauber, curtly. 'We shall have plenty of time for a nice little talk later.'

Gregory had a very good idea what form that 'nice little talk' would take, and wondered unhappily just how much the Gestapo Chief knew of his dealings with Marshal Voroshilov. Without inside information of some kind he could not possibly have arranged the hold-up of the Black Maria, and if he was aware that his prisoners had had three long interviews with the Marshal he would use all the ruthless ingenuity of which he was such a master to extract every ounce of information that he could from them. By comparison with the prospect that now lay ahead of them, a prolonged sojourn in Siberia seemed to offer almost boundless joys.

The launch ran on for about half an hour; then there came a low call of warning from the second sailor, who was crouching on the forward deck. The engine was shut off and for a few moments they drifted silently. Kuporovitch, screwing his head round to peer through a porthole behind him made out the black hulk of a slowly moving ship. When it had passed the engine was switched on again and, slewing round to port, they began to follow in the ship's wake.

In the next quarter of an hour he caught sight of the faint outline of several other vessels; all of them smaller ones riding at anchor and, from his observations, he had now formed a pretty shrewd idea where they were. Leaning his head close to Gregory's in the darkness, he whispered:

'I think we are now passing Kronstadt. It must have been at Oranienbaum that the prison van set us down. From there a spit of sand runs out for about four miles, nearly to Kronstadt Island, and beyond its tip is the only channel out into the Gulf of Finland. Some time back we turned at the point and—'

Low as his whisper was, Grauber suddenly caught it and, jumping down into the well, snarled:

'Quiet, there, unless you want to feed the fishes,' and gave the Russian a heavy kick on the shin.

For another half-hour they sat in silence. Ice was not yet forming on the Gulf, but once they had pssed from under the lee of the island a bitter wind caught them, and the water became choppy. The engine was shut off again and the two sailors consulted together, then the launch was put into a series of sweeps, first in one direction, then in another. This seemed to go on for a long time and, after what Kuporovitch had said, Gregory could guess what was happening. They must have passed through Kronstadt defence boom in the wake of a ship taking supplies to places further along the north coast of Esthonia, where the Russians were still holding out; and now they were searching for a U-boat that had sneaked into the Gulf to pick Grauber up.

His surmise proved correct. At last the sailor on the foredeck gave a hail. An answering shout came from a little distance away. There was a brief interchange that seemed meaningless but evidently embodied some code word for recognition purposes. The launch turned again, ran on fifty yards and there was a slight bump.

'Come along,' said Grauber, getting to his feet, and as they climbed out of the cabin they saw that they were alongside the great curved hull of a submarine. A wood-runged rope-ladder had been thrown out over the slope, and some sailors were standing at its top ready to help them aboard.

Evidently Grauber had no intention of giving either of his prisoners a chance to get away by diving over the side, as he did not unlock the handcuffs that secured them together, but, seeing the difficulty they would have in scaling the ladder, he called out to the sailors to throw down a line. One of the men in the boat caught it, and slipping it round Gregory's middle made fast the free end in a bowline, so that if he missed

215

his footing the loop would catch under his armpits and the sailors above could take his weight until he recovered it. With the launch bobbing up and down and only one free hand apiece to grab at the ladder, the two prisoners found it a tricky business to get aboard, but, partially supported by the line, they managed it without accident.

Keeping a safe distance from Kuporovitch's heels, Grauber followed them; then the launch cast off and drew away into the darkness. On deck the *Kapitänleutnant* commanding the U-boat received Grauber with the formal politeness due to a high official of the Nazi government, and led the way down through the conning-tower hatch to the main operations room of the ship.

Gregory had never before been in a submarine and, although this was one of the smaller non-ocean-going type used for operations in shallow waters, he was surprised at its bulk. From the launch it had seemed almost as long as a small destroyer; yet, below decks, on account of its many little compartments and the narrowness of its passages, one had the impression of being in something hardly larger than a fair-sized bomber.

The captain, a youngish man with close-cropped hair, light blue eyes and a straw-coloured beard, took them along to the tiny Officer's Mess, asked Grauber's permission to proceed to sea, and, on being given it, left them.

After the icy cold outside it was stiflingly hot down there. Grauber peeled off his furs, then unlocked the handcuffs so that his prisoners could take off theirs. Having motioned them to a narrow settee behind a flap-table held rigid by a steel angle-bar, he pressed a bellpush. As they squeezed in behind the table a white-coated steward appeared.

'Food,' said Grauber curtly to the man. 'The best you have, and two bottles of my own champagne. This is an occasion to which I have long looked forward.' He grinned malevolently at Gregory.

'Thanks, *Herr Gruppenführer*,' Gregory replied. 'I hope to return the compliment one day.'

'You would be more sensible to wish that this meal was to be your last my friend. Even your imagination is incapable of conceiving all that I mean to do to you when I get you back to Germany.'

'There is many a slip,' said Kuporovitch belligerently. 'These waters are as shallow as the palm of my hand, and there are many sandbanks in them. If this underwater coffin gets stuck on one, Soviet aircraft will spot and bomb it, and you will never get back to Germany yourself.'

The U-boat's engines were now humming rhythmically, but

was only moving very slowly and Kuporovitch's shot had evidently found its mark, as Grauber blanched perceptibly and hesitated a second before he said:

'Nonsense! *Kapitänleutnant* Bötticher is an officer of great experience and has operated many times in the approaches to Leningrad. We shall have reached deep water long before dawn.'

But the Russian's shrewd attempt to get under Grauber's skin had also badly shaken Gregory. He could already feel his claustrophobia coming on and the terrifying suggestion that the U-boat might get stuck on the bottom made the perspiration break out on his hands and forehead. To take his mind off his nerve-shattering thoughts he asked:

'How did you manage to pull off this extraordinary coup? I've always known that the Gestapo were pretty good, but I hadn't imagined that they were quite up to putting such a fast one over the *Ogpu*.'

Grauber's smile suddenly became quite amiable and he was obviously extremely pleased with himself, as he said: 'Since you will never go back to Russia, or have an opportunity of communicating with any of your friends there, I don't mind telling you. It was, of course, entirely luck that I happened to be in Leningrad myself, but, as you are aware, it is part of my work to supervise all Fifth Column arrangements in cities that are scheduled—'

'There is no Fifth Column in Leningrad,' growled Kuporovitch.

'Isn't there?' Grauber raised his eyebrows with a sardonically humorous glance. 'That is all you know. It is not, I regret to have to admit, as large or as well organised as those I handled in Oslo, Rotterdam, Brussels or Paris, but it is there all right. Anyhow, as I was saying, since Leningrad is scheduled to fall within the next few weeks—'

'It won't fall,' said Kuporovitch doggedly. 'not while Clim Voroshilov is commanding there.'

'He is an old friend of yours, isn't he?' remarked Grauber with smoothness that filled Gregory with quick apprehension.

'What makes you think so?' countered the Russian.

'Oh, my dear General! Because we have never met before, you must not think that I don't know anything about you. It is my business to find out things about people like you: Officers of high rank whose loyalty to their own country is dubious have often proved most useful to us.'

'What the hell d'you mean!' roared Kuporovitch, struggling to get to his feet, but unable to do so immediately owing to the fact that Gregory was sitting between him and the passage

217

between the tables, and the table in front of them prevente[d]
him from springing forward.

As Gregory grabbed his friend's shoulder, Grauber, wh[o]
was sitting in the opposite corner of the little room behind i[t]
other small table, picked up his automatic and snarled:

'Sit down, or I'll put a bullet through each of your arm[s]
You will find that painful, but it will not prevent me from ge[t]
ting what I want out of you.'

Kuporovitch subsided with a muttered curse, and the Ges[-]
tapo Chief went on more quietly: 'As I was just going t[o]
remark, I have quite a nice fat dossier about your past in m[y]
office in Berlin. However, we were speaking of Leningrad
The *Führer* has issued an order to *Feldmarschall* Ritter vo[n]
Leeb that the city is to be captured before the winter sets in
Therefore it followed as a matter of course that I should mak[e]
a short visit there to ensure that all my arrangements for th[e]
final phase are in order. I had completed my work and was jus[t]
about to leave, when I happened to glance through som[e]
papers at my secret headquarters, and on one of them [I]
caught sight of the name Sallust. It was on the list of the
people who had been committed to the Lubianka during the
past twenty-four hours.'

'How on earth did you get hold of that?' Gregory asked[,]
his claustrophobia temporarily forgotten.

'It was quite simple, my dear Watson,' grinned Grauber[,]
evidently pleased at his ability to quote from an English
author. 'There is in Leningrad an old woman whose mother
was a German, and who was herself once married to a German commercial traveller. She is now a charwoman at the
Lubianka. It is not difficult for her, each morning when she
cleans out the hall, to get a glance at the register and make a
mental note of the names of those who have been brought in
during the previous day and night. In that way we often obtain information about agents of ours who have had the misfortune to be caught. We then have a chance of isolating
others working in the same cell before the *Ogpu* can get on
to them and pull them in.'

'Most interesting,' murmured Gregory. 'Do go on.'

'For such a very fat fish—or perhaps, I should say a lean-
jawed dangerous pike—like yourself, I felt that it would be
well worth staying on for a few days to see if I could find out
a little more about what you had been up to. Naturally I put
through a priority call to all my agents in the city. English
visitors to Leningrad are few in these days, so your activities
there must have registered with quite a number of Russians;
and soon little bits and pieces began to come in. I learned
that you had arrived from Moscow by aircraft in the early

ours of Sunday the twentieth and that you had spent the
day at the Astoria Officers' Club. Then, that in the middle of
the night a certain Colonel Gudarniev had arrived and carried
you off somewhere. It was he, too, who a few hours later
handed you over at the Lubianka for incarceration.'

Gregory breathed again. It seemed that Grauber did not,
after all, know of their interviews with Marshal Voroshilov.
The steward came in at that moment and began to lay the
two narrow tables for dinner. Grauber took from him one of
the bottles of champagne and, opening it, filled three glasses.
Raising his, he said, 'Well, here's to a safe voyage!'

'Yes, here's to it,' agreed Gregory, whose dominating
ought now was to get safely out of these close, oppressive
surroundings which seemed to him to be pregnant with a
subtle menace.

'May you die gasping for breath,' said Kuporovitch, his
blue eyes fixed malevolently on Grauber. Then he took a
long pull at his champagne.

'May you die praying for death,' replied Grauber, taking
another swig at his.

The steward produced in turn caviare rolled in slices of
smoked salmon, mushroom soup, salami of duck, an *omelette
au kirsch* and chicken livers in bacon on toast. Having for the
last three days existed on the meagre prisoners' fare of the
Lubianka, Gregory and Stefan did ample justice to this feast,
During it Grauber made no further mention of his activities
in Leningrad and his guests tactfully forbore to question him.
Having cleared away, the steward set one of the many thousands of bottles of Martell's 'Cordon Bleu' that the Germans
had looted out of France on the table, and discreetly withdrew.

While they were eating, the submarine's engines had stopped
and started for varying periods as she cautiously nosed her
way along. The good food and wine had fortified Gregory
sufficiently for him to put the idea of their running on to a
shoal temporarily out of his mind, and as the *Gruppenführer*
poured out three large portions of the excellent old brandy,
he said:

'You were telling us about the achievement of your organi-
zation in Leningrad; do please continue.'

Grauber wiped his little pursed-up mouth on a napkin and
turned in his high-pitched voice:

'One of my people is a mechanic in the garage at which the
police cars of the Lubianka are serviced. It is not difficult for
him to get the times and jobs on which the Black Marias are
booked out. An order to pick up at the Lubianka and drive
to an airfield is an unusual assignment. From a man on the

airfield I learnt that a 'plane was to leave tonight for Irkutsk the capital of Siberia. That, too, is most unusual. I recalle that you, Mr. Sallust, are an Englishman, and that the Genera here had been consigned to the Lubianka under an Englis name. Britain is now an ally of the Soviet Union. It seeme to me that if two Englishmen had been caught poking the noses in where they were not wanted it might occur to th Russians to send them to Siberia. They would be out of th way there and incapable of doing any harm; but if the Britis created trouble about them they could easily be produce with appropriate apologies later. I put a few of my best me on to hold up the Black Maria at a quiet spot just outside th city, and there you are!'

'It was a peach of a job,' murmured Gregory. 'And yo analysis was one hundred per cent correct. We were trying get details of the latest Soviet tanks and they caught us at The situation was tricky for them as we had been sponsore by the British Embassy. Very unorthodox, and all that, b I don't need to tell you how such things are done. Anywa we were rumbled almost immediately we arrived and th produced rather a delicate situation. Naturally the Russia thought twice about shooting us, from fear of a political com back, so they decided to put us in cold storage in Siber until they found out if the British meant to make a fuss thought it more discreet to let sleeping dogs lie. Anyhow, do congratulate you on having got into the minds of the Ru sians so extraordinarily well.'

'Thank you, Mr. Sallust.' Grauber bowed ironically. 'Ho ever I must confess that I find it a little difficult to commi erate with you on your demotion.'

'I don't quite get you,' said Gregory.

'Do you not?' The *Gruppenführer* leaned forward and l voice came like a lash. 'You have the impudence to tell r that you came to Russia to ascertain the details of the late Soviet tanks. Since when has Sir Pellinore Gwaine-Cust se you abroad on such small-time stuff? You, an ace operati working outside the British Secret Service and reporti direct to a man who has immediate access to the War Cabine No, no, you were sent to Russia to bag far higher game; and can tell you what it was.'

'If you think that, do.' Gregory laughed, feeling confide that his enemy could not possibly know, and was about to a clever bluff on him.

'All right, I'll tell you.' Grauber took a gulp of brandy a sat back. 'Your War Office, whose intelligence regardi Russia is about as useful as a sun-helmet in the Alps, believ that the Soviet Armies are already exhausted and due to d integrate any day now. Sir Pellinore, who has a better grasp of *geopolitik* than a dozen of your Generals has his doubts about that. He sent you to Russia in order that you might produce for him an unbiased appreciation of the Soviet's powers of resistance. Am I not right?'

Gregory had now become intensely alert. After many weeks during which he had drunk only very limited quantities of alcohol, the champagne that he had had with his meal had affected him much more than it would normally have done, yet no more than enough to put his claustrophobia out of his mind and make him feel on the top of his form. He thought that Grauber's guess had been a mighty shrewd one, but not outstandingly remarkable in view of the able brain that he knew lay behind the smooth forehead of the sharp-nosed pasty-faced man opposite to him. The tank story was clearly too thin to hold water, so he decided to give his opponent the point, and murmured with a shrug:

'Oh, well, I don't mind admitting that I was asked to keep my eyes open and have a general look round.'

'You are going to admit a lot more than that, my friend, before you're very much older. We shall save time if I prompt you a little. Sir Pellinore propounded three questions and asked you to try to provide the answers to them.'

At this smooth announcement Gregory felt as though a bucket of ice-cold water had suddenly been poured without warning down his spine. His eyes never flickered but his hands clenched spasmodically under the table as Grauber went on:

'Those questions were, One: Can the Soviets train their reserves of man-power quickly enough for them to be of any value to them? Two: What is the real state of Stalin's health? Three: How much territory can they afford to give up before their resources become inadequate to support their armies in the field?'

Gregory's brain was racing. He could understand perfectly well how, with the details garnered from a score of different sources, the Gestapo Chief had succeeded in catching them, but he did not see how he could possibly have become aware of these private instructions issued in London. Making a great effort to conceal the agitation he was now feeling, he answered lightly:

'My dear *Herr Gruppenführer,* those are things that lots of us would like to know.'

'I have formed my own impressions and it will be interesting to see if yours tally with them.'

'I'm afraid mine aren't worth very much. You see, I had hardly had a chance to form any before I was caught out, and plunged into the Lubianka.'

'One can form extremely valuable impressions in a very short time, if only one has the good fortune to contact the right person.'

'So that was it,' thought Gregory. 'Thank God, anyhow, that he did not get his information through a leak in London. He knows that we saw Voroshilov and it is from the same source that he learned what we were after. Next moment Grauber confirmed his idea, by saying:

'While you were in the Lubianka, Marshal Voroshilov visited the prison on two consecutive nights. On both occasions you had interviews with him lasting well over an hour. During those conversations you must have picked up quite a lot of interesting material, and I want it.'

Gregory breathed again. Evidently Grauber did not know that while still free men they had visited the Marshal in his flat. He took a sip of his brandy and shrugged.

'You should know better than I do that interviewing officers do not give away things to prisoners. We were simply being grilled by the Marshal and did not learn a single thing.'

'Ah, but what of the things you learnt before you were arrested? You see, I know the charge upon which you were confined. Special precautions were taken to guard you, and to prevent your talking even to your warders, because it was known that you had gained possession of Soviet military secrets of the greatest importance.'

'What nonsense! We'd had no chance to find out anything. We had been in Leningrad less than twenty-four hours when we were arrested, and during the whole of that time we were confined to the Astoria Officer's Club. We were only pulled in because they got some stupid idea that I was a German. But you know how suspicious Russians are of all foreigners, and if they did take any special precautions to guard us, no doubt that was the reason.'

Grauber leaned forward and the steely note of menace again crept into his voice. 'Do not insult my intelligence by suggesting that Marshal Voroshilov would devote his precious time to interrogating personally a prisoner who was merely suspected of being a German. You are going to tell me what you discovered and the sooner you decide to do so the better.'

Gregory was puzzled as to how Grauber could have found out about the questions when he did not appear to know anything about the answers to them. If the one piece of information had been secured from somebody else close to the Marshal the rest should have followed. But, however that might be, it seemed that he knew nothing of the all-important private interview and was now reduced to guessing; so Gregory decided that the time had come to dig his toes in.

'I'm afraid you are in on a poor wicket,' he said slowly. 'If
e had had a little more time to get going before they pulled
s in we might have something that it would be worth your
hile to screw out of us, but as it is—'

'I want the truth about their reason for pulling you in,'
aarled Grauber. 'And by God I'm going to have it. If not
ow, when we get back to Germany.'

His threat conjured up in both Gregory and Stefan's mind
ague but terrible pictures of the ordeals to which they might
e subjected in some Gestapo torture chamber; but, as if in
nswer to their thoughts, Grauber went on, with a malevolent
huckle:

'I can do better than to get the half-crazy gibberings of a
ain-maddened brain out of you, too. I am convinced that
ou found out the answers to those three questions. Their
alue to Germany is immense, and I mean to have a clear,
oherent statement from you unbefogged by false confessions
nd a confused welter of details extracted piecemeal under
orture.'

They stared at him in surprise and the same idea occurred
o them simultaneously. After a second, Gregory decided that,
n order to learn the worst, it would be worth voicing it, and
aid as casually as he could: 'So you've improved on your old
methods, eh? And now use the Russian Truth drug?'

'The Truth drug!' Grauber hunched his great shoulders with
. high-pitched laugh. 'It has never been proved that the Rus-
ians have it themselves yet. They often dope their prisoners
pefore trial; but in my opinion it is just a clever Bolshevik
ie put out for its mental effect on the prisoner. They give a shot
of something that makes him groggy and the poor fool is
hypnotised into thinking that it is useless to conceal the truth.
No, when we get back to Germany I can produce a far more
certain method of ensuring that you tell me the whole story
without any frills, while in full possession of your right mind.'

'*If* we get back to Germany, you mean,' Kuporovitch put
n acidly. 'Your captain hasn't even dared to dive yet, because
ne knows that the water is so shallow. We may be spotted at
any time by a Soviet aircraft.'

'Not in this weather,' hastily replied Grauber, in an effort
to reassure himself. 'With snow falling, visibility from aircraft
is absolutely nil.'

'All the same, the Gulf of Finland is stiff with Soviet warships.'

'The chances of our running into one are very small; and
again, if we did, the low visibility would help us. The *Kapitänleutnant* got me safely into Leningrad ten days ago during

223

the first snow; there is no reason why he should not get m
out.'

Gregory was torn between two emotions. Grauber's fea
that the U-boat might meet with some mishap was so obviou
that it was fun to see him baited. On the other hand, he him
self felt a horrible paralysis grip at his heart each time th
possibility of his being caught like a rat in a trap down ther
was mentioned.

Since the water was so shallow he wondered how the U-boa
had manged to conceal herself during the daytime while sh
had lain off Kronstadt. Snow could not have been falling a
the time; but probably her captain knew of a deep pock
somewhere along the north coast of the island where she coul
lie on the bottom and her outline would be concealed by th
shadow of the cliffs. The knowledge that the U-boat was sti
cruising slowly on the surface with only a few fathoms c
water below her was some comfort, but that would not b
much help if a Russian destroyer found her and blew a ho
in her side.

Kuporovitch appeared to suffer from none of these fea
and was deriving so much enjoyment from seeing Graub
show funk that he would not let the matter drop. With
maliciousness grin he went on: 'No amount of snow will pr
tect you from mines, and we might easily run into one. The
must be hundreds of them floating about here outside the lar
that is kept clear for shipping.'

He had hardly finished speaking when an electric gor
rang through the ship. There came a sound of running feet c
the bare steel plates that floored the passage outside. Som
one was shouting staccato orders in the distance. The cab
tilted on a forward angle and they felt the submarine goir
down in a smooth shallow dive.

Suddenly there came a dull heavy thud. A second later th
whole ship shuddered, heeled over a little and seemed to slid
sideways to starboard.

Grauber had grabbed the edge of the table. His face wa
white as a sheet and his solitary human eye glared from it
unseeing panic. Gregory felt his own heart hammering wild
below his ribs, and for the first time in his life without havir
something disagree with his stomach, felt that he wanted to l
sick.

Kuporovitch had struggled to his feet. Reaching right ov
Gregory, as far as he could stretch, he struck Grauber a r
sounding slap across the face, and shouted:

'That's for suggesting that I might be disloyal to my cou
try! Now do what the hell you like!'

Grauber let go the table and grabbed up his gun. But

224

that instant there came a second terrific thump; this time much nearer. The U-boat had just flattened out, but as the concussion took her she seemed to heave right up in the water then almost turn over.

Kuporovitch was thrown violently back into his seat; Grauber was flung sprawling across the table; the brandy bottle and glasses flew up in the air then crashed to the floor.

For a few minutes the U-boat rocked wildly from side to side, but gradually she settled down on to an even keel. The engines which had stopped, started again and, at increased speed, she pushed forward through the water. Back in their seats the three men waited with every muscle tensed for the next explosion.

The breath of both Gregory and Grauber was coming in gasps and the sweat was rolling down their faces. Kuporovitch, seated as he was beside Gregory, had not noticed his friend's distress, but he kept his eyes fixed on the *Gruppenführer* with demoniacal satisfaction. When the tension had ceased a little and they were beginning to hope that, after all, a third detonation would not burst the vessel open, he said:

'Don't think you're going to get away with it now. That was only the beginning. Those weren't mines. They were depth charges or bombs. We've been spotted by an aircraft or a ship. Whichever it was will have radioed Kronstadt by this time, and the whole anti-submarine flotilla will be turning out to hunt this U-boat down.'

'Shut up, damn you!' croaked Grauber. But Kuporovitch ignored him and went on:

'At the slow speed we've been going we can't have covered much more than ten miles since we came on board. Aircraft from Kronstadt will do that in about ten minutes, so you haven't a dog's chance. They'll smash in the hull of this thing as though it were made of tissue paper and the ice cold water will come pouring in. You're going to die here, choking out your life like the rat you are.'

Gregory closed his eyes and swayed slightly. Grauber began to curse feebly; then, with a sudden resolution, he stretched out his hand and pressed the bell.

When the steward appeared he said: 'Tell the *Kapitän-leutnant* that I wish to see him. Now! At once!'

'Have you ever experienced what it is like to be choked?' Kuporovitch enquired in a conversational tone. 'One feels as if one's head is going to burst and there is a drumming in one's ears. It goes on for a long time, and one also suffers from most appalling cramps. All that business about drowning being a pleasant form of death is sheer nonsense.'

'Silence!' Grauber roared, bringing his fist down with a crash on the table.

The fair-bearded *Kapitänleutnant* came through the narrow door. 'You sent for me, *Herr Gruppenführer*?'

'Yes.' Grauber mopped his face with his handkerchief, and a whiff of the perfume he always used came strongly to them. 'What happened just now?'

'We were spotted by a Soviet aircraft, and she let go the two bombs she was carrying at us.'

'But how could she spot us through the snow?'

'The snow ceased falling shortly after you came aboard, *Herr Gruppenführer*.'

'But in the darkness?'

'The moon is now up. You will remember that I sent ashore to warn you that you should not delay longer, when you postponed your departure two days ago.'

'Two days can hardly make all that difference.'

'They make a lot to the time of the rising of the moon, *Herr Gruppenführer*, and above it is now almost as bright as day.'

'*Teufel nochmal!*' Grauber exclaimed, now white with fright. 'Then, if they send other aircraft it is certain that we shall be spotted and bombed again.'

'The *Gruppenführer* does not like bombs,' announced Gregory, the sight of Grauber almost dithering with fear having temporarily restored his own nerve. 'I was with him once in London when an air-raid siren went off by accident, and even that false alarm scared him out of his wits.'

The *Kapitänleutnant* gave him a swift sideglance, then replied to Grauber: 'It will be more difficult to spot us than it was before, because we are now submerged; but there are only ten or twelve fathoms of water here so our chances of escaping detection are not very good. Also, I fear that they may send submarine chasers to co-operate with the aircraft.'

'How far are we from the shore?' asked Grauber.

'About a mile; not much more. I dare not go much further out from the coast or I may run into their minefield.'

'Get out the boat then. I am going ashore.'

'But—but,' stammered the *Kapitänleutnant*, 'the *Herr Gruppenführer* does not understand. To get out the boat I should have to surface—to lie still for ten minutes at the least. Other aircraft may arrive in the vicinity at any moment. What you ask would greatly increase the danger of our being spotted.'

Grauber shrugged. 'I can't help that. I must get ashore.'

'*Nein!*' cried the bearded sailor with sudden anger. '*Das kann ich nicht machen!* I refuse to unnecessarily endanger my hip and the lives of my crew.'

Quite slowly Grauber stood up. He was terrified of bombs but he was not afraid of any man living, and there had been times when he had even faced up to Himmler. Huge. gorilla-like and menacing, his effeminate streak lending him an added, unnatural sinisterness, he now stepped up to the U-boat commander. Shooting out a great hand he seized him by the lapel of his uniform and shook him.

'You!' he sneered, his falsetto rising to a squeak in his anger. How dare you tell me what you will or will not do! I am of more value to the *Führer* than ten U-boats, and if your ship is sunk through putting me ashore it will have been lost while employed on important duty. If you refuse to obey me and I survive I will have you flogged in front of your crew for mutiny and I will send every single member of your family to a concentration camp. Now, surface your ship and get out that boat.'

The *Kapitänleutnant*'s resistance collapsed like a pricked balloon. '*Jawohl, Herr Gruppenführer,*' he muttered. 'I apologise for my outburst. I am not accustomed to having distinguished passengers, like yourself, on board. I realise now of course, that your life is more important than the safety of the ship. But the Esthonian coast, here, is in the hands of the Russians. Will you not almost certainly be captured if you land?'

'No,' snapped Grauber. 'I speak Russian fluently, and it would need much more than a lot of *muzhiks* playing at soldiers to capture me.'

'The prisoners? Do you wish to take them with you?'

Grauber cast a malevolent glance at Gregory and Stefan. 'No,' he answered, with marked reluctance. 'I couldn't manage those two in a country infested with enemy soldiers. I must chance your being able to get them through for me. Confine them in your cells, and if you are forced to abandon ship on no account are you to release them. On the other hand, if you can bring them to a German controlled port, hand them over to the Gestapo, and I'll see that you get a Knight's Cross for it. Quick now: go and give your orders about that boat.'

'*Jawohl, Herr Gruppenführer!*'

As the *Kapitänleutnant* clicked his heels, Grauber added, 'And send somebody to take charge of these two men.'

'*Sofort!*' rapped out the sailor, now endeavouring to live down his rash show of spirit by becoming once more an efficient automaton; and, turning, he hurried from the mess room.

Grauber hastily pulled on his furs, then glared again at the prisoners. 'Having caught you at last, there are few things that

I have ever hated to have to do so much as to leave you here

'Then take us with you,' urged Gregory, with a sudden wild hope that he might yet escape from these surrounding that caused such havoc to his nerves.

'*Himmel!* Is it likely? I have to make my way through th Russian lines, and before I could do that the two of yo would find some way to murder me.'

Gregory felt prepared to agree to almost any terms if onl it would enable him to get out once more into the open air

'Let's do a deal,' he cried. 'You're armed, and we're no We'll give you our parole not to harm you or attempt t escape until we sight the first German picket. With your pisto you'll still have the advantage of us and a good chance t bring us in.'

'*Morte Dieu!* You'll go alone then,' said Kuporovitc gruffly. 'I'll be damned if I give him my parole.'

'You must, Stefan, you must! For God's sake don't refuse I can't leave you behind. You know I wouldn't do that.'

'I wouldn't accept it, anyhow,' Grauber said, after a secon 'Once ashore you'd find a way to twist me somehow. The I'd lose you and the information you can give me. For m to leave you here is a far better bet. *Kapitänleutnan* Bötticher is a skilful navigator. If his ship survives the nex hour she will reach deep water, you will be delivered to m from a German port and I shall have lost nothing. If the sub marine is sunk, well, you heard the order I gave him. Yɔ will go down with it, and at least be out of my way for good

As he had been speaking the U-boat had tilted nose up wards. They heard the rush of waters cascading from he sides and knew that she had surfaced. A petty officer cam hurrying in, saluted Grauber, and said:

'The *Herr Kapitänleutnant* says please to come at onc *Herr Gruppenführer*. The boat is now being got out.'

Without another glance at his prisoners, Grauber grabbe a small handbag from a rack, pushed past the P.O. and ra heavily down the passage.

'*Kommen Sie mit!*' said the petty officer, putting a hand t the pistol at his waist, and signing to the others to preced him.

Gregory and Kuporovitch picked up their furs and followe Grauber down the narrow corridor. As they reached th main operations room, in the middle of the ship, they sa that the conning-tower hatch was open. The lights had bee switched off, in order that no beam should strike upwarc through the hatch towards the sky. Instead, a shaft of moor light filtered down, silvering the tubes and crosspiece at th observation end of the periscope.

228

The P.O. hurried them along to the extreme after-part of the ship. Right in the stern he called to a rating and, at his order, the man pulled up a trapdoor in the steel flooring from which a foot wide iron ladder led down to the bowels of the vessel.

'No!' gasped Gregory, 'No!' now almost overcome with terror at the thought of being shut up in that dark abyss.

As he drew back the petty officer kicked him from behind. This act of physical violence provoked his normal courage for an instant, and he swung round to strike the man.

Kuporovitch grabbed his arms, and muttered tersely: 'Don't be a fool. He'd only shoot you. While we have our lives we can always hope; and if it is ordained that we should die, what does it matter where we do so?'

'Thanks, Stefan,' Gregory breathed. The sweat was streaming down his face, but he had used that dictum so often himself that he could not now reject it. 'All right, lead on then.'

At the bottom of the miniature companion-way there was another corridor even narrower than the one above, and so low they could not stand upright in it. On one side of it stood a row of six cupboard-like steel doors, each having a row of slits for ventilation in the upper parts of their panels. They were the cells in which refractory members of the U-boat's crew were confined when necessary. The P.O. unlocked the two sternmost, pushed one of the prisoners into each, re-locked them and clattered away up the ladder.

The cells, like the passge, were too low to stand straight up in, and hardly more than upright coffins in which a man could only just turn round, but opposite the door in each there was a bench-like seat and on these the prisoners at once sat down.

Gregory sank his face into his hands and groaned. After a moment, Kuporovitch's voice came to him, thin but clear, through the ventilators in the two doors. 'Gregory, can you hear me?'

'Yes,' Gregory replied, starting up. 'Let's talk. Anything to take our minds of these ghastly surroundings.'

'They are pretty grim, aren't they? No place to wash or lie down, and right next to the vessel's screws. There! The engines have just started up again and these steel cells will now vibrate like this all night. Well, I suppose it's a good deterrent for the submarine crews if insubordination means being confined in places like this.'

As the U-boat began to submerge, Gregory said: 'That brute Grauber's got off all right. I wish to God he'd taken us with him.'

'The dirty rat! Exposing the ship and crew to additional

229

danger in order to get out himself. We wouldn't have stood much chance if we'd gone with him, though. At least two sailors will have manned the boat that took him ashore and the *Kapitänleutnant* is not fool enough to have waited for them to get back. So we'd have been a party of five or more. They would have shot us for certain before they would have allowed us to fall into Soviet hands again, and when we reached the German lines we wouldn't have been any better off than we were before.'

'I don't agree. My brain simply refuses to function properly when I'm cooped up like this, but once I was on dry land I would have thought of some way of getting out of Grauber's clutches. As it is, we don't stand any chance at all.'

'I think you're wrong there. You heard what Grauber said about the captain of this craft. He knows these waters well, and he must have plenty of experience evading aircraft and destroyers. I think the odds are that he'll get us through. If he does we'll have a much better chance of escape when we reach a port than if we'd gone ashore with Grauber and had the muzzle of his gun in our backs all the time.'

'Yes. *If* he gets us through. But we're not much more than a dozen miles from Kronstadt yet, and he didn't seem at all cheerful about his prospects himself.'

'You're being too pessimistic,' Kuporovitch insisted. 'The worst danger was when we surfaced to put Grauber off. As you say yourself, we're still only about a dozen miles from Kronstadt, so other aircraft must have been up and searching for us by the time they got out that boat. Since they didn't spot us then, the chances are now all in favour of our getting clear away.'

At that second, in flat contradiction of his optimism, the dull thump of another bomb shook the ship from stem to stern.

'Oh, God, they've found us!' gasped Gregory, springing up. 'Now we'll never get out of here alive.'

230

15

Floating Coffin

'Hang on,' called Kuporovitch, 'they haven't got us yet.'

Gregory fell back on his hard seat and bit his lip.

The explosion had occurred at some distance and although the pressure waves had struck the hull a sharp blow, the U-boat was still forging full speed ahead. She now turned sharply, like a huge fish on a line feeling a hook on its jaws and dashing off in a new direction.

Kuporovitch was now sweating too, but he knew that he must try to keep Gregory's courage up as well as his own, so he shouted:

'That's the way! Our captain knows his stuff. I'll bet he's run the gauntlet a score of times before. He's using evading tactics now. We'll get away all right.'

There came a more distant explosion. For an instant they hoped that again they had been found only by a single air-craft, which had now let go both its bombs; but a second later another followed, much nearer, making the vessel's stern heave alarmingly. The prisoners were thrown sideways, hard against the walls of their cells. Thrusting out their arms as they jerked back into their seats they sought to support themselves, while waiting breathlessly for the next shock.

It came, almost immediately. A loud boom rang right through the ship. She shuddered horribly, listed hard to port, then seemed to swing half round. Her engines stopped.

'This is it!' thought Gregory. 'This is it!' They've got her. That last one jammed her propellers or something, and she's a sitting pigeon now. The next one will be a direct hit and the water will come rushing in. Oh, God! This is too awful!'

Two more explosions followed. After each the submarine rocked and vibrated wildly. As she regained an even keel they realised that she was still going slowly forward under her own way and that her nose was now pointed slightly downwards.

For a few moments nothing happened, then there came a very gentle bump and the U-boat stopped dead.

'We've grounded!' shouted Kuporovitch. 'We're on the bottom.'

'I know!' Gregory shouted back in a half-strangled voice.

A new terror had seized him now. He was convinced that the submarine had been put out of action, for although the near miss had not actually sunk them the frightful jolt from it must have damaged some vital part of her mechanism.

Why, otherwise, had her engines stopped? She was stuck there on the bottom and would never rise to the surface again. Instead of the hull being burst open and his being killed instantly, crushed under a mass of compressed steel, or choking quickly as the water poured through some gaping rent in her side, he was now condemned to linger there for hours, or perhaps even days, gradually suffocating in the fume-laden air.

He knew that they were in quite shallow water, and that sunken submarines could be raised by means of camels and buoys; but the Russians were not the people to waste the time of their divers salvaging sunken German U-boats for the sake of rescuing their crews. If they bothered to salvage her at all it would be weeks hence at their own leisure; and by that time every soul in her would have long since been dead.

But no! In these days all under-sea craft were fitted with special escape hatches, though which the crew could one by one be released, so that with their Davis apparatus they shot up to the surface. Probably they were getting out in that way now and the Russians in some torpedo-boat were hauling them up to the fresh air, life and safety. Yet, even if that were the case it could bring no hope to him. Grauber's order had been clear enough. If the submarine was sunk the two prisoners were in no circumstances to be released, but left to drown in her.

His brain was racing with these nightmare thoughts. All that he had read of sunken submarines came back to him. He recalled the grim reports of the imprisoned sailors, tapping out messages in morse code on the hull, and of the divers outside answering. Of how the divers bored a hole through the steel plates and brought down a line to pump in air; but that sometimes the sea became so rough or the currents on the sea-bed so strong that the divers' rescue operations were constantly checked; and that the tapping of the men inside the submarine grew fainter and more irregular, until it ceased. Yet he might tap and hammer until his strength gave out. There would never be any reply, because there would never be anyone there to hear him.

He wondered when the U-boat's batteries would fail, and her lights go out. They had flickered wildly and gone off for a moment once or twice while the vessel was being buffeted by the underwater explosions, but for some moments now they had been steady again and a cheering glimmer coming though the ventilation slits from the electric bulbs in the passage lit the cell with a faint radiance. But long before he died the power would give out and his last hours would be passed in terrifying stygian blackness.

232

Darkness, cold and the reek of poison fumes would be his
st sensations on earth. It was almost stifling now but when
e generators ceased to function, down there on the sea bot-
m, the cold would be intense. His furs now lay on the floor
t his feet. By putting them on he would be able to stave off
e cold for a little, but that would not prevent him from
ying, buried alive in that black, coffin-like pit.

Kuporovitch was very far from being happy but, not being
victim to claustrophobia, he had so far escaped the worst of
ese nightmare fears. He was extremely perturbed by the
urn events had taken, but his mind was still clear, and ever
ince the engines had stopped he had been sitting almost rigid,
stening with all his ears. Soon after they grounded he had
eard three more distant explosions and felt the hull shudder
aintly in response to each, but after that there had ensued
he silence of the grave.

'Gregory!' he called after an interval of about five minutes.

'Yes,' came the hoarse reply.

'You're not scared are you?'

'Not scared!' Gregory replied, with a semi-hysterical laugh.
I'm nearly sick with fright.'

'You needn't be, old chap. Everything's going to be all
ight.'

'What do you mean? We're stuck here on the bottom. We'll
never see daylight again. We're going to die here—to die—to
die in the awful cold and darkness.'

'Shut up!' shouted the Russian. 'Pull yourself together,
man! It's not like you to give way like this.'

'I'm sorry,' Gregory muttered thickly. 'But I can't help it,
Stefan. I've faced death in lots of forms and I've never gone to
pieces like this before. It's being boxed up. If only I could
get out! If only I could get out!'

'Stop it!' came the curt rejoinder. 'Because we are on the
bottom we are not necessarily stuck there.'

'What the hell are you talking about? The engines have
stopped and the ship wouldn't be lying still if they had any
means of getting it going again.'

'Oh yes, she might. A modern submarine takes a lot of
knocking out. and that big bang wasn't near enough to damage
us seriously. The *Kapitänleutnant* has been too clever for the
boys who were after him. He seized on the chance to pretend
they had got him and deliberately went to the bottom. No
doubt he released a lot of oil to make a big patch on the surface so that they'd think they'd bust us wide open and go home
happy. That trick has come off lots of times before now.'

'Do you really think so?'

233

'I'm certain of it. There were no alarm bells or sounds o panic when we hit the sea-bed.'

'Oh, God, I hope you're right. What d'you think they' do now?'

'Lie here for a bit, then go on again. She daren't stay her in this shallow water till morning. Some of the boys wh think they got her are certain to come out to have a look at th wreck. If they found her still whole they'd let her have it, an she'd never get away a second time; so she's got to pu twenty or thirty miles between herself and this place befor daylight.'

Suddenly, as though in deliberate confirmation of Kuporo vitch's statement, the motors started up. Gregory could hav leapt for joy, but the strain upon him had been so great tha he was halfway between laughter and tears.

The submarine rocked then drew astern a little. Her nos lifted and she went ahead. Two minutes later she had fla tened out and was pulsing forward with all the speed he engines could give her.

'It looks—' Gregory hesitated. 'It looks as if we might ge clean away now.'

'I see no reason why we shouldn't,' Kuporovich replie cheerfully. 'If it's been reported to Kronstadt that we wer sunk they won't bother with us any more. This makes th third big victory we've had tonight.'

'Victory!' repeated Gregory. 'Have you gone crazy?'

'No. I said victory and I mean victory.'

'How the hell d'you make that out?'

'Well, first there is the promise we made to Marshal Voro shilov. You remember the terms of our agreement?'

'Yes. We were not to attempt to escape from the prison i Siberia to which he was sending us, and while we were ther we were not to seek to communicate anything that we ha learned from him either by word or in writing to a livin soul.'

'That's it. Well, we haven't broken our promise so far, hav we?'

'No. We made no attempt to escape. We were simply take over by Grauber without having any say in the matter.'

'And as there is not now the remotest chance of our eve arriving at that prison in Siberia, we shall never be in a pos tion to break the promise we made in the future, shall we?'

'You mean that our promise was binding only for so lon as we were detained in a Soviet prison, and that the failure o the Marshal to detain us frees us from it?'

'I do. It is not unfair to say that part of his side of th bargain was to protect us from all future risks to life, lim

nd sanity for the duration. But now, through no act of our
wn, we find ourselves up against the German again; and we
ay yet be hard put to it to withhold his secrets from them.
² we can do that, save our necks and get out of this by our
wn endeavours, I feel that even Clim himself would agree
aat we have a right to cash in on our efforts.'

'You're right, Stefan. As a matter of fact that was the first
aing that occurred to me when we were being taken off in
ae launch to the sub. By allowing us to fall into the hands of
ae enemy the Marshal forfeited his right to hold us to our
romise.'

'Good! Well, that's victory Number One. The second was
ver Grauber.'

'How d'you mean?'

'Why, surely you were not so preoccupied with your own
:ars that we'd never make port in this thing to have failed
› notice how I succeeded in playing on his nerves?'

'No. I was tickled to death to see how you got the brute
attled.'

'But you didn't realise that it was deliberate, eh?'

'I'm afraid, Stefan, that I was very far from feeling like my
sual self, so your tactics escaped me.'

'Well, it *was* deliberate. I realised from the start that we
idn't stand a dog's chance as long as that single basilisk's
ye of his was on us; but I could see he was scared stiff of
aeeting a sticky end under the sea. I felt pretty certain that
² I could play on that fear he would take any risks that there
aight be on shore rather than remain with us. When those
ombs were dropped I got the feel of his soft corn nicely and
rod on it hard. He reacted perfectly and, although he posi-
vely hated leaving us, his fear of his own skin proved too
auch for him.'

'No wonder you dug your toes in when I tried to get him
› take us with him.'

'Yes. I don't like being in this tin kettle myself much, but
d a darn sight sooner be in it without Grauber than on
10re with him. At least—with him and the two or three
rmed robots I felt sure he'd have to take along as well.'

'I don't think it can have occurred to him at the time, that
1e chaps who landed him would not be able to get back to
1e sub,' Gregory said, after a moment. 'If it had he would
robably have taken us. It didn't occur to me either. And
oth he and I thought that two prisoners would be more than
match for him on his own.'

'That's about it. Anyhow, we're rid of him now, and I count
1at Victory Number Two. Number Three, of course, is the
apitänleutnant having foxed the bombers. That was a pretty

235

nasty risk to take, but it was better than going ashore wi
that blood-lusting sub-human, and if he had remained o
board we would have had to face it just the same, anyho
Now, when we do reach port we'll at least have some so
of run for our money.'

'I think you've handled the situation darned well, Stefa
Gregory admitted ungrudgingly. He was feeling much mo
himself now and this conversation had filled him with ne
hope. After all, U-boats often voyaged for many thousan
of miles without coming to grief. Now that they had escap
the Soviet attack and the submarine was going full spe
ahead they should, long before dawn, have passed the out
defences of Leningrad and be cruising opposite the mo
western part of the north coast of Esthonia, which was he
by the Germans. The ship would then have the protection o
the Luftwaffe and the danger of her being further attack
would be reduced to almost nil.

He felt, too, that Stefan was so absolutely right in his co
tention that their chances of escape would be enormously i
creased now that they no longer had Grauber's basilisk e
upon them. On their arrival at the Lubianka, Colonel Guda
niev's order that they were not to be searched had been scr
pulously obeyed. It had apparently not occurred to Marsh
Voroshilov to countermand it later, and Grauber, presumab
believing that he had ample time before him for such matter
had not bothered to do so either; so they still had their pas
ports on them and a considerable sum in both Russian ar
English money. Once they reached a port, therefore, it mig
well prove possible to bribe some of the ordinary guards
whose charge they were placed, or, if not then, during th
long journey down to Germany through the Baltic State
which would almost certainly offer some opportunity for tw
resolute and resourceful men to escape.

For the first time since they had been locked up they no
sat in undisturbed silence for a while, and after it had last
for some time Gregory thought that he could hear a fai
voice calling out in German.

Straining his ears, he listened intently for a few momen
then it suddenly dawned on him that the voice was comi
from a cell further down the row of six, and that the cal
were addressed to him.

The voice kept on repeating: 'You there in number tw
Who are you? What have they bunged you in for?'

He shouted back: 'Number two speaking, I and my frier
next door are political prisoners. We're being taken back
Germany on the orders of the Gestapo.' His German was a

236

excellent that he felt it quite unnecessary to add that he was an Englishman.

'The hell you are!' the voice replied. 'That sounds pretty bad. My mate, in cell six, and me are political prisoners too, in a way; but, praise be, the Gestapo's not yet taken an interest in us.'

'Let's hope they don't then,' Gregory shouted. 'But what have you been up to?'

'Suspected of Communist leanings,' answered the prisoner. 'Pretty thick, I call it. Just because a snooping petty officer found us reading a copy of Karl Marx that we picked up in Tallinn. Old Bötticher's not a bad sort, but I reckon he thought someone would split on him if he ignored it, so he threw us both in the cooler.'

'Are you interested in Communism?' Gregory asked.

'*Himmel, nein!* What have the Communists ever done for their people that the *Führer* hasn't? It was just curiosity, that's all. I reckon we'll be let off with a reprimand when we get back to Tallinn.'

'Is that where we're going?'

'Yes, at least, I suppose so. We've been based on there ever since von Leeb took it. Are you a Communist?'

'No, we're not Communists, but we are anti-Hitler,' Gregory declared.

'May you rot then,' came the voice with sudden anger. 'The *Führer*'s led us to victory, ain't he? I don't hold being jugged against him. It's only the over-zealous little fellows like that snooping P.O. wot makes trouble for nothing. I don't want to talk to the likes of you.'

Kuporovitch was on the far side of Gregory from the two other prisoners so he could not catch what the sailor had said. In the ensuing silence he asked: 'Who's that you were shouting at?'

'There are two matelots in cells five and six,' Gregory replied. 'We are, apparently in one and two, and three and four are empty. They've been put in the bin for reading Karl Marx, but they don't hold with Communism. Like most of these young Germans who have been reared under Nazi influence they think, quite illogically, that Hitler is a great man, without understanding in the least that it is he who has robbed them of the right to read any book they choose, and most of their other liberties.'

'Do you think they heard what we were saying?'

'No. Not at that distance; and, if they did, they couldn't have understood it anyway, considering that when you and I are alone we always talk together in a mixture of mangled French and English.'

They then fell silent and remained so for a little time. Gregory had just looked at the luminous dial of his wrist-watch and seen that it was now just on half past two in the morning, when suddenly the U-boat's engines stopped.

She tilted a little, nose down, and ran on for a few hundred yards under her own way. Then she bumped, slithered and bumped again, coming gently to rest on the bottom.

'What the hell's gone wrong now!' Gregory exclaimed apprehensively.

'Nothing,' said Kuporovitch calmly. 'She went down deliberately; probably with the intention of lying doggo until some ship up above has passed us. She would be able to hear any vessel that was approaching through her hydrophones.'

Gregory was still uneasy. 'She wouldn't bother to stop for an ordinary ship,' he muttered. 'She'd just go on under water. It's much more likely that we've been picked up again by one of those blasted aeroplanes.'

Kuporovitch sat very still. A private theory he had just formed was now making him extremely uncomfortable. After they had first been spotted by the one stray aircraft it was to have been expected that others would arrive on the scene in a quarter of an hour or so, but it would take considerably longer for the Kronstadt anti-submarine flotilla to get under way and then catch up with them. Since the bombers had gone he had been assuming that the U-boat had been reported as accounted for and that, in consequence, the flotilla had put back to port; but now, he feared that he had been counting his chickens before they were hatched. He naturally refrained from passing on his unhappy idea to Gregory, and just sat there with his hands tightly clasped and his thumbs crossed.

And then it came.

Thump, thump, thump—thump, thump. Rumble, rumble, rumble. The anti-submarine flotilla had found them and was putting down a circle of depth-charges round the approximate spot at which they had been located.

The U-boat rocked from side to side, lifted from the bottom and bumped down heavily on to it again.

Thump, thump, thump. Another series of charges had been dumped overboard somewhat further off, but their explosions had a deeper, more powerful note than the bombs had seemed to have.

Gregory had jumped to his feet, but was flung down again. 'Stefan!' he cried. 'Stefan! What the hell's going on up there?'

'Sacré nom! I wish I knew,' Kuporovitch's voice came back, tense with the strain he was feeling. 'I'm afraid the anti-submarine flotilla has got on to us.'

238

Thump, thump—thump, thump, came the charges again; each one nearer. The last forced up the stern of the U-boat till she was at an angle of thirty degrees and as she sank back her nose rose instead. The alternating motion continued for a moment, as though she was a rocking-horse, then another explosion buffeted her sideways. Another and another forced great masses of water against her plates, each causing her to groan and shudder.

Gregory and Stefan were thrown about their cells like loose peas in two pods. Both of them were now scared half out of their wits, but they scarcely had time to think of their fears from the constant necessity of trying to keep their balance.

Suddenly, the submarine's engines started again. Her captain had evidently decided that it was no longer any use trying to pretend that she was not there, and that she would stand a better chance of eluding her attackers if she made a dash for it.

As she lifted, her engines increased in tempo. Even the prisoners could guess that she was now being forced up to maximum speed with a minimum of delay. For a few moments she pushed vigorously ahead. Then the destroyers were after her.

Thump, thump—thump, thump. Thump. A near miss smacked violently at her, forcing her nose ten degrees off her course. She shook as though every plate and girder in her were about to fall apart.

Complete panic had now seized Gregory. He was moaning like a child in pain, with his head buried in his hands. But the shock of the explosion flung him forward on to his knees, and only his hands saved his head from a nasty crack against the door of the cell. His knuckles were badly marked and as he drew one hand quickly back to his mouth the salt taste of blood told him that it was bleeding.

Kuporovitch was cursing solidly and unceasingly in several different languages.

The lights flickered wildly and went out, the engine stuttered; then both went on again and the U-boat forged ahead once more.

There were more thumps, more distant now, but the wash each surged against different portions of her hull, constantly jerking her first one way then another.

A new series of louder detonations came from close ahead. The engine cut out for a second then went into reverse. As the force of the explosions threw up her nose, down there in the cells they could feel the frightful straining of the vessel as the screws fought to check her way, stop her and draw her in the opposite direction to that in which she had been going.

239

Once the force of her forward motion was checked she began to turn, then suddenly, still turning, she began to forge ahead again. The last of the series of charges, which might well have got her had they continued on their former course, now helped her by jerking her nose round a few more degrees. A few moments later she had completed a semi-circle, straightened out, and, with her engines at full speed again, was heading back towards Kronstadt.

Depth charges were still being flung out somewhere astern of them but gradually the explosions grew more distant. With his hands still clasped and his teeth set Kuporovitch slowly counted five hundred, then he drew a deep breath and exclaimed, '*Nom de diable!* I believe he's foxed them again!'

Sweat from Gregory's face was now mixed with the blood on his hands. He felt as though he had been up for days on end, during them, plumbed the depths of hell. Sagging wearily on his seat he muttered: 'D'you really think so? But we're going back towards Leningrad, now, aren't we?'

'What's that?' shouted Kuporovitdh. 'Speak up. I can't hear you.'

'I said—' Gregory began, but he got no further.

THUMP came a depth charge, cutting him short, and the violence of the shock caused the submarine to reel and list to such a degree that they thought she was about to turn turtle. One of the destroyers that was hunting her had detected the *Kapitänleutnant*'s ruse and come racing after her at a far greater speed than hers.

THUMP . . . THUMP . . . THUMP. Three more charges exploded almost simultaneously. There was the sound of tearing steel, the fierce hiss of escaping steam, the wild clanging of alarm bells. The engines stopped and the lights went out.

'Oh heaven!' cried Gregory above the din. 'Get me out of this!'

The U-boat had been flung violently upward, then hurled to starboard, as though she were the plaything of an angry giant. Now, slightly tilted over on her port side, she was slowly sinking.

Gregory began to pound frantically on the steel door of his cell with his fists, yelling at the top of his voice: 'Let me out! Let me out!'

Kuporovitch and the two sailors further along the row were all kicking on their doors and letting forth a spate of blasphemous curses.

They could hear running feet crashing on the steel flooring of the passage above, the alarm bells stopped; then came silence.

One by one they ceased to pound upon the doors of their

cells and, after the uproar, the sudden absence of sound became more terrifying than the preceding pandemonium.

It was broken by another run of depth charges going off ahead of them, as the destroyer above raced on, not realising that she had already hit her mark. The concussions lifted the stricken submarine and tossed her about for a few minutes, as if she were in a heavy gale. Then she began to settle again, listing still more heavily to port.

Suddenly a faint blue light struck through the ventilator slits of the cells.

Gregory gave a gasp of thankfulness. After the pitch-black darkness those faint rays of light seemed positively heaven-sent, and from them he jumped to the conclusion that, after all, the U-boat was not irreparably damaged; but, in fact, the glimmer was caused only through the emergency lighting system having been switched on. Next moment he was cast down from astonished joy to new depths of fear.

For some minutes past he had been subconsciously aware of the sound of trickling water. Now, as he moved his foot slightly, he heard a faint splash. With a terrible contraction of the heart muscles he realised that he was crouching in an inch of it. The submarine was leaking; the bilge was already overflowing; the water had reached the level of the lower deck; the cell was slowly but surely filling up.

One of the sailors had evidently discovered the same thing, as he began to beat wildly on his cell door again. They all joined in and added their screams and curses, which rapidly blended into a soul-shaking overture of horror and distress.

A dull, rhythmic thumping brought a temporary cessation to their cries. The pumps were working and the sailor in cell number five, his difference in political opinion with Gregory now forgotten, joyfully called the news out to him. Yet the water was still rising. It was now up to their ankles.

In an agony of alternate hope and fear they waited to see what would happen next. To the throbbing another note was added. The engineers had got one of the engines going again. The U-boat, still half on her side, began to move slowly forward, then she took an upward slant. Instantly there was a rush of water towards her stern. In two minuties it had risen from their ankles to their knees.

Frantic with fear, Gregory and the sailors recommenced their shouts and prayers to be released; but as the vessel suddenly began to lift upward bodily, Kuporovitch yelled:

'It's all right. He's blowing his tanks! He's going to surface and surrender.'

But the conning-tower had not yet emerged above the water-line. Thump, thump, thump came the depth charges once

241

more. The wounded submarine was hurled round yet again by the concussions and for a moment almost thrown up on end, nose uppermost.

With a hideous roar the water surged through her towards her stern. It almost filled the lower passage and came cascading in fierce jets through the ventilator slits, the keyholes and the hinge cracks of the cell doors. The upending of the ship had flung all the prisoners against the walls of their cells, then to the floor. Instantly they felt the water bubbling up all around them, squirting upon them from a dozen different directions they gave way to a fresh access of panic. Soaked, wild-eyed, panting, they scrambled to their feet to renew their cursing, shouting and hammering.

Swiftly now the water rose from knee to thigh and from thigh to waist level. The U-boat was gradually righting herself again as the effect of the shock subsided. Slowly her bow came down to about ten degrees above horizontal and she heeled over once more to port, but the water did not cease to rise in the cells; it forced its way up only a little less rapidly.

The alarm bells began to ring again; this time in short, strident spasms.

'They're abandoning ship!' shouted the sailor in number five. '*Lieber Gott*, if they forget us!'

For an instant that wild cry gave Gregory new hope. He knew that it was a standing order in all navies that at the order to abandon ship an officer specially charged with the duty came down to the cells and liberated all prisoners, so that they should have an equal chance with the rest of the crew of saving their own lives.

But would the officer come? Perhaps in the excitement he would forget. Perhaps he had been injured or killed when the submarine had been hit. Perhaps he would realise that the after part of the lower deck was already three parts under water and think it too late to make the effort. Perhaps he would not be able to screw up his courage to the pitch of venturing down to that dark waterlogged hole in a sinking ship. Perhaps he had panicked himself, and regardless of all else was even now struggling for a place in the mass of men who must be fighting their way up through the conning-tower.

Then, like a physical blow came the thought that even if the officer did come he would not release the two enemy prisoners. Grauber had made his orders unmistakably clear. If the U-boat was caught and destroyed they were to be left to go down with her.

The water was now well above their waists and still rising, but very gradually. From a roaring spate it had become a gentle, seeping flow with a still, oily surface. Outside there came a sound of splashing, then the pale bluish light was reinforced by a slightly stronger goldish gleam. Someone had splashed their way down the ladder and was now flashing a torch outside the cells.

All four of the prisoners realised simultaneously that it must be someone who had come to let them out, and redoubled their cries for help.

The splashing started again. A new voice was telling the sailors to be patient. Gregory caught something about the keyholes of the cells, being under water which made it difficult to find them. The four prisoners suddenly fell silent, and it seemed a more tense silence than any that had yet occurred.

There was more splashing, then an exclamation of fervid thankfulness as one of the sailors was released. An agonising wait followed, then the splashing again and further cries of relief.

Gregory knew that the crucial moment had come. Were he and Stefan to be freed or left to drown? Once more he hammered on the door and cried: 'Let me out! For Christ's sake let me out!'

'All right, all right,' a voice replied irritably. 'She won't go down for another five minutes.'

Almost collapsing from relief, Gregory swayed and leaned for support against the side of his cell. It seemed an eternity before the man outside could find the keyhole, but at last a streak of light appeared down the side of the door as he sought to drag it open. Jerking his sodden furs about him, Gregory threw his weight against the panel and forced the door outward through the swirling waters.

When he lurched out into the passage he glimpsed the legs of the latter of the two sailors to be freed disappearing through the now strangely slanting trap-door, and saw that the officer, a young *Leutnant* with several days' growth of dark stubble on his chin, was fumbling at the lock of Kuporovitch's cell. His instinct was to dash for the ladder and scramble up it, but by the exercise of almost superhuman will-power he forced himself to stand quietly there waiting for his friend

With a jerk the officer wrenched the door of number one cell open a few inches. Next moment Kuporovitch brought his powerful shoulder against it with a crash and it gave a foot. Turning sideways he squeezed himself through the opening.

Having done his duty the officer did not wait for any thanks, or to see what happened to them. Jamming his torch into his pocket he seized the upper rung of the ladder and swung himself up through the trap-door like a monkey. Next moment his flying footsteps went clanging away as he raced along the steel corridor above.

'Up you go! Shouted Kuporovitch, and Gregory needed no second urging. Pushing his way through chest-high water he grasped the ladder, fumbled with his foot, found a lower rung and thrust his shoulders up through the square hole. As he gained the upper passage Kuporovitch was hard on his heels. Gregory leading, they ran with awkward lopsided steps up the now sloping and tilted corridor.

As they ran they saw that the crew had not yet all left the ship. Ahead of them a little group of sailors were crowded about the foot of the ladder that led up to the conning-tower. Their discipline had not broken under the strain of the action they had just been through, and they were standing there quietly waiting their turns to go up.

Among them Gregory suddenly caught sight of *Kapitän-leutnant* Bötticher, evidently superintending this final parade of his crew before, as captain, being himsef the last to leave the doomed ship.

At the sound of running footsteps he turned and saw Gregory and Stefan. A look of angry amazement suddenly dawned in his pale blue eyes.

They knew what that look meant without any telling. The *Kapitänleutnant* had given no order for their release. They had been freed by his junior, who doubtless had known nothing about them and simply unlocked their cells as a matter of routine. Bötticher might have lost his ship but he was still a well-disciplined German, and he had not forgotten the order he had been given by a man who was not only in a position to break him for good and all, but with a scrawl of a pen could consign every member of his family to a concentration camp. That one look made it as clear as if he had shouted his thoughts aloud, that he meant to carry out the order he had been given and see to it that the two enemy prisoners, although now free from their cells, still went down with the ship.

The young *Leutnant* was now standing at the end of the queue. Bötticher exchanged a few swift words with him, then drew his big service pistol. Pushing past the remaining members of his crew, who now had no eyes except for the conning-tower hatch, he advanced purposefully towards Gregory and Stefan.

They had both halted automatically a little way down the corridor. Neither of them was armed. A few moments ago, on the ending of their terrible ordeal, they had thought that their lives had been spared and that escape was certain. Now, once again, they knew themselves to be in mortal peril.

As the *Kapitänleutnant* strode towards them the submarine

244

suddenly lurched, and heeled over still further to port. Momentarily he lost his balance, and with his pistol still held out in front of him, reeled against the lower wall of the passage.

Gregory, all thought of claustrophobia now banished from his mind, sprang towards him in a desperate attempt to seize his gun. But he, too, stumbled on the sloping floor. The sailor, more accustomed to the swiftly changing planes of a ship's deck, recovered quickest. In the instant he had regained his balance and had them squarely covered again.

Pointing to a door that stood open just beside them, he snapped: 'Get in there, both of you!'

As he saw them hesitate he added, 'Go on, or I'll shoot you where you stand.'

They knew well enough that he was making no idle threat, Behind him all but two of the sailors and the *Leutnant* had now gone up the hatch. The last stricken lurch of the submarine showed that she was now rapidly filling with water, and might plunge to the bottom at any moment. He had only a few moments left in which to save himself. He meant exactly what he said. He was in deadly earnest.

Kuporovitch, with Russian fatalism, felt that the game was up. They had lost out after all, beaten at the eleventh hour, right on the post. Under the menace of the gun, he backed a few steps through the doorway of the cabin.

Gregory, watching his adversary like a lynx, followed suit, and stepped back over the skirting-board.

The *Kapitänleutnant* took two swift paces forward and stretched out his left hand to grasp the doorknob, so that he might slam the door shut and lock them in.

At the same instant Gregory thrust out his right hand and seized that of the German. As his grip tightened on the outstretched hand he flung himself backwards with all his force.

He crashed back against the side of a bunk but the pull of his weight brought the *Kapitänleutnant* flying after him into the cabin. The gun went off with a deafening report. The bullet thudded into a bulkhead. The violence of the movement had thrown both of them off their balance. They fell sprawling to the floor in a tangled heap.

As the back of Gregory's head hit the deck the force of the blow knocked him almost unconscious. For a moment he felt a blinding pain while stars and circles flashed in front of his eyes, and he lay there helpless. The German was face down on top of him, his left hand still clutched in Gregory's right; but in his right hand he still had hold of his gun. With a swift movement he twisted his wrist over on the deck so that the barrel of the pistol was pointing inward towards Gregory's body.

Kuporovitch lifted his heavy boot and brought it down with all his weight on the hand that held the pistol. Three of the *Kapitänleutnant*'s fingers were crushed and mangled between the boot, the weapon and the deck. He let out a scream of pain.

Jerking himself up, he rolled off, Gregory, snatched up the pistol with his left hand and, turning, thrust it upwards towards Kuporovitch. The Russian snatched up a water carafe by its neck from its swinging cradle beside the bunk.

Gregory tried to sit up. The pain in his head was excruciating. The cabin seemed to be going round and round. His eyes would not focus properly. He was now behind the German. He saw his mangled hand, with which he was supporting himself, and saw him raise his pistol in the other. Gregory thrust out his own hand. For a moment it wavered drunkenly, then it grasped the collar of the *Kapitänleutnant*'s jacket and jerked him back.

Again the gun exploded in the air, and the second wasted bullet clanged metallically as it struck a girder in the ceiling. The German was now strained back, his face turned upward. With all the weight of his powerful shoulders behind the blow Kuporovitch brought the water carafe smashing down upon it.

The heavy glass bottle shattered with the impact. The *Kapitänleutnant*'s nose was broken and crushed flat; his mouth was a jagged rent from which blood was pouring; his light blue eyes were starting from their sockets.

Gregory heaved him aside and staggered to his feet. He could see clearly again now, and for the first time in many hours he was smiling. Yet, as he stepped across the German's body, he reeled against the bunk.

Seeing that he was still groggy Kuporovitch cried anxiously, 'You all right?' At Gregory's nod, the Russian added, 'Come on then!' and grasped his arm.

As they turned towards the doorway the submarine gave another horrifying lurch that slumped her over until she was lying nearly on her side. The upper passage was now awash and the side of it opposite to them formed a V-like trench, one angle of which was formed by the bulkheads of another row of cabins and the other by the floor. Down it the oily water was eddying and swirling.

One glance towards the conning-tower hatch was enough to show that the little group which had been beneath it was no longer there. The few minutes of desperate conflict in the cabin had been enough for the remaining members of the crew to make their way up on deck.

As the victors of the fight stepped from the cabin they both

246

slid on the slippery sloping plates and fell with a splash into the waterlogged channel.

At that instant the emergency lights went out. A new terror gripped them as, knee deep in water, they strove to find a footing in the darkness. For a few moments the blackness weighed upon them like a pall of death, then, as their eyes became accustomed to it, they realised that it was not completely dark. Away ahead of them there was a faint patch of greyness. It was the reflected moonlight coming down the conning-tower hatch.

Slipping, staggering, falling, they made towards it, then groped their way awkwardly up the sideways-tilted ladder. As they emerged from the hatch they saw that a Soviet destroyer was lying about a hundred yards off their port beam and that one of her boats was alongside the U-boat, taking off the last half dozen of the crew. A bright moon rode in a clear sky and by its light they could also see two other destroyers and several smaller warcraft in the near distance, slowly circling about their kill.

Clinging to the hand-rails, they hurried along the dangerously sloping deck to the boat and scrambled into it. The other survivors hardly gave them a glance, being too absorbed in their own misery at having just become prisoners. But suddenly, as the boat was about to push off, the *Leutnant* noticed Gregory and, starting up exclaimed:

'What have you done with the *Kapitänleutnant*? Where is he?'

Gregory stared him straight in the face, and replied: 'He will not be coming. He is going down with his ship.'

'But it was you who were to go down with the ship!' cried the young German. 'It was an order! He told me so, and that I had been wrong to release you.'

'That's just too bad, isn't it?' grinned Gregory. 'Well, things didn't pan out that way. My friend bust his face in with the wrong end of a bottle, and we felt no obligation to saddle ourselves with a Nazi murderer.'

Suddenly the *Leutnant*'s hand jerked down to his belt. The Russians had not yet disarmed their prisoners, and he pulled out his gun.

The Soviet sailor who had pushed off the boat saw the gesture and hit him a sharp blow on the wrist with the end of the boat-hook. The gun fell from his hand and clattered on the bottom boards. For a second the young man stared at him open-mouthed, then he burst into tears.

'Come on,' said Gregory, not unkindly. 'Take it easy. You're only a youngster and you showed plenty of pluck in coming down to that stinking hole to let out the prisoners,

247

Your trouble is that you've been brought up all wrong; but by the time you get back to Germany things will be different and you may become quite a decent citizen.'

Ten minutes later they were on the fore-deck of the destroyer being herded together with the other prisoners. Kuporovitch stepped out of the mob and addressed one of the Soviet officers in Russian.

'My friend and I were prisoners on the U-boat. He is an English-man and I too, am British, although born in Russia. We are both war correspondents, and were being taken to Germany. May we see your captain?'

After expressing his astonishment that two British prisoners should have been on board the submarine, the officer took them aft and up to the bridge.

The captain of the destroyer was in a high good humour on account of his recent kill. Kuporovitch congratulated him on it, then told him that Gregory and himself had been captured in Tallinn while reporting on the campaign in the Baltic States. They produced their papers, which were all in order, so the captain saw no reason to disbelieve them, and, after congratulating them on their escape, sent them below with the officer to whom Kuporovich had just spoken.

The officer, having introduced himself as Lieutenant Dakov took them to the mess and gave them half a tumbler of vodka apiece. Then, as they were now shivering with cold, he suggested that they should turn in for a bit while he had their clothes and furs dried. Gratefully they followed him to a double cabin, stripped off their saturated things, and got between the blankets in the bunks. Utterly exhausted, within five minutes they were both sound asleep.

By half past four the destroyer was back at her moorings in Kronstadt bay, but her captain had the kindness not to have his guests called until ten o'clock. Their dry clothes were brought to them and, greatly refreshed by a seven-hours' sleep, they dressed. They were then given a good breakfast in the mess and, as soon as they had finished, Lieutenant Dakov told them he was going to take them ashore.

Their terrible experience of the previous night was still too recent for them to get it quite into focus as yet, and they both felt that they had not actually lived it but, rather, passed through a most appalling nightmare. So far they had had little chance to speak of it to each other, or to make future plans; but immediately they were settled in the boat Gregory said anxiously to Stefan:

'Where is he taking us?'

'To the Naval Governor's office,' Kuporovitch replied. 'Naturally they want an account of how we came to be captured,'

Gregory already knew that the Soviet officer who was with em could not understand French, so he went on, 'What do u suggest telling them?'

'That we were both pressmen working in Sweden, and that hen Hitler attacked Russia we decided to slip over to the altic States, to report the new campaign. That as the Soviet rces were driven back we too fell back, until we were cor-red in Tallinn. Naturally we were anxious to escape cap-re by the Germans, so we tried to get away in a small boat, it we were caught by the submarine and taken prisoners, 'ter all.'

'That sounds a pretty plausible story. The only trouble is at our passports won't bear it out. They have never been anked in Sweden, and they have been franked in the Soviet nion.'

Kuporovitch shrugged. 'But they are visad for Sweden, d in fact, for practically every country that is still neutral Europe.'

'Yes, because old Pellinore had the blessed forethought to alise that we might want to come out of Russia a different ay to that by which we went in.'

'All right, then. The fact that they are good for Sweden is lf the battle. I shall say that since they are diplomatic pass-rts entrance and exit stamps were not considered necessary ere. And by the mercy of God the Soviet Stamp does not ow at what place we entered the Union. I looked at mine is morning. The Soviets took over the Baltic States over a ar ago, so if we had been there it would have been the Rus-ns who stamped them, and there is nothing to show that e came through Persia because, when we did, the country as in a state of upheaval.'

'That's true. And as we were travelling as semi-military rsonnel all the way out from England our passports weren't amped in the Middle East either. Still, Kronstadt is inside e Leningrad defence ring and, except by making one's way rough the German lines, which they would not expect two essmen to attempt, there is no way out—'

'They could fly us out.'

'Yes, I was just about to add—except by air. But that eds a pretty high priority. Naturally we should ask them to y us to Moscow; but if they say that space in an aircraft nnot be spared, what do you propose suggesting that they ould do with us?'

'I shall ask them to let us proceed to Leningrad, in order at we may be attached to Marshal Voroshilov's press bureau d make ourselves useful there, until a place in an aircraft ing to Moscow can be found for us.'

'Right. Now say that they question me separately. How lon
were we supposed to have been prisoners in the U-boat?'

'Let us say for three days.'

'How long were we at sea in the little boat before the su
picked us up?'

'Two days; and we were picked up soon after dawn on th
third day, about thirty miles west of Tallinn. The boat was
small motor-launch. We had plenty of fuel but the engine ha
failed and neither of us knew how to put it right.'

Gregory took up the fabrication. 'We left Sweden in
tramp, two days before the stamps on our passports sho
that we entered Russia, and we went first to Riga. We had bee
working in Stockholm as freelance journalists and thought
a good chance to get a scoop for the British papers because
as far as we knew, there were no official Ministry of Informa
tion correspondents attached to the Soviet forces. We had bee
in Sweden since the fall of Norway. We took refuge there be
cause we got cut off from the British forces operating roun
Trondheim. But how the hell did we get ourselves attache
to the Legation?'

They both thought hard for a moment, then Gregory adde
'I know. We'll say that free-lance journalism is our norm
profession, but it is a precarious existence and the war offere
a chance of steady jobs; so we got ourselves taken on by th
Ministry of Economic Warfare as temporary Civil Servant
As we had volunteered for service overseas we were attache
to the British Legation in Oslo; but, after a bit we got fed-u
with office routine, so when the trouble started there, we wer
off free-lancing again. There's nothing so terribly improbab
about that.'

'No,' Kuporovitch agreed. 'After all, Soviet officers an
officials know practically nothing of how British wartim
Ministries work and the conditions under which they issu
diplomatic passports, so they're not likely to question
much on that side of our story. It is our experiences in th
U-boat which will interest them.'

'We'll say nothing of Grauber, of course.'

'Why not? If we give his description they could send o
an alert to all Soviet forces on the Esthonian coast, and the
might catch him.'

'No. Old man Grauber is as slippery as an eel, and a migh
fast worker. The Russian-held belt is only about thirty mil
deep out there, and I wouldn't mind betting that he's reache
the German lines by this time. In any case the hope of the
picking him up is so slight that it isn't worth the risk of th
trouble we may land ourselves in if we mention him.'

'Why should we land ourselves in trouble?'

250

'Because we'd have such a frightful lot of explaining to do. we were just a couple of strays picked up from a boat how ould we know anything about Grauber? It's a thousand to ne that we'd have spent the whole of our three days in the ck-up, so we wouldn't have even seen him. Even if we had e wouldn't have known who or what he was. And we cer- inly wouldn't know how or when he came aboard the ship left it. We'd have to make up a whole new story to account r such knowledge and that might lead to all sorts of com- ications.'

Kuporovitch nodded. 'You're right. I hadn't thought of at,' and Gregory went on:

'We've got to keep our story as simple as we possibly can. ch a hell of a lot hangs on our being believed. We've had marvellous break but we're very far from being out of the ood yet.'

'Yes, I realise that.'

'Good! Our attitude is that we're only too anxious to help it we know practically nothing, because we've spent the last ree days in the U-boat's cells. We don't know anything about r having picked anyone up off Kronstadt or having put meone ashore further down the coast. If we can put that ver we're as good as free men, and with a little luck we'll get ick to London and complete our mission. But if we fail we'll d ourselves back in the Lubianka; and we can't expect arshal Voroshilov to take any risk of our being taken out Soviet hands again.'

The boat had hove to alongside a jetty while they had been lking, and they finished their conversation only as they were alking up it with their escort.

The scene on the water-front of the famous Russian naval ase was one of great activity. Warships of all sizes lay at nchor in the bay and small craft of all kinds were contin- lly going to and from them. On the quays scores of sailors ere handling stores or passing to and fro along the street. here was only a sprinkling of civilians and women to be en as Kronstadt was a purely naval port and entry to it uld be obtained only by special permit. But Gregory and efan were not given long to observe their surroundings, as few hundred yards from the jetty stood the big Soviet dmiralty building and their guide took them into it.

Having shown his pass he led the way upstairs to the first por, put them into a waiting-room and left them there. He as away for some time and during his absence Gregory uld not help feeling distinctly uneasy. He recalled Mr. Mic- wber into whose mouth Dickens had put the admirable dic- m: 'Income twenty shillings a year, expenditure nineteen

251

and sixpence—happiness. Income twenty shillings a year, e
penditure twenty shillings and sixpence—misery.' He kne
that the coming interview could result in no half measure
Just like having or not having the odd sixpence in hand
the end of the year, they would either get away with it con
pletely and be free to use their wits in devising a good w
to get home, or they would find themselves back in a Sov
prison, as suspects; be identified in due course, have to fa
the merciless wrath of the Marshal, who would certainly t
lieve that they had been in league with the Germans the who
time and had somehow managed to arrange to be rescued
their pay-masters.

At last this period of anxious waiting came to an end. T
officer returned, led them down several passages, and usher
them into a room where a bald, moon-faced naval capta
with prawn-like eyebrows was sitting.

The captain greeted them pleasantly, asked them to sit dov
and listened intently to Kuporovitch's story. Having look
carefully at their passports he handed them back and a
peared quite satisfied. He then asked a number of questio
about the U-boat and their activities in Esthonia. About t
three days they were supposed to have spent in the cells the
was little to be said, and as the Esthonian battle front h
been much like any other Kuporovitch was able to bl
quite convincingly about experiences they might well ha
met with there.

Gregory could not understand what was being said, b
he sensed that things seemed to be going quite well, and f
considerably more cheerful.

Having talked to Kuporovitch for some time, their int
rogator picked up a telephone on his desk and spoke brie
into it. A few minutes later another officer came into the roo
evidently having been sent for, and it transpired that he n
only spoke English but had at one time been a junior nav
attaché at the Soviet Embassy in London. He questioned t
two of them, and particularly Gregory, about the city, a
after a little while reported to the bald man that, whether th
were British or not, they certainly must have lived in t
British capital, as they knew it well.

The bald captain murmured something and the other offic
said, 'Will you please both to remove your collars and ties?'

Gregory wondered what on earth could be the reason f
this strange and apparently ominous request; but there w
no alternative but to obey; so he took the articles off a
handed them over. Kuporovitch did the same and the Englis
speaking officer looked inside the collars at their markings, a
at the labels in the ties.

252

In a flash Gregory realised what the game was. The ex-naval attaché was checking upon where they had been bought. A glow of delighted satisfaction ran through him. He knew that on his return from France Kuporovitch had got himself a new outfit at Harrods, and for many years he had always bought his own shirtings at Beale and Inman's in Bond Street.

The officer handed the things back with a smile and spoke to the captain. The captain smiled too, and said to Kuporovitch in Russian: 'I had an idea that you might be two Nazi agents who had taken the opportunity offered by the sinking U-boat to try to plant yourselves on us. But if that had been the case you would have had no chance to make such careful preparations as getting your clothes in London, so it is now quite clear that you are not. I take it you now wish to get home as soon as possible so I must see what arrangements we can make for you.'

Kuporovitch translated to Gregory and they both laughed heartily at the idea that they might have been Nazi spies. The captain then took some forms from a drawer in his desk and began to fill them up.

When he had finished the English-speaking officer handed the papers to Kuporovitch and said: 'There is a liberty boat. She leaves the main pier for Oranienbaum at twelve midday. You show these passes and take her. These other papers here; they are railway vouchers from Oranienbaum to Leningrad. You take the train. You arrive and you report to the Leningrad Central Travel Bureau. For them it is to arrange your journey to Moscow and next home, if that is possible.'

Taking the papers from him, Kuporovitch expressed his thanks and stood up. Gregory followed suit. There was a general bowing, smiling and shaking of hands. Then Dakov, who had remained silent all this time, accompanied them out of the room, saying that he would show them the pier at which the liberty boat lay.

The three of them went downstairs and out into the street. Gregory felt almost like singing with happiness and Kuporovitch was feeling equally gay. They had made the grade and the cream of the jest was that they owed their liberty, their freedom from the promise they had made to Marshal Voroshilov, and an excellent chance to get home safely with the results of their mission in the bag, all to the machinations of their old enemy *Gruppenführer* Grauber.

As they walked down the crowded quay, Gregory asked Stefan: 'What is this liberty boat we're going on? I thought naval people sent liberty boats off only from ships?'

'Kronstadt is entirely a naval station,' Kuporovitch explained. 'No wives are allowed to live there. They all have home

253

or lodgings across the water in Oraneinbaum. In a way th
two places are like your Portsmouth and Southampton. Al
though Oranienbaum is much smaller, of course, and as fa
as I know there is no ban against sailors' wives and sweet
hearts living in Portsmouth. Still, there is a certain similarity
and that is the reason for the liberty boat, which goes to an
fro several times a day.'

'Ah well,' murmured Gregory happily. 'Anyway, it's th
first stage on our way back to England. Home and Beauty.'

Kuporovitch did not reply. He was staring in fascinate
horror at two men who were approaching along the pave
ment, directly in front of him. One was a short, fat, middl
aged man in a dark uniform; the other was some twent
years younger and a Soviet naval rating. They resembled on
another so strongly that anyone could have guessed them t
be a father who had come to Kronstadt on a visit to hi
sailor son. Both had the yellowish skins, almond eyes an
high cheekbones of Mongolians. The elder was the *Ogp*
officer who, four nights before, had on Colonel Gudarniev
orders booked them into the Lubianka.

Recognition was mutual. Jerking up his arm and pointing
the fat Mongolian began to shout:

'Help, Comrades! Seize those two men! Seize them! The
are the prisoners who escaped last night in the missing Blac
Maria!'

16

Warrant for Arrest

Once more, Gregory could not understand the words, but he
too, now recognised the fat Mongolian-featured *Ogpu* office
and instantly guessed what he was shouting about.

Within twenty seconds his loud cries had caused a score of
heads to turn; within sixty a crowd of half a hundred peopl
was milling round Gregory, Kuporovitch, Dakov, the *Ogp*
man and his sailor son; and from all directions another hur
dred were running up to find out the cause of the commotior
Except for a few longshoremen and two Soviet Wrens th
crowd was mainly composed of fine healthy-looking youn

254

llows with flattish faces and shaven heads, all wearing the
uniform of the Soviet Navy.

Nothing short of being possessed of wings could have enabled the two friends to get away. Even if they had taken to
their heels at the very first shout they could not have covered
twenty yards along the busy quay without being surrounded.
They could only stand there, stricken silent by the overwhelm-
ing disaster which in one brief second had brought their hopes
and plans crashing like a house of cards about their ears.

Brief, excited explanations followed, punctuated by the
angry shouts of the milling crowd. The *Ogpu* man insisted that
they were the escaped prisoners and vouched for having
booked them into the Lubianka himself four nights before.
Dakov told how they had been rescued only a few hours
previously from a German submarine. Just as Gregory had
only too rightly feared, in the case of such a misfortune, it
was immediately assumed that they must be German agents
and that a daring coup had been staged by their Nazi friends
to rescue them.

As scraps of the conversation drifted to the nearest on-
lookers and a garbled version of these were passed back to
those behind the crowd became angrier and angrier. Shouts
of, 'They're German! Hitlerite bandits! Spies! Nazi spies!' began to go up in increasing volume, and it looked as if the two
friends were in grave danger of being lynched.

In vain Kuporovitch strove to drown the uproar by yelling:
'We're British! We're British, I tell you! We were captured by
the Germans and taken aboard the U-boat against our will.'

A sailor struck him a blow on the back of the neck; another
seized Gregory by the arm and attempted to drag him off the
pavement. A dozen hands were stretched out to grab at them
and pull them down.

The situation began to look really ugly, but they were saved
by the intervention of several officers who were among the
crowd. Dakov and the *Ogpu* man called for their assistance.
After a few curt threats that disciplinary action would be
taken if the prisoners were harmed, the sailors suddenly drew
off and made a passage so that they could be marched back to
the Admiralty.

Realising that there was no possibility of their learning the
dénouement of this exciting scene the crowd now melted
away as rapidly as it had gathered, so that by the time they
reached the door of the big block Gregory and Kuporovitch
were accompanied only by Dakov, the *Ogpu* man and his son.
The youngster was sent into a waiting-room while the other
two, having shown their passes, silently escorted the prisoners
upstairs to the first floor.

255

On reaching the door of the room where they had bee[n] interviewed Dakov went in, leaving the others outside in th[e] corridor. The fat Mongolian evidently had no fear that th[e] prisoners might attempt to escape, now that they were ac[-] tually inside the building, and it did not even cross the min[d] of either of them to attempt to do so since he was arme[d] which they were not, and at his first cry help would hav[e] been so readily available to detain them.

The whole disaster had occurred so suddenly, and so litt[le] time had elapsed since their denunciation, that neither [of] them had had a chance to think out a story which might off[er] even the remotest possibility of getting them out of the[ir] mess; but, while he was walking up the stairs, Gregory ha[d] realised that they must at least endeavour to adopt the sam[e] line when questioned, otherwise they would damn themselv[es] irretrievably by contradicting one another. So when they ha[l-] ted in the passage he took a chance that the *Ogpu* man mig[ht] understand French and seized the opportunity to say to Stefan[:]

'Quick! Tell me what course you mean to adopt.'

'We'd better deny everything and refuse to talk,' suggeste[d] Kuporovitch.

'Silence!' snapped the *Ogpu* man, in Russian. Evidently h[e] had not understood, but all the same had no intention [of] allowing the prisoners to formulate a common policy befor[e] they were examined.

Gregory nodded quick approval, just as Dakov reappear[ed] and said:

'The captain has just put through a long-distance call on t[he] telephone, so we must wait five or ten minutes before goi[ng] in to him.'

The little group then remained there for some moments [in] complete silence. As Gregory thought it over he did not fe[el] that in the face of their positive identification by the Mo[n-] golian there would be very much point in denying that. [In] fact, it was absurd to do so since he had booked them into t[he] Lubianka under the same names as they had on their pas[s-] ports. and these were already known to the captain befor[e] whom they were shortly to be re-examined. On the oth[er] hand to refuse to talk at all seemed much the best policy f[or] the present, as if they were left together they might yet hav[e] an opportunity for concocting an account of what had ha[p-] pened which would appear slight less damaging than the[ir] case as presented in the facts known to the Russians at t[he] moment. With that in mind he ignored the *Ogpu* man's ord[er] and said:

'We must admit our identity, but let's say that only Marsh[al] Voroshilov knows the truth about us and that we refuse

256

discuss matters until we are brought before him.'

'Silence!' snapped the Mongolian once more; and, drawing his pistol, he jabbed it into Gregory's side.

Having got his point across Gregory shook his head and smiled at him, as though he had not understood. The four of them then fell silent again.

The thing that worried Gregory so intensely was their apparent complicity in their own escape. There was no avoiding the Naval Intelligence captain learning in the next few moments that they had told him a pack of lies about their having been in Sweden and Esthonia. In consequence, he would be furious with them for having tricked him so completely and immediately become convinced that his first theory, about their being German agents who, on the sinking of the U-boat had endeavoured to plant themselves, was correct. The fact that they had escaped while being moved from the Lubianka the previous night would only serve to corroborate that. He would have every possible reason for condemning them out of hand, and their only tenuous line of temporary safety lay in that, as they had escaped from the Lubianka, he might send them back there to be dealt with. Even if that happened the odds were that Voroshilov would not grant them another interview but order the suspended sentence of death to be carried out at once, merely on the written report that they had succeeded in escaping and been recaptured. The more Gregory thought about it the more slender he felt their chances were.

They had been standing there for about three minutes when Kuporovitch looked at the *Ogpu* man, pointed at the next door along the corridor, and said something in Russian.

There was some lettering on the door which Gregory could not read, but on the Mongolian nodding Kuporovitch moved towards it and Gregory stepped after him. As the door swung open at a touch he saw that the room beyond was a man's washplace and lavatory.

As they went in the *Ogpu* man and Dakov followed them inside. Kuporovitch walked straight over to one of the cabinets, entered it, and shot the bolt behind him. Gregory stepped into the one next door and did likewise.

The bottom of the window was open a few inches. Easing it gently up, Gregory saw that it looked down into a small courtyard surrounded by a well in the building. As they were on the first floor the ground was only about twelve feet below; and the courtyard was empty. The second Gregory realised that, he stepped up, on to the seat and thrusting a leg over the sill began to wriggle through the window. However slender this chance of escape might be, to take it was better than submitting tamely to being shot that night, or at best being sent back to the Lubianka.

Turning over on his tummy, he lowered himself till his hands were gripping the sill and his legs dangling. As he dropped, he blessed Stefan with all his heart for the brilliant idea that had inspired this eleventh-hour attempt to get away, since it would at least enable them to give their captors a run for their money.

He came down feet first, staggered, and fell heavily. In a moment he was up again and looking round for Kuporovitch, whom he had expected to reach the ground as soon as, or perhaps even before himself. He certainly had not had time to get down and out of the courtyard without Gregory catching a glimpse of him as he jumped himself, and not even a projecting limb showed that he was, so far, attempting to get out of his window.

'Stefan!' Gregory cried in a low, urgent whisper.

There was no reply, so he ran back a few paces and looked up again. The bottom of Kuporovitch's window was a little open, just as his own had been. Through it he could see the back of the Russian's neck and the grizzled hair at the base of his skull. Apparently he had simply made a natural request, without the least thought of escape and was just sitting there doing his business.

'Stefan!' called Gregory, slightly louder this time.

Kuporovitch did not even budge.

Gregory cast a frantic glance about him at the surrounding windows. The rooms on the ground floor appeared to be mainly store-rooms. The first and second floors were offices and through some of their windows he glimpsed vague signs of activity, but no one was actually looking down at him.

'Stefan!' he called again, raising his voice to a pitch which made him fearful that half the people in the rooms overlooking the courtyard must hear it.

At last Kuporovitch responded. Screwing round his head he peered out over the sill and, on seeing Gregory, his heavy black eyebrows shot up with surprise.

Gregory ran back to the wall below the row of lavatories, then slid along it to a corner of the courtyard, so that he should be visible from only two of its sides while he waited. For the next few moments he stood there almost hopping from foot to foot with impatience while Kuporovitch did up his clothes. He did not hear the window raised because the Russian was clever enough to pull the plug in order to drown the sound, but next minute there was a heavy thump and he landed within a few yards of Gregory.

Near the far corner of the courtyard there was a door. As

Kuporovitch scrambled to his feet Gregory ran towards it. To his immeasurable relief he found that it was not locked, but gave on his turning the handle. With Kuporovitch now close on his heels, he slipped inside it. The door opened on to an empty side passage, closing it gently behind them they paused for a moment.

'D'you mean to hide?' whispered the Russian, still gasping for breath.

Gregory shook his head, 'No. Once they have a chance to check up that we haven't left the building they'd start a systematic search, and they'd be bound to find us within a few hours. We haven't got an earthly unless we can get out of the building in the next five minutes.'

'We'd have to show passes to get out.'

'Not necessarily. The chap from the destroyer showed his both times when he came in, but they didn't bother him for as he came out. That's the practice in lots of Government buildings. But it means our using the same entrance. D'you think you could find it?'

'First right, right again, left, then right,' Kuporovitch said after a moment. 'That is, if the passages here are on the same as the first floor.'

'That's as I remember it,' agreed Gregory. 'Come on, we haven't got a second to lose.'

As they started off, Gregory went on: 'When we get to the hall we mustn't seem in a hurry and you must be talking to me loudly in Russian. Better choose a subject now. Something we might be arguing about that has nothing to do with the war. I know, you've read Dostoevsky and Tolstoy, haven't you?'

'Of course.'

'Then you can be laying down the law to me that Dostoevsky was a far greater writer than the old Count. If we can raise the nerve for it the strongest card we could possibly play would be for you to grab my arm just as we got opposite the desk, and pull me up for a minute while you angrily hammer home some point or other. I only hope to God that these passages *do* run under those on the first floor.'

The passed a messenger, two girl clerks and an officer, none of whom took any notice of them. While they traversed the echoing stone corridors Gregory was desperately trying to calculate times. After Kuporovitch had pulled the plug the *gpu* man would have given him a couple of minutes, at least, to put himself to rights before becoming suspicious about his non-appearance. The fact that only one plug had been pulled would probably cause their captors to wait a moment or two before doing anything about either of them. The odds were,

259

therefore, that from the time Stefan had dropped out of the window they would have not less than three and not more than five minutes' clear start before the Mongolian began to bang on the doors. They had crossed the courtyard in something less than a minute, their swift conference had lasted about the same length of time, and, at a fast walk, one can cover a lot of ground in sixty seconds. It looked as if they should reach the hall with about a minute to spare before the *Ogpu* man had definitely made up his mind that they were staying in the lavatories too long.

What would happen then? Gregory wondered, his thoughts racing on. The Mongolian might think that they were still in there, having both taken poison, or hanged themselves from fear that, if they remained alive they might be tortured. Both he and Dakov were only visitors in the building. That might make all the difference to the escapers between getting away and immediate recapture. The two visitors would, perhaps, hesitate before destroying Admiralty property by breaking down or forcing the doors of the compartments. They would probably waste precious time in finding someone to summon the guard to do that.

It was possible, of course, that they might look out of one of the other windows and see the tracks of the fugitives in the snow that covered the courtyard, but even if they did, they would not be able to give a general alarm themselves. It was a safe bet that in the Soviet Admiralty some form of alarm system existed at the sounding of which all exits were closed and guards turned out, and it was probably operated from the command post. But the visitors would not know where to find that, so in any case they would have to go to the bald captain's office and explain matters to him before a general search could be ordered.

He had got so far in his agitated speculations when, to his immense relief, they saw that the fourth passage into which they had turned was leading them out into the main hall.

Kuporovitch had realised that at the same instant and immediately began his literary dissertation in a loud voice. As they entered the hall he was declaiming heatedly that the *Brothers Karamazov* was a far greater work than *War and Peace*. Pulling up with a jerk in front of the desk, he suddenly looked straight at the man behind it and appealed to him for his support.

'Do you not agree with me, Comrade? This blockhead here contends that Tolstoy is our greatest Russian writer, while I say there are many superior to him.'

Gregory halted too, and was on tenterhooks at this audacity. He thought it a splendid piece of bravado on Stefan's

260

part but was terrified that they might become involved in a general argument, in which it must soon transpire, that he could not understand what was being said.

The man looked a little surprised, but smiled and said: 'Tolstoy was a fine writer in a dark age, Comrade, but I agree with you that there have been many better since. My own favourite is Maxim Gorky.'

'There!' cried Kuporovitch triumphantly. 'You see!' And grabbing Gregory by the arm he turned him quickly towards the door.

Gregory smiled, shrugged as though he was still not convinced and allowed himself to be led away by his verbose companion. With every step he took he feared to hear the man call out after them to see their passes, but he was just smiling amusedly at their backs. He had recognised them as having enterered the building with the *Ogpu* man and the destroyer officer a quarter of an hour before. There had been nothing to show that they were under arrest or that one of them was a foreigner. Strictly speaking, as they were civilians and had no passes of their own, they should have been seen out by the officers who had brought them in; but officers were sometimes slack about that sort of thing if they were pressed for time, and such minor breaches of the regulations were not infrequent.

When they had passed the sentry on the door their sense of relief was tremendous, but so fleeting as to be gone in a bare moment, since they knew that they had yet to get off the fortress island and that a hue-and-cry might start up after them at any second.

They turned right, as they had done before on leaving the building with Dakov, the same thought being in both their minds—that their one chance of getting clear was to catch the liberty boat before their descriptions had been circulated and the dock police warned to keep a look-out for them.

'D'you know where the main jetty is?' Gregory asked in a low voice.

Kuporovitch nodded. 'I think so; and unless things have changed since I was last here they use as a liberty boat one of those old two-funnelled flat-bottomed ferries, so we ought to be able to spot her. It's five to twelve though, so we'll have to step out of we're to make it.'

Side by side they hurried down the quay. It was still thronged, but the twenty minutes that had elapsed since the mob had surged round them had greatly altered the composition of the crowd. The passing pedestrians who had witnessed the excitement had now left the spot to proceed upon their various activities, and many of the small boats that had then been loading up with stores or waiting for officers from the ships had now put off, others with different crews having taken their places. Nevertheless they dared not break into a run for fear of attracting attention, as some of the sailors who had seen them arrested when they passed that way before might recognise them, and tumble to it that, having eluded their guards, they were escaping.

They reached the jetty at one minute to twelve. There could be no mistaking it as, at its far end, lay the old-fashioned, two-funnelled ferry. Three sailors reached its entrance at the same moment and began to run. Now that they had an obvious reason for hurrying, Gregory and Stefan followed their example.

As they pelted along just behind the sailors both of them were wondering desperately if they would get over the next hurdle that lay immediately ahead of them. Barely eight minutes had elapsed since Kuporovitch had dropped from the window, but by this time it was pretty certain that the *Ogpu* man would be giving excited explanations to the Naval Intelligence captain. Would they jump to it at once that the prisoners had lost not a second in getting out of the Admiralty building, and, having their liberty boat passes still on them, make a desperate effort to get away on her? If so they would telephone to the jetty and the fugitives would be stopped at the control post at its head before they could get aboard. Against that there was a fair chance that the speed and audacity with which they had acted might yet save them. Back at the Admiralty it might not occur to anyone that they could have got out so quickly. In that case the guards would be put on to searching the ground floor storerooms for them and the doorkeeper might not even be questioned for a quarter of an hour or so yet.

Breathless they arrived at the end of the jetty. Two marines were standing in front of the hut there examining all passes. The sailors showed theirs and ran down the gangway. The fugitives had already taken the flimsy papers from their pockets as they ran and pulled up panting to show them. One of the Marines just glanced at the papers and signed to their bearers to go on.

The twelve o'clock hooter blew; the ferry sounded her siren in reply. As Gregory and Stefan charged down the gangplank two sailors were undoing the ropes; the moment the fugitives reached the deck the gangway was pulled in and the ferry put off.

Still panting they looked at one another and grinned. They had performed the almost impossible feat of escaping not only from the Admiralty building but also from Kronstadt

262

island in the brief space of nine minutes. Yet in a moment they were gravely sober again, as they knew that they had still to get through the third barrier which separated them from their liberty, and that their chances of doing so were even less than they had been at the other two.

It was the best part of five miles from Kronstadt to Oranienbaum, and it was unlikely that the old ferry would cover such a distance in less than twenty-five minutes. Before that time had elapsed it was as good as certain that the doorkeeper at the Admiralty would have been questioned and reported their audacious escape. It was possible that it still might not occur to anyone that they had gone straight to the liberty boat, or, since their escape had been made so close on twelve o'clock, that they would have had time to catch it. If so the Naval Police would be put on to comb the town and later the island for them. But if it was once suspected that they had made a dash for the liberty boat the Admiralty would telephone the port authorities at Oranienbaum, and the fugitives would be re-arrested on landing there.

Getting out of the crowd they stood nervously about on a quiet corner of the deck, cudgelling their brains in vain for a possible way to evade the strong possibility that they would be recaptured the moment they set foot on shore.

Kuporovitch suggested that they should hide somewhere in the ferry, go back in her to Kronstadt, then attempt their landing after she had completed her next trip, which would probably start about three o'clock; his idea being that if the port police at Oranienbaum were on the look-out for them now and they did not appear it would be assumed that they had not taken the liberty boat after all, and that nobody would be expecting them when she came into Oranienbaum again about three-thirty.

But Gregory pointed out that the fact of their being in civilian clothes among so many sailors, made them terribly conspicuous, and that it was even more likely that an order would have been given to the Oranienbaum police to keep a watch for them by three-thirty than it was at present. In fact, it was practically certain that precautions would be taken to prevent them getting away from the island in any later boat as a matter of routine; whereas there was still a chance that during the comparatively short space of half an hour nobody would have thought of doing so.

It was now snowing, but as soon as the ferry was half a mile out she lost the protection of the southernmost promontory of Kronstadt island and was fully exposed to a chill wind blowing in from the open gulf. On Gregory's suggestion that they try to find a more sheltered spot they walked slowly aft,

263

still feverishly seeking a way to minimise the risk of their becoming prisoners again in some twenty minutes' time.

As they approached the after part of the ferry, they saw that beyond a set of rails the ultimate section of the vessel's stern consisted of a separate, almost semi-circular platform somewhat lower than her main deck, and that this half-deck was allocated to the transport of vehicles. At the moment it was about two-thirds full, its cargo consisting of some half-hundred bicycles standing in racks, several motorbikes, two small cars and a box van.

The second Gregory's eye lit on the latter he asked, 'What's the writing on that van mean, Stefan?'

'The *Red Fleet*,' replied Kuporovitch promptly. 'That is the name of the newspaper published mainly for the Soviet Navy. As Kronstadt is our principal naval base the paper would be printed in Leningrad, and I expect the van comes out each morning to make deliveries to the shore establishments on the island. I wonder if it is locked?'

The idea of getting into it had occurred to both of them almost simultaneously. Its driver, and those of the two cars, were nowhere about; they had evidently mingled with the crowd on the main deck or, as a large proportion of that was now doing, gone below to get out of the wind. There was no one on the transport deck at all, but unfortunately it was overlooked by the bridge deck of the ferry.

'By Jove! If only we could get into that van unseen!' exclaimed Gregory. 'I bet they never bother to search it at the other end, if it does a routine job, our chances of evading capture would be increased enormously.'

'They wouldn't search it anyhow,' Kuporovitch remarked. 'No one crossing on this ferry has to go through the Customs at Oranienbaum, because they can have come only from the island, and there is nothing dutiable obtainable there for any one to attempt to smuggle across. The van will drive straight up a ramp and back to Leningrad, I expect.'

Neither of them had the least desire to return to Leningrad but where the van might take them when it landed was of small importance compared to the chance of getting ashore unobserved. Both of them turned and gave the forward part of the ferry a quick, anxious scrutiny.

The crowd on deck had thinned considerably and was still drifting below; most of those who remained were now huddled on seats and in corners to the leeward side of the vessel three figures were visible through the glass screens of the bridge, but all of them appeared intent on their business of steering the vessel, so their backs were turned; but there was one little group of sailors still standing within twenty feet of

264

he fugitives and they did not look like moving as they were engaged in a heated argument.

Seeing Kuporovitch's glance come to rest upon the group, Gregory said softly: 'Let's give them another ten minutes or so. Then if they haven't moved by the time the transport deck is coming into view from the shore, we'll have to chance it.'

Barely a third of the time limit he suggested had expired when one of the sailors broke off the argument with an angry shrug and stalked away towards the nearest companion-way. The others followed, more slowly, but in another minute they had disappeared below.

The two friends threw a swift glance at the bridge; the officers on it still had their backs turned. Without a word to one another they both jumped on up to the rail, swung their legs over and slipped down on to the half-deck below.

Controlling their impatience to get under cover, they advanced between the bicycle racks as though simply strolling there, until they reached the van. There were chocks under its tyres, to prevent it moving, and it was facing the starboard rail of the ferry, so its back was sideways on to the bridge; but luckily the rear doors were partially hidden by one of the cars which was parked a little forward of it.

'I'll keep a watch on the bridge,' said Gregory tensely. 'See if the doors are open.' As he stood there staring forward over the car top he added: 'All's well! Go ahead!'

Kuporovitch grabbed the handle of the door, turned it and pulled. To his joy, it swung open. Without losing an instant he stepped inside and, pulling it half-to cried: 'Our luck is in! Come on!'

Gregory gave one last swift glance at the bridge and the upper deck of the ferry, then he turned, followed Kuporovitch into the van, and pulled the door to behind him.

To their great satisfaction they found that the van was absolutely empty, so there was no possibility of its driver coming to get anything out of it, or even any likelihood of his looking inside until he wished either to clean it or load it up again. They sat down side by side on the floor in the semi-darkness and at last relaxed a little. For the first time since they had been recognised by the *Ogpu* man it really seemed that they had a decent chance of getting away.

About twelve minutes later they heard the ferry's engines stop, some shouts exchanged and the faint smack of ropes being thrown down on to her deck, then she bumped gently and came to rest alongside the Oranienbaum jetty. Now that the crucial moment of getting ashore had arrived they instinctively stilled their breathing and grew tense again.

'What shall I say if someone does open the van door?' Kuporovitch whispered.

'Let's lie down and pretend we are asleep,' Gregory sug gested. 'Then you could say that we got in here to get out o the cold, and that having been up all night we dropped off.'

'What reason can we give for having been up all night?'

'Say that we're journalists who have just returned from trip on a minesweeper, and that we made it to get materia for an article in the *Red Fleet*. We can still show our chi for the liberty boat and our vouchers for going on by ra to Leningrad, so those ought to get us through, providing th police are not waiting on the quay to nab us.'

They lay down at full length, closed their eyes and waite A good ten minutes later there came the sounds of bumping o the deck near by as a heavy ramp was lowered to it and mac fast. Suddenly the engine of the van started up. Her clutch wa thrown in and she jolted up the steep ramp on to the quay There she halted for a minute and the gruff voice of her driv could be heard talking to someone. Then she moved on, he speed increased and the two fugitives at last were able to giv free vent to their immense relief, as they felt certain that sh was out of the dockyard and running down a street.

Opening their eyes, they sat up and began to wonder ho long it would be before the van stopped and they had a chanc to get out. As Leningrad was well over twenty miles awa and they assumed that the driver was returning to the yar of the newspaper office there, they expected that the be part of an hour would elapse before he pulled up; but the guess was wrong. Within five minutes of having left the qua the van slowed down, stopped, backed a few yards and cam to a halt.

As it did so they noticed that the light which percolate through the chinks of the door had dimmed. Then came th noise of the driver scrambling down from his seat, footstep and the dragging to of a heavy door. The last light from th chinks disappeared and they were left in darkness.

For a full five minutes they sat on in silence, scarcely breath ing; but as no sound came, Gregory eased the door open crack and peered out. There was a faint light outside, so h pushed the door open a little further and saw that the va had been driven into a garage. The continued silence was clear indication that the driver, having put his van away, ha gone off about his own affairs, so they got out and walke softly over to the garage doors. Kuporovitch gave one o them a gentle push. Their luck was still in; it had not bee padlocked on the outside, but merely shut.

Opening it a few inches, they peeped out and saw that the

266

vere in a mews. No one seemed to be about and the silence
till continued.

'Let's go!' said Gregory, and opening the door wider they
tepped out into the mews.

Further up it a woman was hanging out washing on a line
nd at its far end a few ragged children were busily making
 snowman; but they passed both the woman and the urchins
vithout either giving them more than a disinterested glance.
he mews abutted on a railway goods yard, so evidently, the
undles of papers came from Leningrad by train each day
nd the driver of the *Red Fleet* van collected his quota for
istribution from the station, which they could now see a
ew hundred yards down the street.

Instinctively they turned in the opposite direction. Even if
here had been no risk in doing so they would not have used
ie railway vouchers they had been given, since it woud have
een both pointless and dangerous for them to return to Lenin-
rad; while, as it was, the railway police might by this time
ave been warned to watch for them on the off chance that
iey would attempt to get away from Kronstadt island by
ealing a small boat.

They set off at a good pace, to get well clear of the harbour
nd station area, with lighter hearts than they had had for a
ing time, and Kuporovitch said quite cheerfully:

'Well, here we are, free men again, but with passports that
e dare not use now that the *Ogpu* are after us, still in the
icircled Leningrad area, and several thousand miles from
ondon. Have you any ideas as to how we should get home?'

'Let's be modest,' Gregory suggested, 'and adopt the old
olicy of breaking the faggot one stick at a time. It will be soon
hough to talk of the Vistula when we are over the Rhine, or,
you prefer, of London when we have reached Moscow.'

'Moscow is over four hundred miles away, *mon vieux*. To
:t there we have to pass through the Leningrad defence lines,
hich are about thirty miles deep at this point, then pene-
ate the German-held zone, which probably now extends
out two hundred miles, then get across the main Russian
ront and, finally, cover the balance of another hundred and
fty miles or more.' Kuporovitch had not spoken despon-
:ntly but was making a plain statement of fact.

'I know,' agreed Gregory. 'It's a bit of a teaser, isn't it? Of
urse, if we worked round to the north-east of Leningrad
.e total distance would not be much greater, whereas the
erman-held belt is very much thinner there; probably not
.ore than twenty miles deep.'

'That doesn't seem to offer us any great advantage, since

267

the Russians and the Germans are now equally anxious to have our blood.'

'True, and while the Russians are actively on the hunt for us the Germans are not, so it seems that the more German held territory we cover on our trip the less risk we shall run.'

'What's more, our worst danger lies in remaining in the Leningrad area, and to work our way round to the north-east of the city would prolong our stay in it, so I am in favour of striking the south with the object of getting clear of Clim's command as soon as possible.'

'You're right, Stefan. And there's another thing. As I can't speak a word of Russian, I'm a constant liability to you as long as we remain here, whereas once we are in the German lines I can easily pass for a German myself and you can speak enough German to pose as a Pole of German blood from the Poznan area, or something of that kind.'

'That's so. But one of our worst troubles is lack of transport. Of course, I suppose we could walk the four hundred miles, but it would take us a devilish long time and if the information we've got is to be of any value we must get it to London within the next few weeks.'

Gregory nodded. 'That's been worrying me too. It would be suicidal for us to attempt to use railways in either zone without papers, and at the moment I see no possible means of getting any.'

'We might hop a series of freight cars as the hobos do in America.'

'Yes, that's a possibility. Let's find a place to get a meal and think it over while we eat.'

'If you wish,' Kuporovitch shrugged, 'but personally, I am not very hungry. We didn't breakfast till ten o'clock, and in the middle of the night we had that splendid meal with the *Gruppenführer*.'

'So we did!' exclaimed Gregory. 'Yet somehow that seems days ago. So much has happened recently it seems impossible to believe that this time yesterday we were still prisoners in the Lubianka, and that we only left there in the Black Maria a little over fourteen hours ago.'

'Yet it is true, and today is only the twenty-fourth of September.'

'Since you mention it, I'm not particularly hungry myself, but all the same, I think we'd better have a meal. It is still less than an hour since we escaped from the Admiralty building, so they won't have had time to circulate our descriptions through the local police-stations to the men who are already on duty yet; whereas if we wait until the evening every patrolman in the town will be keeping an eye open for us.'

'You're right, and they are sure to watch the eating-places. So let's fill up while we can, without undue anxiety.'

Two streets further on they found a fairly clean-looking but unpretentious fish restaurant, and going in sat down at a table. Kuporovitch ordered the meal without consulting Gregory, so that it should not become apparent that he was a foreigner, and, for the same reason, they did not converse during it. Although they were not hungry they ate as much as they could manage, as they were well aware of the value of being well lined in such a cold climate, and had no idea when they would see hot food again.

On leaving the place, Gregory said, 'Well, any ideas?'

'Yes,' Kuporovitch smiled. 'Why should we not return to the garage and find the *Red Fleet* van? It is unlikely that the driver will go back there until he has to collect his papers to-morrow morning, and by that time we should be well into the battle area.'

'What then, though? Directly we entered the German zone the *Red Fleet* van would be held up by every enemy patrol we met.'

'Oh, we'd have to abandon it, and adopt other measures from then on—jumping freight trains, perhaps.'

'No. We ought to keep away from the railway if we possibly can, and I think I've got a better idea than that. Let's use the Black Maria that's in Grauber's garage.'

'First we must find it, and that may not be too easy.'

'I know, but think of the terrific advantage it will give us if we can. Anyone can see that it is a prison van from a quarter of a mile away, and who would think of interfering with a van that would presumably have prisoners inside it? In fact, it will have—one, at all events.'

'It sounds a grand idea, but I don't quite get your point about it having a prisoner inside it.'

'Look!' Gregory smiled. 'We'd work it this way. If the van has not been discovered or moved it will still have that dead *Ogpu* guard inside. We'll strip him of his clothes and you can put them on to act as driver, while I'll be locked up but visible through the bars of one of the little windows as your prisoner. The fact of my not being able to talk Russian won't matter then, if you're pulled up and questioned. That, of course, is while we are within the Leningrad defence ring. As soon as we are out of it we'll find a dead German on the battlefield and strip him of his clothes. I put them on and we change places. When we enter the Russian zone two hundred miles further on we swap places once more, and I become your prisoner again for the last lap. How's that?'

'*Sacré nom!* It is a stroke of genius!' Kuporovitch beamed.

269

'Truly a stroke of genius! Let us not delay but set about finding Grauber's garage at once, before the police get after us.'

They had got through their meal as quickly as possible, in order to avoid it being remarked that while Kuporovitch occasionally muttered something in Russian to Gregory, he never spoke but replied only by nods, smiles and shrugs, so it was only a quarter past one, and they returned to the harbour district with a fair amount of confidence that no general search was as yet being made for them in Oranienbaum.

The water-front of the town extended for a considerable distance on each side of the harbour, and, as they had not the slightest idea whether the tumble-down wharf to which Grauber had brought them lay to the west or east of it they were, at first, undecided in which direction to begin their search. It then occurred to Gregory that if the police were already hunting for them on the mainland they would be looking for two men in company, so that they were much less likely to be identified apart from if they remained together. In consequence, it was clear that not only would it be wise for them to separate but that by so doing they might achieve their object more quickly; upon which they agreed that Gregory should take the east side of the harbour and Stefan the west, and that they should meet again in an hour's time outside a decayed-looking onion-spired church near which they were standing when they made the arrangement.

Gregory spent his hour poking about among mean streets and evil-smelling *cul-de-sacs*, but he could find nothing resembling the wharf for which he was seeking, but having had only a glimpse of it in the darkness of a snowy night, he feared that he might have seen but failed to recognise it, and returned in rather a depressed mood to the rendezvous.

Kuporovitch was there and had proved more fortunate. Within twenty minutes he had found the place and had spent the rest of his hour very profitably in buying a roomy hold-all, provisions which would keep them going for several days to go into it, and two new torches. Having announced his good news, he set off for the wharf again, while Gregory followed him at a discreet distance.

The garage proved to be padlocked, but there was no one about, so they forced the doors with a rusty strip of iron that they found in the gutter. To their relief the Black Maria was still there and inside it lay the twisted body of the murdered *Ogpu* guard. *Rigor mortis* had set in hours before, so they had great difficulty in getting his uniform off, but by considerable exertions, and the breaking of some of his limbs, they managed it. Their gruesome task was made slightly less

270

epugnant by the fact that the cold had prevented the onset of decay, so the corpse smelt no more unpleasant than would have a living specimen of unwashed humanity.

Having stripped the guard to his underclothes they carried the body over to a far corner of the garage and pushed it behind some cases that were there. Kuporovitch then proceeded to change into the uniform. It was a chilly business and the guard's tunic proved uncomfortably tight across his broad shoulders, but it would just button up at any time it should seem necessary for him to appear properly dressed. Meanwhile, Gregory remembered having heard Grauber say that the cases contained explosives, so feeling that a few charges might possibly come in useful, he opened some of the cases with the rusty iron and transferred several packages of delignite and fuses to one of the cells of the van.

It was now getting on for half past three but they thought it much too risky to drive the stolen Black Maria through the own in daylight and, knowing that they would be all night, decided to put in a few hours sleep while they had the chance. Owing to the cold they thought it sensible to climb into the van for such little additional protection as it might afford, and on doing so they stumbled on a bonus—in the form of the guard's pistol, which must have jerked from its holster as he fell dead. It was fully loaded and, much heartened at being armed once more, Kuporovitch slipped it back into the holster on his belt. Then they both settled down to sleep.

When they awoke it was a little after seven o'clock. Opening the doors of the garage a crack, they saw that the autumn night had already closed down on the north Russian town, and that it was snowing again. The cover it afforded suited them very well, provided the fall was not too heavy and blocked the roads, but that was unlikely, as winter was only just setting in and every mile would take them further southward to somewhat warmer regions.

The only preparation they had to make was locking Gregory into one of the cells, and, when it came to the point, he found himself distinctly loth to adopt his own suggestion; as, once he was locked in, should anything happen to Stefan his prisoner would be in no position to regain his freedom. They found that the cells had spring locks which there was no way of opening from the inside but could be slipped back from the outside by a pressure of the hand; so they got over the difficulty by jamming one of them with a small piece of wood so that the door could be shut, and appeared to be locked, but could be forced open by a firm pressure from within.

When Gregory had settled himself in the cell, Kuporovitch backed the van out of the garage, got down again to close its

271

doors then climbed into the driver's seat, and they set off on their long journey.

For Gregory the first hour was so uneventful that, in the blackness of his cell with nothing to occupy him, he nearly fell asleep again. For Stefan, it was nearly, but not quite, so monotonous as he had to guess his way as best he could in the snow and darkness. It was easy enough to find the main road that led south out of the town, as they had passed it that afternoon after turning away from the railway station, but once clear of the houses he had to run on blind for a time until he could pick up the distant mutter of the guns as a guide to the direction in which the battle-front lay.

They had covered the best part of twenty-five miles, meeting only a few cars and an occasional column of lorries, and he could hear the guns clearly above the noise of his engine, before he was met with his first challenge. As he pulled up a little party of soldiers, appeared from the side of the road and asked him for a lift.

On getting close enough to recognise the vehicle as a Black Maria, they were greatly amused and started to joke about it. Kuporovitch told them he was taking an important prisoner to headquarters, and that to unlock the back of the van for them was more than his job was worth; so, seeing they could not all crowd on to the box beside him they pressed him no further. He took the opportunity to ask them the name of the next town along the road, and they said that if he drove straight on he would come to Krasnogvardeisk in another three *versts* or so.

From this point on there were increasing signs of military activity, and it was clear that they were now passing through the back area of the defence line. Outside the town he was pulled up again, and twice more while going through it. On each occasion he told the same story and it sounded so plausible that only in one instance was he asked to which head quarters he was going.

'The location of all headquarters are secret,' he replied severely. 'You should know better than to ask.'

Abashed by this rebuke, and no doubt impressed by his *Ogpu* uniform, the leader of the patrol apologised, and Kup porovitch chuckled quietly to himself as he drove on.

From the little he could see of the town and the dim red lights that were placed to give warning of numerous shell craters in the streets, he judged the place to be half in ruins. On the far side of it guns banged every few minutes with increasing noise and about a mile further on he was pulled up again.

When questioned, he made his usual reply, but the N.C.O

in charge of the patrol said, 'if you go on much further in this direction you'll find yourself in No-Man's-Land.'

'I must have taken the wrong turning then, back there in the town,' Kuporovitch growled, adding a fluent spate of Russian curses. 'Is there a by-road leading east before I'm likely to run into the Germans? If so, to take it will save me going back.'

'There's a cross-roads about half a mile south from here. They shell it sometimes, but their patrols haven't yet penetrated that far,' replied the N.C.O.

'Thanks chum. How are things going round here?' asked Kuporovitch in a conversational tone.

'Not so bad,' the N.C.O. shrugged phlegmatically. 'They gained a bit of ground today—took the wood down there in the valley. But we've been shelling it for the last four hours, so they've probably withdrawn by now. If not our boys will have 'em out of it tomorrow.'

'That's the spirit!' Kuporovitch grinned. 'Good luck, soldier!' and with a wave of his hand he got going again.

When he reached the cross-roads he did not turn east, but continued straight down the road. He was praying now that he would not be halted again, as, if he was, he would have to say that he had lost his way, and turn back. The road began to dip gently and he knew he must have reached the edge of the valley.

Suddenly calls to halt rang out from both sides of the road, and he guessed that he must now be running through the main defence zone. He hesitated only a second. The snow was still falling thickly. Visibility was poor and it was all that he could do to make out the road in front with his hooded head lights. Fortunately he was on a long straight strip. Switching out the lights, he jammed his foot down on the accelerator, taking a chance that if the van was shot at in the darkness most of the bullets would go wide.

For a few minutes his heart was in his mouth. It seemed certain that even if the van escaped coming to grief through running off the road some bullets were bound to hit it. But as it had come from the soldiers' rear they knew that it must be a Russian vehicle, so they refrained from firing at it, simply cursing its driver for some poor fool who did not realise that the enemy had gained a mile that morning.

After five hundred yards, Kuporovitch flicked on his headlights to get a sight of the road, narrowly escaped a shell crater and flicked them out again. Then he reduced his speed to ten miles an hour and nosed his way cautiously downhill. Going slowly, the light was just sufficient for him to sense rather than see a steep bank that ran along one side of the road and provided a rough guide to its direction.

Another fainter challenge reached him, doubtless from a picket ensconced in a fox-hole somewhere in the roadside, but again he ignored it. A machine-gun began to stutter.

'Ping . . . ping . . . ping!' Three of the bullets rang loudly on the side of the van and others whistled overhead. But the sound brought sudden comfort to Kuporovitch. It had not previously occurred to him that a Black Maria would be constructed of metal. In order that prisoners should not be able to cut their way out through its sides; and that he was in fact, driving what amounted to a light armoured vehicle which would resist most things short of a direct hit by a shell.

He had accelerated again as the machine-gun opened, but realising that the post could have caught no more than a glimpse of the van through the curtain of falling snow, he slowed down once more, a few hundred yards further on he could dimly make out the forms of trees along the roadside and knew that he must have reached the wood about which the N.C.O. had spoken. Pulling up, he got down and went round to the back of the van to consult with Gregory.

They agreed that they must now be in No-Man's-Land, and that the time had come to change places. Night and the snowstorm rendered any but minor operations impossible, so only the sporadic activity which continues day and night on even the quietest front was in progress. Occasionally a heavy German shell trundled over head in the direction of Krasnogvardeisk and at intervals of about five minutes a Russian field battery was sending salvos crashing into the wood. As swiftly as they could, they changed places and, with Gregory driving set off again.

As quickly as he dared he drove on through the wood, to get away from the crashing of the Russian shells. After a quarter of a mile the road forked, and as Moscow lay to the south-east he took the left-hand turning. From that point the road began to rise again and a few hundred yards further on the wood ended.

They had recently reached open country when another machine-gun opened on them. The bullets went wide, but they were coming from the front so he felt fairly confident that they must be German. As he could not get off the road the only thing to do was to halt, otherwise the Germans would take the noise of the engine for that of a tank or armoured car and, imagining that the Russians were launching a night attack, turn their artillery on to him. At the top of his voice he began to shout:

'Hi, there! Help! I am lost in this blasted snowstorm!'

The machine-gun fired two more short bursts and its bullets spattered down on to the road about fifty feet ahead of the Black Maria. Between the bursts Gregory kept on shouting with all the power of his lungs; then he took a big chance, switched on his head lights and, jumping down ran to the side of the road. Even there, another burst aimed at the lights with a traversing gun might have caught him, but the firing ceased and he recommenced his yelling.

After about three minutes a group of dim figures appeared through the snow. He put his hands above his head and waited, a prey to terrible anxiety. If they were German he had good hopes that things would be all right, but if the proved, after all, to be Russians, the game was up.

To his immense relief one of the figures stepped forward and, covering him with a sub-machine gun, asked him in German who he was and what the hell he was doing there.

'*Gottseidank!*' he exclaimed. 'I lost my way in the storm, and for the last half-hour I've been terrified that I'd be captured by the Russians.' He then went on to explain that he was driving a captured Black Maria with an important prisoner in it, had taken a wrong turning further west, gone down the other fork road into the valley and finding that the wood was being shelled and realised, to his horror, that he was in No-Man's-Land.

In such conditions of darkness and snow the story was perfectly plausible, as the *Unteroffizier* who was questioning him knew that in such weather pickets kept under cover as much as possible, and that if the van had gone down the road further west the outposts there might quite well have taken the noise of an engine for that of an armoured car going forward to reconnoitre.

Having growled that Gregory was darned lucky not to have been captured or shot, he told him that he could proceed, and ordered one of his men to get in the driver's cab as a guide up to company headquarters.

They drove off up the hill, on the brow of which they were challenged by another picket, but the soldier on the box gave the password for the night and half a mile further on, they pulled up at a burnt-out farmhouse.

Against one of its walls a row of rough lean-tos had been erected. From one of them came a few chinks of light and the soldier led Gregory into it. A young officer was sitting dozing there beside a small table that had a field telephone on it.

Gregory thanked his stars that the place was not a house or heated hutment, in which he would have been expected to remove his furs, as his main danger now was that he was not wearing a German uniform, so his furs were his only protec-

275

tion against discovery. When he had told his story again the officer seemed fairly satisfied but demanded to see the prisoner.

Taking him outside, Gregory undid the van, pretended to unlock the cell and exposed Kuporovitch to view. He too, was wearing his furs, but at the sight of his visitors he stood up and let them fall open, sufficient for it to be seen that underneath he had on a foreign uniform.

In halting Russian the officer asked him where he had been captured, and he replied, 'At Kingsiepp on the Luga.'

The officer then asked Gregory where he was taking his prisoner to, and he replied: 'To the Gestapo headquarters in Novgorod. This man is a native of Kalinin and it is hoped that we may be able to get information out of him which will prove useful to our Moscow front—at least that is what my officer told me.'

There seemed no more to be said, so Kuporovitch was again locked in his cell, the officer gave Gregory careful directions as to the road he should take, and, with an immensely lighter heart, he drove off.

The journey from Oranienbaum and the crossing of the front had taken only a little over two hours, so it was not yet half past nine and they still had the best part of the long Russian night before them. As they penetrated further behind the German lines they now and again met a convey bringing up supplies and passed occasional cars or solitary lorries, but no one bothered any longer to challenge them, taking it for granted that any vehicle in that area must be German.

Gradually the sound of the guns grew fainter until they could no longer be heard. Soon after midnight the snow ceased falling. Every few miles they passed through a village or small township but all of them consisted of the blackened shells of buildings, having been burnt out in accordance with the scorched earth policy. At a quarter past two in the morning, on passing through a long street of scattered buildings, many of which still had their roofs on, Gregory felt sure that he was entering the north-eastern suburbs of the ancient city of Novgorod, once the capital of all northern Russia. They had accomplished the first hundred miles of their journey in seven hours, and seeing the state of the roads, he was well satisfied.

His main fear now was that he might run into a Gestapo man who would be intrigued by the sight of a Russian Black Maria and pull it up to ask awkward questions. Fortunately, it was still the middle of the night, and the only people about were a few belated soldiers but, feeling certain there would be a police post in the centre of the city, having driven a little way into it, he took a turning to the left and continued on by

276

a succession of by-ways, until he had worked his way round to its south-western suburbs. He lost half an hour in this manoeuvre, but eventually found his way back on the main road to Kresti, Kalinin and Moscow.

Since the snow had ceased he had been making much better going, and two hours after leaving Novgorod he reached the outskirts of the little town of Kresti. Here he followed the same manoeuvre as in Novgorod, but the place being much smaller, did not lose so much time by skirting it, and was clear of the town by five o'clock.

He was very tired now after seven and a half hours' continuous driving, but he knew that if he could cover another twenty miles or so he should reach the Valdai Hills, where there would be woods, and good cover in which to lie up during the daytime. By six o'clock he was leaving the flat plain behind and entering an undulating area of broken forest land. At twenty past six he found a turning to the right which would bring him deeper into the hilly area. Two miles down it he found a by-road leading east, so he drove some way along it until he was deep in the forest, then finding a track took the van in among the snow-covered trees and pulled up. Dawn was only just breaking and during the long night they had successfully negotiated some hundred and eighty miles.

When he entered Kuporovitch's cell, Gregory found the old campaigner curled up in his furs, sound asleep on the floor. On being wakened he declared that he had had a very good night, and that from about an hour after the German officer had come in to look at him he had only one prolonged period of wakefulness.

As they breakfasted off some of their iron rations they congratulated themselves on their good fortune to date, and discussed the future. They agreed that had it not been for the snowstorm they would probably have had much difficulty in getting through the battle zone that now lay a hundred and fifty miles behind them, and that they could not count upon a repetition of such luck when they made their bid to cross the other, which lay forty to sixty miles along the road to Moscow.

However, as Gregory pointed out the two fronts differed considerably. The one about Leningrad had formed into a solid ring, whereas the main line of conflict was so immensely long that it was occupied in strength by either army only in certain strategic areas. He likened the situation to two forks with a great number of irregular prongs pointed at one another, and constantly being jabbed together so that some of the points met with a clash while other went a little way into the empty spaces between the opposing prongs.

Kuporovitch nodded. 'Yes. That must be so; otherwise nothing like so many prisoners would be taken or spearheads cut off. And if only we can find a space between two German prongs, with luck we'll get through unmolested.'

'Exactly! So our best plan is to keep well away from strategic areas like Kalinin, through which the main Leningrad-Moscow railway runs, or Staritza and Rahev, further south.'

'Staritza is the best part of fifty miles south of the railway and there is nothing worth capturing in between; so we should stand a good chance of slipping through there. You'll be driving again until we know that we're in Russian-held territory, I suppose?'

'Yes. But it shouldn't take us long to cover fifty miles, so we won't start till dusk. It's too risky since I've had no chance to get a German uniform off a stiff, as I had planned.'

'Perhaps that's just as well.' Kuporovitch said thoughtfully. 'I'm inclined to think that on the route we mean to take you will be in more danger from the Partisans than from the Germans.'

'We must chance that. Anyhow, it's a good thing that I drove most of last night as I can get a sleep now while you keep watch, then if a band of them is lurking in these woods, and some of them come to investigate, you can explain matters to them in their own lingo.'

With a tired sigh Gregory got into the Black Maria, curled himself up, and was almost immediately asleep.

When he awoke it was well on in the afternoon. To his considerable interest Kuporovitch reported that a little band of ragged Partisans had appeared on the scene shortly before midday, but they had been perfectly satisfied on his telling them that he was a Russian officer trying to get through to Moscow and that he had stolen the Black Maria from a park of vehicles captured by the Germans. They had said that he could drive on for twenty-five miles at least, without fear, as not a single German had been seen in the whole district for days.

They had another meal and, in view of the information of the Partisans, decided to set off immediately dusk began to fall, so by five o'clock they were on their way. A little under an hour later Gregory turned off the main road and began to run through by-ways in a generally south-easterly direction.

A few miles further on, just as it was getting dark, a group of men and women ran out of a roadside coppice, and brandishing an odd assortment of weapons, yelled at him to halt. Instead of doing so he increased his speed. As a result a spatter of duck-shot rattled against the van. Momentarily, he was alarmed by the thought that some of the pellets might have punctured a tyre, but the old Black Maria continued to run on steadily and after another mile or so he knew that his fears had been groundless.

Soon after nine o'clock he found himself on a straight road leading directly towards a town which, it appeared, there was no way of avoiding. In consequence, just before reaching the first houses, he pulled up and went round to the back of the van to consult with Kuporovitch.

They were now in something of a quandary as, according to their calculations, they should by this time be out of the German zone, but not far back Gregory had passed a string of lorries that, even in the semi-darkness, he felt fairly certain had been German and it might prove that in the past week, the enemy had made a considerable advance on this sector.

As it was of paramount importance to find out which army held the town it was decided that Kuporovitch should go forward on foot to reconnoitre. He returned half an hour later having questioned some of the inhabitants, to say that the town was Torshok, and that it had recently been captured by the Germans. The front was now fifteen miles beyond it.

The question now was whether to go back and try another way or risk being pulled up at a German police post. Their success so far had, perhaps, inclined them to rashness and they decided to go on. As they entered the small square of the half ruined town they were called on to halt and, in a wave of fresh apprehension, cursed their temerity.

Gregory told the usual story to two military policemen, but they asked him for his area pass and, as he could not produce one, they at once became suspicious.

In his cell Kuporovitch could not hear what was being said outside, but from the longish halt he sensed that Gregory was in trouble, so he began to shout and bang violently on the side of the van.

On hearing the noise the two policemen made Gregory get down from his seat and take them round to his prisoner. While doing so he protested vehemently that he had had a pass, but somehow mislaid it. As he opened Kuporovitch's cell door the Russian, seeing the two Germans behind Gregory, struck him in the chest and, still shouting, attempted to force his way out.

With the assistance of the policeman, Gregory forced him back into the cell and relocked it. But Kuporovitch's demonstration had convinced the two Germans of Gregory's *bona fides*, as it seemed to them that none but a genuine prisoner would behave with such violence, and that Gregory's obvious business as a driver of a Black Maria was to take him from one safe place to another.

One of them asked what the prisoner was shouting about, and Gregory replied in a surly tone that he did not speak the fellow's filthy language, but perhaps it was because he had not been given any food all day, and added that he did not believe in wasting food on dirty Russians.

This sentiment so warmed the German hearts of his listeners that they not only agreed to his proceeding, but the senior even wrote out for him a temporary area pass on a perforated sheet of his field pocket-book.

Mutually cursing the country, the weather, the Russians and particularly such Russians as the violent prisoner in the van, they parted, and Gregory breathed again as he drove out of the town.

Having extracted an area pass from the German military police gave him special pleasure; but he was never called upon to use it. He passed some artillery tractors and a squadron of tanks some way outside the town, but covered another twenty miles without being challenged. Then, feeling that he must, at last, be out of the German zone, he pulled up again. They ate another scratch meal from their provisions, after which Gregory shut himself into the cell and Kuporovitch took the wheel.

As they had supposed, the front was fluid almost to the point of non-existence in this sector without objectives. His first indication that they had actually entered the Russian zone was when some soldiers at a cross-road shouted at him to know if he could direct them to a village of which he had never heard. After that his principal anxiety was petrol, since the engine was already being fed from the reserve tank which he knew must now be getting low.

Half an hour after having taken over from Gregory, Kuporovitch found himself running into another small town. Pulling up in its centre, he boldly shouted to some men who were standing about a row of lorries, parked in its square asking to be told where the nearest filling station was to be found. They directed him to it and five minutes later, the tanks of the Black Maria were being filled up. He learned that the town was called Ivanitch and was one hundred and seventy-five *versts* from Moscow, the equivalent to one hundred and twenty miles. The church clock was striking eleven as he drove out of it.

After that, everything was plain sailing. Soon after three in the morning he was within a few miles of Moscow, and could just make out against the starry night sky the vague outline of its massed buildings, domes and spires. Pulling in to the side of the road, he got off the box and went round to rouse Gregory.

It was clear that to drive into the capital in the Black

280

Maria and abandon it outside the British Embassy would have been positively suicidal. The vehicle that had proved such a godsend to them was so conspicuous and unusual that even to abandon it anywhere in the neighbourhood of Moscow might easily set on foot enquiries which would disclose its origin, lead the Leningrad *Ogpu* to conclude that Gregory and Stefan had used it as a means to get through the German zone, and result in an intensive search being made for them in the whole of the Moscow area. In fact, their only hope of permanently retaining their hard-won freedom seemed to lie in the total destruction of the van, and, at first sight, this seemed almost impossible of achievement.

They both thought hard for a moment, then Gregory exclaimed: 'I've got it! I felt sure that those explosives of Grauber's would come in handy sooner or later. Let's blow the old bus up.'

'*Nom d'un nom!* What a splendid idea!' Kuporovitch laughed. 'Get in the back again and I'll drive her well off the road into a field.'

Both of them had often handled explosives before so it took them only about ten minutes to arrange the charges and, while Gregory set the fuses, Kuporovitch hastily changed back from his *Ogpu* uniform into his own clothes. Leaving the uniform on the floor of the van they closed its doors for the last time and, side by side, ran for the road.

They had scarcely reached it when the Black Maria went up with a fine bang, but they had no fear that this would cause undue excitement, and bring people hurrying to the scene as German aircraft often dropped bombs on the outskirts of Moscow, and the bang might easily have been the explosion of a time bomb dropped several nights before.

Under a starry sky they completed the last five miles of their journey on foot, arriving at the British Embassy as the bells of Moscow were chiming five o'clock.

They were very tired, very dirty, and with a five days' growth of stubble on their chins; so at first the porter regarded them with some suspicion, but on their producing their passports he let them in. Going straight up to their little office at the top of the building, they found it just as they had left it only six days—although it seemed to them like six weeks—ago. Sinking into their chairs, they put their feet up on their desks and slept.

After dozing for a few hours, as soon as they thought the Press Attaché would be in his office, Gregory rang through and asked him to come up to see them. He arrived a few minutes later and, on seeing their bedraggled appearance, gave them a surprised and rather anxious grin.

Gregory explained that they had succeeded in their mission but at the price of falling foul of the Soviet authorities.

'You can't stay here then,' the Attaché said in quick alarm 'It would make the Ambassador's position extremely difficul' if you are traced to the Embassy.'

'I know that,' Gregory agreed. 'But it's very unlikely tha we shall be traced, providing that nobody here gives awa' the fact that we are back in Moscow. That is why we did no go to the annexe when we arrived early this morning. W dare not risk any indiscretion by one of the Press Sectio' which might lead to General Alyabaiev learning that we hav returned. What we have to do now is to get to London by th' quickest possible means.'

'That is not going to be easy, since His Excellency is in nc position to help you officially. In fact, I don't think I ough' even to inform him that you are here.'

'I'm afraid you'll have to. The information that we have is o' the very greatest importance. Of course it can be sent tc London by Most Secret Cypher Telegram, but I imagine that only he can give authority to use one-time pads. And that's the way our stuff must be sent.'

'In that case I'll do my best to arrange matters,' the Attaché agreed. 'But the trouble is that the whole Embassy is in a flat spin at the moment owing to the arrival of this War Cabinet Mission the day after tomorrow.'

'What is the reason for the Mission?' Gregory inquired.

'Lord Beaverbrook and Mr. Averill Harriman are arriving for a Three-Power Conference on aid to Russia. The Russians want Britain and the States to supply the Soviet with masses of tanks, lorries, aircraft, and all sorts of other war equipment, and the whole matter is to be thrashed out here.'

'Is it, by jove!' exclaimed Gregory with a quick grin at Kuporovitch. 'Then you needn't bother the Ambassador after all. But you must get us an interview with Lord Beaverbrook before the Conference opens. If you say that we have information which may be of assistance to him in his Mission, and that we have been travelling in Russia on behalf of Sir Pellinore Gwaine-Cust, I feel sure he will give us half an hour. In the meantime the fewer people who see us the better, so we had best remain in this room.'

The Attaché obviously felt that he was taking on a pretty heavy responsibility in agreeing to their remaining at the Embassy without the Ambassador's knowledge, now that they were wanted by the police; but he gamely consented to the proposal. Then, having seen that the coast was clear, he took them down to the next floor, so that they could have a bath and shave, and collected their bags from his office, which

...abled them to change their underclothes; after which he ...omised to bring some cold food up to them himself from ...me to time, in order that as few people as possible should be ...t into the secret of their return.

It was the morning of the Saturday, the 26th of September, ...d the three days that followed provided a strange interlude. ...hey had nothing to do but chat and doze, yet they were not ...ored. In the preceding six days they had had enough excite-...ent for six months; their self-imposed prison was far from ...omfortable, but it was positively palatial compared with the ...nderground cells of the Lubianka, and they were perfectly ...ontent to spend the long hours quietly recovering from the ...ppalling strain through which they had gone.

On the Monday night, round eleven o'clock, the Press ...ttaché came to fetch them for an interview with Lord ...eaverbrook. In spite of the tiring and hazardous flight he ...ad made that day, followed by a long conference with the ...mbassador, the indefatigable statesman gave them two and ... half hours, and showed no trace of fatigue at the end of it. ...e asked innumerable questions and with an extraordinarily ...uick grasp for each situation extracted every ounce of in-...ormation they had to give. When they finally left him at ...wenty-five to two in the morning he spoke glowingly of the ...reat help their information would be to him, and they knew ...hat their mission had been well and truly completed.

Next morning they again raised with the Press Attaché the ...natter of their getting safely back to London. As the impera-...ive need for speed was no longer a factor they were less well ...laced than ever to ask the Ambassador to compromise ...imself by giving his assistance; so it seemed that the only ...hing for them to do was to set off under their own steam, and ...hey agreed to start as soon as darkness fell that night.

The Attaché still knew nothing of the secret of their mis-...sion, but their two and a half hours with Lord Beaverbrook ...he previous night was sufficient guarantee that they had done ...some very special job of work, and, in any case, as a patriotic ...Briton the thought of two of his compatriots falling into the ...nands of the *Ogpu* worried him considerably. In consequence, ...at the risk of losing his own post he made a spontaneous and ...very handsome gesture.

As they were about to leave that evening he produced two ...British passports which had been issued in Moscow to ex-...members of the Consul-General's staff and said:

'It may prove a bit dangerous to show your own passports ...anywhere in the Soviet Union now, so I thought you might ...like to use these instead. I selected them from a pile that had ...been sent in for cancellation, and although the descriptions

283

and photographs don't fit too well, I think they'll pass at push. But for goodness' sake don't let anybody know that gave them to you.'

For this invaluable help they could not thank him enough Then, having done their best to express their gratitude, the left the Embassy by its back door.

They had had ample time to plan their journey and ha decided against attempting to go straight through on th trunk railway to the Russian frontier. Foreigners travellin direct to and from Moscow were sufficiently few to be subjec to careful scrutiny, as they knew from their journey to th capital, so they had agreed to take only local trains and hitch hike wherever possible.

By these means, and using their priceless supply of soa for bribes, wherever necessary, having left Moscow on th evening of the 29th of September, and averaging a little unde a hundred miles a day along by-routes, they reached Astra khan on the morning of the 11th of October. It took them tw days to find a tramp going south across the Caspian, and be fore they could leave the port they had to secure exit visa from the Soviet Emigration authorities.

At Gregory's suggestion, inspired by his sardonic humour they posed as two English Communists who, now that Russi had been attacked by Hitler, had decided that they ought t wind up their affairs there and go home to fight for Britain This absurd illogicality, having the backing of a world-wid appeal by the Comintern, met with such an excellent recep tion that the passports given to them by the Press Attach were scarcely glanced at, and with great inward relief the went on board.

For three days they were running down the vast inland sea, and on the fourth landed at Bandar Shah, the northern extremity of Persia's only mainline railway. Three days o rail travel brought them to its southern extremity. Bandar Shahpur, at the head of the Persian Gulf. Thence, they con tinued their journey northwestward via Basra to Baghdad, where they had to wait for a series of aircraft to take them via Damascus and Jerusalem down to Cairo.

Having reached Middle East Headquarters on the 26th of October their hopes were high of arriving home by the end of the month; but these were doomed to grievous disap pointment. The situation in the central Mediterranean had materially worsened in the past two months and the line of Imperial Communications now hung on by a hair. Aircraft were still going through every few days but only Generals and other key men needed in London on the highest priority could secure passages. Not only all munitions, food and stores, ut also the entire personnel needed to maintain the British Forces in the Middle East, were now having to be brought cross eleven thousand miles of sea, right round Africa.

Gregory thought of cabling Sir Pellinore, but, on reflection, decided that he ought to save such appeals for cases where either real urgency or an imperative need for help required them. The only alternative was to return home via South Africa and, on reaching this decision, they were at least spared the long trip by ship down the Red Sea and East Coast. After a wait of only four days they got seats in an aircraft going down to the Cape, and having left Cairo on the 1st of November they reached Cape Town on the evening of the 5th.

A return K.L.M. Convoy was coming round from Durban almost empty, so they had no difficulty in securing berths when it called at the Cape on the 8th. West Africa still being in the hands of the Vichy French no alternative route by air up the West Coast was possible, so for three weeks, they had to submit to the dreary routine of constant boat drills, airless cabins, blacked-out portholes and a prohibition against smoking on deck after dark. At last, on the 29th of November, they docked in the Clyde.

Their baggage was so light that it took them only a moment to pass the Customs, but at the passport office they were temporarily held up. Having looked at Gregory' passport the man behind the guichet asked him if he and his friend would mind waiting for a minute, as he had a message for them.

Mildly surprised, they allowed one of his colleagues to usher them into a small room, but Gregory knew that all sailing lists were cabled from the Cape, so he assumed that Sir Pellinore, having learned from Lord Beaverbrook that they had completed their mission, had since been watching such lists for their names, and, on learning that they were travelling in the convoy, had chosen this means of communicating some urgent news to one of them.

They were somewhat perturbed that the message might be to go to Gwaine Meads at once, as either Erika or Madeleine was seriously ill, and they were still speculating when, a few minutes later, a police inspector walked in.

'Good morning sir,' he said to Gregory. 'Are you Mr. Gregory Sallust?'

'I am,' replied Gregory.

'And you, sir,' he turned to Kuporovitch, 'will be Mr. Stephen Cooper?'

'That's right,' Stefan agreed, after only a second's hesitation.

'Well gentlemen,' the inspector went on, 'I must give you the usual warning that anything you say may be used in evidence—'

285

'God's boots!' exclaimed Gregory 'What the hell are you talking about?'

The inspector was a kindly-faced, grey-haired man. 'I hope you don't mean to make any trouble, sir,' he said quietly. 'But I have a warrant here for the detention of you and this other gentleman under Eighteen-B.'

17

Poison

'This,' said Gregory, the scar above his left eyebrow going white, 'is one of the big moments of my life! Our country asks us to go to Russia. We spend days in aeroplanes at considerable risk of beng shot down by the Germans. We have interminable arguments with security officials. We motor through wild mountains where we are liable to be robbed and murdered by Kurdish tribesmen. We suffer cold and discomfort in Moscow. We fly by night across the German lines to Leningrad. After fifty-three days and a journey of over seven thousand miles we reach our destination. On the return trip we make our way through the shot, shell and machine-gun fire of two battle zones back to Moscow. By train, car, lorry, ship and on our own flat feet, we eventually bribe out way through to Persia. Again for days on end, we fly about in aeroplanes, then, for three weeks we are cooped up in a ship liable to be sunk by U-boats. After a further sixty-seven days and another journey of fifteen thousand five hundred miles we get home. One hundred and twenty days of it, and a grand total of twenty-two thousand five hundred miles! Very nearly the circumference of the earth! And during this delightful little joy-ride what happens. We are arrested by the *Ogpu* and sentenced to death. We are seized by the Gestapo and sentenced to death. We are threatened with indefinite exile to Siberia. We are drugged and imprisoned, and half frozen, and people try to drown us. Yet we get home! And for what? To be arrested on landing under Eighteen-B!'

The inspector grinned 'You certainly seem to have had an interesting time, sir.'

'On the contrary!' Gregory's eyes flashed. 'The interesting rt is just about to begin. I haven't shot anybody on is trip, but when I've had five minutes with the oaf who ued that warrant you'll be wanting me for murder! What's e charge, eh? I suppose some nosey parker, who doesn't ow there is a war on, has found the sugar and tinned ton- es that I had the sense to lay in before the war started, in y store cupboard, and I'm accused of hoarding. Or is it that e National service age limit has gone up since I've been vay, and you want to chain me to a factory bench? If that it I'm your willing victim.'

'No, there's no specific charge. It's just an order to detain u.'

Gregory looked at Stefan. 'It seems that we have conspired ;ainst the safety of the Realm. Why we never thought of)ing so before, I can't think. Poor muts that we are, we sked being sent to Siberia, when all this time we could have en enjoying peace and plenty in the Isle of Man. There is) queueing there, but the best food in Britain; and we'll have ts of time to plan a revival of the legend about what a kind veet gentleman Adolf Hitler really was, after the brute is efeated. With a little luck we might even think up a way of ersuading people that the Germans ought to be allowed to ep their bombers and U-boats so that the poor dears' na- onal pride is not offended.'

'Come along, sir,' said the inspector. 'You're only wasting me, and we have a train to catch. I'm not taking you to the le of Man, but to London.'

'May one ask why?' Gregory enquired.

'I really don't know. To be questioned, I expect.'

'I've a question or two to ask myself,' muttered Gregory ngrily, as they followed the officers from the room. 'May I elephone my friends?'

'I'm afraid not, sir. But you may send telegrams if you like imply stating that you have landed, and, if you like, asking a egal representative to get in touch with Scotland Yard.'

On reaching the station Gregory telegraphed Sir Pellinore nstead of his lawyer; and then sent two other telegrams to Erika and Madeleine to say they hoped to be at Gwaine Meads the following day.

The train was crowded, but they travelled down in comfort, s a compartment had been specially reserved for them. At he London terminus they were met by a police car that wiftly conveyed them to a big building in South Kensington. There, they were put into a sparsely furnished room and told o wait.

They had spoken little on the long journey south owing to

287

the presence of the inspector, and even now speculation ove the cause of their arrest seemed rather futile, when Kupore vitch said, 'What do you think can be behind this extrao dinary business?'

'Heaven alone knows!' Gregory shrugged. 'The whole thir is probably a stupid mistake.'

At that moment Sir Pellinore entered the room. Towerir in the doorway, he seemed almost to fill it as he beame upon them, and cried with hearty joviality: 'Strap me! B it's good to see you fellows again! Till you were reported me as sailing in that convoy I was wondering what the deu had become of you. I'll explain later why I had to have yo arrested.'

'So *you* were at the bottom of it!' Gregory replied acidl 'Have you come to apply the hot irons in person?'

'Ha-ha!' Sir Pellinore guffawed. 'That's good! No. Dinn first and hot irons afterwards. Come along. Car's outside.'

'Does this mean that we are free men?'

'More or less; more or less. I expect you will be after I' read the Riot Act and you've agreed to toe the line. With word of thanks to the inspector, who had appeared behind hi the tall, white-haired man led the way out to the street.

'What the hell are you talking about?' Gregory asked, they got into Sir Pellinore's huge Rolls-Royce. 'Anyone wou think that while we were in Russia we had joined the Comi tern.'

'No, no! You put up a marvellous show! Absolutely ma vellous! The Beaver told me the bare bones of it after I and Harriman returned from Moscow; but I can hardly wa to hear full details. Their Mission, by and by, was an eno mous success, and the Bolshies are being given practica everything they asked for. No, it's not what you've done, n boy. It's what I feared you *might* do, on your return England, that caused me to arrange to have you both p under preventative arrest. After all, you've suffered no inco venience, and it was the quickest way of getting you to Lo don.'

'But why?' Gregory persisted. 'Why were you in such a almighty hurry to see us? Erika's not ill, is she?'

'Not as far as I know.'

'Or Madeleine?' added Kuporovitch.

'No. Fit as a fiddle. At least she was when I last heard fro her, about a fortnight ago.'

The car sped swiftly and almost silently through the da London streets. Sir Pellinore proved adamant in his refus to say any more, and five minutes later they pulled up outsi his mansion in Carlton House Terrace.

Immediately they were settled upstairs in the big library with a decanter of fine sherry before them, Gregory renewed the attack; but Sir Pellinore imperiously waved his question aside.

'Dinner first, thumbscrews afterwards,' he declared. 'Just so as not to put you off your oats I'll tell you this much. While you have been away, the Germans have laid a very clever trap for you, and I didn't want you to fall into it before I'd had a chance to put you wise. Come now! Another noggin of this old Amontillado, then we'll dine.'

'Oh well, if that's all, there is to it . . .' Gregory shrugged and by the time they went down to dinner he was his cheerful self again.

Over the meal he and Kuporovitch gave a detailed account of their adventures, punctuated by ejaculations from Sir Pellinore of: 'God bless my soul! The devil you did! Well I'll be jiggered!' When at last the recital was concluded and the port put on the table. Kuporovitch said:

'And now tell us, please, something of what has been happening here.'

Sir Pellinore took a swig at his port. 'Well,' he replied, having swallowed it with loud appreciative noises, 'as you'll have heard over the ship's radio, we launched our new offensive in Libya about ten days ago. The first phase looked pretty successful. The Tobruk garrison broke out, and on the third day linked up with our main forces. The New Zealanders captured Bardia with great *élan*, then came up to assist in the fighting round Sidi Rezegh. But since then things haven't been going too well. Somehow there doesn't seem to be the Wavell touch about that army any longer, and it looks to me as if this feller Rommel is proving more than a match for 'em. I may be wrong. Hope in God I am. Anyhow we'll see.

'At home here there's been a big shake-up among the Generals. John Dill has been retired from C.I.G.S. on having reached the age limit. Pity that, I think. Dill is a very able feller, and it's absurd to suggest that because he has reached sixty he is no longer capable of advising the Prime Minister. These bureaucratic rules governing promotions and retirements are bad enough in peacetime, and they may prove highly dangerous in war: it's said they are sending him out as Governor of Bombay, but I hope they have the sense to use his very able brain in some more important capacity. He's been succeeded by Alan Brooke, who was C.-in-C. Home Forces, and Bernard Paget has taken Brooke's place. They're both said to be good men; but, again, we shall see.

'There was a great dust-up about Sir Roger Keyes. He was

forming this new Commando outfit for Combined Operations but they've given him the sack, at least, that's what he says himself. The little Admiral is a great fire-eater and I have an idea he wanted to go ahead too quickly for Whitehall. Anyway, I believe Special Service troops are going to prove immensely valuable in the future.'

'How about America?' Gregory asked. 'Is she any nearer to coming in?'

'Yes. Quite a bit. Those idiot Germans never seem to be able to learn a lesson. It was their sinking American shipping that brought the U.S. in last time, and they're at it again now. The amendment of the Neutrality Act in the middle of this month shows how American opinion is hardening and they've already started to arm their merchantmen against the U-boats.'

'Any other good news?'

Sir Pellinore helped himself to some more port and pushed the decanter round. 'The Navy's been doing good work in the Med., although recently we really did lose the good old *Ark Royal*. But the R.A.F. is still the only weapon we've got with which we can really make the Germans squeal. It is bigger than the Luftwaffe now. For the past two months it's been knocking blue blazes out of Hamburg, Bremen, Stettin and all those Baltic ports from which the Nazis send their stuff up to the North Russian front.'

'Thank God for that!' murmured Kuporovitch. 'Things don't look too good in Russia now, from what one hears over the radio.'

Sir Pellinore cocked a bright blue eye first at him, then at Gregory. 'Um!' he muttered, meditatively, 'we'll be in a pretty pickle if it turns out that Voroshilov led you two up the garden path after all.'

'I'd stake my last bob that he didn't,' said Gregory quickly.

'Well, I'm not yet rattled myself. But I know plenty of people who are. And we've gone to town on your word, remember. I've never lost a night's sleep over anything yet; but by jove! I'd have had plenty of cause to these past two months if I'd been that way inclined. Just look what's happened since you gave Beaverbrook your appreciation. Budenny managed to get away from Kiev with about two-thirds of his army, but he lost the city and the Ukraine with it. Kharkov's gone too; one of the greatest industrial centres of all Russia. In the south, the Germans have captured Odessa and over-run the Crimea. Timoshenko's counter-offensive against Rostov is not going too badly, but the Germans are round his southern flank, so he won't be able to keep it up, and before we know where we are the Nazis will have their hooks on Stalin's oil.'

Gregory shook his head. 'I think you're wrong about that. Their main object in holding Stalingrad is so that the oil can continue to come up the Volga, so defending one commits them to defending the other.'

'Hm! The Germans are darn near within range of Stalingrad now.'

'So I gather, but I don't believe they'll ever take it.'

'And how about Moscow, eh? It's getting on for seven weeks since Hitler personally launched his great offensive against the capital. No battle in the whole history of the world can compare with this one for the area of territory being fought over or the destructive power of the huge forces engaged. By comparison it makes our little effort in Libya look positively Lilliputian. And, so far the Germans have won all along the line. It's costing them a packet of course, but they're well past Kalinin in the north and they've got Tula in the south. Moscow has been abandoned as the capital and the Government has retired to Kubishev. They got out weeks ago, and that shows how worried they must be. The latest reports say that the Nazis are now within thirty-five miles of Moscow; so it's beginning to look as if you'd sold us a pup, my boy; and if you have, it's a pup the size of a bulldozer.'

'I gave no guarantee that they would hold Moscow,' said Gregory doggedly. 'I simply stated my belief that they would, somehow manage to maintain themselves on the line of the Volga, and that its key point, Stalingrad, would be held at all costs. If Stalingrad falls you can hang me out with the washing on the Siegfried line; but not till then.'

Sir Pellinore nodded. 'Well, it's some comfort, anyhow, that you've so far proved right about Leningrad. The War Office thought the city would fall a couple of months ago, but Voroshilov is still hanging on.'

'And he will continue to do so,' Kuporovitch put in, with sublime conviction. 'If Leningrad falls you can hang me out with the washing too.'

Having sent what was left of his third glass of port to join its predecessors, Sir Pellinore wiped his white moustache and said: 'Well, as the fate of the civilised world may hang on this Russian armageddon, I find it more comforting to talk to you fellers than to the Chiefs of Staff. Let's go upstairs and drink a spot of Kümmel.'

'The original pre-nineteen-fourteen Mentzendorff?' asked Gregory with a smile.

'Yes, drat you! The bin's getting down near empty now; but I knew I couldn't fob you off with that muck we have for parties, and we'll need something pretty potent handy, in view of what we have to talk about.'

Upstairs, the long-necked, dust-encrusted bottle repose upon a silver salver with three glasses and a corkscrew place before it. Picking up the bottle and the corkscrew, Sir Pell nore advanced to the fire-place and began gently to tap o the wax seal.

'Never believe in doing anything myself that I can get othe people to do for me—with one exception,' he muttered. ' won't let servants open old bottles. Servants these days don understand how to handle fine liqueur. This cork's gone t powder, like as not, and if I allowed them to monkey with they'd let the cork dust ruin the drink.'

Having gently inserted the corkscrew he pulled it with swift sideways twist and the crumbled cork was flicked clear on to the hearth. Then he filled the three glasses with th syrupy white fluid, and lifted his own.

'Well, here's luck to your next venture. You'll need it.'

They drank in silence. The thirty-year old Kümmel, was a soft as cream but had a concealed punch that sent a gloriou warmth through them as it went down. Gregory let out ar appreciative sigh, and said:

'Your toast inferred that you already have in mind anothe job for us. If that's so, unless it's something terribly urgent I'd rather we didn't discuss it for a week or two. Stefan and have had a pretty sticky three months of it, and I think we'r entitled to a spot of leave now. Naturally he wants to see hi wife, and you know how mad I am about Erika.'

'Of course, of course; a very reasonable request.' Sir Pelli nore began to stride up and down the big room with his hand in his trousers pockets. He remembered few things in his life that he had so much hated to have to face as his present task of breaking the news about Erika to Gregory. He would have liked to have gone to meet him on the dock and get it over there, but had felt that the blow might be softened just a little if it was delivered in these familiar surroundings after a good dinner. He had not enjoyed a single mouthful of the meal himself, but it had enabled him to ply Gregory so heavily with good wine that he was in hopes that by the time they got to bed nature would take charge. A few hours' sound sleep after the shock was the best prescription he could devise for restoring the victim's equilibrium, and he meant to send Gregory to bed more or less tight, if he could possibly do so. After a moment he went on:

'I take it you still want to marry Erika?'

Gregory looked up from his Kümmel in surprise. 'Yes, of course. We'd get married tomorrow if only she were free.'

'Quite! Well, there were developments about that soon after you left England. A letter reached her, via the Swiss Legation, from her husband, offering to give her a divorce.'

'By Jove! How terrifically exciting!'

'I've got it here.' Sir Pellinore paused in front of his desk, took two letters from a drawer, and handed one over. 'She left it with me, and I think you had better read it.'

Gregory's face remained quite expressionless while he read the long letter, but, when he had finished, it was very glum as he said: 'Divorces usually take the hell of a time. It says three months here, but I should have thought it would mean much longer than that. I suppose you're trying to break it to me that Erika went abroad to get her freedom and is not back yet; so I won't be able to see her before I have to go off myself on this new job you've got for me.'

'That's it!' Sir Pellinore refilled the Kümmel glasses and there was a moment's silence.

Suddenly Gregory sprang to his feet. His face was dead white and the weal of his scar showed strongly. Letting out a peculiarly blasphemous and unprintable oath that he used only on rare occasions,, he cried: 'You said something about a trap before dinner. You don't mean—you don't mean—'

Sir Pellinore nodded. 'Yes, I'm afraid so. Words can't express what I feel for you, my dear boy—but none of us could have foreseen it. Erika went to Switzerland on the tenth of August. She wrote to me from St. Gall on the twentieth, and I have not heard from her since. Here is her letter. When you've read it I'll fill in the gaps as well as I can.'

With a trembling hand, Gregory took the second letter. His eyes blurred over as he read the familiar, dearly-loved writing, but having to concentrate on it saved him for the moment from visualising the worst that might have happened. When he had done, he said:

'So she went into Germany, to get the low-down on this new weapon. Of course, that's all baloney, it doesn't exist. The divorce was the bait to get her to Switzerland, and this new gas, or whatever it is, the bait to get her across the frontier.'

'I wonder if you're right about that,' Kuporovitch intervened. 'The Germans have not only their own scientists but also Czechs, Norwegians, French and many others whom they compel to work for them now. With such resources they might easily become possessed of some scientific secret that would change the whole course of the war.'

'I've always feared that myself,' Sir Pellinore agreed. Whether von Osterberg knows anything really worth getting hold of, it is impossible to say, but he may. The R.A.F. recently reported the development of a great new experimental station up at Peenemunde, on the Baltic, and Erika says that by his own account, von Osterberg was employed somewhere up in the north before he escaped to Switzerland.'

'Escaped my foot!' exclaimed Gregory. 'He was deliberately planted there by Grauber to pull Erika in.'

'No. You were the big fish that Grauber was after. He reckoned that you would accompany her to Switzerland, and that when von Osterberg had said his piece, it would be you who would go into Germany to get those notes.'

'Yes, I suppose so.' Gregory glanced at Kuporovitch. 'I can see daylight now about what Grauber meant when he said in the U-boat that once he got me back to Germany he'd make me talk without resorting to torture. The swine had got Erika already and he was contemplating flaying her alive in front of me if I refused to spill the beans.'

'You are right,' Kuporovitch agreed. 'But from that emerges one comfort for you. It means that Erika is still alive and unharmed. To exert maximum pressure on you he must produce her well and with her beauty unmarred to start with, when he catches you, as he no doubt still hopes to do.'

'Yes—she is the bait now,' Sir Pellinore agreed. 'And evidently, in anticipation of your getting back safely from Russia the trap has recently been reset.'

'What do you mean?' Gregory asked quickly.

Sir Pellinore walked over to his desk and produced a third letter. 'This reached me early his month, again via the Swiss Legation, and it is another letter from von Osterberg. But before you read it I'll tell you the very little that I was able to find out subsequent to Erika's disappearance. As you'll have gathered, I set young Piers—what's his name—out to Switzerland with her; so he was able to give me the lie of the land on his return. I was deuced worried when I learnt that Erika was going into Germany, but by the time I had her letter she had crossed the lake, and there was nothing I could do about it. Still, for once I put the national interest second to yours and I laid Piers off the job he was going to do for a bit. After a week, having heard nothing more from Erika, I sent him out again. He reported that on the evening of the twenty-second of August the launch from the Villa Offenbach was seen going out, apparently on a fishing expedition, with two men and a girl in her. As far as is known the launch did not return, and the Villa remained unoccupied. On learning that, I realised that either the whole party had been caught or that Erika had been betrayed by her husband, so I recalled Piers and proceeded to await events.'

'D'you mean to tell me you've sat here for three months and done nothing!' Gregory cut in angrily.

Sir Pellinore spread out his large hands. 'What could I do

294

ny boy? I felt that it was all Lombard Street to a china orange that we'd been had for mugs and that Erika had been deliberately snared to bait a fresh trap for you. Therefore, that he was a prisoner, but safe for the time being.'

'You could at least have tried to find out the concentration camp to which they had sent her.'

'That was next to impossible. As I've often told you, our Secret Service performs miracles in keeping us informed of the enemy's military moves, but it seems to know next to nothing about what goes on inside Germany. I could have sent young what's-his-name or someone like that but I didn't dare to risk it. None of them is in your class, and if they had mucked the thing up and got Erika killed while trying to get her out you would never have forgiven me. No, I felt confident that no harm would come to Erika as long as Grauber had a use for her, and that you'd want to handle this thing yourself. So I waited for you to return.'

'Yes, you were quite right about that,' Gregory admitted rather grudgingly.

'Good! Well, although I couldn't do anything about Erika, I had a watch kept on the Villa Offenbach. It was reported to me that on or about the twenty-fifth of October the Villa was reoccupied by two men answering the descriptions of von Osterberg and Einholtz. In the light of what we now know, it looks as if, by that time, having got back to Germany himself, Grauber had learned through one of his agents in Leningrad that you had escaped being drowned in that U-boat. He'd conclude that you'd probably be back in London by early November—as you would have been had you been able to get an aircraft from Cairo. So he packs von Osterberg and other feller off to set the trap again. As soon as they're settled in, the Count writes this letter; it reached me ten days later.'

Gregory took the letter, which was in German, and read it out, translating as he went along:

Dear Sir Pellinore Gwaine-Cust,

'During several conversations that I had with my wife here in mid-August she mentioned, more than once, the great kindness that you had shown her as an enemy alien while domiciled in Britain. It therefore seems probable that before leaving England she told you that she was going to Switzerland for the purpose of coming to some arrangement with me about our future relations.

'Our discussions on the subject proceeded very amicably but, most unfortunately, they were complicated by another matter which resulted in our deciding to risk a short trip into

295

Germany, for the purpose of recovering certain personal papers from my old home—Schloss Niederfels.

'We crossed the lake on the night of August twenty-second and reached Niederfels in safety. Both of us had naturally assumed that the staff of old family servants there would prove completely trustworthy, but by a most tragic piece of ill luck my mother had recently taken into her service a new lady's maid. The girl's last place was in Berlin and, I gather, she was the mistress of an S.S. man there. In consequence, she denounced us to the local headquarters and we only narrowly escaped being captured in the Castle.

'In our flight we had the further misfortune to become separated. I took refuge with an old friend of mine and he concealed me for nearly two months, after which I succeeded in making my way back here. What has happened to Erika I do not know. The friend with whom I was in hiding told me that there was a great hue-and-cry after us both, but no report of her ever being captured. It therefore seems reasonably certain that she also took refuge with one of our tenants and is still in hiding somewhere in the neighbourhood of Niederfels, but afraid to leave the temporary security that she has found.

'If I am right in this I do not doubt that by discreet enquiries I could soon find her; and I feel very strongly that it is my duty to go back and help her to escape from Germany, which should not be very difficult now that the hue-and-cry for us has had time to die down. But, I am ashamed to say, my courage is not equal to undertaking such a trip alone.

'You see, I am not a man of action. Most of my adult life has been spent in scientific research and few men could be more ill suited to undertake such a venture as myself.

'However, Erika was extremely frank with me when we discussed her future. She freely admitted that in the event of her obtaining her freedom it was her intention to marry a Mr Gregory Sallust. I understand from her that he is a journalist and war correspondent, whose assignments in many countries have called for a most active and enterprising nature. In fact that he has all those qualities which are so lamentably lacking in myself.

'I have no animus whatever against Mr. Sallust on account of the fact that he is in love with my wife, and it has occurred to me that if he is still working in Fleet Street, or could be recalled from some front on which he may be reporting the course of the war, he would perhaps, welcome the opportunity of affording me the assistance which I regard as essential, if I am to go back to Germany on an attempt to rescue my poor wife.

'As I have no idea how to get into touch with Mr. Sallust

*direct, I have taken the liberty of writing to you, in the hope
that you will be able to communicate the contents of this
letter to him.*

'*I am, etc., etc.*'

Gregory flung down the letter in disgust. 'The dirty, double-
crossing swine! But Grauber is behind it, of course—and it's
as clear a case of "Come into my Parlour said the Spider to
the Fly" as ever I've seen.'

'I wouldn't quite say that,' Kuporovitch demurred. 'The
way we are looking at it one naturally smells a rat. But what
real grounds are there for doing so? Only, I think, the boast
that Grauber made in the U-boat; yet he may have had in
mind some quite different method of making you talk.'

'Hm! Von Osterberg's first letter was plausible enough,'
grunted Sir Pellinore.

'So is his second,' Kuporovitch went on. 'We have no evidence at all that this von Osterberg set a trap for Erika, or
that Grauber is behind him. Everything might have happened
just as he says. Had they talked as old friends he would naturally have asked her about her time in England. He knew already that she had been working in the hospital at Gwaine
Meads, so there was no reason why she should not have mentioned Sir Pellinore's kindness in giving her a home there.
They had already agreed to a divorce, so it does not seem to
me strange that he should have asked if she had any plans for
the future or that she should have told him that she intended
to marry a Mr. Gregory Sallust. You will note, too, that
he appears to know only that Gregory is a journalist and war
correspondent. As Sir Pellinore acted the part of guardian to
her while she was here, the Count would be quite justified
in assuming that he would know of her affair with Gregory
and be able to get in touch with him. We all know that von
Osterberg is a scientist, and most scientists are far from being
practical men of the world, let alone of the resolute and audacious type capable of taking on and outwitting the Gestapo.
What could be more natural than, feeling so helpless himself,
he should propose that a man accustomed to action and danger should go with him, when that man is his wife's lover
and has more to gain that he has by rescuing her?'

'What about this chap Einholtz?' said Gregory. 'He went
in with them the first time and, from the report, returned
with von Osterberg to the Villa at the end of October. Don't
you consider it suspicious that no mention at all is made of
him?'

'It was what Erika said in her letter about Einholtz that somehow made me suspect it to be a trap,' grunted Sir Pellinore.

'Perhaps it was his being out for filthy lucre that made me feel he was a fishy customer. It's certainly suspicious that von Osterberg doesn't mention him in either of his letters.'

'Not necessarily,' Kuporovitch countered. 'It may be tha having little courage himself, von Osterberg would not go without this friend of his on the first trip, and they got away together, but Einholtz now feels once bit twice shy, and wil not go again. After all, it is no affair of his, so why should he? And why should von Osterberg complicate his letter by dragging him in since he played only a subsidiary role?'

'Something in that.' Sir Pellinore took another swig of Kümmel. 'Maybe I've been barking up the wrong tree. That's what comes of having a suspicious nature. Of course, the fact that made me jump to conclusions was Erika's disappearance. She took a big risk going in anyway; and she may have been put on the spot by the old woman's abigail, as her husband says. Still, the moment I learnt that she hadn't returned with the other two I had a hunch that there was some deliberate devilry at the bottom of it all, and my hunches aren't usually wrong.'

Kuporovitch's eyes narrowed. 'I don't say that it isn't a trap; only that, if it is, it's a very well laid one. You see, if Grauber had got Erika he might quite well have found a way to force her to write a letter to Gregory himself saying that she was in hiding somewhere and needed his help to get back. But it seems to me that if he is behind it he has been more subtle than that.'

'I don't see that it matters who wrote the letter,' Gregory shrugged. 'He would know that the moment I got it I should set off for Switzerland. Turning to Sir Pellinore, he added, 'When is the earliest you can get me a 'plane?'

Sir Pellinore sighed. 'I still think you'd be walking straight into a trap my boy. And if Grauber has set it deliberately to snare you I'd rather put my head in the jaws of a shark. If you go to Switzerland the odds are that you'll never come back.'

'I'm going there all the same. If I'd known about this when we docked this morning I would have begged, borrowed or stolen an aircraft and been there by now.'

'I know. That's why I had you arrested. As you'd completed your mission I thought you might not bother to come to see me right away. After all, landing at Glasgow, Gwaine Meads was on your way south. You might easily have decided to stop off there to see Erika.'

'If I had I'd only have learned that she left there three months ago, and I should have come hurtling down here on

he next express to find out from you what had happened to
er.'

'Maybe, maybe not! I naturally replied to von Osterberg's
etter. Told him that you were abroad for the time being,
ut that as soon as you got back I'd pass his letter on; and
at in the meantime I hoped he'd have some news of Erika.
ut that is close on a month ago, and I've heard nothing since.
t's on the cards that he may be getting impatient. He may
ave got the impression that I was stalling him and had de-
berately refrained from showing you his letter. If so, he may
ave written to you direct by now. A letter might have arrived
rom him by any post at Gwaine Meads, or at your club. If
ou'd gone to either of them before seeing me you might
ave stolen an aircraft, just as you say, and been in Switzer-
nd by this time. You see, I know just what you must be feel-
g, and just the sort of mad-hatter tricks you might get up to
fter such a shock.'

Gregory gave a faint grin. 'You're right, of course. If I'd
und out about this on my own I should have been too im-
atient to wait, and certainly have done something pretty
azy.'

'Well, you won't when you get to Switzerland,' Kuporo-
tch put in. 'I'll take care of that.'

'D'you mean you're coming with me?'

'Of course. You are in no fit state to be allowed to go any-
here alone.'

'That's darn decent of you, Stefan.'

'Nonsense!' the Russian shrugged. 'You would do the same
r me at any time. And the sooner we start the sooner we
all get back.' He looked at Sir Pellinore. 'When will it be
ossible for us to start?'

'You must have proper papers, and tomorrow's Sunday.
t awkward that. Some of the people I'll need to get hold of
ay not be in their offices. Still, by pulling every gun I've got,
ought to be able to get you off by Monday afternoon.'

'Thanks,' said Gregory. 'I'm sure you'll do your best for us.
Sir Pellinore emptied the remains of the Kümmel into their
asses. 'I suppose so,' he grumbled unhappily, 'but I know
hat I ought to do with you two lunatics.'

'Lock us up, eh?' Kuporovitch smiled.

'Exactly! But I'm getting old; that's the trouble. I'm allow-
g sentiment to overrule my sense of duty, by all the laws of
e Medes and Persians I ought to have you both clapped into
e Isle of Man for the duration. I'm not yet certain that I
on't, either.'

'Thanks,' said Gregory curtly. 'But personally I have no
esire to be prevented from risking my life against my will.'

299

The elderly Baronet raised his bright blue eyes and stare at him angrily. 'It's not your life I'm worrying about, yc young fool. It's what the Gestapo might get out of you you're caught. Surely you two realise that your recent succe in Russia has turned you into dynamite. You're both fle and blood, like anyone else. Those fiends may do things you until you're both driven out of your minds. Then ye won't even know *what* you're saying. And under your bo nets you've now got the whole of Russia's future strateg Why, damn your eyes! If the Nazis get that out of you v might lose the war. Hell's bells! The very thought of takin a risk makes me sweat.'

'You're going to take it all the same.' Gregory stuck out l lean jaw.

'Yes, I'm going to take it.' Sir Pellinore's voice had nc dropped several tones, and he spoke very quietly. 'I'm goii to take it on one condition; and in order to be in a positic to insist on this was the main reason why I had you arreste I'm going to give you both some capsules containing cyani of potassium. If you go into Germany you will carry them your mouths. One gulp and death is instantaneous. You' got to give me your word that if you're caught you'll swallc them.'

18

Back into Germany

When Sir Pellinore Gwaine-Cust had privately made up mind that any particular person should do a certain thi they almost invariably did it; so that night or rather at abc two-thirty on Sunday morning, Gregory, having partak after the old Kümmel of the brandy champagne, more bran and finally a mixture of the two, swayed his way upstairs, j managed to undress, flopped into bed and swiftly passed in oblivion.

But not so Stefan Kuporovitch. He had gone upstairs nea five hours earlier; not because he wanted to but because

Pellinore had taken occasion to tip him off that he wished to be left alone with Gregory. The news about Erika had appalled him, and privately he had little doubt that she had fallen into the hands of the Gestapo; his arguments as to the possibility of von Osterberg's letter not being a trap had been put up solely in the hope that even the chance she might still be free, although in hiding would prove a comfort to his friend.

Yet once having accepted the situation with true Russian fatalism, he had imagined that he was in for a very good evening. He loved fine liquor and, knowing Sir Pellinore's boundless hospitality, had felt that many good things would follow the Kümmel in a possibly melancholy, but nevertheless enjoyable, drinking party. Good-natured as he was, he could not but feel a little resentful at having been packed off to bed, still as sober as a judge, at a quarter to ten. But he consoled himself with the thought that he was at least now free to ring up Madeleine and have a long talk with her.

On opening the door of his room his frown gave place to a slow smile. Beside the large, comfortable-looking Queen Anne bed stood a wheeled tray. On its two shelves reposed a cold lobster, salad, a *foi gras*, some hothouse fruit and, in an ice bucket, a magnum of champagne. Stefan was fond of drinking much more for the sake of good company and good talk than for drinking itself, but, all the same, he thought it a darn decent gesture of Sir Pellinore's to provide him with such an excellent cold supper.

His eye then fell on a chair at the far side of the high-canopied bed. Upon it were neatly arranged an array of feminine clothes, with the silken undies uppermost. His dark eyebrows shot up and he gave a low whistle of surprise. For a second he thought that he must have got into the wrong room. Despite his age, Sir Pellinore's extraordinary virility and great wealth suggested that he might still keep a beautiful young mistress. But Stefan saw that the meagre outfit with which he had travelled from Cairo was also in the room. He then jumped to another conclusion. To his pre-Revolution Russian mind, there was nothing particularly strange in a great nobleman like Sir Pellinore providing a little feminine entertainment for his guests.

His ear caught a faint splashing in the adjacent private bathroom, then, as he closed the door behind him, a gay voice called:

'Stefan! C'est toi chéri?'

In one bound he was across the room. In another, he was through the bathroom door, and a second later, he had his beautiful but wet young wife in his arms.

The explanation of her presence was very simple. Earlier in

301

the day Sir Pellinore had telephoned to her to come at once to London. On her arrival he had told her that her husband would be back that night but that he did not wish Gregory to see her, because the sight of her and Stefan together would have made Erika's absence so much harder for him to bear. Sir Pellinore had added that if they cared to consider themselves prisoners over the Sunday in the suite he had placed at their disposal this would be all to the good, and he would see to it that they lacked for nothing which would make their captivity endurable.

Had they arranged matters themselves, or possessed Aladdin's lamp, there was nothing more that they could have desired or asked of the all-powerful Jinni.

Sir Pellinore had popped a dose of veronal into Gregory's last drink, so he slept until nearly midday. On waking he felt pretty heady but he remembered perfectly clearly all that had taken place the night before. For a little he lay in bed torturing himself with thoughts of what might be happening to Erika; but, after a bit, he realised that he was acting like a fool, as unnerving speculations about her could do neither her nor him any good, and that his best hope of defeating Grauber lay in regarding the problem of her rescue as coldly and logically as if it was no personal concern of his at all.

After a bath he felt slightly better, then, downstairs, he had a Pim and three cocktails with Sir Pellinore which made him feel more his own man.

When they had lunched Sir Pellinore provided the best possible antidote to his guest's depression. Upstairs in his library he had a fine collection of maps, both historical and modern and he produced a great pile, all showing either Lake Constance or the ancient Kingdom of Württemberg, in which Schloss Niederfels lay. Work, and work connected with the hazardous journey he was soon about to undertake was the very thing Gregory needed to occupy his mind. He spent most of the rest of the day concentrating on memorising the names of German villages, the by-roads that connected them and the situation of wooded areas which would give good cover if required.

On the Monday morning Sir Pellinore introduced both Gregory and Stefan to a clever-looking little man wearing thick-lensed spectacles. He had at one time been a dentist but, owing to the war, had gravitated to certain highly specialised duties connected with sabotage operations. From a little box he produced some small square of hardish, jelly-like substance each of which had a little lump in its middle. The lump was the cyanide of potassium and its coating so composed that, with a little pressure, it would stick to the side of a back tooth and, nce stuck, would need a really hard thrust of the tongue to dislodge.

'If you—er—get into trouble,' he explained gently, 'you simply rip it off with your tongue and bite throught its centre. The result is very swift and, I believe, affects the user only by a sudden contraction, as though he were about to give a violent sneeze.

'You will see,' he went on, 'that they are of two colours. The green ones are dummies for you to practice with; the red ones are the real thing. Both kinds can be kept permanently in the mouth for a considerable time without any likelihood of their dissolving and becoming dangerous. But, if necessary, I advise that you should replace a used one by a new one after a fortnight. Now, I'd like to look at your mouths to decide the most suitable places for you to wear them.'

Having asked on which side of their mouths they chewed by preference, he made a very careful examination of their teeth, and affixed two of the dummies. Then, wishing them good luck he departed.

At first, both of them felt as though they had had plum stones stuck in the sides of their mouths. It was difficult for them to keep their tongues from worrying the capsules and they could not help thinking that the bulges in their cheeks must be obvious to anyone. But Sir Pellinore assured them that his was not so and, somewhat to their surprise, they found at lunch they could still eat without undue discomfort.

Sir Pellinore had told Gregory on the Sunday of Madeline's presence in the house, and she joined them for the meal. Afterwards, Kuporovitch had half an hour to say good-bye to her, then Sir Pellinore accompanied the two friends in his car out of London to the airport.

They met with none of the delays that had so irritated Erika and Piers four months before, as Sir Pellinore, who never did things by halves, once he had made up his mind on a matter, had laid on a special aircraft for them.

It was the 1st of December and a grey, depressing winter's day, but up to the very last moment he never ceased to joke with them and speak with bluff good humour of the great time they would all have at Gwaine Meads over Christmas. It was only as the 'plane lifted into the air that his bright blue eyes grew misty. For once, he was really feeling his age. He loved Gregory as a son and, despite all his confidence in his courage and audacity, he doubted very much if he would ever see him again.

That evening Gregory and Stefan were safely landed in Switzerland. They spent the night at a quiet hotel and next morning went on to St. Gall. There, they put up at the Pension

303

Julich on the very slender chance that Erika might have found means of sending out of Germany some message to the proprietor, which he, for some reason, had failed to relay to London. But this frail hope of a clue to her whereabouts proved abortive. The proprietor remembered the lady well, and produced the suit-case that she had left behind. Gregory was so moved at seeing her things that he could not bring himself to go through the case; so, instead Kuporovitch did so with the proprietor; but there was nothing in it from which they could make fresh deductions.

On the Wednesday morning Gregory wanted to go straight down to Steinach, but Kuporovitch persuaded him that, since von Osterberg was supposedly still in hiding from the Gestapo, a visit by strangers to the Villa Offenbach would more suitably be made at night. In consequence, he waited until the evening before taking the little local train down through the bleak wintry weather to the lake-shore and, at Stefan's suggestion, he went alone, so that it should not yet emerge that he had brought a friend with him to Switzerland.

Although only seven o'clock it was already full dark when he reached the Villa, as the moon had not yet risen to silver the snow-capped mountains and turn the landscape into a fairy scene.

He rang twice at the door, then Einholtz opened it.

'May I ask if I am addressing the *Herr Graf* von Osterberg?' Gregory enquired in German, although he knew that it must be Einholtz to whom he was speaking.

'I regret, but there is some mistake. This house is occupied by Dr. Fallström,' Einholtz replied, with a suspicious look

'I am from London,' Gregory persisted. 'A letter that the Count wrote to a friend of mine there has recently been passed on to me; and in it he expressed a wish to see me. My name is Gregory Sallust, and—'

'*Ach so!*' Einholtz broke in. 'I am so sorry, but we have to take precautions here. The Count is far from well. His experiences have unnerved him, and at times you will find his manner strange, but, all the same, I am sure he will be delighted to see you. Please to come in, *Herr* Sallust.'

As he stood aside for Gregory to enter, and closed the door after him, Einholtz went on: 'Let me introduce myself. I am Fritz Einholtz and I know all about poor Kurt's affairs. You see, I, too, am a scientist, although a very minor one compared to him. I was his assistant and we escaped together from the Nazis. Then I accompanied him and his wife back into Germany, last August. *Ach!* that was a terrible experience. We became separated from the Countess and we have been distraught with anxiety on her account ever since. But we still hope that she is hiding with friends. We had to hide, ourselves, for two months before we dared to attempt the return trip. This way, *Herr* Sallust. Please to come in.'

As Gregory listened to these eager confidences it occurred to him that, after all, Kuporovitch might be right. One of the points that had seemed most suspicious about von Osterberg's letter had been his omission to make any mention of Einholtz, yet here was the man himself filling in the gap quite spontaneously about the subsidiary part in the affair that he, apparently had played.

On entering the sitting-room of the house Gregory saw a rather frail-looking man considerably older than himself, and with two small scars from student duels on his right cheek, sitting by a log fire reading a book. In spite of the fact that it was quite warm in there his knees were covered with a blanket.

As he looked up Einholtz said cheerfully: 'Kurt, this is *Herr* Sallust. You know how anxious you have been at not hearing from him, but now he has arrived in person. Is not that splendid!'

Von Osterberg stood up, brought his heels together, bowed, and said with formal politeness, 'Mr. Sallust, you are very welcome.'

Gregory smiled. 'I'm sorry that I've been so long in getting here, Count, but now I have, I do hope that we may succeed in tracing Erika and getting her out of Germany.'

'Erika,' von Osterberg repeated. 'Yes, yes, poor little Erika, I dare not think what they may be doing to her.'

'Now don't be silly, Kurt,' Einholtz said sharply. 'You keep on imagining things that have not the least foundation. She may not be comfortable, living in some barn perhaps, but there is no reason at all to suppose that she has been caught. In fact, if she had, we should have been certain to have heard of it before we left Germany.'

While speaking he had rearranged the chairs and now held one for Gregory, opposite the fire. As they all sat down Gregory said:

'I know only the bare facts that you put in your letter, Count, and in view of your state of health I can well understand your feeling that this thing is too much for you to take on alone; but if I'm to pull my weight I ought to know the full details of all that has happened up to now.'

With hesitations here and there von Osterberg gave the outline of the story. The hesitations were easily ascribable to his highly nervous condition, and Einholtz helped him out with fuller accounts of all points where Gregory put in a question.

They told how they had crossed the lake to *Freiherr* von Lottingen's summer villa, borrowed a car there and reached

Niederfels without accident a few hours later. The Count's mother had given them a late supper and the old lady had been so pleased to see him that they had allowed her to persuade them to stay for twenty-four hours, instead of returning that night, as had originally been intended. The only people who were aware of their presence there, as far as they knew, were old servants whose loyalty was beyond question. The sleepy castle, surrounded by its forest-clad heights, had seemed, as Einholtz put it, a thousand years and a million miles from modern war and totalitarian politics. The *Frau Gräfin* Bertha was getting on in years and might never see her son again. How could they refuse to take what seemed an almost negligible risk of remaining with her till the following night?

But the next afternoon while they had been sitting in the sunshine on the battlements they had seen two cars coming up the winding road that led to the Schloss. They were full of police and in the back of one of them had been sitting the *Frau Gräfin's* personal maid. The old lady knew that when the girl was in Berlin she had had an S.S. trooper as a lover, but the man was now far away on the Russian front, and the old Countess was so out of the world at Niederfels that it had never even occurred to her that men or women once infected with the Nazi virus could never again be trusted. Yet here was her maid in the very act of betraying them.

Only Kurt and Einholtz had been with the old lady at the time. Erika was resting on her bed to fit herself for the exhausting night that lay before her. The *Frau Gräfin* had insisted that the two men should take to the woods at once while she went to warn Erika. They had already arranged that in the event of any unforeseen visitation they would rendezvous at a place in the forest some two miles away, where they had hidden the car.

They had reached it without being spotted, and they had waited there all night, but Erika had not come. In the dawn they had driven to the house of an old bachelor tenant-farmer whom the Count had felt confident was to be trusted. He had agreed to take them in, hidden them in a loft and concealed their car in the middle of a hayrick. They felt certain that Erika had not been caught because the whole district had been placarded with notices offering a reward for her capture as well as theirs, and they thought it even possible that she was still at the Castle, having been hidden by the *Gräfin* in one of its many secret rooms. After remaining concealed for two months they had decided to try to recross the frontier. No one suspected that they had been using the *Freiherr* von Lottingen's car, and when they returned in it to his villa they found their launch still in the boathouse, and got away in her.

The whole story was so circumstantial that Gregory found difficulty in disbelieving it. Of one thing he was certain. Von Osterberg was no conspirator. His mind was too obviously unbalanced by his experiences for him to be capable of trapping anybody. About Einholtz, Gregory was not so certain. He thought the Count's tall, semi-bald companion just a little too glib and ready with explanations; but it appeared that he was more or less a dependent of von Osterberg's, so the way in which he so often spoke on his behalf might be no more than a desire to save him fatigue and, at the same time, ingratiate himself with their visitor. Gregory found the swathe of thin hair pasted across his scalp rather unattractive and the flashy amethyst ring that he wore on his left hand suggested that he might be a pansy; but, even if that were so, it would be no indication of his secret political convictions, as for several generations past a high proportion of German males had begot children from their women while seeking their pleasure in perversion.

With a view to testing the situation further Gregory asked them about their first escape from Germany.

'We were transferred from Krupps to a new experimental station in the north—' Einholtz began.

'At Peenemunde on the Baltic?' Gregory put in quietly.

They both started, and stared at him, but he simply laughed and said: 'There's no reason to be surprised at my knowing about that. My work as a journalist often takes me to the Air Ministry and sometimes the people there show me their most recent photographs. A few days before I left London I saw one of this new place there, that's all.'

'Well, yes. That's where we were,' Einholtz admitted. 'Does your Air Ministry know about the work that is being carried on there?'

'I shouldn't think so,' Gregory shrugged. 'It's hardly likely that they would be able to deduce that simply from a few photographs of a lot of camouflaged buildings, and, even if they did, they certainly wouldn't tell anyone so unimportant as myself about it.'

He hoped that future air reconnaisances would not meet with stiffer opposition owing to his deliberate indiscretion, but that was, to some extent, offset by Einholtz having confirmed that the buildings at Peenemunde were, in fact, a scientific experimental station, and his having done so quite readily seemed further evidence of his own honesty.

Von Osterberg seemed a little more at ease now that they were no longer talking of Erika, and he related the story of

307

their escape from Peenemunde and journey south with com
paratively little aid from Einholtz. When he had done, Gre
gory said:

'I take it that you never succeeded in recovering your note
from Schloss Niederfels, after all, or you would have sai
something about them in your letter?'

'No,' replied the Count, 'we didn't get the notes.'

'We had our chance, but most stupidly lost it,' Einholt
added. 'You see, we didn't expect to leave till midnight an
Kurt was so occupied with his *Frau Mütter* that he had nc
even visited his laboratory before we saw the police speedin
up the road. And then, of course, we had to run for our lives

'They should still be there, then?'

Einholtz shook his head. 'They may be, but I doubt it. Afte
our visit it is pretty certain that the S.S. would have blown ope
the safe to see if there was anything worth pinching inside i
and have burnt or removed them.'

He spoke without emphasis and while staring thoughtfull
into the fire. Gregory, who was watching him narrowly, fe
that if the German was attempting to deceive him he wa
doing a beautiful job of work. If, too, Grauber, was really a
the bottom of all this he would know that the fact that Erik
was a prisoner would alone be quite sufficient to lure hi
enemy into Germany, but, all the same, it seemed strange tha
they should deliberately play down one of the principal in
ducements to make the trip. Although he felt only a reluctan
pity for the Count and a vague dislike of Einholtz he wa
tending more and more to the opinion that the two men wer
really anti-Nazis, and were telling the truth.

Einholtz suddenly asked him if he would care for a drink
'Would you not like some *Glühwein* perhaps?' he added. 'I
is a good thing to warm one up on a cold night.'

Gregory hardly hesitated a second. Even if his hosts wer
in active league with the enemy the odds against their attemp
ting to drug or poison him were enormously high. He had
already expressed his willingness to go into Germany of hi
own free will, so there was no point in undertaking the la
borious business of shanghaing him there. And as they coul
not have had any warning of his visit no preparations to tha
end could have been made.

'Thanks,' he said, 'I should love some.'

'Kurt will oblige us, I'm sure,' Einholtz smiled at the Count
'He has his own recipe and makes it better than anyone
know.'

Von Osterberg came to his feet at once. 'Of course,' he sai
quickly. 'I like to make *Glühwein*. It is always so good.'

When he had left the room Einholtz remarked in a con

versational tone: 'It is over five weeks now since Kurt wrote to Sir Gwaine-Cust. We were beginning to think that either the letter had gone astray or that having had Kurt's message you intended to ignore it.'

'I was in Russia,' Gregory replied frankly. 'For two months I was working in the Press Section of our Embassy there.'

'How very interesting. Do tell me what you think of those strange people and the situation there.'

For a little while Gregory discoursed quite truthfully on Moscow and the Russians. Then von Osterberg returned with a large jug of mulled red wine and three tumblers. As he poured out the steaming drink his dull eyes took on a sudden lustre and the reason for the alacrity with which he had agreed to make it was soon apparent. With his eyes glued to the remaining contents of the jug he hurriedly sipped away as quickly as he could at the near-scalding liquor in his tumbler, evidently intent on getting in first for a second helping. As Gregory watched him covertly, he thought, 'Poor devil, he's certainly been through the mill all right, and drink is about the only thing that can make him forget.'

The conversation having turned to Russia, Einholtz kept it there. He made no secret of the fact that, although he was an anti-Nazi, he was infinitely more violent anti-Communist.

'Those barbarous swine!' he exclaimed. 'Well, however much we may dislike Hitler's methods in our own country, at least he will crush the Bolshevik menace for us. They'll cave in when he takes their capital. I expect; and it is pretty certain now that he will be in Moscow before Christmas.'

'I don't agree,' said Gregory quietly. 'I'm no lover of the Bolsheviks either, but I'm certain that their army is a long way from being beaten yet; and, if Hitler is not careful, having gone into Russia may yet prove his Waterloo.'

'But that is absurd!' Einholtz protested. 'The Russians, so far have been defeated in nearly every battle. Already half their principal cities are in our hands, and it is quite clear that they cannot possibly resist the assaults of our magnificent German Army. They have no organisation.'

'Oh yes, they have,' countered Gregory. 'And in its own peculiar way it may prove more efficient than yours, in the long run. I was lucky enough to obtain private interviews with some of their top men when I was in Moscow and I know what I'm talking about.'

Einholtz proved dogged in his disbelief and Gregory could not resist the temptation to play with fire. He felt now that all the chances were that anything he said would go no further as who was there that mattered to whom this friendless exile could repeat it—if he were a friendless exile? If he were not, well, this was an opportunity which should not be neglected, however slender the chances of its bearing fruit. He told Einholtz the real truth about the organisation of the Soviet Army and repeated, almost word for word, everything that Marshal Voroshilov had said about it during their amazing talk in Leningrad, when the Marshal had been under the influence of the Truth Drug.

Einholtz did not interrupt with any questions but just sat there drinking in every word. Von Osterberg had gulped down his second tumbler of the now tepid mulled wine and fallen fast asleep in his armchair.

When Gregory at last fell silent Einholtz said: 'This is amazing—if it is true. But tell me, how is it that the Russians who are normally so secretive should have disclosed all this to you—a journalist?'

Gregory gave him a curious sideways look and replied:

'I managed to secure the information partly because they wanted to impress me. You see, they are now very anxious to stand well with Britain. Partly, too, because I *am* a journalist, and to succeed at my job you have to be a highly trained observer, capable of putting quite small things together and worrying them out until they make sense. But on top of that, in wartime, journalists are often asked to step out of their own rut a bit, and for the past two years I haven't been strictly confining myself to journalistic activities all the time.'

It was as good as an admission that he was a secret agent, but Grauber knew that already, so even if Einholtz, after all, proved to be 'the enemy' Gregory was giving nothing new away about himself.

'Since you found out so much I'll bet that you couldn't rest until you had discovered where the Reserve Army of shock troops was located,' Einholtz said, with the air of 'the man in the street' who is being let into fascinating secrets.

'Yes, I found out all right,' Gregory gave a self-satisfied smile. 'It's sitting pretty in an area about a hundred and fifty miles to the south-east of Moscow, all ready to spring. That's why I'm convinced that Moscow won't be taken. Your people have been putting everything they've got into this drive for the past six weeks. They must be pretty tired by now. They'll never be able to stand up to this terrific counter-offensive that is about due to be launched against them. The Soviet striking force consists of an entire Army Group, every man of it trained to Guards' standard, and equipped with up-to-the-minute weapons as fine as anything that has ever been turned out by Krupp or Skoda. From south of Moscow this terrific mass of men and metal will be hurled north-west to save the city, and it will tear up the whole central German front as though it were only paper. Believe me or not, as you like, but I'd bet my last cent that that's what will happen within the next two weeks.'

Einholtz had gone quite white; the hand with the amethyst ring was tapping nervously on his knee. The picture that Gregory had drawn was not a pretty one for any German, whether pro- or anti-Nazi, as it envisaged a major defeat of the German Army; that Golden Calf that the German people of all shades of opinion had set up and worshipped as an idol for many generations, because deep down they all believed that Might was Right and that the short cut to affluence lay in the subjugation and robbery of their neighbours.

There was a short silence, then Gregory said: 'Well, I didn't come here to yarn about my own rather queer activities, or about the war. How soon can we start on our attempt to trace and rescue the *Gräfin* von Osterberg?'

'The moon would be bad for you at present,' Einholtz replied. 'It will be much better this time next week. Then there is the question of Kurt's health. You can see for yourself that he is in a pretty poor state. I'll nurse him for you as well as I can during the next few days, but unless I can get a bit more life into him before you start you would run the risk of having him collapse while you are in Germany; and that would be disastrous.'

Gregory glanced at the sleeping Count. 'It certainly would. And from what you've just said I gather that it's not your intention to come with us. I had been hoping that you meant to do so.'

Einholtz shook his head. 'I'd like to help, but it isn't really my affair. And if we were caught—well—I gather that death in a Nazi concentration camp can be pretty terrible.'

For a moment Gregory considered the situation afresh. The fact that Einholtz apparently did not wish to go with them impressed him strongly. Von Osterberg was obviously quite incapable of either arresting him or efficiently leading him into a trap when they reached the other side. If, therefore, they were working under Grauber's direction it seemed essential that Einholtz should be in the party to stage-manage the Judas act. Otherwise, if he, Gregory, decided to quit von Osterberg at any time the Gestapo would lose track of him, and the last thing Grauber would want was for him to be on the loose in Germany. Einholtz's refusal to go in therefore seemed a spontaneous testimony to his honesty. And if he was on the level, and Grauber was not at the bottom of the whole thing after all, his presence with the party would prove invaluable. Although he had not actually said so the inference was clear enough that it had been his initiative and

311

courage which had twice brought the weakling Count and himself out of Germany, and, much more important, he knew the lie of the land at Schloss Niederfels. Therefore, it now seemed that no price was too big to pay for his help.

'I can well understand your not wanting to go back again,' Gregory said. 'But, all the same, I wish you would. It looks to me as if von Osterberg is going to be more of a hindrance than a help. If only we could come to some arrangement I'd far rather leave him behind and take you with me.'

'What do you mean by "some arrangement"?'

'Well, before going into Germany the Countess wrote to Sir Pellinore Gwaine-Cust, giving him particulars of certain financial arrangements she had made with you in the event of your securing von Osterberg's scientific notes. From what you say the prospects of doing that now seem very remote; but I take it you are still in need of money. You must know the Niederfels district pretty well by now, so, if you'll accompany me there and back, I am willing to pay you that ten thousand pounds myself, providing we succeed in bringing the Countess safely to Swiss soil.'

Einholtz nodded. 'Yes. As long as Kurt and I stay here there is always a danger of our being kidnapped and taken back to Germany. We need money to get right away to South America and start our lives afresh. But even if I went with you we'd have to take him too. You see, although I know the Niederfels district I am still practically a stranger there. I don't know any of Kurt's tenants and if one of them is hiding the Countess, or knows where she is, they would never take the risk of disclosing it to you or me. Whereas, if her own husband was searching for her their attitude would be quite different. They would talk then, freely enough.'

'Yes, I quite see that. All right then, the Count must come in any case. But in his present state it would be dangerous to leave him alone, and he would be a heavy liability if I get mixed up in a fight. It may happen that I might wish to act independently, and, if so, I'll badly need someone I can trust to leave him with temporarily. If I undertake to handle any situation that looks dangerous on my own, will you come to look after him?'

'I don't know. I must have time to think about it. The money would be immensely useful, but the risk ...' Einholtz shuddered.

'Gregory stood up. 'Well, I'm staying at the Pension Julich in St. Gall. When you've made your decision perhaps you'll let me hear from you. Can we fix a provisional date now for my going in?'

'The moon will be right a week hence, so, if Kurt is fit enough, any night from then on would be suitable.'

'Then let's say the tenth. In any case we'll meet to discuss details before then. We've talked so long that I'm afraid I've kept you from your dinner.'

'No, no,' Einholtz smiled. 'We live very simply here and had finished our evening meal before you arrived; later we have only coffee and a *brötchen* before going to bed, otherwise I would ask you to stay.'

He moved over to rouse von Osterberg, but Gregory said: 'Please don't wake the poor fellow. Just make my adieus to him when he wakes of his own accord.'

Einholtz nodded and they went quietly out into the corridor. At the front door they shook hands, then Gregory set out on his way back to St. Gall.

The moon had now risen, silvering the lake, and as he walked rapidly back into Steinach he was thinking over his long talk with Einholtz and the Count. It was quite natural that after Erika's disappearance Sir Pellinore should have jumped to the conclusion that the whole set-up was a trap but it seemed almost certain now that he had been wrong. There had not been a single suspicious circumstance in the whole discusssion. Von Osterberg was much too ill to be the pivot of any complicated conspiracy and Einholtz's interests were evidently tied up with those of the Count.

Gregory hoped that Einholtz would decide to go into Germany with him. He was not a particularly likeable man, but what German was, at bottom? And anyhow, the fellow had his wits about him, was the lean, strong type that stood up to hardship well, and, having risked his neck twice already to get away from the Nazis, evidently had plenty of guts.

As he glanced at the moonlight on the lake Gregory shivered. It reminded him of the moonlight that night in the Gulf of Finland, when he had so nearly lost his life in the U-boat. His thoughts turned to Grauber, and he recalled the *Gruppenführer*'s strange boast that he would make him tell everything he knew coherently without using torture. What could he have possibly meant by that, if it were not that Erika was already his prisoner and that he would threaten to torture her instead? She might, of course, have been caught without von Osterberg and Einholtz knowing anything about it. But they had not got out of Germany until long after Grauber had made his boast and, according to them, a reward was still being offered for Erika's apprehension at the time they escaped. The two sets of premises did not fit as they should have done.

Fifty paces further along the road Gregory came to an

abrupt halt. When Grauber had made his boast there ha
seemed no possibility whatever of his prisoners escaping fro
the U-boat, so it would not even have occurred to him tha
he might need to set the trap, if it was a trap, at the Vill
Offenbach again. By the time he wished to do so he woul
probably have forgotten that he had ever made such a strang
boast at all, much less have calculated the deduction that h
ex-prisoner might draw from it. In baiting such a trap h
would certainly realise that where many men would risk goin
into Germany to find the woman they loved if they though
her to be in safe hiding with friends, even the bravest migh
hesitate to attempt her rescue if they knew her to be in th
hands of the Gestapo. The difference in the risk was immens

Turning round, Gregory began to walk back towards th
Villa. As he recalled Grauber's horrid chuckle he felt mor
strongly than ever that such evil gloating could have bee
inspired only by the fact that he had got Erika. If so, the
Einholtz had lied about those posters offering a reward for h
capture. What possible reason could he have had for doing s
—unless he was Grauber's man? If he was he would take im
mediate steps to inform his master that, at last, the fly wa
buzzing round the web.

It was no more than six or seven minutes since Gregor
had left the Villa. When he had returned to within fifty yar
of it he stepped off the road and crossing a strip of coars
grass, concealed himself among a little group of trees tha
were growing quite close to the water's edge. From his pos
tion he could see the back of the Villa clearly in the moo
light, and the boathouse, which lay a little way below it. Tak
ing a fat Sullivan from his cigarette-case he turned his bac
to the Villa, lit it, cupped the burning end of the cigarette i
his open hand, turned round again, and waited.

For ten minutes nothing happened, and there was no sig
of life in the house; then a door banged and there came th
sound of quick footsteps on a gravel path. Einholtz's tall figu
emerged from the patch of shadow at the back of the Vill
Purposefully he strode down to the boat house and disap
peared inside it. A minute or two later an engine started u
then a long launch, with Einholtz at the wheel, left the she
and nosed her way out into the lake.

Gregory smiled to himself in the darkness. He was thinkin
how very nearly Einholtz had put it over him; only his eager
ness to let his chief know that the success of their plot no
appeared imminent had proved his undoing. That he mean
to cross the lake to Germany Gregory had no doubt at al
The launch was a fast one and could no doubt hold her ow
with any Swiss patrol boat that might challenge her; moreove

314

r exhaust had been muffled. Besides, Einholtz would have
d ample opportunity to make a study of the times and
aces where they operated, and when he reached the middle
the lake he would have nothing more to fear, as, after that,
would be in Nazi-controlled waters.

As it appeared so easy for Einholtz to cross, even in moon-
ght, Gregory began to wonder why it should have been sug-
sted that he should not make his own crossing for a week.
rhaps that had been one of Einholtz's many artistic touches
, had he really been on the level, he would naturally have
voured a dark night as offering the best chance of running
e gauntlet of the Nazi patrols. In fact, it would have been
urting disaster to attempt to get through them on a night
e this. But Gregory thought there was probably another
ason for the proposed delay. Grauber would want to handle
is matter personally, and the *Herr Gruppenführer* was a
ry busy man. He would require a week or so's notice before
had a free date on which he could come down to Württem-
rg to savour to the full the capture and final humiliation
his deadly enemy.

Pulling freely on his Sullivan now, Gregory started to
eculate on what part von Osterberg was playing in all this.
seemed beyond dispute that the Count must have been a
rty to the plot from the beginning. The idea that he was low
ough deliberately to have enticed his own wife from her safe
fuge in Britain to Switzerland, in order to hand her over to
e Nazis, made Gregory's fingers curl with the itch to get
em about the Count's lying throat. He wondered if he was
ally as ill as he looked. For such a delicate-looking man to
am illness would not be difficult. Perhaps he was shamming so
at his apparent state would be used to postpone the trip to
ermany until it was convenient for Grauber to receive them
the other side. It would be interesting to find out if von
sterberg was really ill or not. Gregory decided to pay the
ount a little visit.

Slipping over a low bank, he got down on to the foreshore
d began to walk cautiously along it. After passing the boun-
ry fence of the small garden he climbed up the bank again
d walked along a strip of lawn, past the patch that led
wn to the boathouse, till he reached the long low window.
There were chinks enough between the curtains to show
at the light in the sitting-room was still on, but he could
t no more than a slit-like glimpse of the room through any
them. Treading as gently as he could, he moved further
ong the wall until he reached the back door. It had a yale
ck, so, if von Osterberg had not bolted it on the inside after
inholtz's departure, getting in would prove easy. Taking an

inch wide strip of strong celluloid, which he always carried f
this purpose, from his pocket, Gregory inserted its end in t
crevice and pushed gently, until the natural spring in the cell
loid forced back the spring catch.

Still holding the celluloid in place with one hand, he no
pressed with the other, and the door gave at his touch. N
light showed through the crack of the opening so he dre
the celluloid out. As the latch slipped back with a faint clic
he waited, holding his breath. No sound broke the stillnes
He then took from its shoulder-holster, under his left armp
the nice new automatic with which Sir Pellinore had fu
nished him before he left London. Having made sure that
was ready for instant action and adjusted its silencer he ti
toed inside.

The moonlight from the open door behind him showed th
he was in a small scullery and that the kitchen lay beyond
Cautiously as a cat he made his way through both rooms to th
far door of the kitchen. His free hand closed on the doorkno
and with one firm movement he turned it. The door creaked
little as he eased it open and again he remained quite still for
moment, listening intently.

No sound came. There was no light on in the passage and
with his gun held ready, he advanced into its deeper shadow
To his left some cracks of light gave him the position o
another door, which he knew must be that of the sitting-room
One step at a time, and pausing half a minute between each
he advanced towards it. Again he listened, but the house wa
absolutely silent. He began to wonder if von Osterberg ha
left by the front door while he was making his way round th
back, or if the Count was still, perhaps, asleep.

Pleasant as he had felt it would be simply to walk in an
wring the Count's neck, he had dismissed the idea instantly
To show his hand yet awhile, and to disclose that he had not
after all, been completely duped, would have been to giv
away a most valuable advantage. If he could, he wanted
while remaining hidden himself, to get a good look at von
Osterberg, so as to see if the Count was still sitting mourn-
fully about or hopping round the place as lively as a cricket
Not being able to see anything through the window had been
a big disappointment, but the easy lock on the back door had
proved too tempting to resist and he had gone in with the
hope that he might yet catch a sight of von Osterberg through
a half-open doorway. That hope, to, had vanished, and it
seemed to Gregory that he dared not now risk intruding any
further, or he would be bound to be seen himself, and thus lose
the advantage that he had over his enemies.

He was just about to make a stealthy withdrawal when he

thought he heard a gentle snore. After a moment it came again. Von Osterberg was, then, in there and still sleeping. Gregory folded his hand round the doorknob, pressed gently with his shoulder against the door so that it would not budge and turned the knob. Then, millimetre by millimetre, he pushed the door inward until it was open a few inches. Screwing his head round, he peered inside.

The Count was sitting in the same chair and, apparently, had not woken since Gregory's departure. His thin face was lined, his grey hair untidy, and he certainly looked very ill and worn. In any case he had certainly not been shamming sleep after his two goes of *Glühwein*. As Gregory was about to close the door again his eye caught the glimmer of firelight on some shining object near von Osterberg's right foot. For a second he stared at it unable to make out what it was; then, suddenly, he recognised the form of the thing he was looking at. It was a nickel-plated handcuff; one of a pair, and it was round the Count's right ankle. The other was round the thick rail between the front legs of the old-fashioned wing chair in which he was sitting.

Gregory carefully reclosed the door, stole away down the passage, gingerly crossed the kitchen quarters and left the house, gently closing the back door behind him.

As he regained the road and walked out to Steinach he congratulated himself on the success of his second visit to the Villa. From it he knew now just how the land lay. Einholtz was a Gestapo man acting under the orders of Grauber. Von Osterberg was just a poor weak stooge who had allowed himself to be caught up in their filthy web. They had evidently terrified him into writing those letters, and acting a part when the two people they were intended to snare had appeared on the scene. That he had resisted, to some extent, was obvious from the fact that they still kept him a prisoner, and he had become genuinely ill from strain and fright. But what a poor fish he must be, Gregory reflected, not to have been able to think up some way of warning his wife before she went into Germany or, when in neutral territory and left alone for hours only shackled to a heavy chair, not to have the guts even to get hold of a hacksaw or a hatchet and free himself.

For anyone, so lacking in spirit Gregory could only feel complete indifference as to whether they regained their freedom or allowed themselves to be beaten to a pulp. But von Osterberg's betrayal of Erika made him see red. Anyone, he believed, might be tortured into finally admitting anything, but to remain a semi-prisoner for weeks and take no step of any kind to warn an old friend who was running into danger seemed to him absolutely unforgiveable. Through the Count's own lack of will and decency he had made himself a pawn in the game, and Gregory had no hesitation in making up his mind to treat him as such, with complete unscrupulousness should the need arise.

It was nearly midnight when he at last got back to the Pension Julich, but Kuporovitch was waiting up for him and had, moreover, had the forethought to have some cold supper left for him on a tray. While Gregory ate it in his bedroom he gave his friend a full account of all that had passed that evening.

'I think you have got a long way in a very short time,' was Kuporovitch's comment, when Gregory had finished his recital. 'But it seems that we shall not be called upon to take any active steps for several days to come. So let us sleep on it and discuss the whole situation in the morning.'

Gregory agreed that this was excellent advice, and having slept well, woke up to find, as so often happens, that the previous night's events had sorted themselves in his mind and now stood out in much clearer perspective. After breakfast they put on their overcoats and went out, not because either of them liked walking in wintry weather, but because they felt that only in the open could they talk freely without fear of eavesdroppers.

The salient points that had emerged from Gregory's visit to the Villa Offenbach were: That two traps had definitely been laid there. Into the first, Erika had walked, and, in consequence, was now almost certainly a prisoner of the Gestapo. Into the second, Gregory, so his enemies happily believed was, quite unconscious of the danger, now walking. Einholtz was a clever and dangerous agent of the Gestapo von Osterberg was his unwilling but completely subservient accomplice, and a prisoner whose shattered nerves made him unreliable and of little further value to either friend or foe. The story about the scientific notes in the laboratory safe at Niederfels was all balony. They had probably never existed. But Peenemünde was an experimental station where a new gas or weapon was being perfected and it seemed certain that the Count had worked there. Einholtz had crossed to the far shore of the lake during the night to warn his colleagues that the fly was shortly about to take a header into the web, and probably to arrange that when he touched down the Chief Spider should be there to receive him. The enemy was, however, still presumably ignorant that he was not working entirely on his own, but had brought Kuporovitch with him to Switzerland. They had several days before them in which to make a counterplot, as, either for the sake of artistry or on account of orders from above, Einholtz had no intention of

318

owing Gregory to set out on his venture for another week
least. When he did go von Osterberg would definitely ac-
mpany him and now, it seemed, Einholtz also, since, if the
ter still took the precaution of handcuffing the former to
eavy armchair during a temporary absence, it was most un-
ely that he would let him go off as a free man alone with
egory.

The major facts which emerged from all this were: that
ika was not simply in hiding, and, once found, could be
t out of Germany with comparative ease. If she was to be
cued at all she would have to be snatched by force or
ckery from under Grauber's own eyes. And that if Gregory
nt through with the arrangements already tentatively agreed
on he would go into Germany, not with one or more friends
help him, but in the company of those whose object was
death and, moreover, be a marked man—his every move-
nt watched by a score of unseen eyes—from the first mont that he set foot on Nazi territory.

Gregory and Stefan thrashed the problem out for the best
rt of three hours and two among the numerous decisions
ey reached were: that Kuporovitch must leave the Pension
lich at once, so that his presence on the wings should con-
ue unknown to Einholtz, if the Gestapo man called to see
egory. That he should move down to the little hotel Stein-
a and endeavour to rent a small furnished house or cottage
ere, if possible, among the straggling properties to the west
e of the village, among which the Villa Offenbach lay, in
der to be as near the scene of action as could be managed.

After lunch Kuporovitch packed his bag, paid his bill at the
nsion Julich, let it drop at the desk that he was going down
Zurich, and departed. Gregory spent most of the afternoon
his bed, trying not to think of Erika.

Next day, to distract his mind, he bought some large sheets
paper, a ruler, indiarubber and pencils, and began to draw
plan of the sort of house he would like to own if he eventu-
y decided to build instead of buying one.

That was on Friday. On the following Sunday, 7th of De-
mber, 1941, he was still at it, when the momentous news
shed round the world that, in defiance of all decency, hon-
y and humanitarian considerations, the Japanese, a race of
lly disposed, lying, cheating, treacherous little yellow apes,
ving only a remote outward resemblance to human beings,
d, without warning, bombed the United States Fleet in
arl Harbour and, equally without warning, simultaneously
acked Singapore.

Very soon it was known that Britain had joined the United
ates in the war against Japan and that the great American

319

people had joined the British Empire and the Soviet Union i
their determination to remove the curse of Hitlerism from th
earth.

Gregory knew that the Anglo-Saxon peoples in the Fε
East were now in for a very thin time indeed. Nobody but
fool could have imagined that after two and a quarter yeaτ
resisting the might of Germany, and for a year of that on i
own, the British Empire could have any but the most meagτ
forces merely keeping watch and ward against a possible co
tingency down there in Malaya. But America, with her hundre
and twenty million citizens, her fine fleet, her rapidly expanε
ing Army and Air Force, her vast wealth, her enormous inflι
ence in neutral countries, her huge stores of raw materials, hε
immense agricultural potential, and her staggeringly va
capacity for producing the most modern weapons of war—
was in. That was what mattered, and there was some real hoρ
now of putting all that was left of both the Germans and th
Japs behind the bars within a foreseeable period.

With a spontaneous happiness that he had not felt fc
months he broke into the old American marching song of th
last war: *'Tramp, tramp, tramp, the boys are marching; Joh
Bull, America's in with you! Tramp, tramp, tramp, the boy
are marching; just to help you see this through!'*

Kuporovitch rang up, equally delighted with the news. H
also had news of his own. He had succeeded, the previou
evening in persuading a French writer to rent him a cottaε
on the lake shore that was only about half a mile further out c
Steinach than the Villa Offenbach, and was moving in thε
afternoon. Having described its appearance and whereabouτ
he suggested that, after dark, Gregory should come down an
join him there for a picnic meal to celebrate America's entr
into the war.

Gregory agreed and arrived about seven o'clock with tw
bottles of French champagne under his arm—Krug, Priva
Cuveé, Vintage 1928, no less. Kuporovitch had already laid
three bottles of his favourite Chambertin and two of ol
brandy, so a good time was had by all.

Kuporovitch related that he had set his heart on this litt
cottage, as it was some distance from any other dwelling y
adjacent to the lake and almost within a stone's throw of th
scene of operations. The Frenchman, who had rented it fc
the duration, was a man of mixed ideals, being both a Con
munist and a Pacifist. He had not wanted to sub-let, but h
was poor, and Kuporovitch had at last induced him to do :
by offering for a month, with immediate possession, a su
that would pay his rent for a year.

They drank innumerable toasts, forgot their worries for

w hours, and Gregory having decided to spend the night
ere, in the early hours saw one another several times to bed.
On the Monday morning Gregory returned to the Pension
lich and, somewhat lackadaisically, resumed his efforts as
1 amateur architect. In the afternoon Einholtz called to see
m.

The German said at once that he had now made up his
ind to join Gregory in the venture, and some little time was
ccupied in discussing means by which he could be certain of
curing the promised payment in the event of the trip proving
success. As Gregory had anticipated Einholtz's decision he
id already thought out certain proposals to this end, and
ter a few minor points had been settled he agreed to make
e necessary arrangements. Both of them knew that there was
ot the remotest possibility of the sum being collected, but
ey both had to appear seriously concerned about the matter
r fear of giving away their secret intentions to one another.

Einholtz then went on to the real purpose of his visit. He
id that von Osterberg, although more normal, was still far
om well, but that if he were given a few days more should
: in far better shape to make the trip. He therefore proposed
at they should cross the lake on the night of the thirteenth.
Inless,' he added with a smile, 'you are superstitious and
ould prefer to make it the fourteenth, as an extra day will
ake little difference to the conditions we may expect.'

'No,' replied Gregory, 'I'm not superstitious. Let's make it
e thirteenth. But I'd like to hear the programme that you
ve in mind.'

'Even if it is a clear night with no cloud,' Einholtz told him,
ie moon is not due to rise until just before dawn. I suggest
at we should start about ten o'clock. I have watched the
viss patrol boats go by so often that we should have no
ouble with them. By midnight we should be off the German
ast. It will be too late then for many people to be about.
wing to the headland that juts out into the lake some miles
the east of Friedrichshafen we should have no difficulty in
ding *Frieherr* von Lottingen's summer villa, since it is only
st round the corner. There were three cars in his garage last
ne we visited it, and as that was only about six weeks ago
ere is every reason to suppose that at least one of them will
ll be there. We borrow it as before, and drive to Niederfels;
it not to the Schloss itself. We make for the home of the
nant-farmer who hid Kurt and myself. Having spent so long
th him I have no doubt at all that he will prove willing to
elter us again for a few nights. Using his farm as our base, we
gin to make our enquiries for the Countess. When we have

found her we wait for another dark night and return by the same route.'

'That sounds all right,' said Gregory. 'In fact I don't see how it can be improved upon.'

As they drank two steins of lager they talked about the war. At their first meeting Gregory had taken a malicious delight in watching the German squirm, as he forecast disaster to the German armies in Russia.

That had, at first been his only reason for letting himself go on the subject, since at that time he was ninety-eight per cent convinced that Einholtz really was an anti-Nazi refugee and that anything said to him was most unlikely to reach the enemy. But Gregory had a saying, 'Scratch any German and you'll find a Nazi', which could well be interpreted as 'Once a German always a German'—Nazism being simply the frankest expression yet achieved of the basic instincts of the German race. In consequence, his final statement that the Soviet Reserve Army Group was situated south of Moscow and would strike north-west to shatter the German central front had been pure invention.

It had been inspired simply by the fact that the most serious inroads into the defences of Moscow were being made from the north-west, and if during the final phase of the attack the *Wehrmacht* could be induced to withdraw large formations from that area to reinforce the southern end of their central front Moscow might yet be saved. At the time he had felt that the odds against what he had said ever reaching the German High Command and causing it to alter its dispositions were terrific; and, even now that he knew Einholtz to be a Gestapo man, he considered that the chances of his casually thrown out remarks having a disastrous effect on German strategy were still extraordinarily small.

Today, however, with no even vaguely ulterior motive in mind, and with even more gusto, he was able to enjoy a good half-hour's sport dwelling lightly but pointedly upon just how disastrous America's entry into the war must ultimately prove for Germany. He was able to do so quite pleasantly on the assumption that Einholtz was an anti-Nazi who desired the speedy defeat of Hitler in order that a free German Republic might be more speedily reborn. Realising this, Einholtz was forced to suppress his gall and painfully screw up a series of false, twisted smiles of agreement.

In spite of the seething rage that inwardly consumed him he managed to prevent himself from giving way to an outburst that might have betrayed his real feelings, and they parted ostensibly good friends, pledged to risk their lives together on a most dangerous expedition.

On the Tuesday morning Gregory went down to see Kup-vitch. At midday they took a motor-bus going west along lake-shore to the little town of Arbon. There they bought picnic meal and took it down to the harbour, where they ed a motor launch. As the weather was chilly and there s a slight drizzle the boat-owner thought them insane, but egory did not seek to disguise the fact that he was English, owing that on the Continent the legend still persists that Englishmen are mad, and that it had often served to ex-se his apparent vagaries in tricky situations.

Visibility on the lake was poor, but the weather cleared mewhat in the late afternoon, so they got a fairly good view the smoke-belching chimneys of the great munition plants Friedrichshafen and of the coast up to the headland to uth-east of it. Through a pair of binoculars that Gregory d bought in St. Gall, they could make out a rambling uilding just west of the headland that they felt certain must Freiherr von Lottingen's summer villa; but on their at-mpting to go nearer in, a German patrol boat came out and rned them back. As soon as she had left them Gregory took veral compass bearings, which he carefully noted down. hey then returned to Arbon, and so to their respective domi-les.

On the Wednesday Gregory worked at his house-planning r the best part of the day, then, when darkness had fallen, ;ain went down to Kuporovitch's cottage. By half past seven ey were in Arbon talking to the boat-owner, whom, without fficulty, they had traced to a wharfside café. At first, he as most loth to hire them his launch on a winter's night, sus-ecting that it could be required only for some illegal purpose. ut luckily, the night was fine and starlit, and Gregory finally icceeded in jollying him into it by playing the rich, eccentric nglish 'Milor', and offering him an outrageous price with a efinite promise to bring the launch back at midnight.

At their first attempt to get out into the centre of the lake ey were turned back by a Swiss patrol boat, but on their econd they succeeded in getting to within two miles of the German coast without interference. They could have gone urther in but did not wish to risk the possibility of landing hemselves in serious trouble. So Gregory took some more ompass bearings of the blast furnaces and such other lights s were visible, and they then turned back to Arbon.

On the morning of Thursday the 11th, Gregory sent a tele-ram which read: FALLSTROM. VILLA OFFENBACH, STEINACH, BEI ORSCHACH. IS THIRTEENTH DEFINITELY AGREED ON. SALLUST.

By midday the reply reached him. YES, ALL SET FOR THIRTEENTH, FRITZ. He had spent the morning completing the

323

plans of the house he might one day build, although he do
ted if he would ever do so, as he felt he would greatly pre
an old house with well-grown trees in its garden, if he co
find one that he really liked; but drawing the plans and m
ing things fit had proved an excellent and amusing distracti
In the afternoon he slept.

At five o'clock he set off for Kuporovitch's cottage.
Russian was expecting him, and, being a very passable amat
cook, had prepared an excellent meal. They washed it do
with some bottles of Chambertin, and afterwards sat talk
cheerfully together until a quarter to eight.

Then they went out and walked along the grass verge of
road towards the Villa Offenbach. As they neared it Kupo
vitch dropped a few paces behind and halted in the deep sh
dow made by the angle of the porch, while Gregory stepp
forward and rang the front-door bell.

After he had rung a second time it was opened by Einhol
Seeing his visitor, the German's face expressed surprise, b
Gregory did not give him a chance to ask any questions.
had been holding his automatic ready in his overcoat pock
Pulling it out, he jabbed it into Einholtz's stomach and sai
'Stand still! Come on, Stefan!'

Kuporovitch pushed past them holding a length of co
one end of which was already prepared in a slip-noose. Gra
bing one of Einholtz's wrists, he slid the noose over it a
jerked the cord tight. Seizing the German's other arm,
wrenched it round behind his back and swiftly secured t
two wrists together. The whole action had been so rapid th
Einholtz had his hands tied behind him almost before he ha
time to begin letting out a spate of curses.

As Kuporovitch pulled out his own gun, Gregory turn
away and walked down the hall. The Russian dug the barrel
his pistol into Einholtz's ribs and said the one word, 'Follow

Still dazed from the shock of his swift capture, and all t
fight temporarily gone out of him, the Gestapo man walk
down the passage after Gregory to the sitting-room. All thr
of them entered it and Kuporovitch closed the door behir
them.

Von Osterberg was sitting in his usual chair. He looked u
with a start as they came in and nervously shuffled to h
feet.

'Good evening, Count,' said Gregory. 'There is no need
be alarmed. As you see, your gaoler is no longer in a positio
to harm you.'

'I—I don't understand!' stammered the Count.

'It is quite simple,' Gregory replied firmly. 'We know wha
has been going on here. The Gestapo forced you to write thos

324

letters, to help in trapping Erika, and to attempt to trap me. But the trap has worked the other way—this time. I repeat that you have no more to fear from this man Einholtz, and I now want you to tell me as clearly as you can exactly what did happen when the two of you took Erika into Germany.'

Kuporovitch had given Einholtz a push that sent him sprawling into an armchair, so that with his hands tied behind him he could not get up without considerable difficulty.

Von Osterberg stared at him wild-eyed, then looked back at his captors and gasped:

'Do you—do you mean—that I'm free?'

'More or less,' said Gregory laconically. 'Come on now! I've got no time to waste, and I want your story.'

For a moment von Osterberg remained silent, evidently trying to collect his wits. Then he began to talk in short, jerky sentences. He told them everything, just as it had happened, from the time of his first being intimidated into serving the Gestapo, right up to Erika's capture and the infamous supper-party which had followed at Schloss Niederfels.

'So that's how Grauber learned about the three things that I had gone to Russia to find out,' commented Gregory. 'What did they do with her then?'

'They locked her up in one of the dungeons,' replied the Count slowly. 'It wasn't too bad a prison, as it was quite dry. At one time we had used it as a store room. Next day they gave her a bed and a few pieces of furniture and they continued to keep her there. She was still there when we came back here.'

'Do you think she is still there, now?'

'I don't know. I suppose so. As they had kept her there for the best part of two months there doesn't seem any reason why they should have moved her since.'

'All right,' Gregory stepped over to an open desk upon which were some sheets of writing-paper and a pencil. He gave them to von Osterberg and added: 'Now you will be good enough to draw for me a series of plans of the Castle—particularly the part of it in which this dungeon is situated.'

With pencil and paper before him the Count seemed to take on new life. For twenty minutes he sketched and wrote rapidly, while Gregory sat beside him watching and asking questions from time to time. At length Gregory was satisfied, and sweeping up the papers put them in his inner pocket. Then he said:

'Before the Gestapo got to work on you, you were doing a job at the experimental station at Peenemünde, weren't you?'

Von Osterberg nodded.

'What was this experimental work that you were engaged on?'

The Count shook his head. 'I cannot say.'

'Oh yes you can,' Gregory said threateningly. 'Come on now! What was it?'

At the same moment Einholtz spoke for the first time. 'Keep silent, Kurt. If you speak you will live to regret it.'

Von Osterberg stood up. 'I am a German,' he declared, 'and a patriot. I refuse to talk.'

'Well said, Kurt, well said,' cried Einholtz.

Gregory, too stood up. Looking the Count full in the face he said: 'I don't care what you are. You're going to tell me what you know.'

'Nothing will make me do that. Nothing!'

Gregory hit him a resounding slap across the face. 'Talk, damn you!' he roared. 'Or I'll beat you to a jelly.'

Von Osterberg crumpled up and fell back in his chair, but he still violently shook his head and refused to speak.

'I suppose you're still scared of Einholtz' Gregory muttered 'All right, we'll deal with him first.'

Turning to the Gestapo man, he ran quickly through his pockets. Among their contents were the handcuffs, a special pass showing him to be an S.S. Lieutenant-Colonel, and a wad of a dozen letters. Gregory put the whole lot in his own pocket and snapped:

'Stand up!'

Einholtz struggled to his feet. 'You'll pay for this in the long run,' he growled. '*Herr Gruppenführer* Grauber will see to that.'

'Never mind Grauber now,' Gregory said with menacing quietness, 'I am dealing with you. Do you know about this work that is going on at Peenemünde?'

'Yes, I do,' Einholtz gave him a twisted grin. 'Not much, but enough, at all events, to be certain that all your hopes of Russia are pure moonshine, and that with this wonderful new weapon we shall destroy all your English cities long before America can come to your aid.'

'Are you going to tell me about it? To talk might be worth your while.'

'Is it likely?' Einholtz sneered.

'You can take your choice. You are either going to talk or die.'

Einholtz went very white. Then he moistened his lips and muttered, 'I'll see you damned first.'

Gregory lifted his pistol. 'Are you quite sure? I mean what I say.

'Certain,' gasped the German.

'Then, as you are a member of the Gestapo, which has wilfully inflicted terror, humiliation, unbearable pain and death

n countless innocent people, I, taking this deed fearlessly
pon my own soul, condemn you to die, in agony, yourself.'

Gregory squeezed the trigger of his pistol, and shot Ein-
oltz through the stomach.

The German doubled up, slid to the floor with a screech
f pain and lay there twisting and whimpering.

For a moment Gregory stood there watching him with com-
ete detachment, then he put a second bullet through his
ead. Einholtz jerked and lay still.

Von Osterberg, gripping the arms of his winged chair, sat
rward in it staring in fascinated horror at the bloody corpse
a the floor. Gregory turned back to him and went through
s pockets. They were completely empty.

'Now!' he said. 'You see that Einholtz will never be able
repeat anything you may say. I give you my word my friend
d myself will never disclose the source from which we ob-
ined our information; and if you will tell us what we wish to
now I will guarantee that you shall be provided with ample
nds to start life afresh in South America.'

But the Count only shook his head and, averting his eyes
om Einholtz's body, looked dumbly at the carpet.

'So you refuse to play,' Gregory snapped. 'It's time that I
arned you, then. You've seen what happened to Einholtz. I've
enty of bullets left and I can quite well spare two for you.'

'Shoot me then,' gasped von Osterberg, in a half-strangled
ice. 'I have no future; and, for me, life is no longer worth
ing. Shoot me!'

At that cry from the heart Gregory knew that to persist
rther was useless. He was up against, not a man, but a wreck
o no longer cared if he lived or died.

Switching over the safety-catch of his gun he put it back in
s pocket, and said: 'Stand up!'

Slowly the Count obeyed.

Putting his hand into another pocket Gregory drew out a
k handkerchief. Folding it carefully into a bandage the ends
which were formed by two of its corners, he wrapped it
und the knuckles of his right hand, then clenched the part
at was inside his palm so that the swathe across his knuckles
came tight and firm.

He looked for a moment at von Osterberg, then he said:

'You regard yourself as a man of honour, don't you; be-
use you have just refused to betray your country's secrets.
et you betrayed the woman that you once loved and, like
veritable Judas, led her by the hand to torture and death.
hen Hitler and his gang are dead; when the brutal tradition
  Bismarck and the harsh philosophy of Neitzsche are at
st forgotten; when all that are left after this war of the

327

stupid, brutal German people have been sent back to labour o
the soil for five generations, then, and not before, we ma
hope to educate a new and cleaner race of Germans to sha
in the benefits of modern civilisation. For you, civilisation ha
meant the employment of your gifts upon a horrible weapon
destruction. For you, honour has meant the acceptance
such scars as I see on your cheek in senseless student due
Well, I am going to give you another scar, and one that yo
will bear for all that remains of your miserable life. Each tim
you look at yourself in a mirror you will think of the betray
of your wife, and remember that you received it for that
the brand of dishonour.'

As he finished speaking Gregory drew back his silk-covere
fist and struck von Osterberg a glancing blow from temple
chin. The silk, catching under heavy pressure on the ski
ripped it open as though it had been slashed with a knife ar
blood poured from the gaping wound. It was a trick that Gr
gory had learnt long ago in Paris, from an Apache.

With a cry like a wounded animal von Osterberg slumpe
backwards in his chair and buried his bleeding face in h
hands. But Gregory stepped forward immediately, grabb
him by the arm, jerked him to his feet, and said:

'Where's your bathroom? Pull yourself together and ta
us to it.'

Moaning and staggering, the Count led the way upstai
supported by Gregory, who, when they reached the bat
room, pushed him inside it. As he collapsed on the floor Ku
orovitch took the key out of the lock, reinserted it on the ou
side of the door, and locked him in. Then the two frien
went downstairs again.

Kuporovitch took the shoulders of Einholtz's dead boc
and Gregory the feet. Between them they carred it out throu
the kitchen scullery and back door, down to the boathous
While Kuporovitch was getting it on board the launch Gr
gory went back to a woodshed that was affixed to the side
the house. Flashing his torch round he found a chopper an
picking it up, hurried back to the boat with it.

He spent the next few minutes examining the engine of t
launch and seeing that the tanks were full of petrol. Mea
while Kuporovitch hunted round till he found an old anchc
and attached it firmly to Einholtz's feet. Gregory then to
from his pocket a small envelope which contained the cyani
of potassium capsules. Opening his mouth he carefully fix
one of the red ones to the outside of one of his back tee
Having practised wearing one of the green dummies ever sin
he had left London, he was now so accustomed to the feel

328

e small pellet that he was rarely conscious that he had it in
s mouth at all.

'I must say I am glad that I'm not called on to use one of
ose things,' Kuporovitch said, with a smile.

Everything had gone with such clockwork precision that it
as the first remark either of them had made to the other
nce they had entered the Villa.

'All I hope is that I am not called upon to bite it,' Gregory
inned back.

Stepping down into the launch he raised one of Einholtz's
ms and laid his hand on the gunwale. It was the hand on
hich the amethyst ring glittered dully. Raising the wood-
opper, Gregory struck at the dead German's wrist with all
s force. the chopper severed it at a single blow; both the
nd and arm fell back into the launch.

Picking up the hand, Gregory wrapped it in a piece of
led silk and rammed it into his pocket.

Kuporovitch had opened the outer doors of the boathouse,
regory started up the launch's engine.

'Good luck, dear friend! Good luck!' called the Russian.

'Thanks! I'm on the top of my form tonight,' Gregory
outed back. 'See you in two days' time!'

And the long low launch slid out through the smooth water
n her way to Germany.

19

At the Eleventh Hour

regory had good reason to be pleased with himself. So far
verything had gone according to plan and without the slight-
t hitch. By his surprise tactics he had beaten the gun, and
as going into Germany two days before he was expected.
Ioreover, his guess that Erika was still most probably at
iederfels had been confirmed by von Osterberg.

That, so far, was the real high spot of his good fortune. He
ad feared at first that Grauber might have sent her to some
oncentration camp hundreds of miles deep in Germany,
id her rescue from a well-guarded camp would have proved

immensely difficult. But, on reasoning the matter out, he ha
reached the conclusion that if Grauber wished to maintain th
impression that Erika had not been caught he would not mov
her. The beautiful Erika von Epp, being such a well-know
person in Germany, if moved, might be recognised in trans
and, later, her presence in a concentration camp for sever:
months would be almost certain to leak out through guard
and others talking and might get back to Switzerland, wherea
the Castle itself offered every facility for a safe and secr
prison.

In consequence, his plans had been made on the tentativ
assumption that she was at Niederfels and this now seeme
highly probable.

It was the night of Thursday, December the 11th, and it wa
most unlikely that Grauber would arrive at the Schloss befor
the evening of the 13th. If the situation there was the same a
it had been when von Osterberg left, and there seemed n
reason why it should be, the old Countess's personal mai
Helga Stiffel was still Erika's chief gaoler. No doubt Helg
had assistance of some sort, as Grauber would not have riske
the possibility of so valuable a captive escaping through th
slackness or complacency of one woman. On the other hand
he would certainly not have allocated S.S. personnel to such
backwater job, as, now that Germany was holding down ha
Europe, trained Gestapo men were far too scarce and valuabl
Therefore, Gregory felt, by going in before Grauber and hi
personal staff appeared on the scene he should have a ver
good chance of effecting Erika's rescue.

Another thing that pleased him greatly was that he ha
been able to keep Kuporovitch out of this desperate gamble
The Russian had grumbled a lot at being left behind, an
Gregory knew his worth as an ally too well not to be sorry o
that account; but he had felt that he owed it both to his loya
friend and to Madeleine that Stefan should be protecte
against his own courageous inclinations. This venture wa
different to all others that they had undertaken, in that the
had given Sir Pellinore their word that, if captured, they woul
commit suicide by swallowing the cyanide globules. Gregor
had no illusions about the fact that, although things had star
ted well, he was still only at the beginning of the job, and tha
once in Germany the risk of being caught before Erika coul
be got out of the country was very considerable indeed.

They had, however, gone to the Villa Offenbach that nigh
with the definite intention of killing Einholtz; and whateve
their personal views might be about the justice of giving th
Gestapo thug his deserts, should the Swiss authorities com
to hear of it they would unquestionably regard the deed a

330

·der. Gregory intended to dispose of the body himself;
it had also seemed an essential precaution that all traces
he crime should be removed from the Villa and impera-
to ensure that von Osterberg, half-crazy from fear of the
zis on the one hand and Einholtz's killers on the other,
uld not be allowed to stagger into Steinach and, having
ght the protection of the Swiss police, spill the whole story
hem. So, when making their plan, it had proved possible
ersuade Kuporovitch that, much as he wanted to come to
many, it was far more important that he should remain
witzerland; if only for the purpose of taking charge of von
erberg and seeing to it that if Gregory succeeded in his
he would not return only to find himself faced with a
rge of murder.

t was that thought which kept him extra alert as the launch
led out into the lake. Ordinarily, to have been stopped in
ss waters would have meant no more than being turned
k and, after an annoying wait, to give the patrol boat a
nce to pass out of the area, another start; but, if he was
pped with Einholtz's body on board and the lake police
de even a casual inspection of the launch to see that he was
endeavouring to run contraband into Germany, he would
n for the high jump.

he time was only about half past eight but the winter's
nt was very dark, the reflection in the water of a few lights
ther along, from houses in Steinach, seeming only to make
arker; and the exhaust of the launch's engine was muffled.
s would, Gregory knew, reduce her speed a little in an
ergency, but he felt, as evidently Einholtz had before him,
t a greater degree of safety lay in the good chance of es-
ing detection altogether through having a comparatively
seless engine than having a few extra knots' pace if once
llenged.

Having covered about three miles without misadventure, he
pped the motor, dragged Einholtz's body from the small
in to the launch's gunwale and pushed it over. At the
nd of the heavy splash it made he felt considerably relieved.
e old anchor that Kuporovitch had attached to the corpse's
t would keep it on the bottom for many weeks and by the
e it broke away, if it ever came to the surface at all, it would
so only as a hideous piece of fish-nibbled pulp far beyond
recognition. Its safe disposal was another hurdle passed,
ich added to his feeling of satisfaction.

Restarting the engine, he turned the boat's nose northwest,
l kept her going roughly parallel to the lake shore for some
miles, until he came opposite Arbon. He had no difficulty
picking up the little port, as the lights were full on in all the

331

Swiss towns and villages, in order that their lack of black
should reveal them to Allied bombers as in neutral territ
Here, he stopped again, took several compass bearings, wh
he compared by the light of a hooded torch with the notes
had previously made, adjusted the launch's position by a qu
ter of a mile, then set a new course, north-east, for the C
man shore.

After he was halfway across the lake he shut off his eng
every few moments to listen. Twice he caught the faint th
of another engine and each time refrained from switch
his own on again until the throbbing had faded into siler
The Swiss villages were now too distant for their glow to sl
any reflection on the water and the only light came fr
patches of stars occasionally revealed through gaps in
scudding clouds. Straining his eyes into the darkness he at
succeeded in picking up the headland south-east of Friedr
shafen and, turning the launch again, began to nose his
round it.

It was now that his daylight reconnaissance proved inva
able. Instead of running aground below a small bathing ch
as he might otherwise have done, he realised that its r
against the skyline was not large enough to be that of the v
he had seen through his binoculars. A quarter of a mile
ther on the more spacious eaves of von Lottingen's sum
residence suddenly showed up against a belt of stars, and
turned in towards it.

As he neared its waterfront the unexpected plop of a le
ing fish made him start, and he realised that his dram
half hour at the Villa Offenbach had keyed his nerves up
an unusually high pitch. The next hurdle was going to
one of the nastiest he would have to face, so he delibera
checked the boat's way before he need have done, and slo
counted a hundred before giving her a final impulse towa
the shore.

He had spent many hours considering every aspect of
project and had reached the conclusion that, even if Er
proved still to be at Schloss Niederfels, however early a s
he made it was not a practical proposition to attempt
whole operation of getting there, rescuing her and recross
the lake with her in one night.

Given a car, which there was good reason to suppose
would be able to secure from von Lottingen's garage, it
not the distance and time factor which would invalidate s
an attempt, but the fact that if he made it he would have
enter the Castle in darkness, without having carried out
previous reconaissance of it; and that had seemed to him
big a risk to accept.

He had abandoned the idea of a one night's *Blitzkrieg* only with the greatest reluctance, as, if it could have been done, it offered so many advantages. With luck, he could have moored the launch, stolen a car, got there and back and recrossed the lake again without anyone at von Lottingen's being aware that a stranger had made use of the premises.

On the other hand; a two-night job meant that he would have to leave the launch at von Lottingen's all next day, and that he dared not risk stealing a car from the garage, as the discovery of its loss would be sure to result in a widespread search and, if coupled with the finding of the launch might even cause one of Grauber's people to cross the lake the following night to investigate at the Villa Offenbach. Then, when Einholtz's disappearance was reported, those in the know about his mission would put two and two together, realise that Gregory had outwitted the Gestapo man, rob him of his advantage by arriving at Niederfels before he could get away and block his line of retreat across the lake.

Nevertheless, on balance Gregory had decided that he might live to rue it if he rushed his fences. Niederfels was the key point of the whole operation, and to have plenty of opportunity to nose around it in daylight before going in would probably mean the difference between success and failure. He felt confident that he would be able to steal a car somewhere further afield than the lake shore, and the only really serious snag to the more lengthy job was that he would have to leave the launch for some thirty hours in von Lottingen's boathouse. But hidden there, if the boats were used only infrequently, as was probably the case in the depths of winter, there was a good chance that she would remain undiscovered. If she was discovered his line of retreat might be cut, but, even if it was, he could still have a chance to find other means to bring Erika back across the lake to safety. The thing now was to get the launch into the boathouse without arousing anyone who might be in the Villa.

The place was in darkness, but as the whole of the German shore of the Bodensee was subject to the wartime blackout, that was no guarantee at all that there were not people inside it. Having shut off his engine some way out, Gregory, using a bottom board as a paddle, gently steered her in towards the boathouse, the outline of which he could now see faintly.

When the prow of the launch bumped gently against it, he went forward and secured her with the painter. With mixed feelings he found that the doors were secured inside with a chain and padlock. That seemed to indicate that the boats were not used with great frequency. On the other hand, it meant some delay before he could get the launch inside.

Stepping ashore, he tiptoed round to the other entrance. He found it unlocked. Opening the door gingerly, he went in and along the skirting boards to the water-gate. Shining his hooded torch on the padlock, he found that it was quite an ordinary one. It took him only two minutes to pick it. He then drew the launch inside beside two others that were there.

Taking Einholtz's letters from his pocket he glanced swiftly through the packet and noted that the handwritings on all of them appeared to be those of women. Removing the envelope from one he crumpled it up, and dropped it in the stern of the launch. He had no great hopes of it proving a very odorous red herring, but there was just a chance that, if the boat was found the following day, the people in the Villa might deduce from the envelope that Einholtz had crossed in her but re-frained from letting them know of his arrival, having some business on shore that brooked no delay.

Having refastened the padlock Gregory closed the shore-wards door of the boat house carefully behind him and walked cautiously up the path, past the garage, to the road. Once through the gate and on to it he smiled to himself in the darkness. Another tricky fence had been crossed without accident.

His next risky undertaking was to steal a car, but he did not intend to attempt it anywhere near von Lottingen's villa, or even in the neighbourhood of the Bodensee. To have done so, should the launch be found, would be to connect the two inci-dents, and possibly set the local Gestapo thinking on lines which he was most averse should occur to them. In conse-quence as a first step, he set off at a quick walk towards Fried-richshafen.

He had proceeded barely a kilometre when, as he had hoped, he was able to pick up a bus which took him into the town. When he alighted he made his way at once to the railway sta-tion. It was ten minutes to eleven, so he was in ample time to catch the night train, as he had provisionally planned, leav-ing Friedrichshafen at eleven-ten for Ulm, Stuttgart and the north.

The station was not crowded, and his impeccable German enabled him to take a ticket without the booking-clerk giving him even a second glance. Punctually at ten minutes past eleven the train steamed out with Gregory occupying the cor-ner seat of a first-class carriage in it.

When planning his trip he had felt that in either Ulm or Stuttgart he would be able to secure a car without any likeli-hood of its theft being connected with the unheralded arrival of the launch at von Lottingen's villa. Had he been forced to take the slow train, that left half an hour after midnight, the

nroad into his time would have necessitated his alighting at
Ulm; but as he had managed to catch the express he felt that,
despite the additional three quarters of an hour's rail journey,
his purpose would be better served if he went on to Stuttgart.
The capital of Württemberg was a somewhat larger town,
which meant that a higher percentage of cars would be about
the streets in the early hours of the morning, and, also, although it was no further from Niederfels, it was considerably
further from the Bodensee, which was all to the good.

Alighting at Stuttgart, he made his way to the centre of the
old town. It was now just after two in the morning and
obviously the night life of the place was extremely limited.
Nevertheless, within a stone's throw of the *Klosterkirche* there
were two places from which he could hear the sounds of dance
music and laughter, and each of them had a row of cars outside.

With a slightly rolling gait, which would enable him to
plead the excuse of a mistake through drunkenness if a policeman emerged from the shadows, he approached the less conspicuous line of parked cars. Using a flexible strip of ser-
rated steel, made for the purpose, he found no difficulty in
getting the doors of those at the head of the line open. The
first two he tried had had their ignition keys removed, but the
owner of the third had been careless and left his in. That saved
quite a lot of bother, so, since it was a Stutz and the indicator
showed that there was plenty of petrol in the tank, Gregory
got in and drove away.

His study of the maps of the district had imprinted them so
firmly on his mind that he never had to hesitate for a moment
about his route. By way of Echterdingen, Waldenbach,
Tübingen, Hechingen and Schomberg he reached the village
of Wilflingen, near which Schloss Niederfels lay. Most of his
sixty-mile journey was along deserted roads through the dark
forests of the Schwarzwald Kreis, so even on those by-roads
he was able to maintain a good pace, and a little before five
in the morning he could see the grim, stark silhouette of
Schloss Niederfels towering against a starlit sky over the tree-
tops above him.

One of Sir Pellinore's many maps had been a walking-tour
guide of the Heuberg for *Wandervögel*, and Gregory's memory
of it was so photographic that, after passing through the village, he turned off, instinctively, up a narrow woodland track
that led through the heart of a forest area lying adjacent to
the Castle but along which there were no buildings for several
miles. About two miles due east of the Castle, and on ground
nearly as high as it stood itself, he drove the car off the track
in among the trees; then pulled up.

335

Although the first snow had not yet fallen it was bitterly cold there, but he took a long pull from his flask of Swiss *Brann twein* and, arranging himself in the back of the car under two rugs that were in it, soon dropped off to sleep.

He woke a little before nine, found an icy brook in which to splash his face, shaved with a pocket razor and cream from a tube, then made a meal off some of the cold meat biscuits and chocolate he had brought with him.

It was the first food he had had since fixing the red-coated cyanide capsule in his mouth. Practising with the green one during his ten-day sojourn in Switzerland had made him so accustomed to the little bump beside one of his back teeth that during most of his journey he had completely forgotten that if he now had an accident he might swallow the deadly poison. If he did, and the capsule went down uncracked, it might possibly pass harmlessly through him, or be recovered by a doctor with a stomach pump, but, on the other hand, it might not, and having to resort to a local doctor would have upset all his plans; so he now ate with special care.

By ten o'clock he had repacked his knapsack, hidden it under the seat of the car and, taking enough cold food with him for another meal, was setting off on a reconnaissance of the Castle. First, he climbed another mile up through the wood in which he had spent the latter part of the night, until he found a vantage point where a break in the trees gave him a good view of his objective. He was now a little higher than the base of the Schloss and it lay some two and a half miles away from him across the valley. It was a clear, cold winter's day and through his powerful binoculars he could see the whole of the eastern side of the huge rambling pile with great distinctness. At intervals, for over an hour, he swept its battlements, towers and windows, but could not see a single sign of life.

This lack of activity was most satisfactory, as it now seemed clear that the Castle had not been taken over by the Nazis as a headquarters, or to house a department from one of the ministries, as he had feared might prove the case. A closer reconnaissance was now indicated, but before making it he decided to go through the papers that he had taken from Einholtz's pockets.

Apart from the S.S. pass there were no official documents; the rest consisted of two bills and a number of letters, all from women. Some, like the one envelope of which Gregory had left in the launch, had been addressed to Einholtz in his real name while still in Germany, but three, more recent ones, all in the same hand had been directed to him at the Villa Offenbach under the assumed name he had used there.

Starting with the earliest in date, Gregory read them through and it was soon clear to him that Einholtz had been something of a Don Juan. Two of the writers had illegitimate children by him and a third was expecting one in the coming January. Gregory knew that there was nothing exceptional about that as Nazi policy encouraged all S.S. men to have as many illegitimate children as possible; the mothers were excellently cared for and granted special privileges by the State, and much propaganda had been used to impress German girls with the idea that it was an honour to bear illegitimate children to the private army of the Nazi Party. But his interest quickened when he found that the three letters addressed to the Villa Offenbach were from Helga Stiffel, the ex-lady's maid who was now Erika's wardress.

She said little about Erika, although Gregory was comforted to note that the girl did not seem to bear her prisoner any malice, and wrote of her as in good health and giving no trouble. The letters were, however, long ones and would have made a less hardened sinner that Gregory blush to the ears. As it was, he found them somewhat primitive, but in parts amusing. Helga omitted no detail of the jolly little games that she had played with Einholtz when he had been living at the Schloss, recalling the high spots with abandoned gusto, and suggesting even more lavishly erotic excitements that they might enjoy together on his return.

The letters, also gave Gregory some valuable information. From them, it was clear that during the two months between Erika's capture and Einholtz's return to Switzerland he had been stationed at Nürnberg, which was only about a hundred and forty miles from Niederfels, and that he had come over to spend most of his week-ends with Helga. Further, it emerged that as a convenient method of helping Helga to guard Erika, without committing special men to such a time-wasting job, had been arranged that four local policemen should be billeted at the Schloss. They were road patrol police, and as they took turns of duty by night and day it appeared that there were never less than two of them off duty at the Castle who could be called upon to assist Helga in an emergency, and that the senior of the group made a routine visit to Erika each morning, which, it seemed, Helga resented as an insult to her own capabilities as a gaoler.

It looked therefore, as if Gregory would have to outwit only Helga and two or three local policemen. Such luck seemed too good to last, but with a light heart he set out down the hill and, after a four-mile tramp across the valley bottom, emerged soon after one o'clock, under the walls of the Schloss. The woods were mainly pine, so, although it was winter, they still gave adequate cover, and this was supplemented by large clumps of brambles and holly which grew among the trees fairly close up to the Castle walls. Having made his way round to the south side of the pile, where it descended in terraces to meet the woods, he selected another good spot for observation and, while eating his lunch, studied the more modern part of the building through his binoculars.

Once he caught a glimpse of a female figure pulling some curtains aside, and a little later on an old lame manservant hobbled out on to one of the terraces, looked up at the sky shivered and went in again. After his meal, Gregory, now feeling very cold from having sat still, took a pull at his flask and set off to make a complete circuit of the great building.

As he came opposite the banqueting hall his heart began to pound more quickly, for a double reason. From von Oster berg's account of what had really happened on that night last August, he knew that it was from one of those tall window high above him, that Erika had faced death in making her ter rible leap. He knew too, from the Count's drawings, that i was in one of the dungeons below the banqueting hall tha Erika now lay confined.

He would have given a great deal to be able to get a word o comfort to her; to let her know that he was there, within a hundred feet of her, and meant to attempt her rescue tha night. But the trees ended in an abrupt line some yards from the Castle wall and their bare trunks gave little cover. He posi tively dared not jeopardise the whole venture by risking some one looking out of one of the upper windows and seeing him snooping there. Moreover, although he had detailed plans o the inside of that part of the Schloss, he could not be quit certain which of the line of low, barred windows about ter feet from the ground gave on to her cell; so even had he been able to approach nearer without danger he would not have known into which of the windows to throw a written message With a sigh, he withdrew further in among the trees and con tinued his circumnavigation of the pile.

It was half past three by the time he had completed hi inspection and, during it, he had reached the conclusion that i would be flying in the face of Providence to neglect to make use of the new information that he had been so fortunate in securing through Helga Stiffel's letters to Einholtz. His secre knowledge of their intimacy opened up the possibility of ac tually obtaining a glimpse of the inside of the Castle in dayligh which he would otherwise never have dared to attempt.

Making his way back to the great courtyard, he passed i and entered a smaller one flanking the kitchen quarters. Cross ing the flags in a postern door that stood partly open, he pulled

338

old iron bell-pull that hung beside it. The bell jangled
intly in the distance. After a minute he heard footsteps, then
fat, middle-aged woman, wearing no apron, appeared and
oked at him enquiringly.

'Is *Fräulein* Stiffel at home, and if so, can I see her?' he
quired.

'Yes, she's at home,' the woman replied, none too graci-
usly 'But if you're a friend of hers you should have come to
e front door. She's the lady of the place these days. D'you
ind coming through this way?'

'Not a bit,' smiled Gregory, as he thought what a fine time
ascists or Communists and their girl-friends had when they
anaged to get their hooks on a country through pretending
at they were the champions of the working people.

'All right, I'll show you,' said the woman, wiping her hands
n her apron, and Gregory followed her inside.

He had already observed that the bars had long since been
emoved from the windows of the kitchen quarters; and that
ne window-sashes being warped with age and having only
ld-fashioned catches, it would be a simple matter to force
n entry through any of them. Now, as he followed the fat
voman through a series of stone passages, his quick eyes took
n a score of details which would be of the greatest value on
he unannounced visit he intended to make that night.

At first he had a little difficulty in orienting the place in his
mind with the plans that von Osterberg had drawn for him;
but as they entered the main hall of the Castle he realised
hat, just before doing so, he had actually passed the door
hat led down to the cellars, which one of the plans showed
o be connected by a short passage with the dungeons under
he banqueting room.

Crossing the hall, the woman threw open a low door, said
in a surly tone, 'Gentleman to see you, *Fräulein*,' and left him
to announce himself.

The room was one of the smaller drawing-rooms of the
Castle. Its walls, hangings and principal pieces of furniture
showed that it had originally been designed by a von Osterberg
who had probably brought back ideas with him from France,
after visiting Versailles and Trianon in the latter part of the
eighteenth century. But the elegance of the French style had
been marred by German bad taste and this had been accen-
tuated by the more recent addition of several mid-Victorian
monstrosities.

Gregory thought it a perfect setting for the young woman
who, propped up by a pile of cushions, was reclining on a
chaise-longue in front of a roaring wood fire, with a litter of
cheap film papers on her lap. She was a well-made girl with

339

good legs and provocative breasts. Her dark hair was draw
back from a central parting. Madonna fashion, with lit
clusters of curls behind her ears, which were small and w
modelled. Her brown eyes, under carefully plucked brow
were full of vitality, but her good looks were a little marr
by the heaviness of her jowl and the over-fullness of her li

Having seen mouths and jowl lines like that on women l
fore, and knowing the sensual proclivities of their owne,
Gregory, with the wildly erotic passages of Helga's love-lette
still fresh in his mind, was not at all surprised to see su
features on her.

She was dressed in expensive clothes that were a little o
fashioned and a bit too tight for her, making her breasts star
out almost indecently. Gregory had little doubt that th
clothes, and the short mink cape beside her, which she ev
dently used when moving about the colder parts of the Cast
were from the pre-War wardrobe that Erika had left behir
her for use on her occasional visits there.

Drawing himself up in the doorway, he clicked his heel
bowed stiffly from the waist and, introducing himself in th
German fashion, uttered the one word 'Möller', which wa
the name he had decided to adopt for this occasion.

She gave him a quick glance and, obviously liking the loo
of his lean virile face, followed it with a smile that showe
her strong even teeth. Then, attempting the *grande dame*, sh
said, 'To what do I owe the pleasure—'

He smiled in reply. 'I am a friend of Fritz Einholtz. I saw hir
a few nights ago, and as he knew that I was coming to Niede
fels he suggested that I should pay my respects to you.'

Her smile broadened. 'Oh, how nice! Do come in! But fir
take off your things, then come and make yourself comfortabl
by the fire here.'

Murmuring his thanks, he advanced a few paces, bowe
again and, knowing that since she could hardly be used t
such courtesies, she would be likely to appreciate it all th
more, he took her hand and kissed it. He then took off hi
overcoat, carried it out to the hall, had another quick loo
round there, and came back to seat himself, near her in a
armchair.

'Do tell me about Fritz,' she said, as soon as he was settled

Gregory had not the least compunction about lying to her
so he replied glibly: 'I saw him in Friedrichshafen. He was ove
only on a flying visit to see somebody at the local headquarter
there, but he hopes to be back here tomorrow night.'

'Oh, how splendid! It's terribly dull here, and for the past
six weeks I've been simply dying for a little amusement.'

340

'Yes, I expect you must get pretty bored here with nothing to do.'

'Oh, there's plenty to do. You see, I run the Castle now, more or less, and the servants take quite a bit of looking after. It's just that when Fritz is away there's no fun to be had here, and myself, I've always been one for a gay life, as they say.'

'So have I,' Gregory agreed heartily. 'Still, poor old Fritz is having a pretty dull life at the moment.'

As he spoke, he had a swift mental picture of Einholtz, his jaw hanging limply open, his blue eyes bulging, as he swayed gently to the pressure of the current at the bottom of Lake Constance.

'How was Fritzie?' Helga's question cut in on his macabre thoughts. 'Did he say much about me?'

'Oh, he's fine, and just longing to get back to you. Pretty naturally, he's hated having to kick his heels all this time in Switzerland, looking after that goofy Count.'

Helga shot him a cautious look. 'You know about that, then?'

He nodded. 'I've been mixed up in it myself, to a certain extent; and it was to make some arrangements in the village for tomorrow night that I've come here in advance. The job is as good as finished now, and it looks as if after tomorrow Fritz will be back for good.'

'That's fine,' she said, and added thoughtfully, 'in some ways.'

'Why? I thought you were simply dying for him to get back.'

'Oh, I'll be glad to see Fritz again. But if his job is nearly finished, it means that I'll be out of a job in a day or two myself.'

'You mean that you won't be required any longer to act as gaoler to the Countess Erika?'

She gave him another quick look. 'So you know about that, too?'

'Of course. I've been mixed up with the whole business from the beginning. How do you get on with your prisoner?'

'Not too badly. I must say she's given me very little trouble. She's a real lady; I will say that for her. She's been quiet and just kind of natural. I let her have books from the library and she spends most of her time reading. Not like the old Countess. She was a real tartar.'

Gregory noted the past tense and said, 'So she played you up, did she?'

'The old girl played herself up in the end,' Helga laughed. 'Didn't Fritz tell you? Her temper was something awful. One day she threw a plate of stew at me, so I slapped her face, and it seems she had a heart attack. It came on quite sudden

341

and I didn't know what was wrong with her at first, I just left her, to learn her manners, and the next time I went down to give her a meal there was the old bird dead on the floor.'

Gregory could be a very good actor when the need arose, and he laughed as though he thought the episode intensely funny. After a moment he said: 'I expect that after tomorrow night they will send the Countess Erika to a concentration camp. Will you be sorry?'

Helga took the question to apply not to Erika but to herself. 'It all depends,' she said, a little pensively. 'I wish I could read the stars a bit and see what life has to offer me round the corner.'

'Fritz might find you a job in Nürnberg,' Gregory suggested.

She stretched her arms above her head, and folded her hands behind her neck, the thin stuff of her blouse becoming taut across her bosom, as she replied.

'If it was something exciting I'd like that. On the other hand, I wouldn't mind staying on here if he could come over and see me frequently. It's pretty cosy living here as the *Hockwohlgeboren* used to, even though we're left with a war time staff. Nürnberg would certainly be nice and cheery, whereas most of the time this place is so dull, with never a man about. I'm sort of torn between two stools as they say.'

'What about the police boys who are billeted here?' Gregory asked. 'Don't they ever provide you with a little mild entertainment?'

'Oh, them!' She shrugged contemptuously. 'They're not S.S. but old fogies, or middle-aged; and no class, anyway I wouldn't let any of that lot so much as put a hand on me.'

'Don't be unkind. I'm getting on for middle-aged myself,' Gregory grinned.

'I wouldn't say that,' Helga gave him an arch smile. 'You're different, too. Anyone could see that much. And, after all, age doesn't count if you're the right sort, does it? I think you're nice.'

'Thanks.' Gregory smiled. 'That's a charming compliment, coming as it does, from a very beautiful girl.'

'You'd better be careful,' she admonished him coyly, 'or you'll have Fritz on your tail.'

'I'm quite capable of taking care of Fritz,' he said lightly, but with far more reason than she knew. 'And I'm glad you think I'm nice—because I think you're an absolute stunner.'

He had struck the right note and Helga was now thoroughly enjoying herself. But with the natural female desire to play any new and good-looking fish that appeared to be nibbling at her line, she sat up, and, pushing a bell beside the fireplace, made a pretence of changing the conversation, by saying:

'I'm sure you'd like some coffee. The old geezer who has been butler here for the best part of a century is just about due to bring it.'

'Thanks, I'd love some.' He deliberately offered her his cigarette-case, although he knew that it contained only Sullivans. She took one without noticing; he lit it, and as she drew in the first mouthful of fragrant smoke, she exclaimed:

'Hallo! What's this?'

'Something that will make you forget Fritz and see me as twenty years younger than I am,' he laughed.

'Really!' Her dark eyes looked into his quite seriously.

'No. Not really,' he admitted. 'They're just some very fine oriental cigarettes that a friend of mine in the Marines, who doesn't smoke, sent me from a captured British ship.'

She smiled at him. 'Well, I wouldn't want you to be twenty years younger, anyway. I never have found it amusing to be practised on by boys just out of their *Gymnasiums*.'

The old, lame man that Gregory had seen through his binoculars on the terrace earlier in the afternoon came in with a well-laden tray, and set it down on a small table near Helga.

'Thanks, Johann,' she said pleasantly, but he did not smile or reply by a single word, and walked stiffly from the room.

Helga made a grimace behind his back, then smiled at Gregory as she began to pour the coffee, and said:

'See what I've got to put up with. The only staff we've got left are a lot of old doodlers like that who have been growing gay in their hair at Niederfels most of their lives. They don't much like my being mistress now, and I have to show a pretty firm hand to keep them in their places.'

'I should have thought they would be glad to have a change of mistress, after being under that tyrannical old harridan for so long,' Gregory replied.

'You would, wouldn't you? After all, I'm easy enough to get on with.'

'I'm sure you are. Perhaps it's that they rather resent you acting as gaoler to the Countess Erika.'

'Maybe there's something in that; although she scarcely ever came here, so most of them hardly know her.'

'I wonder,' said Gregory, between two mouthfuls of sugared cake, 'that you ever came here. Why did you take this place with the old Countess originally? A smart girl like you ought to have been going places in Berlin.'

'I was,' Helga laughed. 'until I was caught out using the lady's frocks and she refused to give me a reference. Then my godfather, who's head-keeper here, wrote about this place. He has got quite a bit put by, and no children of his own, so it will come to me if I play up to the old so-and-so. Not that

that matters now, but at the time it seemed important; so I came here and stuck it for a year. Anyhow I've since had my own back on the old woman; and now I'm on the up and up, as they say.'

'You certainly are,' agreed Gregory, drinking up his coffee 'A lovely person like you ought to go a long, long way.'

'You're kidding,' she murmured. 'Still, every girl likes to hear that sort of thing. And I'll bet you've got lots more pretty speeches where that came from.'

'It's just the simple truth,' Gregory assured her.

'You're telling me!' She gave him a mocking glance from under her long black lashes, as she lit a fresh cigarette from the one she was already smoking.

'I mean it,' he persisted. 'And if Fritz weren't coming back tomorrow night I'd have liked the chance to tell you lots more truths like that.'

She drew her feet up on the *chaise-longue*, clasped her hands round her knees, rested her chin on them, and gave him a long, steady look from her dark eyes, as she asked, 'Are you afraid of Fritz?'

'No, I'm not the least afraid of Fritz,' he replied with perfect candour.

'Then why not stay and have dinner with me here tonight? she said quietly. The new attitude she had just adopted had he knew, been purposely designed to give him a good sight o her silk undies, and an alluring glimpse of the insides of he plump pink thighs, just above where her stockings ended It was clear that the invitation was not confined to dinner.

He hesitated only a second. To be actually in the Castl when the time came to attempt his coup would simplif things enormously. But he felt that there were certain snag attached to the invitation. He had now extracted from Helga all the information that she could give him, and if he dine with her it was obvious that she would expect him to mak love to her. He could have dealt with that and, for the mo ment he could not actually put his finger on what other snag there might be; yet some sixth sense warned him that to accep would land him into unforeseen difficulties.

'No,' he said. 'Thanks all the same. I'd simply love to, bu the trouble is that there are certain arrangements that I hav to make down in the village tonight.'

She pouted prettily. 'Oh, come on. Why not? I'll see to that the servants put their backs into giving us a jolly goo meal, with lots of the Count's best drink; and we might—wel we might have a bit of fun afterwards. Surely you can d whatever you've got to do in the village tomorrow morning?

He shook his head and stood up. 'No! Honestly! It's a

uch as my job is worth not to get those arrangements made
night. I'm sure Fritz won't be occupying all your time and
at we could have lots of fun together. Leave it to me, and
ter tomorrow night's business is over I'll get in touch with
ou.'

'What about coming back later on tonight?' she enquired.

The last thing he wanted her to do was to stay up for him,
he said: 'I shan't be through before two o'clock at the
rliest. We had much better make it another time.'

'All right,' she agreed reluctantly. 'Still, if you find that you
n get back earlier—'

'That's sweet of you,' he smiled. 'But I doubt if I can. I've
ot the hell of a lot to do, and I simply must go now.'

As he moved towards the door she accompanied him, and
the hall outside helped him on with his coat. Then she
ened the front door for him.

'I'll be seeing you,' he smiled, as he stepped out into the
urtyard.

'*Auf Wiedersehen!*' she called, letting her eyelashes fall in a
st gesture of renewed invitation.

He nodded, blew her a kiss, and crossed the big echoing
rd. He would have preferred not to go down the main road
the village, but felt that he must do so because she might
ill be watching him from a window.

As he walked down the curving slope he was thinking what
arvellous luck he had had so far. When he had set out from
ondon it had seemed that he had set himself an almost im-
ossible task. Yet, he had had one good break after another.
here was the cardinal fact to start with that Erika was still
Niederfels and in good health, instead of a poor helpless
reck in some heavily guarded concentration camp deep in-
de Germany, as she so easily might have been. Then his
rning back after his first visit to the Villa Offenbach, to see
inholtz setting off across the lake and von Osterberg hand-
ffed to his chair, had given him an enormous advantage
ver the enemy. The raid on the Villa had gone without a
ngle hitch. He had met with no difficulty in disposing of
inholtz's body. He had reached von Lottingen's villa with-
t even being challenged by a patrol boat. No one had spot-
d him coming ashore. Everything had gone according to
an once he was inside Germany, and he had got away with
first-class car. To cap it all he had learned from Helga's
tters that Erika was guarded only by herself and two or
ree middle-aged road patrol men, and those letters had
abled him to reconnoitre the inside of the Castle in day-
ght.

Look for the snags where he would he could not see them,

and the job now seemed unbelievably easy—if only his luck would hold for another few hours.

He was halfway down to the village, and just about to turn off into the woods to recross the valley, when he caught the purr of a powerful car approaching. Swiftly as he jumped aside into the fringe of trees the car was almost upon him. As it raced round the bend he had a full view of its occupants. Inside, with their backs to the driver, sat two heavily jowled Gestapo thugs. Facing them was a handsome young S.S. man whose face had obviously been painted, and beside him sat *Gruppenführer* Grauber!

Gregorys' coat collar was turned up and the brim of his soft hat pulled down over his eyes, as some protection against the cold; so even if any of them had noticed him, he didn't think there was any chance that he had been recognised. But the very sight of Grauber was for him, at that moment, like a terrific punch landing straight on his heart.

Only a moment ago everything had looked so easy. Now, by arriving on the scene a night earlier than Gregory had expected him, Grauber loomed like a dark and terrible menace over any prospect of spiriting Erika simply and swiftly away.

Instead of the occupants of the Castle going to bed at the early hour usual in the country, with Grauber there they would be sure to sit up until midnight or later, talking and drinking. When Gregory stealthily made his way to Erika's dungeon he might find it empty, as it was quite possible that Grauber would have her upstairs to taunt and torture her with the news that her lover would also be a prisoner by the following night. Worse, Helga might mention his recent visit.

He had told her that he was making certain arrangements in the village in connection with the trap. Grauber would know that no instructions of that sort had been issued to any of his people. He would ask Helga to describe her visitor and from the description he would recognise Gregory at once. If that happened when he made his way to Erika's dungeon, they would be there in the dark, waiting for him. The trap would close with a snap. It would then be impossible for him to make any second attempt to rescue Erika, and he would have to bite through the capsule of poison that he carried in his mouth.

In a terrible wave of depression he knew that he had been counting his chickens too soon. His luck had now run out.

20

The Long Night

Slowly and dejectedly Gregory walked across the valley
bottom and up its further slope, to the car. Darkness had
fallen by the time he reached it, and glancing at the luminous
dial of his watch he saw that the time was twenty-five to
seven.

Thinking matters over, he realised that just before he had
seen Grauber, he had had one last piece of luck. His refusal
of Helga's invitation had been nothing less than a miraculous
preservation. Had he accepted it, or even lingered with her
for another ten minutes, Grauber would have arrived to find
them together, and the game would have been up. As it was,
he was at least still alive and free.

While he was still cursing the *Gruppenführer* for his most
untimely arrival Gregory had formulated a probable reason
for it. At first, he had jumped to the conclusion that something must have gone wrong at the Villa Offenbach and Grauber had somehow found out that he had entered Germany
forty-eight hours before he was expected. But it could not
be that. Einholtz was safely in a place where he would never
more tell tales, and Kuporovitch could be trusted to look after
von Osterberg. Even if Stefan had conceivably slipped up and
the Count had escaped he had neither the guts, the means nor
any incentive to make his way back to Germany and, for the
sake of reporting Einholtz's death, place himself once more in
the hands of the Gestapo. Even a surprise visit to the Villa by
one of Einholtz's colleagues could have revealed nothing of
Gregory's own plans. He was quite confident of that.

Therefore Grauber's arrival could have no ulterior motive
behind it, and Gregory recalled having glimpsed some gun-
cases among the luggage strapped at the back of the *Gruppen-*
führer's car. In consequence, it seemed almost certain that he
had simply decided to take a day off. He had brought his
pansy boy-friend with him to provide amorous entertainment,
and meant to spend the following day shooting in the woods,
as a pleasant relaxation before glutting himself with sadistic
pleasure when his enemy was brought in as a prisoner on the night
of the 13th.

The odds were, then, that unless Helga had spoken about her
other visitor and described him, Grauber was still in ignor-
ance that he had as yet left Switzerland. The possibility of
Helga talking remained a terrible imponderable which it was

Impossible to assess; but, fortunately, Grauber was not terested in women and probably still regarded her as l more than a servant. The fact that he had not bothered notify her of his impending arrival could be fairly taken some evidence of that.

On the other hand, she was Einholtz's girl-friend Erika's gaoler, so Grauber would be certain to have so conversation with her. Still, like most people with whom one-eyed *Gruppenführer* came into contact, she would pr ably be frightened of him, and refrain from volunteering information for which she was not asked. As the girl was m or less a nymphomaniac her thoughts, too, would proba now be centred on alluring one of the hefty Gestapo m whom Grauber had brought with him. Such a woman wo be certain to have in instinctive dislike of perverts, so, if choice lay with her she would probably have as little as p sible to do with Grauber, and if he confined his remarks to to formal enquiries as to Erika's safe keeping and hea Gregory felt that there seemed a fair chance of getting in the Castle while his presence in the neighbourhood was s unsuspected.

It occurred to him that his chances might be better if put the job off for a few nights, until Grauber got fed up w waiting for him, and departed. But he soon realised that to so would not really make his prospects any better, and mig even make them considerably worse. When Einholtz failed appear on the following night Grauber would know at on that his plans had miscarried. A search of the Villa Offenba would reveal nothing, but he would guess that somehow l enemy had proved too clever for Einholtz; and the discove of the launch in von Lottingen's boathouse would be a pret good indication that Gregory had used it to enter German That would cause Grauber to order a maximum state of ale ness; triple guards of his own men would be put on Erik and every policeman in Württemberg would be ordered join in a grand battue to hunt Gregory down. No, he de cided, the attempt must be made that night or never.

As huddled in his overcoat, he ate another cold meal, h pondered a further problem that worried him considerabl This was the time factor. If he did succeed in getting Erik out of the Castle, they had to accomplish the journey bac to von Lottingen's and recross the lake before dawn. Fortur ately the winter nights were long, but, even so, allowanc must be made for unforeseen delays, and that meant a fairl early start.

It was as good as certain that Grauber would not go to be before midnight, and by that time they ought to have reache the car and just be setting off. He had planned to go in about eleven o'clock, but to do so now meant taking a great additional risk of being caught on the spot. On the other hand, if he postponed his attempt until he could be ninety-nine per cent certain that everyone in the Castle was asleep he would have to put off his time of going in until about three o'clock.

If he waited until then all hope of getting safely across the lake the same night would be gone. Even in the most favourable circumstances, Erika's rescue, getting from the Castle to the car and the sixty-odd miles by by-roads from Niederfels to von Lottingen's would occupy three hours; and if they did not reach the lake side until six o'clock they would find it already stirring into its daily activity, dawn would be breaking and all attempts to evade the German patrol boats rendered hopeless by the morning light.

As a last alternative he considered going in at four o'clock —the optimum hour of unpreparedness of the inmates of the Castle—getting well clear of the Niederfels district before dawn, then lying up in some quiet spot for the day and making his bid to recross the lake the following night. But that, too, had to be dismissed. The moment Erika's escape was discovered Grauber would have the police of the whole countryside in a ferment. He would instantly assume that Gregory had beaten him to it and was responsible for the rescue. The theft of the car in Stuttgart the night before would be linked up with him and become a redhot menace unless he abandoned it. Investigation would reveal the Villa Offenbach's launch in von Lottingen's boathouse and their retreat by means of it would be cut off. They had no friends with whom they could seek shelter, very little food, no ration cards and no identity papers. With such appalling handicaps and the police in every village searching for them, in a few days, at most, they were bound to be captured.

In vain Gregory racked his brains. His original plan was the only one that offered the least chance of success, so he must go through with it. Once more he went into times and decided that about half an hour after midnight was the latest he dared to leave it to go in, but the odds were that Grauber and his friends would not be in bed by then, if they were on holiday and there was no cause for them to get up early the following morning. Moreover, even if he succeeded in reaching Erika's dungeon without being detected, he might meet with unforeseen difficulties and delays in getting her out.

His final decision, therefore, was that on balance he would do better after all, to go in as soon as the servants could be expected to be out of the way, around eleven o'clock, as he would then, at least, gain an additional hour and a half's lee-way against unexpected contingencies later in the night.

His hours of waiting seemed intolerable and never-ending. The devastating break in his luck now seemed a presage of final misfortune and defeat. The cold was bitter and with the coming of night both the temperature and his spirits sank towards zero. But even the longest wait has an ending, and at last it was time for him to set out on his terrible gamble.

At half past ten he edged the car back on to the forest track and drove it at a moderate pace down through the village, then some way up the winding road to Schloss Niederfels.

About two-thirds of the way up he came to a place where the rough road widened, so he slowed down, turned the car round, and eased it in as far as he could under the shadow of the trees, with its bonnet now pointing down to the village. Getting out, he made certain that his pistol, torch, skeleton keys, chisel, pliers and file were all in their right places on his person; then, little realising that he was standing on almost the identical spot on which Erika had stood one hundred and twelve nights before, he did just as she had done when Einholtz had left her with the car and pretended to go forward to reconnoitre. Craning his head backwards, he stared up above the opposite tree-tops at the faint outline of the Schloss.

For a moment he stood there, his thoughts for once tenuous and confused with vague speculations as to whether this would prove his last night on earth, and a half-formulated prayer that the gods would aid him to restore the liberty and happiness of the woman he loved so desperately. Then he turned, and set off with firm steps up the hill.

On reaching the wide approach to the Castle he began to tread more gently. Skirting the great main gateway, he entered the smaller courtyard that he had used on his visit in the afternoon. Pausing for a moment, he gave the façade above the kitchen quarters a swift but careful scrutiny. No light showed, no sound reached his ears. Going softly forward, he reached the postern door at which he had talked with the fat woman. Trying it, he found it locked, so he moved along to the right, looking at the windows as he went. The third had been left a little open, so there was no need for him to force an entry.

For a second he hesitated, suspecting a trap. Then he cursed himself for the state that he had allowed his nerves to get into. Of all the possible entrances to this huge pile how could Grauber conceivably guess that he would elect to come in by one of the kitchen windows? If Helga had mentioned his visit, and a trap had been prepared for him, it would be somewhere down near Erika's dungeon that those Gestapo gorillas would

w be waiting to spring upon him out of the darkness and
in him with their blackjacks.

Easing the upper half of the window down he levered him-
lf up and over it. As he felt about with his feet they came
contact with a sink, so his descent to the floor was easy
d almost noiseless.

Pausing, he listened intently for half a minute, then took
it his pistol and flicked on his torch. Flashing it round he
w that he was in the scullery, but only a few yards from
n the door to the kitchen stood half-open.

His rubber-soled shoes making no sound on the ancient
ones, he passed through it and crossed the kitchen. Its fur-
er door creaked a little as he opened it. Again he listened
t the silence was absolute. Stepping out into the passage,
walked slowly along it, taking paces of a fair length and
tting each foot down squarely so that its sole and heel
ch bore a portion of its weight. Following the same route as
had taken with the fat woman that afternoon, he came to
e door that he knew led down to the cellars. It was neither
cked nor padlocked, and on his turning the handle it opened
th out a sound.

Again he suspected a trap. He had had to pocket his gun
order to open the door. Thrusting his foot forward, so
at it should not slam to, he jerked out his automatic and
un round, to stare into the shadows behind him. There was
movement, and no sound. Again he cursed silently and
ove to reassure himself. There were several entrances to
e tortuous underground passages of the Schloss, and he
ght have chosen any one of them. It was not here that
auber would set his trap, but down there near the dun-
ons.

Cautiously he edged through the door, went down two steps
d closed it soundlessly behind him. Shining his torch down-
rd he safely negotiated the flight of broad stone stairs and
me out under an arch into a wide vaulted passage. On either
le of it there was a row of wooden doors with airholes in
em. There, he knew, were the wine cellars. Further on the
ssage opened out into a sizeable low-ceilinged room. Three
es of stout scantlings ran from end to end of it, and upon
em there still reposed a number of casks; great aums and
aller hogsheads that had once held hock, moselle, and stein-
in, now mostly mildewed and presumably empty.

Turning left he went through another arch. A dark hole
ped at his feet, and recalling the plan that von Osterberg
d drawn for him he realised that it was the circular stairway
at led down to the foundations of the Castle, in which the
re ancient and primitive dungeons lay. At that still lower

351

level human beings had once been chained to the walls fro
which must ooze a perpetual slime and moisture, while ra
scampered unchecked in the darkness and, when driven to
by hunger had gnawed the toes from the prisoners' livi
feet. Gregory shuddered, thanked all his gods that Erika ha
at least been spared such horrors, and, skirting the dark we
turned right into another vaulted passageway.

At its entrance he paused once more. According to vo
Osterberg's plan this passage ran below the centre of the ban
queting hall, and it was in the last vault on the left that Eri
was confined. There was no other entrance to this double ro
of basement rooms, so it was here, if a trap had been laid, th
the enemy would be lurking for him.

He tried to think how he would have laid such a trap if l
had had to set it himself, and had the answer in an instant. I
would have placed his men in some of the vaults at the e
of the passage where he now stood and when the midnig
visitor had passed their hiding-places it would be simple
ABC for them to spring out and corner him further down t
corridor.

Yet, a second later, he saw that such a plan was far fro
perfect. The men would have to open the doors to come o
Unless done with extreme caution that would make enou
noise to warn the intruder. He would have time to swi
round, and if armed, shoot down his attackers as th
emerged before they could shoot him.

No. The place to have laid the ambuscade was in the b
open cellar. A dozen men could have hidden behind those c
casks without being seen. After the intruder had passed th
could have sprung upon him before he had time even to le
a weapon.

Gregory breathed a little more freely. He had passed u
heeding through the place where the maximum danger mig
have been expected to lie; so perhaps Helga had not talk
and there was no trap after all.

Then it came to him that although Grauber and his m
might have concealed themselves in the big cellar that was n
necessarily where they would have staged their attack. Tho
casks would give good cover for a man who was hunted
well as his hunters. Given even a moment's warning he mig
have had time to slip behind them, then he could have led l
ambushers a macabre and deadly dance, shooting several
them before they could finally locate and kill him. And, he w
little use to Grauber dead. Grauber wanted him alive, so t
task of securing him without being injured themselves wou
in such a case, have proved an exceedingly difficult one.

No. They would want to catch him in the open; in

352

lace where no means of retreat lay open to him and there
as nothing that he could dodge behind. The far end of the
assage where he now stood would be perfect for that. Per-
aps they had been behind those casks all the time, had seen
im go by and were, even now, preparing to corner him.

At that thought the cold perspiration broke out on his fore-
ead. He strained his ears, endeavouring to catch a whisper, a
ootfall or the scrape of a boot; but he could hear nothing—
nly the beating of his own heart as the blood pulsed in swift
ythmic jerks up to his brain.

After a few moments he felt a shade more confident that
o one was creeping up behind him. Yet his nerves were still
lmost at breaking point and to test the situation, he took a
w steps boldly down the passage, then with his gun levelled
witched round.

Still no sound broke the eerie silence, so he turned again
nd, treading more cautiously, moved like a ghost down to
ie end of the corridor. The door of Erika's dungeon proved
• be made of stout old oak, and as he shone his torch on the
eyhole in it he gave a low groan of despair. The door had,
s he had expected, a mortice lock, but this one needed a key
ine inches long and with a three-inch-square grid to open it.

None of the skeleton keys that he had brought would be the
ast use and, although the lock must turn fairly easily from
aving been so frequently used, his pliers were not nearly big
1ough for him to exert the pressure on them necessary to
1ove this ancient and formidable example of the locksmith's
·t.

He knew there was only one thing for it. He must chisel
way at least eight inches of the solid oak doorpost to extract
ie socket of the lock, and that would take him anything up-
ards of an hour. Had he been faced with such a lengthy
.sk at one in the morning the game would have been up,
1t it was not yet half past eleven, and he had every cause to
less his decision to come in early, as he had originally plan-
ed. On the other hand, in the next hour or more it was quite
1 the cards that Grauber might still send one of his men down
• bring Erika up for his amusement, if he had not already done
); and if that happened the intruder would be caught red-
anded.

Still holding his torch in his left hand he pocketed his gun
ith the other; and, deciding that it was only sensible to find
ut if Erika was still inside before he started to work with
is chisel, he knocked gently. There was no response, so he
10cked again, a little louder.

Suddenly, things began to happen behind him to his right.
is hearing and sight were hit simultaneously with a rapid

succession of new impressions. A soft footfall was instantl
followed by the creak of an opening door. A glimmer of ligh
gilding the door a few yards further up the passage was obl
terated as it came streaming through the opening doorway.

Quick as he was in flicking out his own torch, backing u
against Erika's door and thrusting his hand into his pocket fo
his gun, before he could get it out he found himself menace
from the next doorway along the passage.

Helga stood there. She was wearing feathered mules and
satin nightdress, with a fur coat draped over her shoulder
In her left hand she held aloft an oil lamp and in her right sh
grasped a gun that was pointing straight at his heart.

'So you came back after all,' she said, in a tone that expres
sed interest, but conveyed nothing to him. From it, he coul
not tell if she had spoken with Grauber, so now knew that h
was Erika's lover, and his return in an attempt to rescue he
was expected; or if she still regarded him as one of Grauber
people and thought that he had returned to make love to he

'How did you find your way down here?' she asked.

'They told me,' he said, hoping for the best.

She smiled and lowered her pistol. 'Well, that's fine! B
you were knocking on the wrong door. Fritz has often warne
me that the Countess Erika's boy friend might attempt her re
cue at some time or other, and for a moment I thought thos
noises outside her door might be him.'

'What an idea!' He forced a laugh that he hoped migh
sound natural.

Her dark eyes again took in his lean good looks with appr
ciation as she said: 'It's been one of the snags to this job, a
along, my having to live down here. But Fritz insisted on i
You see, he knows that I'm a light sleeper and that any nois
outside in the passage would wake me at once. He reckone
that the boy-friend would never guess that I was in the roo
next door to her, and that I'd be able to give the alarm. The
ran a telephone line down for me, so that I could ring up th
traffic cops who sleep upstairs if I had need of them, but whe
I heard you just now I thought it would be a feather in m
cap if I could catch the boy-friend all on my own.'

Gregory's brain was racing. Helga had not spoken of h
visit and described him to Grauber. She had no idea at a
that he was the Countess Erika's boy-friend whom she ha
hoped to catch. There was no trap with yawning jaws waiti
for him. Grauber had no idea that he had left Switzerland, ar
was upstairs either asleep or inflicting repulsive caresses c
the young S.S. man with the painted face. Erika was still
her cell. If only he could deal with this damnable woman wh
stood fluttering her charms in front of him there was a goo

354

ance that he could release Erika and get clear away with
er.

Helga, meanwhile, was going on. 'I'd have liked to use the
ountess Erika's bedroom, upstairs. It's nice, that. Still, the
pper dungeons here are quite dry and pretty roomy, so I had
er carpet and most of her furniture brought down. I've three
stoves too, so it's really rather cosy. It was a shame you
uldn't have dinner with me, but I've been consoling my-
lf with a naughty book that I found in the library. It's by a
an called the Marquis de Sade and all about the queer
ings he used to do to his girl-friends. It's got pictures, too. I've
en thinking of you while I was reading it, and, better late
an never, as they say. Anyhow, now you're here, do come

'Thanks,' said Gregory, 'I'd love to, but I can't. I really did
me down to see the Countess Erika. I've been ordered to
ake a medical examination of her, and report.'

'Ooh!' Helga's eyes widened 'Are you a doctor, then?'

He nodded. 'Yes, I'm the chap who tickles them up when
ey refuse to talk. But the first thing I always have to find out
how much tickling they are likely to stand up to.'

Helga's mouth went sullen with disappointment. 'Then you
dn't come down to see me after all?'

'No. I'm afraid I didn't,' he admitted. 'But never mind.
e'll just have to look on our getting together as a pleasure
eferred. As I said this afternoon, I'll get in touch with you
 the earliest possible opportunity. Then we'll have some real
gh jinks. At the moment though, I'm on duty. Can I have the
y of the Countess Erika's door?'

'I suppose so,' she pouted. 'Still, if you've got to make a
edical examination of her that will take a bit of time. Surely
u can skimp it a little so as to spend ten minutes with me.
me on, and I'll show you some of those pictures. They're
vfully well drawn, and no end of an eyeful, as you might
y.'

Gregory saw that there was nothing for it but to accept,
, pocketing his torch, he followed her into the room. It was
 stone-walled, vaulted apartment, with only one window,
rred and set high in the wall. There was no fireplace, but
e oilstoves made it quite warm in there, and Helga had
rtainly made her unusual quarters much more comfortable
an might have been expected. A thick carpet, two-thirds
dden with fine Persian rugs looted from all parts of the
stle, covered the floor, the bed was of simple design, but wide
d looked most conducive to slumber. The other furnishings
ere all elegant and in excellent taste. He guessed that they
d been chosen by Erika, and he felt a surge of hatred rise in

355

him for this good-looking nymphomaniac who had stolen a
was profaning them.

Setting down the oil-lamp, Helga slipped off her fur co
and got into bed, where she had evidently been reading.

'Come on,' she said, picking up the book. 'take off yo
overcoat for a few minutes and be matey.'

Gregory shook his head. 'Really, I mustn't. *Gruppenführ*
Grauber is waiting for my report; and he's such a hell of
big shot, I simply daren't keep him waiting.'

'Yes. Even Fritz is scared of him,' Helga admitted, with
little grimace. 'By the by, if Fritz does get back tomorr
night, you won't tell him anything about us, will you? H
terribly jealous of me.'

'Of course not,' Gregory raised a smile. 'Is it likely? I
no more anxious than you are to land a nasty quarrel on r
hands just because I like a bit of fun. But look, I simply mu
get on with my job. Where's that darned key?'

'It's hard luck, isn't it,' she sighed. 'After you and me mee
ing for the first time like that and taking such a fancy to ea
other. Still, I suppose we've got to grin and bear it, as they sa

As she spoke she leaned over, opened the top drawer of
small cabinet beside her bed and produced a huge, rusty ke
almost large enough to have served to open the gates of a
old fortress city. She weighed it in her hand for a momen
then she said:

'It's some key, isn't it; but the lock is well oiled so it turn
all right, with a bit of pressure. Don't go doing things yo
didn't ought to with the Countess. She's a good looker enoug
to tempt most men; but if you're a doctor I suppose you on
look on most people as cases.'

'That's right,' Gregory gave her an answering smile as h
took the key and thrust it into his pocket.

It was at that second that he caught the sound of footstep
in the distance.

'Someone's coming!' exclaimed Helga. 'Surely they can
be chasing you for that report already?'

'I must go,' he said quickly; but all the same he did no
move. His luck had run out again, and at the worst possib
moment. He was in a ghastly quandary. The heavy footfal
now entering the passage could be those only of an enemy
Everything now hung on his next action, and he had only
few seconds to make up his mind what course he should tak

Helga might yet be tricked or coerced into proving
friend, or, if he left her to tackle the men coming down th
passage, she might suddenly become a terrible menace in h
rear. His automatic had its silencer on, so, without arousin
the suspicion of the approaching enemy he still had time t

356

shoot her in cold blood. That was the wisest course, but she had hardly merited that, and it went against the grain. If he whispered to her now to imply that he was her lover; that he had come there only to see her, and would explain later, there was just a chance that she might play. He could reinforce the plea by a whispered threat that if she let him down he would kill her. Perhaps the footsteps were those of someone only coming to pay her a midnight visit in the hope of a little amorous dalliance. If so, the man would go away disappointed. Then the awful danger would have been averted, Helga could be dealt with and Erika freed.

While those swift thoughts raced through Gregory's mind the man had taken some twenty paces. He was now about halfway down the passage.

Suddenly he called out in a guttural voice: '*Fräulein Stiffel, sind Sie da?* The *Herr Gruppenführer* has ordered that the *Frau Gräfin* be brought up to him.'

In a flash Gregory realised that his swiftly-thought-out plan for using Helga was now useless. Once Erika had been taken upstairs his chance of freeing her might be gone for good. He looked at Helga and their eyes met.

Instantly she realised that something was wrong. In his brown eyes there now lurked something akin to murder. Her mouth opened as Gregory leapt.

'Help!' she screamed, and flung herself sideways to grab for her gun.

With one blow he sent it spinning to the far side of the room. With another he caught her a glancing cut across the side of her chin. Her head jerked backwards, struck the bed-head with a thud and she rolled over, temporarily knocked out.

Swinging round, he thrust his hand into his pocket for his pistol and jerked it clear. At her scream the ponderous steps outside in the passage that a moment before had sounded like the footfalls of doom broke into a heavy run. When Gregory had followed Helga into the room he had left the door half open. It must have been the light coming from it that had told the man coming down the passage, that Helga was still awake, and caused him to call out. Next second he had thrust it wide and come charging into the room.

He was a typical bull-necked Prussian of about thirty-five, fattish but muscular and with the battleship jaw of a prize-fighter. His coarse flushed face showed that he had been drinking, his black and silver S.S. tunic hung unbuttoned, showing beneath it a rather grubby white shirt, and he was not carrying a gun.

357

As the door swished open Gregory was just on the point o raising his pistol. At that instant he saw Helga lurch up into sitting position, shake her head dazedly, and stretch out a han for the telephone that stood beside her bed.

It was a horrible moment. The Gestapo man had to cove only a dozen feet to cross the room. Yet if Helga succeede in ringing through to give the alarm, Grauber, his boy-frien and two or more of the road patrol men would come dashin down to the dungeons within the next few minutes. Such odd Gregory knew, would be utterly beyond his powers to com bat. There was only one thing for it.

Lowering his pistol, he leant over and with his left han snatched the telephone receiver from Helga. Throwing him self back, he tore at it with all his strength. It was a house lin with only a single wire and the jerk ripped the instrume from its connections breaking the wire with a snap.

Before he could turn round the Gestapo man was upon hin The thug caught him with a terrific punch behind the ear, an he went down with a crash. For a moment he saw stars an circles flashing in a black, void before his eyes, but instin tively he rolled over, and strove to protect his head.

As his sight came back he glimpsed a heavy boot comin straight at his face. Twisting sideways he grabbed at the ank above it with his left hand and thrust it aside. The Gestap man lost his balance and went sprawling in the floor.

Gasping for breath, Gregory stumbled to his feet. The Ge man was up almost as quickly, but now the corner of the be was between them, and Gregory had somehow managed t retain a hold upon his gun. Helga had slid off the bed on th far side, and, without waiting to pull a coat over her nigh dress, was running towards the door.

Once again, if she were allowed to contact Grauber, com plete and final disaster threatened. Jerking up his pistol, Gr gory shot her through the back.

With a scream, she flung up her arms and collapsed.

But the vital instants needed to stop her dashing upstai had again lost Gregory his temporary advantage. Before h could turn his weapon on his assailant the big tough had jum ped round the corner of the bed and struck at him a secor time.

He had no chance to guard his face and this time the blo caught him squarely between the eyes. He staggered bac felt his head swim and his knees grow weak, then sank dov as though a ton weight had suddenly descended on his shou ders,

For a moment he was out, and with a roar of triumph the erman came at him again. His heavy boot thudded into regory's side. The kick drove the breath out of Gregory's ody but the agonising pain brought back his senses. As his ssailant drew back his foot to deliver another kick, he hun-ed up his knees and thrust his head under the bed.

Instead of landing on his ribs a second time the kick caught m on the thigh. It hurt as much as a blow from a road-ammer, but with the instinct of getting away from further nishment he forced his body under the bed, wriggled side-ays, and drew his feet in after it.

A temporary stalemate ensued. Gregory lay on his face der the bed, striving to get his wits and his breath back; e German stood beside it panting heavily and wondering w to get him out.

'*Teufel nochmal!*' exclaimed the thug suddenly. 'Come out that—damn you!'

Gregory made no reply. From where he lay his head was ly about thirty inches from the German's feet. Drawing up s gun hand he took careful aim at the man's right ankle and lled the trigger.

The cough of the weapon was followed instantly by a roar agony. As his enemy jerked up his shattered leg Gregory ed again, at the other ankle.

With a howl of rage the German, both his feet shot from der him, collapsed like a pricked balloon. A second after his ad hit the floor, Gregory fired a third time, putting a bullet ht through it. The Gestapo man jerked once and was dead.

Still sobbing for breath, Gregory crawled out from under e far side of the bed. His ribs were paining him terribly d he felt certain that one or more of them were broken. As came to his feet his eyes fell on Helga. She was lying on her ck, moaning faintly.

Her eyes were open and her arms were twitching, but the ver part of her body lay quite still.

'I can't move my legs,' she moaned, as she stared up at him, can't move my legs.'

He knew at once what had happened. His bullet must have oken her spine. As gently as he could he turned her over. e no longer felt any animus against her for having purloined ika's things In all other ways she seemed to have treated r prisoner decently enough. As for the *Gräfin* Bertha, Erika d told him long ago what a tyrant the old woman could be. lga was no more than an over-sexed young animal, and an underdog who had taken the chance to get her own bac[k] without deliberate malice.

Ripping away her nightdress he looked at the wound. A[s] he had thought, the bullet had gone clean through her spin[e] in the region of her kidneys. It was highly probably that sh[e] would die from it, and, even if she recovered, the lower part [of] her body would be paralysed for life. The lower part of he[r] body *was* her life to Helga, and she wouldn't be much use t[o] anyone or herself without the use of it. He knew what h[e] would have wished himself had he been her. Putting the poin[t] of his gun within a few inches of the base of her skull he ble[w] out her brains. He felt no compunction at all about the ac[t]. It was the merciful thing to do.

Having reloaded his pistol to capacity, he picked up the dea[d] girl's weapon from the floor, pocketed it, got out the gre[en] key of Erika's dungeon, went out into the passage and fitte[d] it into the lock.

As he turned the key his heart was beating fast again; n[ot] with fear now but with terrific excitement. They were not o[ut] of the wood yet by a long way, but he felt that they were ge[t]-ting on for halfway through it. He had intended to speak [to] Erika through the door, just calling out, in German, 'are y[ou] awake?' or something of that kind, in the hope that his voi[ce] would strike a chord in her memory, and thus prepare h[er] for the shock of her release before she actually came face [to] face with him. But there was no time for anything of that ki[nd] now. Pushing the heavy door open, he walked in.

The room was lighted by a single oil lamp, and Erika w[as] sitting up in bed. Her hair was done up in little plaits rou[nd] her head, making her look very young and girlish. Her bl[ue] eyes seemed enormous as she opened them to their full[est] extent in surprise, and gasped, 'Darling!'

'My precious!' he murmured, and next moment he had h[er] folded tight in his arms.

Yet he broke their first hungry kiss off abruptly, knowi[ng] that their lives might hang on a matter of seconds.

'You shouldn't have risked your life to find me,' she smil[ed] up at him. 'But all the same, I always knew you'd come.'

'Listen,' he said. 'Grauber's upstairs and he's just sent one [of] his thugs down to get you. I killed the thug a few momen[ts] ago.'

'So that's what was happening!' she exclaimed. 'I went [to] sleep about ten o'clock, then just now I was awakened [by] screams and shouts next door. I thought that someone w[as] beating up Helga.'

'They were! I was! I had to kill her, so she's dead too. B[ut] when Grauber's man fails to return with you he'll send som[e]

360

ne else down to find out why; or come himself. So we've got
get out of here in double quick time. Come on, Jump out
bed and get yourself dressed.'

'I can't, darling! They took all my clothes away, except my
dies and a dressing-gown. I suppose it was part of their
an to make it difficult for me to get away. Then there's this.'

Thrusting down the bedclothes, she drew up her right foot,
d showed him that round the ankle was a handcuff attached
a long steel chain.

'It allows me to move about the room,' she went on, 'but
t to get within four feet of the door. It was Einholtz's idea,
prevent me from attempting to push Helga one day when
e brought me my food. That, and having no clothes, is why
have never attempted to escape.'

Gregory's luck now seemed to be swaying in the balance.
e had got himself out of a most desperate situation only a
w minutes ago, yet now his hope of getting Erika clear of
e Castle before Grauber sent down to find out what had
appened to his thug was menaced by new, unforeseen delays.

'I'll fix that,' he said quickly. 'Get out of bed and put your
ot up on to it.'

As she obeyed, he glanced swiftly round and snatched up a
mall thick diary that was lying on a table beside Erika's bed.
e thrust the diary between Erika's ankle and the loose steel
rclet that girdled it, so that the thick wad of paper should
revent any particles of steel flying into her foot.

'Stand quite still,' he murmured, and, pulling out his pistol,
e shot away the end of the chain that was attached to the
andcuff; the bullet thudded into the bed.

'Now for clothes,' he went on hurriedly. 'Helga has a lot
f your things next door. You must use those.'

Together they ran out of the sparsely furnished room, along
e passage, and into Helga's luxurious apartment. The clothes
e had used that day were flung heedlessly over a chair-back.

Averting her eyes from the two dead bodies, Erika began
put them on as quickly as she could. Meanwhile, Gregory
ood in the doorway, dreading to hear the sound of fresh
otfalls. If Grauber was fairly well occupied with talk and
ine it might not even cross his mind for twenty minutes or
that the man he had sent down for Erika was a long time
eturning. In the worst case, assuming her to have been asleep,
e would allow ten minutes for her to dress and make herself
resentable, and the long walk through the cellars and upstairs
the banqueting hall would occupy another four or five. At
est it might be half an hour before he sent someone else
own; at worst fourteen from the time his first messenger had
ome charging into Helga's room. But a very great deal can

happen while anyone counts eight hundred and forty at the slow pace of seconds, and Gregory did not think that his desperate encounter had occupied more than four hundred seconds, or his swift exchanges with Erika more than another two hundred. A further two hundred were need for her to pull some clothes on, and that left a margin of only forty. It was, in all conscience, narrow enough, but it just might serve to give them a flying start.

As Erika grabbed up the fur coat Gregory turned back into the room, kicked over the oilstoves and sent the two lamps crashing from the table to the floor. For a second the room was plunged in semi-darkness. then the flames began to give out a lurid glow as they ran hungrily across the carpet, caught Helga's nightdress and licked at the coverings of the bed. Since the chamber had only the one small window high up in the wall at its far end, he knew that the smoke would soon billow out and fill the passageway. That might gain them the start they so badly needed, as when Grauber's next messenger arrived on the scene he would not know that Erika was now still locked in her dungeon and, if the smoke had become dense enough, might even have to go back to fetch a gas mask before he dared penetrate it, for fear of suffocation.

Erika now had the coat on. Leaving the door open they ran out into the passage, and Gregory thrust Helga's gun into her hand.

'You know how to use one,' he said tersely. 'And if we get really cornered I want you to use it on yourself. I shall take that line. I know too much to fall into their hands alive, so I had to promise to before old Pellinore would let me come.'

As he was speaking he ran along to her door, relocked it and thrust the key in his pocket. If they could get clear of the Castle, before Grauber arrived in the smoke-filled corridor he would believe Erika to be still locked in her dungeon and when she failed to answer, imagine her to have been overcome by the fumes of the fire. Then, expecting to save the precious bait in his trap, he would order the heavy door to be broken down, and that was going to keep his people busy for quite a time.

'Don't run,' he cautioned, taking Erika by the arm, 'but there's no need for us to waste time creeping along now. If they are on their way down here and hear us approaching at a sharp walk they'll think it is that thug returning with you and Helga.'

In ninety seconds they had reached the foot of the cellar stairs.

'Quietly now!' he muttered. 'It's going to be tricky if we

in into them up there; and we don't want them to hear us on
ur way out.'

Letting go her arm at the top of the stairs, he listened for
moment, eased open the door, and listened again. The upper
assage was still in darkness and no sound reached him from
cross the hall. There was no fear of an ambush now, so he
rew Erika quickly through the door and pulled it gently to
ter her.

Flashing his torch, he tiptoed with her down the passage to
e kitchen, crossed it, and reached the scullery sink. The win-
ow was open, as he had left it.

'Up you go!' he whispered. 'Wriggle out feet first. It's only
three-foot drop.'

As she squirmed out over the window-sash he followed her
o on to the sink. A moment later they were side by side
ut in the yard. Quickly but cautiously they crossed it, then,
reaking into a run, fled down the drive.

An awful thought suddenly struck Gregory. When he had
ft the car down there where the track widened out he had
mpletely forgotten the road patrol police who were billeted
the Schloss. He had seen two of their motor-cycles parked
ear the front entrance of the Castle when Helga had let him
ut that afternoon, but after that he had never given them
other thought. If one of them had passed, either going on or
oming off duty during the hour he had spent in the Castle,
ey could hardly have failed to notice the car. Finding it aban-
oned, they would have driven it either up to the Schloss or
own to the local police-station. If that had happened his line
f retreat was cut.

As he ran on he cursed himself for underrating his enemy.
hat was the way people always came unstuck. One concen-
ated so much on the big fences in a problem that one was
ot to forget the little ditches that might trip one up. Like a
ol he had thought only of outwitting Grauber and Helga,
d contemptuously ignored their satellites. It would have
en so simple to have left the car properly hidden further
ield, and cost only a little time in getting back to it. Where-
now, one of those dull, middle-aged country policemen
ight prove his complete undoing.

Hardly able to contain his anxiety, he raced ahead round
e last bend before the open space; then stopped dead with a
asp of relief. The car was still there. He could see its outline
aguely, in the half-light.

'What is it? What's the matter, darling?' panted Erika, as
e caught up with him.

'The car,' he laughed, catching her arm and pulling her up.
was afraid the traffic cops might have found it.'

Then a new thought struck him. Perhaps they had. If so, a road police they would be certain to have the numbers of a stolen cars, and the number of the Stutz would have bee circulated that morning at latest. Perhaps one or more of them were posted there in the darkness, behind the car, among the trees, hoping that the car thief would return, s that they could catch him.

There was no time now to sneak round through the tree and take them in the rear. Besides, if they were there they mu already have heard the running feet coming down the track and now be on the alert. The only thing was to go forwar and attempt to bluff it out. As they advanced again, in th hope of putting anyone that might be lurking there off thei guard, he called out in a friendly voice:

'Don't get excited. It's only us!'

There was no reply, and nothing stirred. He knew then tha his fears had been groundless. A moment later they were i the car, speeding round the corkscrew bends towards the vi lage.

From Wilflingen, Gregory had a choice of ways of gettin back to von Lottingen's Villa. He could either go south-eas through the Hauberg to Beuron, then in a curve via Sigmarin gen, Herbertingen and Saulgau to Ravensburg, from whic a by-road would take him to just the point on the lake h wished to reach; or he could go south to Spaichingen, Tuttlin gen and Stockach, then follow the road that ran right alon the north shore of the lake.

The former was slightly longer, but the latter had the dis advantage that he would have to pass through Friedrichshafe and he thought that the police in the big frontier town wer much more likely to be on the *qui vive* for the stolen car tha their colleagues in the small island towns and villages. H hated to have to give extra time to the additional half-doze miles, but he felt that as a precaution it was wise to do so Therefore, on leaving the village he took the road south-eas that led up into the higher parts of the Hauberg.

Owing to his inspiration of starting the fire he now felt tha they still had a sporting chance of getting clean away from Grauber. When the Gestapo man had first entered Helga' room it had flashed upon him that, although there was stil a chance that he might get Erika out of the Castle, the game was up as far as any hope of crossing the lake in the Villa Offenbach's launch was concerned. Whatever happened, it seemed that within half an hour at most Grauber must learn either of his enemy's presence in the Castle or Erika's escape, and that it was her lover who had rescued her. In that case he would guess at once that Gregory had fooled Einholtz and immediately telephone Friedrichshafen for a squad of men to go out and surround von Lottingen's boathouse.

Gregory had had little time to realise how very nearly his line of retreat had been cut, but he saw now that it might yet hold long enough for him to get across it. When Grauber learned of the fire there was no reason why he should connect it with either Gregory or Erika. He still supposed the one to be enjoying his last night of freedom in Switzerland and the other to be safely locked in her dungeon. There was no water handy down there, and all Helga's loot in clothes and furnishings would keep the blaze going merrily, so it would be very difficult to put out.

Even when they had broken down Erika's door and discovered that she was no longer inside, they would probably assume that the Gestapo man had taken her into Helga's room to dress and that all three of them had been trapped there by a sudden outbreak of fire, through one of the lamps being knocked over. But by that time the room would be a raging furnace. It would be impossible to get at the bodies before the fire had died down. That might not be for several hours, and only then would they find that the charred remains left one woman unaccounted for.

They would jump to it then, that, somehow, Erika had succeeded in escaping during the confusion resulting from the fire. But there would still be no reason to suspect that Gregory had played any part in her escape. It would be regarded as the spontaneous seizing of an opportunity, and thought that she was either seeking shelter at some neighbouring farm or hiding in the forest. In consequence, there seemed no reason at all why Grauber should take measures to have von Lottingen's boathouse guarded.

But, once more, everything hung on the time factor. How long would it take them to break down the door of Erika's dungeon? How long to get the bodies out of Helga's still smouldering room? It should be an hour at least, probably two, perhaps even several. And there was always the chance that once both Erika and her charred body were found to be missing Grauber's alert mind might jump to Gregory right out of the blue. Moreover, when the two remaining bodies were properly examined it would be found that the victims had not met their deaths through fire at all. The Gestapo man's ankles had both been broken by bullets and his forehead smashed in; Helga's spine was broken and the base of her skull shattered. Even the roasting of their bodies would not permanently conceal that. If Erika had managed to get hold of a gun, could she have succeeded in doing such deadly execution? On that count Grauber's mind would jump to Gregory on a basis of reason. It seemed certain then that the moment it was discovered that Helga and the Gestapo man had met their deaths by shooting would also be the moment when the danger bell would ring for the escapers.

Knowing that, Gregory drove with the maximum speed that could possibly be combined with safety. His ribs pained him badly, but he was too elated by having Erika once more beside him to think much of his pain. Yet they spoke little. Without any explanations she guessed the terrible necessity for speed and, much as she longed to hear how he had succeeded in finding her, she knew that for both their sakes she must leave him to concentrate on his driving. Instead of saying anything she kept her hand on his leg, just above the knee, and, now and then, gave it a fond little squeeze.

It seemed to him, now that he had got her safely out of Niederfels, that the luck was running with him again. The feeling strengthened when they had got clear of Sigmaringen, which was the biggest town through which they had to pass, without being challenged, since the fact that they were using a stolen car was now their greatest danger.

But three miles outside the town, on rounding a bend, they suddenly came upon a farm wagon full of boisterously singing yokels. Drawn by two hefty, slow-moving horses in tandem, it occupied the middle of the road, and there seemed no possible way of avoiding it.

Only Gregory's magnificent driving saved them from complete catastrophe. Braking fiercely, he skidded the car half off the road up on to a low bank. There was a loud bang and the car almost turned over; but it righted itself again, and ran back on to the road. With a sinking heart he brought it to a standstill a hundred yards further on. He knew only too well what that bang had meant. When skidding, he had burst one of his back tyres.

The farm cart too, had stopped, the singing ceased, the yokels climbed out and came straggling up the road towards them. Gregory was already out of the car and preparing to change the wheel. It emerged that the yokels were belatedly returning from a wedding party in the neighbourhood. Most of them were drunk but they willingly offered their help and, although it was rather doubtful if they really helped or hindred the spare wheel was fixed with the minimum possible delay With a wave of good-bye to their bibulous helpers Gregory and Erika drove on again, but the accident had cost them a precious quarter of an hour.

They passed through Herbertingen and Saulgau without event, and having accomplished four-fifths of their journey into Ravensberg, but their run of bad luck had not ended. In the

366

suburbs of the old town there lay a railway crossing and its gates were closed against them. Annoyed at this new delay, but unperturbed, Gregory pulled up, expecting that in a few moments a train would pass and that then the gates would be opened. Instead, four uniformed men ran out from the shadows of the gate-keeper's lodge and jumped upon the running-boards of the car.

'Got you!' exclaimed a fat man who seemed to be in charge of the party.

'What the hell!' cried Gregory. 'What the devil do you mean?'

'It's a fair cop,' laughed the fat man. 'You nearly ran down a wedding party some thirty miles further back, didn't you?'

'Yes. What of it? No one was hurt.'

'Maybe not. But by a bit of luck the village policeman was in the party. He thought at the time the number on your car seemed somehow familiar, and when he got home he looked up his list of stolen cars. This Stutz was stolen in Stuttgart last night. He telephoned round for traps to be set for you and we're the lucky lads to pull you in.'

While listening to him Erika felt as though she would sink through her seat with mortification and distress, to have survived so much only in the end to be caught through a village policeman was unutterably galling. But Gregory was now speaking again, coldly and angrily.

'This car was not stolen, Sergeant, it was commandeered. I am a Lieutenant-Colonel of the S.S. and I needed it for an affair of the greatest urgency.'

'What! With the lady?' The sergeant laughed. 'You can tell that one to my officer. Come on! You're going to drive us to the station.'

The fat man shouted to the signal-box, then climbed into the back of the car. One of his men got in with him, the other two remained on the running-board and hung on to the wings. The gates of the railway crossing swung open. Gregory realised that it was useless to argue further with the sergeant and, having registered a most vigorous protest, drove on into the town under his direction.

On arriving at the police-station they were put into a small room while the sergeant went to report Gregory's protest to the night duty officer. As the minutes ticked by they felt an increasing perturbation; yet they knew that the one thing they dared not do was to lose face, so Gregory began to call out, demanding attention.

The result was that a few minutes later they were taken into an inner office to confront an inspector. He was a lean, grey, tired-looking man.

'What is this story about your being an S.S. officer?' he asked at once. 'Have you your papers to prove that?'

Gregory bowed from his waist, snapped, 'Einholtz,' and producing the dead Gestapo man's pass, laid it firmly on the desk in front of the inspector.

He looked at it for a moment, then handed it back, remarking quietly: 'That's all in order. But you will agree that one does not often see S.S. officers out of uniform, and, beyond question, the car you are using was taken without any legal authority.'

'The S.S. does not need legal authority.'

'Still, I require further proof of your identity before I can consider letting you go.'

Pulling Einholtz's letters and bills from his pocket, Gregory flung them on the desk with an angry gesture:

'All right! Look at those, and if your curiosity carries you so far, read them. But I warn you that you are exceeding your authority. I am an officer of the Gestapo Department U.A.-1, and many of my duties have to be carried out in plain clothes. I have shown you my pass, and that should be sufficient.'

The inspector glanced at the superscriptions of the letters then handed them back. 'Those appear all right, too,' he said, 'but, like the car, the whole lot may have been stolen. I propose to detain you.'

'You! Detain me?' Gregory thundered. 'By God, if you do that will be the end of you! Can't you get it into your thick skull that I am on an urgent mission? If you don't believe me ring up my chief, *Herr Gruppenführer* Grauber!'

It was the supreme bluff, and Gregory gambled everything upon it. If it worked they would be freed. If it did not, and the inspector put a long-distance call through to Berlin that would avail the prisoners nothing, as the Alexanderplatz would inform him that the *Gruppenführer* was at Schloss Niederfels. Another call would be made and within an hour or so Grauber would arrive in triumph to collect them.

Gregory was banking entirely on the fact that, at heart, all German officials are bullies, and when they get up against a bigger bully they invariably cave in. Yet every nerve in his brain was alive with apprehension as he waited to see the inspector's reactions.

After a second he saw him blanch slightly. The dread name of Grauber had rung a bell with the inspector. Like all civil police officers, he loathed the privileged S.S., yet went in fear of them. He was old enough to remember another, freer Germany of the Kaiser's day. He had had to join the Nazi Party to keep his job, but he was old-fashioned and did not

368

ike their methods. Now that Hitler had gone to war with Russia, he secretly believed that the Nazis were leading Germany to destruction. But they were still the masters, and their power was absolute. If the man before him was a car thief he would be caught again, sooner or later. If he was, as he declared, a Lieutenant-Colonel of the S.S., detaining him might lead to the officer responsible losing not only his job but his pension. On long-distance calls there were often considerable delays. It might take an hour or more to get through to Berlin; and if the Colonel was on an urgent mission such a delay might cause its failure. Then there would be hell to pay. No, obviously, the risk was not worth it.

'All right,' he said, after a moment, 'I must accept your word, *Herr Oberstleutnant*. The car is still outside. You are free to go.'

'*Ich danke Ihnen*,' replied Gregory frigidly. With a stiff bow he stalked arrogantly from the room, leaving Erika to tail along behind him.

As they drove down the street in the car they both let go a heavy sigh, and smiled at each other in the darkness.

'Heavens! That was a near thing,' Erika murmured.

'It certainly was,' he agreed. 'And even though we got out of it, the car number being spotted by that blasted village constable has cost us half an hour of our invaluable time.'

The last lap, from Ravensburg to the lake, was a matter of only fifteen miles. After turning into the lakeside road they drove along it for a little way; then Gregory ran the car through an open gate, into a field, and they got out. He looked at his watch and saw that it was a quarter to three.

Instead of the journey taking two hours, the burst tyre and their temporary arrest had caused it to take two and three-quarters. However, the moon was not due to rise until a little before dawn, so they still had several hours of darkness before them. There remained the awful question as to how long it would take Grauber to get the fire under control and make damning deductions from the charred bodies. If he had managed to do so already the boathouse at von Lottengen's would now be surrounded, and prove another trap, but Gregory still felt that it would be well on towards morning before the fiery furnace he had created in Helga's room would be cool enough for anyone to enter it. So, in good heart, they set off on foot to cover the last third of a mile to von Lottingen's.

The injury to Gregory's ribs had made his breathing painful for the last three hours, and now that he was walking the pain became considerably greater. Yet the imperative necessity for keeping his wits about him helped to take his mind off it.

As they approached the Villa they began to go forward very cautiously, but the road was entirely deserted, and for the last hundred yards a tall hedge gave them excellent cover. When they reached the gate they waited beside it for a moment, listening for any sounds that might give them warning if an ambush had been laid. It was very cold. Erika shivered slightly and drew her fur coat more closely about her. Gregory took a step forward, and, raising himself a little from a crouching position, peered between the ornamental, wooden bars in the upper part of the gate. No lights showed in the house and there was no sign of movement among the deep banks of shadows in the garden. With his gun ready in his hand he lifted the latch of the gate and opened it a little. Slipping inside, they closed it after them.

Side by side they stole down the garden path to the garage. Before passing round its corner they paused and listened again. They could now hear the lapping of the water across which lay life, freedom and happiness, but no other sound disturbed the stillness. Again they advanced, like two silent shadows.

As they neared the boathouse, Erika could feel her heart beating wildly, and her scalp began to prickle. The summer night, now months ago, when she had crept down that path was still vivid in her memory. Although she had not yet reached it she could already see in her mind the darkened interior of the big shed, and feel again the brutal kicks and blows that she had received there.

Motioning her to stay still, Gregory covered the last few paces to the door. Opening it gently he stood a little aside, thrust in his torch and flicked it on for a second. The eerie stillness remained unbroken. He flashed the torch again and shone it round, although, as only his extended hand was behind it, he could not yet see inside. The ruse brought no shot or sound of movement, and a great surge of hope lifted his heart. If Grauber's men were lurking there it seemed certain that at the sight of the light they would have sprung into action.

'I think it's all right,' he whispered, and stepping from behind the door he walked softly through it.

With her pistol held ready in her hand, Erika followed him in. He flashed his torch again, and shone it round. His heart seemed to sink right into his stomach and she smothered a little cry of dismay. The boathouse contained no ambush; no enemies were waiting there to spring upon them. The place was entirely empty; but all the boats had been taken away.

For a moment they stood there, stunned by this terrible misfortune; but Gregory guessed at once what had happened. The one link in his plan which he had always known to be

veak had given way. During the previous day the launch from
he Villa Offenbach had been discovered there. Whoever occu-
ied von Lottingen's house had become suspicious that the
aunch was being used for some illegal purpose; and, in order
hat the user might not reclaim it, or take one of the others,
vithout going to the house to give an explanation of what he
vas up to, had removed them all.

Gregory took Erika's arm and squeezed it. 'Cheer up,' he
aid. 'This is a bad break, but at least Grauber can't have
;uessed yet that we're together, and trying to get back to
switzerland; otherwise the place would have been full of his
eople. We'll get a boat somehow.'

'But how, darling?' Erika tried to keep the despondency she
vas feeling out of her voice.

'We'll go along the road to the next villa and try there. All
hese places on the lake shore have boathouses.'

Still treading gently, they left the boathouse and made their
way back up the garden path to the gate. At the very moment
hat they reached it a voice rang out from behind them:

'Stay where you are, or I shoot!'

Erika swung round and saw that in the porch of the house
there were now several dim figures.

Gregory grabbed her arm and dived for the gate. He had
scarcely pulled her with him one step towards it when the gate
was flung open, and they found themselves facing another
squad of men who covered them with sub-machine guns.

A whistle blew, and at its shrill blast pandemonium broke
loose. Lights were switched on in the villa. Torches were
flashed in their eyes, motor engines roared up the road; some
of the men in front of them sprang forward, others from the
Villa came dashing at them from their rear.

The first vehicle to arrive was a lorry, on which was mounted a searchlight. It's powerful beam lit the small garden with
a blinding glare. Three cars drove up and squads of men tumbled out of them. But before they could even reach the gate
Gregory and Erika had been surrounded, seized, and disarmed.

Against such numbers any attempt to put up a fight would
have been utterly hopeless; but as, still half-blinded, Gregory
gazed around he felt that, to ensure his capture, his enemy
had paid him a remarkable tribute. The place was now swarm-
ing with Gestapo men, and the arms they carried were sufficient for them to have taken on a whole platoon of soldiers.
It looked as if the entire S.S. Headquarters of Friedrichshafen
had been called out to participate in this snaring of one man
and a girl.

Such a force could not, he knew, have been concentrated

there through the simple finding of the launch, or even th
discovery of Einholtz's murder and the connecting of th
launch with it. Such excessive precautions against their get
ting away could only have been ordered by *Gruppenführe*
Grauber. It seemed certain now that he had got the fire unde
control fairly quickly and telephoned through at once.

Gregory did not think there could have been much of
margin and supposed that the arrangements for the ambush
had probably still been incomplete when he and Erika had
first entered the garden, the finishing touches had, no doubt
been added while they were down at the boathouse. Still,
didn't matter now how the trap had been prepared. The grim
fact was that it had worked; they were caught, and Grauber
would be arriving on the scene to claim them in something les
than two hours' time.

Those were the thoughts that spun through his mind as h
and Erika were hustled towards the Villa. They entered it
small, rather ugly hall and an S.S. officer waved a hand fo
them to pass on into a room on the left. As Gregory stepped
through its doorway he came to an abrupt halt, and gasped
with amazement.

There, beyond a small dining-table, with one of his heavy
jowled adjutants behind him, stood Grauber himself.

As the door closed behind them Grauber surveyed his pri
soners with his solitary baleful eye.

'So we've got you at last,' he piped.

'Yes, you've got us,' Gregory agreed in a tired voice. Th
hurly-burly of the last few moments had temporarily taken hi
mind off the ache in his ribs, but it was gnawing now at him
again. 'Still,' he added, 'I'd be interested to learn how you
did it. Or, rather, how you managed to get here ahead of us?'

'It was quite simple, my dear Watson,' Grauber grinned
'We were held up by the smoke in the cellars for a bit, and th
door of the Countess's dungeon took some hard work to
break down. But once we were inside I found the broken chair
which had secured her to the bed. It had been shot through
with a pistol. I found the bullet in the mattress. As she had no
weapon and no clothes I felt certain that she could not have
severed the chain and got away on her own. Naturally, know
ing that you were due at Schloss Niederfels tomorrow night
my mind flew to you. I realised that, as you have always liked
to play the lone wolf, you must have decided to leave th
others behind and go into Germany on your own, two night
ahead of schedule.

'Fortunately, as I was on the spot, I was able to deal with
matters. I telephoned to the Villa here, where we have alway
had a man, and learned from him that the Villa Offenbach'

launch was in the boathouse. It needed only that to confirm my theory. I telephoned Friedrichshafen to make the necessary arragements, got into my car and drove here by the shortest route myself. I imagine that you must have taken a longer one, as by the time I got here I expected you to be already a prisoner. But as it was, I beat you to it by a good quarter of an hour. By the by, I hope you appreciated my artistic touch in instructing my people to let you go down unchallenged to the boathouse, so that, just as you thought you had beaten me, you should find there were no boats.'

'It was typical of your kindness,' said Gregory.

'I am kindness personified,' leered Grauber. 'In fact, so kind that, as I told you when we met in Russia, I am not going to hurt one hair of your head—yet you are going to tell me all you found out there.'

'And if I refuse?'

'Then the charming Erika will give us an exhibition of a mad animal gibbering to be put to death; and I assure you that it will be a very lifelike exhibition indeed.' Grauber ran his tongue over his thin lips, then suddenly added:

'Either I'll call my men in to strip her and begin, or you'll talk at once. I've no time to waste in fooling about tonight.'

'Neither have I,' replied Gregory, with equal firmness. 'I don't want to be stopped by the Swiss patrol boats, so we've got to be across the lake before dawn.'

Erika was staring at Grauber in fascinated horror. At Gregory's words she turned and gave him an incredulous look.

'Don't be a fool,' snapped Grauber. 'I mean exactly what I say.'

'So do I,' Gregory countered swiftly. 'And what is more, you are going to cross the lake with us. At least, you will if you wish to retrieve anything out of the mess that Einholtz has made.'

'Einholtz?' Grauber repeated in a puzzled voice, a faint uncertainty suddenly showing in his single eye. 'D'you mean that you didn't just decide to slip into Germany on your own; but realised that there was a trap set for you, and that Einholtz was one of my men?'

'I do.'

The uncertainty in Grauber's eye deepened. 'When,' he said slowly, 'when did you find out about Einholtz?'

'The very first night I met him,' Gregory replied amiably.

'So!' exclaimed the *Gruppenführer*. 'And you talked to him about Russia?'

'I did. I told him every single thing I knew, and—er—just a little more.'

'*Zum Donnerwetter!*' Grauber roared, smashing his fist down on the table.

For a second he paused white-faced and trembling, then he swung round to his adjutant.

'Kobler! Get me on to the *Führer*'s Headquarters. At once! Instantly! Use the highest priority! Clear all lines!'

As the adjutant dashed from the room Gregory laughed and said: 'So Einholtz *did* pass on that false information I gave him about the impending counter-offensive from south-east Moscow. And you passed it on to the *Wehrmacht*, eh? I wonder if they acted on it? If they did I'll have killed a hundred thousand of you filthy swine before Christmas, and saved Moscow. My God! If Erika and I have to die, that will be something worth dying for.'

'Oh, darling!' Erika cried, clasping his arm. 'Oh, darling! What an amazing feat!'

'You *are* going to die,' snarled Grauber, the sweat pouring down his face. 'But I'll see to it that neither of you finally expire for months, and that every minute of every day of those months shall be passed in a living hell.'

'We are *not* going to die!' Gregory flung back. 'We're going across the lake to Switzerland; and unless you're more of a fool than I take you for, you're coming with us.'

'Why?' panted Grauber. 'Why? What other devilry have you been up to?'

'I take it you'd like to fetch von Osterberg back?'

'Von Osterberg?' The puzzled look crossed Grauber's face again. 'What the hell would I want with that wreck of a man?'

'I should have thought you would have been pretty anxious to get him back into Germany.'

'What for? He is on a string. Einholtz has charge of him. In due course Einholtz will bring him back.'

'Are you quite sure of that?' asked Gregory quietly.

'Certainly I am. Einholtz may have done something to give himself away to you; but in all essentials he is absolutely reliable, and a very able man. He knows the importance of maintaining control of von Osterberg and you could neither bribe nor trick him into neglecting that.'

'You agree, though, that it is important to you that Einholtz should have maintained control of the Count?'

'Well, perhaps,' Grauber admitted. 'As an able scientist we may find some further use for him.'

'What would you say if I told you that I had kidnapped von Osterberg?'

'Firstly I should say that you were a liar. Secondly, that even if you have it will not do you the least good. You see, I know that you are lying. For you to have slipped through

374

Einholtz's fingers is one thing, and for you to have kidnapped the Count from under his very nose is quite another. Einholtz has orders to live with the Count, to sleep with him and to shoot him if he attempted to escape. So you see, it is no use your trying to put over this useless bluff.'

'I fear that you have made the fatal error of slightly underrating my capabilities, *Herr Gruppenführer*. Believe it or not. I succeeded in kidnapping the Count.'

Grauber shrugged. 'Your persistence in this matter is quite pointless. The Count is of little value to anybody; so what could you hope to gain by such an act? Anyhow, I know you to be lying. Because, if you had done as you say, by this time Einholtz would have informed me of it.'

Gregory's hand went towards the left pocket of his overcoat.

'Don't move!' snapped Grauber, lugging his pistol from its holster. 'I suppose there were so many of those fools outside that each thought the other had searched you for weapons.'

'It was rather a *mêleé*,' Gregory agreed, and added sarcastically, 'but I feel that I ought to compliment you on having captured me without having to call in the *Wehrmacht*.'

Slipping round the table, Grauber muttered: 'Anyhow, it's not too late for me to rectify the omissions of my subordinates. I'll have that gun.'

As he spoke he thrust his hand into Gregory's pocket. It came into contact with a large flat packet.

'What the hell is this?' he asked, pulling it out and throwing it down on the table.

'I was about to give it to you myself,' Gregory said quietly. 'You'd better unwrap it and see.'

The packet was not tied up. With a quick movement Grauber jerked away the loose wrapping. On to the table there rolled out a bloody severed hand, upon which still sparkled a large amethyst ring.

'Einholtz!' Grauber gasped.

'Yes. Einholtz. And if you want the rest of his body you'll have to go and dredge it up from the bottom of the lake.'

'So he let you kill him, eh? The stupid fool!'

'Yes. He wasn't quite such a good watchdog as you seemed to think. Anyhow, that's proof enough that I dealt with him according to his deserts; and perhaps that will convince you that I'm not bluffing when I say that I've got the Count.'

Grauber looked Gregory squarely in the eyes. 'Well—what if you have? That's not going to save your skins. the loss of one scientist, more or less, makes no difference to Germany.'

'Doesn't it?' Gregory's glance held the single eye. 'Listen my dear Holmes, it's time that I let you into a trick or two.

Have you ever heard of a place upon the Baltic called Peene münde?'

'Peenemünde!' Grauber's eye wavered for a second, then he suddenly gripped the edge of the table with both hands and leaning over it, shot at Gregory:

'What do you know about that?'

'Nothing much,' Gregory shrugged. 'Except that it is a new experimental station, and that before you got hold of von Osterberg he was working there.'

'What do you know?' snarled Grauber, beginning to sweat again.

'Very little,' admitted Gregory. 'But whatever you may do to the Countess and myself, unless you can regain possession of von Osterberg the British Government will learn quite a lot. You see, I have made arrangements that if Erika and I are not back at the Villa Offenbach by dawn today, the thirteenth of December, the Count will be taken over by a British agent and questioned at leisure.'

Grauber relaxed and smiled faintly. 'My dear Mr. Sallust, I congratulate you, in that for a moment you succeeded in frightening me. But I see now that I have no cause for alarm. I feared that you had somehow induced von Osterberg to talk, yourself. Yet it is evident that you have not done so. Poor specimen as he is, the Count is still a patriotic German, so we can rely on him to keep his mouth shut, I regard this capture as most regrettable, but, fortunately, it is against the principles of the British Government to employ torture to their prisoners, so Germany's secrets will remain quite safe.'

He paused for a moment, took from a leather monogrammed case one of his big cigars, and lit it; then went on: 'It was a clever line that you endeavoured to sell me, but I am not a buyer. Your Intelligence people can have the Count, and welcome. You and the charming Countess will not cross the lake tonight, and I shall not go with you. Instead we shall remain here for our nice little talk. We have wasted a great deal of time in this pointless discussion, but we will waste no more. You will now tell me about your journey to Russia and—'

The door was flung open and his adjutant came stamping in.

'*Herr Gruppenführer!*' he cried, as he saluted. 'A line to the Führer's Headquarters is now at your disposal.'

Temporarily, Grauber had evidently forgotten the report he had to make. The blood drained from his pasty face. Then with a cry of 'Keep an eye on these people!' he ran heavily from the room.

There were innumerable questions that Erika wanted to ask Gregory. But in the presence of the adjutant there was little

hat she could say. After a moment, hoping that the man
ould not understand, she leaned towards her lover and whis-
ered in English:

'Grauber's pretty rattled now. You've put up a marvellous
how. Do you think that, even yet, you might—er—persuade
im to let us go?'

Gregory took her hand and pressed it, as he whispered back
don't know. I've used my best ammunition, but there's still
1st a chance. Not a very good one; but keep up your heart,
y sweet.'

He had given her such comfort as he could, but his own
eart was very low. All along he had been counting von Oster-
erg as one of the highest cards in the pack and had believed
hat if Grauber did catch Erika and himself, playing it might
vin them the last trick. Yet it seemed that he had overrated
s value. He had played it and Grauber had not reacted as he
ad expected. That could only be because the *Herr Gruppen-
ührer* believed he would already have endeavoured to make
on Osterberg talk himself, and that, if he had failed, short of
sing torture, no one else would succeed in doing so.

Gregory passed his tongue over the red capsule in his mouth,
nd wondered how soon he would be called upon to tear it
ree and bite through it. But about that he now felt little con-
ern; he was so desperately worried about Erika. They had
oth been disarmed so he could not shoot her, and she could
ot shoot herself. He wondered if he could possibly manage
o kill her in some other way, he glanced round the room for
ome means of attempting it.

His eye fell on the mantelpiece; at each end of it there stood
heavy candlestick. If he could get hold of one of those he
ould perhaps bash out her brains before they could stop him.

He turned and smiled at her. 'You must be tired. Won't
ou sit down?'

As he spoke he stepped round the table and held a chair
or her. The movement brought him within a few feet of the
nantelpiece. It now needed only one more step for him to
each the nearest candlestick, and he would be able to strike
er with it from behind. One swift stroke should do it, and
he would never know what had hit her.

Just as she sat down. Grauber strode back into the room.
Ie was looking frightful. His eye was bloodshot and his pasty
ace was wet with sweat. The information he had sent in
vould, Gregory knew, have been collated with all other avail-
ble material, and it would have been the responsibility of
he General Staff to accept it or reject it; so he would not bear
he sole responsibility. But it was certain that he would have

marked it as coming from an A-plus source, and it was clear that his masters had given him a terrible dusting.

Gregory still had one card left. He did not rate its value a very high, but he fought down the pain in his ribs, and made a great effort to pull himself together in order to play it with maximum effect.

As Grauber stamped past him to the table he said:

'Let's get things clear. Then, if you are determined to get yourself broken for good and all, you can do your damndest on us. You will admit that Einholtz is dead, or at all events that I got the better of him?'

Grauber seemed to be trying to collect his thoughts. He pointed to the dead hand on the table, and muttered, 'Yes— that's proof enough that you put him out of the game.'

'Exactly! That's why I've been carrying it in my pocket for the past two days. I knew that, if I had to, producing it was the only way I could convince you that I had also got the Count where I wanted him. I take it you accept it that I've got him on a string?'

'Yes—you're not the man to have let such an opportunity slip.'

'Good! And you agree that von Osterberg is dynamite as far as Germany's new method of warfare is concerned?'

Grauber's eye flashed, and he seemed to regain some of his old spirit as he sneered: 'He would be, if our positions were reversed and he was an English scientist in my hands. I'd make him talk! But your people won't. You must have tried by persuasion and threats, already. He is a loyal German, and where you failed your official Intelligence people won't succeed.'

'You haven't got the situation quite right,' said Gregory quietly. 'If Erika and I do not return von Osterberg won't be handed over to our official Intelligence people. But he'll talk all the same. I didn't come into Switzerland alone on this trip, I brought Stefan Kuporovitch with me. You will remember meeting him in Russia?'

A queer look came over Grauber's face. 'Yes,' he murmured. 'I remember him.'

Gregory was very tired now, and the pain in his side was excruciating. But he drew himself erect and threw his last card on the table.

'Well, it is Kuporovitch who is taking care of von Osterberg. Stefan is a Russian, and he is not troubled with the childish scruples that the foolish British handicap themselves with in their wars. If Erika and I are not back across the lake by dawn Kuporovitch will know that you have got us; and he will begin to take the Count to pieces, limb by limb.'

378

Grauber stared at Gregory in hatred and dismay. His hands trembled, and he seemed to sag.

'You—you Machiavellian devil!' he breathed.

'We haven't got much time to lose,' added Gregory firmly, feeling now that he was going to win out after all. 'If you want to save your skin from Himmler, you'd better order somebody to bring round a boat.'

For a moment Grauber hesitated, then he nodded at his silent adjutant. 'Go on, Kobler. Tell someone to get a launch. I daren't let that Russian get to work on von Osterberg. He'd never stand it. We've got to let them go.'

'That's better!' said Gregory as Kobler saluted and left the room. 'And now you'll be good enough to give us back our guns.'

Grauber swung round and snarled at him: 'Is that likely? D'you think I'll risk you having shoot me in the back when we get to the other side?'

'Well, I'm not going to risk you shooting me in the back just as I get out of the boat, either. If you prefer it we'll both go unarmed. Put your gun on the table.'

'As you wish,' Grauber shrugged, and taking out his pistol he laid it down beside the dead hand. Gregory watched him make the gesture with supreme satisfaction. It was so complete a testimony of abject surrender.

'Come on,' he said. 'Let's get down to the boat.'

Erika stood up and led the way. It seemed to her almost unbelievable that she was at last to walk down to that boat-house without fear.

Two minutes later they reached it. The Villa Offenbach's launch had been brought round. A man in a yachting cap was ready at the wheel, and three Gestapo thugs stood on the landing-stage.

When Erika, Gregory and Grauber had scrambled down into the stern of the launch the three men made to follow, but Gregory said quickly, to the *Gruppenführer*:

'Oh no, you don't. This party is to consist of you and I and Erika and the boatman. You are quite capable of looking after von Osterberg on the return trip?'

'I insist on having at least one man with me,' said Grauber. 'I won't go otherwise. I'll not risk you playing me some trick and taking me prisoner.'

'All right,' Gregory conceded. 'One man, but tell him to leave his gun behind.'

Grauber looked up at the little group. 'I'll take you, Kobler. Leave your gun.'

Suddenly, just as Kobler had handed his pistol to one of the other men, and was stepping down into the boat, Grauber

379

gave a cry, and sprang to his feet.

'*Lieber Gott!* I must be mad! This Russian business h;
caused me to lose my wits. Get out of the boat, both of you

Gregory felt the blood drain from his face. What hellis
inspiration had come to the *Gruppenführer* at this the very la
moment of the eleventh hour which might yet spell ruin, to
ture and death for those who thought that they had tricke
him?

'Quick, Kobler!' shrilled Grauber. 'The game is still in o
hands! Get thirty men. Have them take five or six launche:
The odds are that the Swiss will never know of it. Even if th
do and there is an incident with their Government, who t
hell cares about that? We will surround the Villa Offenba
raid it in force, kill the Russian, and bring von Osterbe
back.'

Grabbing Erika by the shoulders, he added: 'You heard m
Get up! Get out of the boat!'

Erika's heart contracted with a spasm of despair. Only
moment ago her hopes had been so high. The cruelty of t
blow was unendurable. Grauber had outwitted them on t
straight run home. Even her brave and resourceful lover cou
have no way of defeating this new plan. She was engulf
anew in a fresh wave of agonised fear.

Then Gregory laughed. It was the quiet laugh of one st
supremely confident, and he said:

'My dear *Herr Gruppenführer*, you can raid the Villa Offe
bach if you like; but you won't find von Osterberg there.
know you Germans don't give a straw for neutrality, and
was surprised that you didn't think of this idea before. An
how, I provided against it. Kuporovitch has got the Cou
quite safely in another place, and you could hunt all night wi
a hundred men but you wouldn't find it. I'll give directio
how to get there when we are within half a mile of the Swi
shore.'

Grauber was beaten, and he knew it. With a blasphemo
curse, he released Erika and ordered Kobler back into t
boat. The man in the yachting cap started the engine, a
the launch chugged out into the lake.

A mile out a German patrol boat caught them, but Graub
showed his pass, and with deferential salutations from the la
police, they were allowed to proceed.

It was a quarter to six in the morning when they appro
ched the Swiss shore. Clouds obscured the low moon, but
greyness in the eastern sky showed that the winter's dawn w
not far off. Under Gregory's directions the launch was broug
opposite a strip of grass that lay a little to the west of Kupor
vitch's cottage. He took out his torch and began to flash it.

efan and von Osterberg had been waiting there for sev-
al hours. The Russian flashed a torch in reply.

'How is the exchange to be made?' asked Grauber dully.

'Erika goes ashore first,' Gregory replied. 'then von Osterberg comes on board. You'll still have me as guarantee for his
doing so. Then I'll land myself.'

Grauber nodded his agreement. The launch was nosed into
the shallow water. Erika lowered herself over the side, splashed
into it and waded to the beach. Across a thirty-foot-wide
strip of foreshore she could now just make out a bank, and
above it two dim figures at the point from which Kuporovitch had flashed his torch. Stumbling a little, she clambered
up the bank, and as the Russian, giving a cry of joy, sprang
forward to help her, she fell fainting at his feat.

Von Osterberg, knowing that Kuporovitch meant to torture him to death if he refused to go, came reluctantly down
the bank. After a moment, as he crossed the foreshore, his
outline could be made out by those in the boat, and they
could all see that he was limping badly. As he splashed out to
the launch, he almost fell, but Kobler pulled him aboard.

Suddenly, the second von Osterberg was over the gunwale,
Grauber came to life. Flinging himself on Gregory, he shouted

'Quick, Kobler! Quick! We've got this one anyway!'

It was the one move that Gregory had not foreseen. Once
again he had made the mistake of underrating his enemy. He
was so tired and pain-racked that during the crossing of the
lake his mind had lost its alertness, and he had thought that
Grauber, too, was too dead beat to try any tricks.

As he crashed backwards under the attack a frightful pain
seared through his side. While he fought for breath he could
hear Grauber snarling at the boatman:

'Turn round the launch! Turn round the launch! Head for
Germany and go like hell. That fellow on shore may start
shooting at us!'

Gregory was underneath. He kicked out violently, but his
kicks met only with empty air. Then he brought up his knee
and jabbed it hard into Grauber's groin. The *Gruppenführer*
let out a squeal of pain and relaxed his grip.

The engine of the launch had been switched on again. As
Gregory struggled out from beneath his attacker he could
feel the boat backing away from the shore. He had no sooner
got his head up from under Grauber's shoulder than Kobler
hit him. The blow caught in on the temple and made his senses
reel.

The launch was turning now, and Grauber, his pain forgotten in this last-minute triumph, flung himself again on
Gregory's half-prostrate form, his great hands clawing for his

enemy's thoat. As they closed about it Gregory knew
the game was up. He no longer had the strength to fight
the two of them. He had saved Erika but the Spider had got
him instead. Kuporovitch was over a hundred yards away
up on the shore, and in the still uncertain light was too far off
to see the boat, and, even if he could hear the sounds of the
struggle going on in her, was too far off to help. All Gregory
could do was to force down his chin and, with his remaining
strength, endeavour to break Grauber's grip. But he knew
that nothing short of a miracle could save him now. As from
a great distance, he heard Kuporovitch calling:

'Gregory! What is the matter? Why do you not come?'

Then Grauber's own words of a moment before flashed
again through Gregory's tired brain. He had said, 'That fellow
on shore may start shooting at us.' But they could not see
Kuporovitch, and would not know how he was armed, or what
instructions he had been given for the night's work. With a last
desperate effort, Gregory wrenched his head free, and gasped:

'Stop! For God's sake stop! Or you'll get us all killed!'

Kuporovitch's voice came again:

'Gregory! What is happening down there? Are you all right?'

Raising his own voice, Gregory yelled: 'Hold it Stefan!
Don't shoot for another minute!' Then he panted at Grauber:
'Kuporovitch has got a machine-gun up there. I told him before I set out I'd rather be killed myself than let you take me
back to Germany. If you don't stop the launch he'll mow the
whole lot of us down.'

Grauber's physical cowardice in the face of real danger
prevailed. Releasing Gregory, he stood up and shouted a furious order to the boatman. The launch turned back towards
the shore. Gregory pulled himself up into a sitting position
and a moment later the boat bumped on the mud, As he
flopped over the side Grauber snarled:

'This is not the end! I'll get you yet!'

'Oh, we'll meet again,' Gregory wheezed. 'But it is I who
will get you!'

Still breathless and shaken with pain he staggered to dry
land. The foreshore seemed a quarter of a mile in depth as
he wearily dragged himself across it. Kuporovitch hailed him
anxiously. He mustered a cheerful cry of response, lurched
up the bank, and collapsed beside Erika.

'Are you wounded?' the Russian enquired with quick concern.

'No, Stefan,' he smiled. 'I've only got a couple of cracked
ribs, but we've pulled it off, so nothing else matters now.'

'Have you heard the great news?' Kuporovitch asked ex-
citedly.